CAPTAIN MOONLIGHT

by

ETHEL MANNIN

"... Liberty was all his cry!"

THE BOOK CLUB
121, CHARING CROSS ROAD, LONDON, W.C.2

This Edition, 1943

' Whatso looks lovelily
Is but the rainbow on life's weeping rain.
Why have we longings of immortal pain,
And all we long for mortal ? '

(FRANCIS THOMPSON.)

BOOK
PRODUCTION
WAR ECONOMY
STANDARD

This book is produced in complete conformity with the
authorised economy standard.

MADE AND PRINTED IN GREAT BRITAIN BY
THE HOLLEN STREET PRESS LTD.,
LONDON, W.1.

CONTENTS

PART I

DEDICATION

To ROGER CRAVEN

PART I

QUEST

"... a world whose beauty is desire,
A twisting flux where nothing is complete
And life's one hope is hope's eternal fire."

I

FOR a long time both for Jesse and Jessica Hallard all compensation was centred in Oldport, with its narrow alleyways and its streets of steps, its twisted apple-trees topping grey stone walls springing with red and yellow wallflowers, white and pink valerian, its swinging signs of tavern and ale-house, its dark little casements that leaned out across the cobbles to gossip with each other like old women, with its constant traffic of swarthy, ear-ringed sailors, and in the harbour the tall swaying forest of the spars of ships that sailed to fight the French. Two miles away across the fields from Valley Farm the little town, a jumble of red roofs and broken walls scrambling up from the harbour, an untidy pyramid with a church at the top, rose up like an enchanted castle with towers and battlements and drawbridges ; rooks rose above it, and mastheads, and sails that from a distance were caught in the clouds, and the fields ran out to meet it golden with the perpetual summer of childhood. It was girdled by the horizon-wide adventure of great ships, top-heavy galleons of glory, and the heart of it held the dashing, breath-taking excitement of the arrival of the stage-coach.

It lasted them till puberty. Then they became aware of the island. Until then Oldport, islanded in the flat green sea of the countryside, was escape enough.

Earliest memory held the recurring need for escape. Particularly for Jesse. John, two years younger, knew no such need. It was Jesse and Jessica who were the wild ones, whose high spirits and daring and stubborn wills must be quenched with good thrashings. John was never disobedient, was never involved in escapades, never whispered or giggled in chapel. He was a good, quiet, obedient child, and, as he grew older, primly aware of his virtue. His manner demanded, smugly, of his brother and sister, ' Why can't you be *good*—like *me* ? ' so that they hated him, and persecuted him to the best of their ability, and the more they hated him the closer they drew together. That these two were ' limbs of Satan,' as their mother was always declaring, was apparent in the flash of their eyes and their rigid resistance to all authority. They had, too, a wild, dark, ungodly beauty which at times almost frightened their mother, and from which she was convinced no good could come. They attracted attention everywhere, those two—particularly the boy. There was something a little furtive about the girl ; she was always looking out from behind a tangle of black hair like a wild thing from a thicket, her eyes full of the slyness of the wild thing's profound mistrust of the human race. The boy's beauty challenged and defied ; where Jessica hid in the thicket, Jesse was always poised for flight in the open. But their eyes held the same dark secretiveness, their manner the same withdrawnness and they were inseparable.

The boy never cried when he was thrashed ; his cheeks would flush and his lips tighten and his eyes become black fires, but there was never even a whimper. But the sight or sound of Jessica being beaten would drive him crazy. Then he would sob himself to exhaustion, crying out in an agony of fear and hate. John would go a little pale and frown hard. Occasionally one or other of the children would be sick when one of the others was beaten. Mrs. Hallard would give the sick child a powder for its stomach. Both she and her husband believed as implicitly as they believed in God that to spare the rod was to spoil the child. And when you had two wild ones like Jesse and Jessica what could you do but thrash the wickedness out of them and, you devoutly hoped, the fear of God into them ? All decent, God-fearing, Christian parents brought their children up in this way.

If the Hallards were a little stricter than some, even in an age which believed in the rod, and in the idea that children should be seen and not heard, they were also, perhaps, more pious in their austere non-conformity. Morning, afternoon and evening they drove over to chapel in Oldport on Sundays, in the black, high-seated trap in which the milk was taken in ; they went in all weathers, except when a child was ill or a cow calving, and even then one of them would go, that the house of Hallard might be represented before God on the Sabbath.

They were sharply aware of the wickedness all round them, and would have regarded it as laxity in morals to give anyone the benefit of the doubt—for who knew but what the conferring of that benefit might not be in fact a condoning of sin ? That dressmaker widow in Oldport who walked arm in arm with the man she called her cousin and who lodged at her house—was it not all too clear that they were living in sin ? That couple who in middle life had adopted an infant—it was common ' knowledge ' that the child was the husband's by another woman—some said (on their way to chapel) by an actress from a troupe of players who visited the town, to corrupt the morals of decent people. Satan was always on the prowl, and when a company of strolling players visited the town you could almost smell the brimstone.

Would any sensible Christian person attempt to deny that the frequency with which theatres caught fire was anything but an act of God, an expression of His anger at the wickedness they represented ? Mr. Astley's Amphitheatre was burned twice, once in 1794, and then again in 1803, when Jesse was three years old. Two years later the Royal Circus was burnt out, and in 1807 there was the great fire which destroyed Covent Garden Theatre. Two months after the foundation stone of a new Covent Garden was laid by the Prince of Wales, behold, Drury Lane was ablaze and burnt to a cinder. It was all very well for Mr. Sheridan to make light of it, with a joke about warming himself at his own fireside ; any God-fearing person could see the hand of God operating directly in the whole business.

Dancing was another sulphurous affair, not to be tolerated by decent people. As to the new valse, its indecency was such that decent folk did not even refer to it. Whatever went on in that great gaslit—so they said—Babylon that was the city of London, with its glittering, sinful pleasure gardens, Vauxhall and Ranelagh, Oldport had no part in such immorality. ' Serious ' music in the privacy of the family circle might be permissible, but the Hallards preferred to take no risks of ensnarement in sin and contented themselves with the harmonium and evangelical hymns, thereby setting an example to the countryside, as befitted the master and mistress of its most prosperous farm.

Not that they were liked. No prosperous farmer was liked. He was lucky if he escaped actual hate and open hostility. The first summer and autumn of the century saw riots in various parts of the country because of the scarcity of corn and the high cost of living, and the year closed with bread riots in London. The price of wheat went up and up, and the Earl of Warwick declared in Parliament that the farmers were making two hundred per cent profit. They were further assisted in their profiteering by the fact that the Continent had also suffered from bad harvests, and despite the Government bounty there was very little imported corn. At home the farmers were doing so well that they could afford to leave acres of their land uncultivated and did, in spite of the great national need, and the quartern loaf rose from sixpence to one-and-ninepence, and the food riots continued. The quartern loaf went up to half-a-crown, and the King issued a proclamation urging the strictest economy in every kind of grain, no pastry to be made, and no more than a quartern loaf allowed for each person per week. There was no proclamation, and no government measure, compelling the farmers to grow more corn and bring it to market, despite the Earl of Warwick's repeated protests.

No one could accuse the Hallards of playing guinea whist or mixing brandy with their wine, for there was not a playing-card in the house, and no alcohol but good home-brewed ale ever passed their lips, not even at harvest-time or Christmas ; they could not be accused of that extravagant living with which the Earl indicted the farmers generally, but that they prospered on the common misfortune as much as the other big farmers was not to be denied, though they lived with an ostentatious plainness. William Hallard had the reputation of being a grasping man, for all his piousness ; some—the ungodly—said because of it.

After the birth of Jessica, a year after John, Mrs. Hallard lived in continual dread of having another child. She had never wanted children. There had been ten in her own family, and as a young girl she had been sickened of the everlasting ' new baby ' in the house ; as the eldest of the family her role became that of unpaid nurse. When William Hallard had asked her to marry him she had at first refused, telling him that she did not wish to marry because she did not wish to have children. She had accepted him finally under pressure from her family—to be mistress of Valley Farm was no mean thing—but had asked him to promise her that there should be no children. Only the utmost desperation could have driven her to make so indelicate a request. William had been unable to give any such promise ; the farm needed an heir, and the more sons a farmer had the better ; he was, moreover, a lusty man. They could but hope not to have too large a family, he said, and in this pious hope she consented to become his wife.

She had hoped that after producing two sons she might be excused further obligations, but William always hoped there would be a daughter, and two was not much of a family. After giving him a daughter Mrs. Hallard became a little hysterical, urging the sinfulness of repeated carnal relations other than for the procreation of children, and now they had enough children. She quoted St. Paul continually —and not without effect. William Hallard fought his carnal impulses and disposed of his surplus nervous energy in an intensified religiousness and a passionate determination that his children should grow up in the path of righteousness, even if he had to flog them every day to achieve it. Always after thrashing Jesse he would feel a tremendous upsurge of spirit, an excitement as of voices lifted up to God, of triumph over the sinfulness of the flesh. He would feel strong and virile and carnal, but conscious of his mastery over desire, as though he had offered up his potency to the service of the Lord. Then he would bring out the huge family Bible and read from St. Paul denunciation of the sins of the flesh, proud that he was not amongst those who had not the gift of continence, full of a thunderous anger against those whose flesh was weak.

Mrs. Hallard would feel flushed and excited, her nerves tingling, proud of her man, of his righteousness before the Lord, of the purity of their Christian marriage and parenthood. From the room above would come the sleeping whimpers of Jessica, if it was Jesse who had been thrashed, or of the boy's hiccuping sobs, shaking him even in sleep, if it had been Jessica. John, who never gave trouble, should undoubtedly have been the eldest son. Mrs. Hallard had no doubt that her two ' bad ' children were God's punishment for her own wickedness. It was her bounden duty to God to strive to bring up the children in the fear of the Lord. In the living-room of the farm she hung the text, ' *God is the Head of this House ; the Unseen Guest at every meal ; a Silent Listener to every conversation.*' Over the four-poster marriage-bed red and gilt letters intertwined with forget-me-nots warned that, ' *The wicked shall be cast into hell.*'

John, who had nothing to fear from the ever-watchful ways of God, was frightened by these texts ; they made him constantly aware of the awful presence of God ; God knew everything, saw everything, heard everything. He could not remember a time when he had not lived in that terrible shadow of God's presence. He was a grave, quiet child who wept secretly over his sins and was mortally afraid ; afraid of God, afraid of his parents, afraid of the school-master, afraid of the dark. Jesse and Jessica had everything to fear, but defied God, comforting themselves with the reminder that they would be cast into hell together. For the most part they did not think about it ; God was as remote and unreal as death and the Judgment Day. Their lives abounded in the realities of childhood's fantasy world, which was first Oldport and its tall ships and crazy red roofs and stone walls, and then the dim blue mystery of the island, so far out from the mainland that it was no more than a misty mound floating on the horizon.

When he was about thirteen the island stood for Jesse for all the romance and adventure and mystery and freedom his imagination could evoke. One day he would land on its shores. In this fantasy Jessica never came with him. He never told her this, but his heart insisted. The whole essence of escape was that he should go alone. Everything else they could share, but not the island, and he would want Jessica not to look at it, not to talk about it—because it made him ashamed that he did not want to share it with her, and he could give her no reason, because he could give himself none.

He would be filled with remorse looking at her when the island

9

mood was on him, the little sister looking out like a small wild animal from a thicket of hair, and the more remorse worked in him the more he loved her. At that time she was all he did love.

2

He had not gone far into his teens before he became aware of two things, the tragedy of the land, and his effect on the opposite sex. He had been only five years old at the time of the battle of Trafalgar, and the victory of Waterloo, viewed from Oldport, was mostly a matter of singing, drunken sailors, and rockets bursting in the sky, but even before Waterloo he had been aware of the changing face of the countryside. He had seen one small farm after another swallowed up in bigger farms, because the tenant farmers could not meet the high rents, or under a bill of enclosure. He saw, without understanding, the land swept away from the peasantry. He saw the cottagers and the squatters robbed of their little plots of land, their small-holdings, their gardens, he saw the fences going up and the cottages going down. He watched the disappearance of the common lands on which the peasantry had been wont to turn out their geese, their goats, their pigs, their cows—seldom more than one cow to a family, but the family's most precious possession. With the passing of the commons and wastes he saw the common people robbed of their free pasturage, of furze and fern and turf. He saw them robbed of their independence, of their foothold in society. Men he had known as a child as small farmers or small-holders he saw in his teens as gaunt, hungry-looking labourers. He saw what he did not realise he was seeing, a whole countryside being slowly divorced from the land that was its subsistence. And heard, afar-off, the whirring wheels of machinery. Stories of children forced to work in mills and factories. Stories of machine-breaking riots, in the Midlands and the North. He saw the slow pauperisation of the countryside, and a growing ragged regiment of landless men, who first sent futile, bitter, despairing petitions to Parliament, then, their spirits broken, fell back upon the ale-house and parish relief. And all the time, rents and the cost of living went up, and wages went down. People blamed it on to the war with France. But it was more than that. It was the slow, steady, relentless march of the industrial revolution, and side by side with it, the agrarian revolution.

Young Jesse Hallard knew nothing of all this; his life was merely part of the history that was in the making. But he saw men who had themselves once owned or rented a little land working for his father as common labourers ; he saw his father refusing to sell milk, butter, hay, to people who came to the door, because he could get a better price for it in the town. He saw his father hissed in the market-place by a knot of sullen-looking men who had once touched their hats to him. He saw those same men, joined by others, and armed with reaping-hooks, hatchets, cudgels, tearing the enclosure notices down from the church door. Then, incredibly, there was no longer a broad sweep of open fields, of common land, between Valley Farm and Oldport. The land was still there, but it was no longer open. Men came and put up a fence. Other men came and tore it down, and what had once been a common became a battle-field. A troop of yeomanry arrived on the scene, the Riot Act was read, and the mob was marched away under escort. The fences went up again on the common, and the sheep and cattle that had once grazed there were sold, because their owners had nowhere else to graze them, and it was impossible for poor people to buy or rent land even if any were available. Families whose ancestors had belonged to the valley for hundreds of years began to drift away to the towns, where the smoke pouring out of the tall chimneys meant money, a new life—a grey, grimy, enslaved life, but at least escape from the starvation and hopelessness of the country-side. The young people were the first to go ; there was nothing for them on the land except a farm labourer's pittance ; they would never own a patch of land, never milk a cow that was their own ; for them the land was finished as it was for their fathers. They were the children of the industrial revolution, and their heritage was the machine.

All this made a profound impression on Jesse Hallard. He was fifteen, and awake and aware. He could not get out of his mind the memory of the look on the faces of the men who had hissed his father in the market-place, and torn down the notices from the church door. The look of men fighting for their rights. The look of men at bay. He expressed it as his opinion that the taking away of land from the cottagers and squatters and small farmers was unjust. His father informed him, curtly, that he didn't know what he was talking about, and commanded him to hold his tongue. There were thousands of acres of land in England lying fallow for want of enclosure, whilst we imported corn to the tune of a million sterling from abroad. The land had to be worked, and it could not be properly worked tied up in small parcels, a few acres here, a few roods there, or running to waste in commons for the benefit of the poor and their few mangy horses and scraggy cows. The land had to be put into the hands of responsible people who knew how to get the most out of it with up-to-date methods of drainage and cultivation. It could then be let at high rents. Apart of course, from the value of its productiveness to a needy country.

Jesse could not hold his tongue. He burst out passionately, " But if you take the land away from the people how are they to live ? I was down at Mortimer's this morning and the children were crying with hunger. They used at least to have enough to eat ! "

His father banged his fist down on the table so that all the supper dishes rattled.

" Those who aren't content to be agricultural labourers can always find work in the towns these days, can't they ? But the rascals prefer to sit in ale-houses, concocting petitions to Parliament, and living on the Poor Rates ! There's too much pampering of the poor, with all this Poor Law Relief. Let the Mortimers and the rest of 'em do an honest day's work for once, and bring their children up to honest labour ! What are they now ? Hedge-breakers, idlers, poachers ! "

Jesse was silent. It was never any use trying to argue with his father. But young Jim Mortimer had been his friend, and now he had gone away to work in a mill in the North ; and his older brother, Jack, had only taken to poaching since the common had been enclosed and they had had to sell their cow. Jesse felt that he understood. A fence made you feel you wanted to trespass, for one thing ; and since hunger and dispossession had come to the valley men who had lived honestly enough before began poaching ; who could blame them ? Only those who could not imagine what it felt like to be hungry and dispossessed. That neither of his parents had any imagination worth speaking of Jesse discovered quite early on. It was not, he thought, trying to make excuses for them, that people meant to be unjust and cruel, but they just could not, it seemed, put themselves in the other person's place. Tom Mortimer, the head of the Mortimer household, was serving a year's imprisonment for his part in the fence-breaking on the common. But on moonlight nights small parties of men and lads would go out and break up the fence again. Jesse, hearing of these acts of defiance, would thrill with excitement and long to join in them, but he was never allowed out after dark at that time, and had not yet discovered defiance in himself. He had an instinctive sympathy with rioters and poachers and men against the law. It was something his father had driven into his blood at the end of a leather belt.

Then in May, 1816, when he was sixteen, came news of the rising in the Eastern counties, of the firing of ricks and barns and houses by angry labourers demanding work, and those in employment demanding increased wages, and all of them demanding a lower cost of living. ' Bread or Blood ' was the slogan on their banner, and they were armed with sticks to which iron spikes had been fixed. There were fifteen hundred of them, and they threatened to march on London. Jesse, when he heard the news, wanted to spring up and cheer. He hoped

12

wildly that something of the kind would happen in the valley. They would march up out of the valley, their spiked sticks glittering in the cold sunlight of that bitter spring like lances ; they would march up into Oldport and take their stand in the market-place and compel the landlords, the shop-keepers, the farmers, the prosperous, bland Quakers, to come to terms ; the land would be given back, the fences taken down, wages would go up, the price of meat and bread and flour come down ; there would be no more strained-looking women, angry-looking men, and children crying with hunger in the valley.

' He came out of his excited fantasy to be aware of his mother's pallor, his father's frown.

" D'you think we shall have trouble here ? " his mother asked, anxiously.

" If there is we shall know how to handle it ! "

Mrs. Hallard saw her husband glance at the gun-rack. She said, faintly, " Oh, William—'twill never come to that, surely ? None of our people would turn against us ? They respect us—we have always been just——"

She had no idea what the Valley Farm labourers were paid. She was not permitted to know anything about the farm's business side, and as a good wife, who knew her station, she did not expect to be allowed to know. All that was not a woman's business. Of industrial and agricultural unrest she knew only what her husband read out to her from the papers, and never dreamed of questioning his views. For her he was the supreme authority on all such matters. The rise and fall in the price of corn was a subject upon which she heard her husband hold forth continually, but for her it was all part of an inexplicable something called ' politics ' and she made no attempt to understand. She found it impossible to imagine outside affairs affecting the stability of Valley Farm. William complained bitterly of the falling prices of that year, but the Hallards had never lived in great style, never kept liveried servants ; they had always gone in for solid comfort rather than show, and the slump when it came did not seriously affect them. The slump and the riots might touch other farms, but surely not Valley Farm, whose history went back to the Domesday Book ?

She turned to her husband now for reassurance, but he swept aside her questions impatiently.

" Oh, to your own affairs, woman ! 'Tis time enough to meet trouble when the Lord sends it."

He pushed the paper from him and glowered round the room at his children, staring at him in fear and awe.

" ' *As our days, so shall our strength be ! ' * " he thundered at them, and strode out of the room.

His anger was the expression of his refusal to acknowledge that he was scared. So far there had been no trouble in that district, but unrest was infectious, and there was too much talk of wages amongst the labourers—he was not deaf on market-days, nor blind to the sullenness in gaunt faces. He regarded himself as a just man and refused to be bullied by the mob. No one should dictate to William Hallard what wages he should pay his own workmen.

In spite of this it was a relief to read that the yeomanry, dragoons, and militia were called out against the men armed with spiked sticks. Two rioters were killed and seventy-five taken prisoner. A Special Commission sat in judgment on them ; five were sentenced to be hanged ; of the twenty-five capitally convicted five were transported for life, one for fourteen years, three for seven years, one for four years, and ten were sent to prison for a year. In the opinion of the court they had no just cause for their conduct, they were receiving ' great wages,' and to lower the cost of food would merely provide them with more money to squander in drunkenness. . . .

When his father, with great satisfaction, read out the sentences, and the Chief Justice's closing speech, Jesse felt stunned. Could men really be hanged, and deported for life, merely for demanding the right to live ? For that was what it came to. These men wanted, when all was said and done, just that—the right to live. Their cry was for bread—such as his mother threw out by the sackful for the horses and hens.

He felt sick with anger and a wild sense of injustice. Was there no fairness anywhere ? He desperately wanted someone to discuss it all with, but he never discussed anything with John—in any case he was always on his father's side—and Jessica was too young. The boys at the school he attended in Oldport were tradesmen's sons for the most part and not interested in agrarian riots and their causes. They accepted their fathers' and the newspapers' views that the rioters were a lot of damned rascals stirred up, said the better informed, by rags like Mr. William Cobbett's *Political Register*. . . . Jesse would have liked to have been able to have accepted this view, because it would have enabled him to have dismissed the whole thing from his mind, but he had seen too much at first-hand to be convinced. He had seen people robbed of their land and grow poor and shabby and hopeless, humbling themselves to the parish officer for three shillings a week. And he could not get out of his mind the thought of the five who were to be hanged. To be condemned to die because you had demanded the right to live . . . his young mind groped after meaning and found none. He could only feel, deep down in him, that he could never be heir to the prosperous Valley Farm ; that he belonged with the exiled, the dispossessed, the ragged army of the disinherited.

14

All this unease of spirit was a big part of his adolescence. But there was something else which filled him not with uneasiness, but with a curious, exciting sense of power, and that was his growing awareness of the fact that he attracted females, girls of his own age and younger, and women old enough to be his mother, and older. Little girls flirted with him unconsciously, the older ones consciously—he was easily the best-looking lad in the valley, or in the whole parish for that matter. Women looked at him with a curious wistfulness and remarked to each other what an extraordinarily attractive lad he was, and what a ' heart-breaker ' he would be when he got older. Something stirred in them, looking at him ; in fantasy they were girls again and this dark youth with the sense of latent power in his strong, slender, coltish body their lover. He played up to them, instinctively ; he had been doing this ever since he had been an admired child, but at sixteen he began to look for this admiration, this feminine homage, and he never looked in vain. With less charm he would have been intolerably conceited ; as it was no one ever made that charge against him, and in a sense it was true that he was not conceited ; he was too easy-going and good-natured.

It was merely a confirmation of something he unconsciously—perhaps half consciously—knew already, when Jessica told him, with a child's directness, " All the girls want to kiss you, Jesse ! "

He went red, and told her not to talk foolishly, but there was a stirring of pride and gratification in him, and after that he began to show off a little in the presence of females ; but never with Jessica. He began to be aware of the swelling breasts of girls and women under their tight bodices, and longed to touch. He became aware of Jessica, and once, wrestling with her in play, laid a hand on her. Instantly her nails drove into his wrist and her teeth bared like a young animal suddenly attacked. It was the end of all childhood between them. Everything finished in that moment. After that he was the enemy. In the violence of her reaction against him she went over to John, ready to share his view that Jesse was bad ; ready to let him ' save ' her from a badness that till then had matched Jesse's. She let him teach her hymns and to weep for her sins.

Jesse's sense of guilt was intense, but it did not make him want to pray or sing hymns or weep. It was not of God he craved forgiveness, but of Jessica. He would have moments of intense longing for things to be as they were, the two of them unself-conscious, unaware of their changing bodies, children, excitedly awaiting the arrival of the stage-coach, fascinatedly following the rat-trap dealer with his live rats demonstrating the efficacy of his wares, mocking the man who called

'Bellows to mend,' peering into the gloom of the blacksmith's shop, making fun of the woman who sold what she called 'water-creases,' watching the ships, dreaming of the island. . . . At such times he would long for the feel of her thin arms round him again in clumsy childish embraces, and to know again the earthy smell of her hair against his face.

That he was damned he was quite sure, but what tormented him by day and by night was not the threat of hell-fire and brimstone hanging over him, but the fact that now when she passed him Jessica tossed her head, that now she was always at John's side. He had long ago grown used to his brother's dark eyes looking at him coldly, but now they were always paired with Jessica's. It seemed to him that now they stood always side by side, their faces turned coldly to him, two pairs of accusing dark eyes. His own burned with a dark fire of misery and rage and despair. He was glad that he was old enough to leave school before his brother and sister. Once he and Jessica, gaily loitering in the cobbled alleyways of streets of Oldport, laughed at the sedate John who always went straight to school, and straight back home afterwards. Now Jessica walked arm in arm with John, sharing his rectitude.

Mrs. Hallard believed implicitly in the value of book-learning, having none herself, and took great pride in the fact that John was a good scholar ; it compensated for Jesse's lack of interest. Jessica was not expected to acquire book-learning, but only 'refinement.' The wild thing had to be tamed. Mrs. Hallard never knew why the girl suddenly stopped allying herself with Jesse and went over to John, but it was a source of great satisfaction to her. John would be as good an influence as Jesse had been a bad one ; indeed his good influence was already being manifested by Jessica's new attention to lessons and to prayers. Through some mysterious agency Jessica was a brand plucked from the burning. It was too much to hope that a similar miracle might be performed in Jesse's case. He was too wild, and quite sinfully good-looking. Only through great piousness could he expect to overcome the temptation his good looks represented, and he was utterly lacking in piousness ; so there was no hope for him. He was a black soul, lost and damned. She asserted this, continually, to all the people who expressed their admiration for his attractiveness and charm.

"That's a fine lad your Jesse has grown into, Mistress Hallard."

"John is worth ten of him," she would reply, vehemently.

But nothing could turn people against Jesse, it seemed. People liked him—and the poor even forgave him the fact that he was William Hallard's son, which was a very great deal, considering how high feeling ran in the valley against landlord farmers. He had a natural courtesy of manner, and a smile that was like the sun coming out. When he smiled it was as though he carried a secret sun of happiness inside himself, and this was its emanation. His father insisted that he was lazy, but the general opinion was that Jesse worked harder than any of the Valley Farm labourers, and that William Hallard should be proud of his fine, strapping, eldest son. John was a poor thing compared with him, pale and studious, and over taken up with religion for one so young. It was a wonder, some said, that Jesse's spirit was not broken, between the labour his father put upon him, and his mother's scolding, and her favouritism of her younger son.

Jesse's spirit, however, was a long way off being broken. He did not expect anything else from his parents except toil and disapproval, but he lived in a perpetual dream of escape. He would not always be bound to the farm with its labour and restrictions. One day he would set foot upon the island. . . .

As to Jessica, since he was no longer permitted to love her he hated her. To his brother he was merely indifferent, because he had never had any deep feeling for him ; but Jessica he could hate because once he had so wildly loved her. Jessica was all he understood of love, since love had never entered into his relations with his parents. He could not remember gentleness and softness from either of his parents. His mother's cold, hurried goodnight kiss on his forehead as a child was meaningless. He had no memory of games with his parents. Yet that his mother had a capacity for maternal love, for tenderness, he knew ; he had seen the gesture with which she would brush back John's hair from his forehead ; seen the softness in her eyes resting on him as he pored over his books. She addressed him in a quite different tone from that which she used to anyone else. But for Jesse and Jessica there had always been each other and their lack of parental love had never mattered. When Jesse suddenly became the enemy, John naturally took his place for Jessica. For Jesse there was no one in place of Jessica, and for a little while he was intensely lonely.

He was not lacking in friends and affection. Every house in the valley was open to him, and there were girls a-plenty who would have given him more than affection and friendship, but he smiled down at them in a way that melted their blood, and that was all. There was not one of them he even remotely wanted, for all he dreamed of women and their full bared breasts. None of the girls who invited him with their eyes were what he wanted. He hardly knew what he wanted ; he only knew that he had not yet found it. But he was completely incapable of not returning a friendly smile, or of being anything less than gallant where the opposite sex was concerned.

He enjoyed popularity as a cat enjoys the warmth of a fire, and because of the lack of warmth in his own home it was necessary to him.

17

He would go into a cottage kitchen and stretch himself out on the bench along the wall, or on the straight-backed settle in the ingle-nook, and in the meanest home would come over him a sense of well-being he never knew in his own home like a creeping of mulled wine in the veins. Merely to be amongst people who liked him, who did not criticise, who did not remind him of the hell-fire damnation to which he was doomed, who smiled at him—this was happiness. To be sure all the families he knew were as God-ridden as his own, and the same grim texts hung in their rooms, but they gave him the warmth of their liking and their welcome ; they accepted him as on their side in their bitter struggle for an existence on the land, and it was all he asked.

Not that he had much time for visiting—his parents between them saw to that. When his father could find him nothing further to do at the end of a day which began at dawn and finished only with darkness, his mother could—there would be fruit to prepare for preserves, or wood to chop, or butter to churn, or brass or silver to polish, or apples to sort over in the attic. John was excused all such evening tasks on the grounds that he had his Latin to prepare for the next day ; he was the scholar of the family, whereas Jesse could not even spell properly, and had no interest in books. Mrs. Hallard cherished a secret hope that John might become a school-master, or a minister ; he would certainly become a lay-preacher. . . . Jesse, on the other hand, was destined to become the master of Valley Farm, carry on the house of Hallard ; it was essential he should learn farming. Jessica spent the evenings doing the embroidery she learned at her school for young ladies, the purpose of her education being to make a gentlewoman of her, so that she might eventually make a good marriage—to a gentleman farmer, a squire's son, or a wealthy landlord.

Sometimes Jesse would look across the table at the dark heads of his brother and sister bent over their work, and Jessica, impelled by his gaze, would raise her head and look at him, momentarily, then lower her face to her embroidery again, and it would be as though she had looked at a stranger, or there would be hostility in her eyes. Jessica who had once made excuses to get out under the stars with him, away from the lamplight and the studious John and the constraint of the home atmosphere. Gipsy Jessica being made into a lady ! You might as well try to bind the wild briar ! When he could escape himself it would seem strange to him that she was not at his side, laughing, twisting her fingers in his, suggesting some devilry. She belonged out there in the moonlight with him, to the blossomy moons of the Spring-time, or the frosty moons of Autumn and Winter ; not to the lamplight and the shutters closed against the moon. Jessica, the little sister, lost to him forever. Because once in a heady moment he had touched her soft young breast. Damn her ! Damn her ! Let her pray her

18

way to heaven and leave him to burn in hell—what did he care? Now she was always washing her face and hands and brushing her hair and folding clean white handkerchiefs over her breast, very severe and prim; now she was like any other dull, pious girl in the valley; now it was always 'Yes, Mamma,' and 'No, Mamma,' and 'Very good, Mamma,' and frowning at him when he clumped in with boots caked with cow-dung from the yard, and because he sat down to a meal in an old coat that smelled of stable and byre. Very refined and delicate she had become, with her brushed hair and her white fichus, her samplers, her embroidery, and her prayers, and he despised her, and went out of his way to shock her new fastidiousness, to let her know that he despised her.

But not all the fierce angry things his mind said to her and of her could prevent the unacknowledged aching of his heart where the loss of her was concerned. She was all he knew of love, both given and received. Somehow he had to get her back. He told himself that it was to spite John.

Then, suddenly, a magic casement opened on the foam.

II

In spite of Mrs. Hallard's devotion to learning there were no books—other than the Bible and a few religious books—at Valley Farm. It had never occurred to anyone to acquire any. William Hallard read the paper and the Bible; Mrs. Hallard did not read at all. John had his Latin books and grammars, but nothing else.

Jesse owned a Bible given to him as a birthday present by his mother when he was twelve. He had never read it for pleasure, but once, bored during chapel, he turned the pages, desultorily, aghast at so much printed matter and so much boredom, and to his amazement found something he liked, something that meant something to him, deeply, so that he carried it in his mind: '*A garden inclosed is my sister, my spouse; a spring-shut up, a fountain sealed.*' He thought about it, endlessly, seeing a walled garden, a dammed-up spring, a waterless fountain. And that is what Jessica was since she had gone over to John; she had been a spring bubbling with life; she had been a fountain spraying in the sun, full of laughter and sparkle; she had been the common, flowing away in freedom to Oldport, before the fences went up round it, enclosing it. A wild and lovely garden she had been, and they had played in it together; now she was a garden enclosed, like it said in the Bible, and he could not get over the wonder of finding

19

it in the Bible, all so perfectly expressed, in language he could never have found for himself. And then the impassioned invocation, ' *Awake, O north wind ; and come thou south ; blow upon my garden, that the spices thereof may flow out.*'

The words thrilled him, like the ' Bread or blood ' slogan of the rioters. It was fine. Let the winds blow upon the garden, blow down the fences ; set everything free. After that he read the whole thing, laboriously, for as his mother was always complaining, he was ' no scholar,' not understanding except in part, yet receiving flashes of beauty that moved and stirred him.

The Bible, then, was not all dreary or terrifying commands and promises of punishment. It was not the vast thou-shalt-not it always seemed in chapel, and when his father read it aloud in the farm-kitchen. Here was something which spoke of wine and spices, of thighs and breasts, and love and desire ; of everything that was beautiful and forbidden. Did his parents know that all this was written in the Bible ? he wondered. He could not believe that they did. His discovery excited him. It was a revelation—and a secret. He knew now how to pass the dreary time in chapel, and on Sunday evenings when everything was forbidden except the reading of the Bible.

For days he went about with his head full of a confused golden fire. ' *Who is she that looketh forth as the morning, fair as the moon, clear as the sun, and terrible as an army with banners ?* ' He knew nothing of poetry ; all that belonged to a world of books and learning in which he had no part. He did not know that this was poetry. It certainly meant nothing to him translated in terms of the Church. He accepted it all paganly ; his blood accepted and comprehended even where his intellect faltered. He longed to tell someone about it, to share it with someone, but there was no one. This was not something to be spoken of to the people whose doors were open to him. This was something Jessica could have shared with him, but she was gone from him, become a garden enclosed, a spring shut up, a fountain sealed.

And the springs of his own youth were open, flowing ; all the time he was working in the fields, or seated with his dark head against a cow's warm flank, or cutting up a slaughtered pig, or bringing cattle in, or taking them out, guiding a plough, scything the grass in the June fields, or the ripe corn in August ; all the time, in everything he did, unknown to himself. All the time he was drinking ale with the other labourers under the hedge ; leaning up against a wall cleaning a gun : spreading dung ; branding cattle ; shearing sheep ; tramping in the mud of the market-place ; sitting in the lamplight of the farm-kitchen whilst his blood raced out to the moonlight and his home became a prison. All the time. Behind his charming, absent smile ; behind

all his dreamy preoccupations ; behind all his placid outward acquies-
cence to the farm routine.

That he should work on the farm when he finished with schooling
seemed natural to him ; but he could never visualise himself stepping
into his father's place. His friends were all of the poor, the dispossessed ; if he belonged anywhere in the valley it was with them. The
idea of himself as a landlord farmer, as Jesse Hallard of Valley Farm,
was utterly unreal. On market-days with his father in Oldport he
would look at the sailors, and the masts of the ships in harbour, and
know a fantasy in which he sailed away to that blue edge of the world
where an island lay folded in mist. He was glad now, in his estrangement from her, that Jessica had never been a part of the island
dream. It was always with an effort that he brought his mind back
to the business in hand, to bullocks and sheep, the prices of fat pigs, of
hay and corn, and the provisions to be taken home. By the time he
was released from all this he was too tired for thought, and would
plunge into the feather-mattress and down through the black darkness
of exhausted, dreamless sleep.

But day found him vulnerable again in his unarmoured youth ; vulnerable to the unpitying pain of the dying countryside, to the hunger
evoked by the heedless bodies of women, to the impassioned beauty of
the *Song of Songs*, and the sea-dream of ships and an island that was
borne inland by every gull wheeling above the valley.

When he was seventeen the twenty-five-year-old wife of one of the
Valley Farm cowmen took him to her bed whilst her husband was
away attending a calving cow.

2

The three children were asleep in a dark corner of the room, where
the eaves sloped down like a tent, and he was fearful of disturbing them,
and of the master of the house returning. He knew suddenly that this
was not what he wanted, to keep another man's bed warm. He
whispered to her to come outside with him ; out under the open sky,
in the wide fields, the dusky woods, he was at home. She laughed at
his fears ; her husband would not return till dawn, for sure ; as to the
children they slept like the dead. Who would wish to lie out under a
hedge when there was a feather-bed ?

Anna Holding had been married five years and been tired of her
husband for four. Many an evening she had watched young Jesse
Hallard lounging at the door of the cottage talking with her husband,
or playing with the children beside the fire, and been aware of such
things as the fall of dark hair across his forehead, the evenness of his

teeth when he smiled, the studded leather belt that emphasised the litheness of his body. She thought of him endlessly, the tall, slim dark boy who could have had any girl in the valley, yet had no one, who chatted with the men-folk and played with the children, and smiled at the women as though he joyed in each and every one, yet cared for none of them. Always when he had been to the cottage it was as though he had left something of himself behind. If only she were single! What, after all, was twenty-five? But she was married, and had three children. . . .

Her husband was a short, thickset man; once the heavy, bull-like strength of the man had fascinated her—until she began to realise the slow animal mentality that went with it. Then Jesse Hallard grew up like a colt, with all a colt's grace, and when she looked at him she had the sense of her blood melting.

Jesse had had no intention of calling at the cottage that evening; he knew very well that Nat Holding was at the farm, and had no particular interest in Nat's wife. He had been on his way down to the Mortimers' when she had hailed him from the door. He stood chatting with her and then she asked him in, on the pretext of looking at a sickly duckling she was trying to raise; she had it in a box in the chimney-place and wanted his advice, she said.

When she handed him the box containing the duckling she leaned forward so that her hair brushed his face and he saw the valley between her breasts. She let her hand touch his. They stood together looking down at the duckling, then she took the box out of his hands and replaced it on the shelf in the chimney-place and came back to him and took his hands, saying his name, softly, and drawing him to her.

He responded instinctively. He had dreamed for so long of a woman's body pressed close to his that when it became a reality it did not take him by surprise, though he had no clear recollection of how it had happened. One moment they had been chatting at the door in the mellow summer evening sunlight, and then they had been inside looking at the duckling, and then she was, somehow in his arms.

When she whispered to him of the bed in the room above, and led him by the hand towards the steep stairs, he followed her as he had followed women in his dreams. But the sight of the wide four-poster bed with its two pillows and its creased, used sheets, and the stir of a child in the dark corner of the room, dispelled the dream. And the reality was not what he wanted.

She pulled him down beside her on the bed and fumbled at the bodice of her dress; now her breasts were naked under his hands, but behind all the wild clamour of his blood something in him insisted, almost as wildly, ' Not here.' She laughed at him, she tried to per-

22

suade him, she entreated, but it was all no good. He was like a wild thing brought into a house and blindly seeking a way out. The hot tide which had leapt in him ebbed and grew cold and he was aware of the coarseness of the woman's skin, the heaviness of her body, the straggle of her hair escaped from its pins, the ponderous domesticity of the wide bed, the sour-sweet smell of the warm unwashed bodies of the sleeping children. . . . He reached the point at which he no longer wanted her even to come out into the fields with him. She taunted him with not being a man, and it didn't matter. He wanted only to be gone and never to see her again.

When he was alone, striding through the cool dusk that smelled sweetly of honeysuckle and cleanly of hay, with the occasional warm milky smell of cattle, his blood tingled again with the memory of naked woman's flesh under his hands, and eager lips fastening on his own, but he had no desire to turn back. The woman he had just left was not woman as he had dreamed of her, fair as the moon, clear as the sun. For a moment his blood had deceived him, but now he knew. He did not merely want a woman ; he wanted someone to share things with— as once with Jessica. He wanted—needed—someone to whom everything in himself could flow out freely, to be given again.

3

The encounter nevertheless unsettled him. He began going into Oldport in the evenings that summer, when he could escape from the farm. He would retire to his room on the pretext of getting to bed early, and then slip out down the back stairs that led into the back kitchen, with its scullery and pantry, and the dairy, out of which opened a room used for storing meal and chicken corn and such things. A door from this room led out into the rickyard, which was not over-looked from the farm living-room, and he could cut across it unseen to the cart-track that led away across the farm fields and out to the road and freedom.

Oldport allayed his restlessness. He enjoyed its movement, the clatter of horses' hooves on the cobbles, the busyness of the quays, the sound of laughing and singing from the sailors' taverns, the silken swish of skirts of the women of the town. They were pretty, some of them, he thought, with their painted faces and darkened eyelids, and their bonnets gay with flowers, and there was a lightness and gaiety in their manner which appealed to him. But they were not for him because he had no money.

His father did not reckon to pay him. After all, the boy had his keep, and the farm would be his one day. When he wanted clothes his father bought them for him. What did a boy of his age want with money? Those who had no money had no temptations. Blessed are the poor—if only they would realise it.

But Jesse began to feel the need for money in his pocket. Sometimes he would fall into talk with a sailor down by the harbour, and the sailor would end up by taking him to an ale-house, and it was humiliating not to be able to stand his host a drink in return. Besides, money would buy more than a few drinks; it would buy one of the painted ladies. He was not looking, now, for the fairest among women, but merely for a woman, and it was not necessary to look far in Oldport if you had the money. That he could have Anna Holding for nothing was an idea that occurred to him only to be rejected. Even if she attracted him, which she didn't, he couldn't go back to her now.

That there was a way of making money other than by what was called 'honest work' Jesse knew well enough. He had not worked with common labourers, and consorted with those who had suffered under the enclosures schemes, for nearly two years without discussion of the various Game Laws. He knew all about the savage Act of 1816 by which any person found at night, unarmed but with a net for poaching, 'in any forest, chase, or park,' was to be transported for seven years. He knew that men poached in spite of it, though they could be hanged merely for wounding a keeper, and though the game preserves abounded in spring-guns which killed a man without warning or maimed him for life. The bill was modified the following year, so that a man must be carrying 'an offensive weapon'—firearms, crossbow, bludgeon—as well as a net before he could be liable to transportation. In June of that year Mr. Curwen made a passionate protest in the House of Commons over the use of spring-guns, declaring that it were better that the whole race of game should become extinct rather than that it should owe its preservation 'to such cruel expedients.' Lord Holland called them 'these diabolical engines,' but no bill was passed to prevent their use, and men did not stay home at nights because of them. There was always the grim satisfaction that sometimes a gun went off and killed a keeper or one of his underlings instead of a poacher. . . .

Men risked their lives poaching because they could not live on the wages they were paid, not even when it was supplemented by the miserable sums doled out from the Poor Rates. It was better to take a chance than to sit by and watch your family starve. Jesse knew that most of the men in the valley went ferreting, or after pheasants and hares, at one time or another, and that there had been an increase of it in the last year. He was even more aware than was his father of the poaching on the Valley Farm acres, and had many a time turned a blind eye to the wires he had found in the grass. But for himself he wanted something more than rabbits ; he wanted what paid best ; he wanted some of the squire's pheasants. He decided to ask Jack Mortimer to accept him as a member of his gang when the season began.

He was impatient for the falling of the leaves. Young Mortimer advised against taking anything before then. If you were poaching for the pot, of course, it was different ; you took what you wanted when you wanted. You might even take a chance of a crack at a hare or a pheasant in broad daylight. But if you were going in for the thing ' proper,' selling to the big poulterers, working it through the coachmen and guards on the mails and vans, you wanted to wait at least till acorn-time and the proper season.

The young labourer was full of poacher's wisdom. It was his boast that even as a young boy he had poached everything poachable, even a swan off the lake in the squire's pleasure-grounds adjoining the park. It ate very nice, he said, like goose. The eggs were good, too, if you could get them. He and his father had once got away with a deer out of the park ; all you wanted was a double-barrelled gun and someone waiting handy with a cart. His father had taught him to poach, in the ' famine ' years of the ' bread or blood ' riots. It was a great adventure then, for a boy, but now it was more than that. Now it was a question of the empty belly and of spiting those who called themselves the working man's ' betters,' whilst they stole his land and his common rights.

He preferred to take pheasants by hand, or with a net, he told Jesse. You could work silently that way. Besides, it didn't do to get caught with a gun nowadays. You wanted a good silent cur to drive the birds down their runs into the net, or a single bird into a noose ; or you went out without a dog and took the birds by hand as they roosted—but you could only do this, of course, whilst the leaves were still on the trees to give you cover. You took the bird by the feet, the way you might take a roosting hen out of a fowl-house, and you wrung its neck before it had time to start squawking. You had to work quickly and silently, and you had to know every inch of the ground before you started. Working round and about you had plenty of opportunity for that. You had to watch out for where the pheasants roosted. For rabbiting you wanted a good moon, or you couldn't find the buries, but for pheasants, provided you knew your way about, you didn't want too light a night, or too still a one ; a bit of a wind stirring the dry leaves underfoot, and the branches all round, covered your own movements. A night with a cloudy moon and a rainy wind. . . . But after Jesse had been out with the boys a few times he would soon learn the tricks of the trade. You could go after salmon in November, with a lantern and a gaff ; there was nothing to it ; you just stuck them as they came up ; just below the weir was the best place. You were best working alone on that job ; once the keepers got wind of anything going on you dursn't go near the river, and with the water rushing you couldn't hear anyone coming up on you ; but the job itself was dead easy.

But pheasants, and any other kind of feathered game, was the best work, taken all round. You got a good six months' market ; a lot of the stuff never reached the towns, but went to the inns along the road. The coachmen and guards made their arrangements with book-keepers and porters. Pheasants were easiest to get, too. Once you knew how. You never went into a preserve without a crêpe mask on, of course ; you couldn't afford to take any chances. Not if you didn't fancy being brought up before a J.P.—one of the landed gentry himself, or as likely as not a whole bench of 'em—and a trip in a transport ship. You had to get to know the habits of the keepers on the land you proposed to work ; there wasn't the keeper living who would stop up all night, or could be in two places at once ; and if he had a whole squad of assistants they couldn't cover an entire estate. It wasn't enough just to know the runs and roosting places of the birds ; you had to know the keepers' runs—and when they roosted. And you never talked in the ale-house, because you never knew but what there was an eavesdropper from Bow Street passing himself off as something else. When you could you took a stroll in the daytime in the rear of a keeper, following him on his rounds, so that you knew where the alarm-guns were set, and all such useful information touching his lordship's land. . . .

The whole business excited Jesse like the thought of women. Mortimer assured him that there was no one in the valley nowadays who poached for the love of adventure, but solely out of dire need, but Jesse felt that even if he didn't need money for his secret life as much as the other men needed it for their families he would still be unable to resist the excitement of stalking pheasants under a poacher's moon. Jack Mortimer became a hero in his eyes, like the men who led the bread-or-blood riots, and the remote dim figure of the fiery Mr. Cobbett. He never tired of listening to Mortimer's stories, of raids carried out in broad daylight, and with guns ; of cords tripped over in dark woods, setting off alarms that started the keepers' dogs barking, signal for a cross-country race between poachers and keepers ; of skirmishes with keepers and breathtaking escapes ; of men hanged for wounding keepers in self-defence, aye and young men at that, married, with wives and babes ; sent to the gallows, or to the other side of the world for seven years—which meant for ever, for how many could ever earn the fare back ? All for a few rabbits or hares, which belonged by rights to nobody but God; who had made them to run wild about the country-side ; or for a few fancy birds raised for the guns, for gentlemen's pleasure, whilst all around the men who worked the gentlemen's land by the sweat of their brows lived in wretched hovels, earned five or six shillings a week, and starved, they and their children. But let any of them knock over a hare, or put a wire down for a rabbit, or take a pheasant or two, and raise a hand against the gentleman's stooge who caught him at it, and he was for the transport ship or worse. . . .

All the bitterness of a hopeless, defeated countryside would be in Jack Mortimer's voice as he told of these things, and Jesse would listen with a heart stirred by anger and revolt. He began to realise something of the unceasing civil war between gamekeepers and poachers—fundamentally a class-war involving the whole unjust system by which men lived—and the savagery of the convictions under the Game Code. These men were not stealing, he told himself, passionately, they were merely taking back what enclosure had taken from them.

Jack Mortimer's 'gang' consisted of seven men beside himself. Two were working on the roads, navvying, and earning from half-a-crown to three shillings a week ; one was a dispossessed tenant farmer turned labourer ; three were young farm labourers, one of them married ; the other was a dispossessed small-holder, a married man with a wife and four young children. They all belonged to the valley. They went after everything that was going ; they went after rabbits with ferrets and a net ; they went after partridges and pheasants with nets, and guns when they dared ; they put wire nooses down for hares ; occasionally they bagged a fawn from his lordship's park—you could get a nice price for venison. Each man did a little on his own, for the pot, occasionally, but they worked together to keep the driver of the mail-coach supplied—what he did with the stuff was no concern of theirs, whether he sold direct to poulterers in some town, or to the book-keeper or porter of an inn on his route ; he paid the head of the gang, Jack Mortimer in this case, and he in turn paid the other men, equally dividing out the money.

When Mortimer's gang learned that Jesse Hallard proposed to turn poacher they were instinctively suspicious. Why should any son of Farmer Hallard need to go a-poaching ? they demanded. To which Jesse replied, grimly, " Because he is Farmer Hallard's son and therefore hasn't even half-a-crown a week to call his own ! Young Luke here works for my father for three shillings a week. I do the same work for nothing."

" Ye get yer food," the ex-tenant farmer reminded him, dourly.

" A man needs more than food ! " Jesse flashed at him.

" Does a man risk his neck to go a-whoring ? " one of them demanded.

" Aye, if his name's Jesse Hallard," Mortimer said, curtly, then rounded on them. " Ah, leave him be, can't yer ? What is it to do with anyone else how a man spends the money he comes by ? 'Tis what we all suffer from—people always interferin' and trying to tell us what we ought to do. Aren't we always being told how the poor squander their money—as though only the rich have any right to spend their money how they choose! Whether Jesse Hallard spends his money in the ale-house or the bawdy house, or puts it in the collection-bag at chapel, 'tis nobody's business but his own! Jesse Hallard is working along with Jack Mortimer's gang, and any man that doesn't like it can get out!"

Nobody got out; they all knew and liked Jesse, but they were determined not to have him work with them at nights; he was, after all, William Hallard's son, and there was no farmer in the parish more determined to keep his shooting to himself and to support the gentry in upholding the Game Laws; how could they be sure that he was not at heart his father's son, and not acting for his father, out to spy on them and get them run to earth? Apart from that, several of the older ones resented his motives; the ex-tenant farmer was an ardent Primitive Methodist and could not get over the abomination of the idea that Jesse Hallard wanted any money he made from poaching for riotous living, for drinking in taverns and whoring after strange women. To allow him to work with them would be to sanction that, nay, more, collaborating with him in the wickedness of his ways. Jack Mortimer might say it was none of their business, but the Mortimers were Catholics, and everyone knew that Papists thought you could break all the commandments so long as you went to confession. Others, less concerned with morals, argued that an inexperienced man in the gang might make a false move that would imperil them all. It was altogether risking too much to take young Hallard with them when they had serious business on hand.

Mortimer had to acknowledge the validity of this objection. Also he did not want to fall out with the older men who made the moral objections, because they were the men with the most experience, and one of them was a close friend of the coachman through whom they sold the game. Mortimer suggested to Jesse that they should go out together a few times, just the two of them, and that after that Jesse should work on his own. Jesse agreed that all things considered it was the better plan. For one thing it gave him more freedom; he could never be sure of getting out on a certain night. For another he had qualms about operating on the Valley Farm land; he had neither affection nor respect for his father, but was surprised to find that he had some sort of feeling for the farm itself. He could not say exactly what it was; he only knew that he discovered an obscure aversion to the idea of poaching so much as a rabbit on Valley Farm. Others could do it and he would not interfere; but for himself some curious sense of loyalty was involved.

He was relieved when on their first night out together Mortimer took him away over to some country at the other side of Oldport. Mortimer had been working there and knew a little copse to which the pheasants came to roost, strayed away from the manor preserves after the berries in the hedgerows; he had been encouraging them for the past week, throwing grain down. They were to be had for the taking, like so many sitting hens. The advantage of casual labouring was that it gave you a chance to get to know the countryside. . . .

There was a hedge skirting the wood, and you could get right up to the birds at the other side of the hedge without they knowing you were there. There was a gap in the hedge at the very place where they went to roost—he had seen to that. They could crawl in under the hedge and put their hands up as easy as under a willing wench's petticoats. Then they would take the stuff into Oldport and dispose of it right away and get the money then and there. After that, said young Mortimer, 'the pleasures of the town.' . . . He could do with a night out himself.

III

OF that night of dual initiation Jesse remembered the dark little wood with which he began the night better than the dark little room in which he ended it. By the time he reached the sailors' brothel in the narrow back street behind the Oldport quays his brain was fuddled and his senses numbed. When he crept out of his room and down the back stairs, across the stone-floored back kitchen and out to the rickyard, to meet Jack Mortimer down by the river whilst the night was still young, every nerve in his body was tinglingly aware. He had the feeling that never in his life before had he felt so intensely alive; as though until then he had been moving in a dream. Tonight everything was new; when the night was over he would be launched upon strange new seas of living; tonight the closing of the rickyard gate behind him was a leaving of the harbour.

Then there was the river and the murmur of it in the darkness, and the rank smell of elder bushes, and a sudden pungency of wild mint crushed out under their feet as he and Mortimer dropped down over the low grey stone parapet of the bridge and on to the enclosed common. There was the satisfaction of using the common again, of asserting a common right. There was the smell of sea on the air as they bore down on Oldport, and the taste of it on their lips. There was the moon climbing up, golden as harvest, so brilliant you could have sworn a warmth came from it. Then there was the white line of the sea, and the voice of the river growing louder as it ran out to meet it. And after that the skirting of the town, the blackness of fields lying in its shadow, a blacker darkness where the road ran through woods, and a plunge across marshland to avoid the turnpike. There was the thatched huddle of a village and a drifting smell of wood-fires and a barking of dogs, and then they were cutting across fields again, keeping under the hedges, out of reach of the moonlight. Then a belt of trees flanking a field of stubble, and the two of them standing flat against the hedge listening not merely with their ears, it seemed to Jesse, but with their entire skin's surface. He had the sense of being aware of every sound for miles around, the stir of a leaf, the crackle of twigs and dead leaves when something stirred on the ground, the movements of sheep and cattle and horses out of sight. His senses were keyed up like an animal's for scents and sounds and faint move-ments, every nerve of his body on the alert. Then they were moving soundlessly, invisibly, along the hedge, under the hazel-nut trees and the hawthorns, here and there caught by brambles or thorns, moving across the sandy face of rabbit buries, and always, every few silent steps, stopping and listening so intently they could hear, it seemed, the blood running in their veins and the throb of their hearts loud as a horse cropping in the next field. They found the gap under a clump of nut-bushes and pressed through into the copse and stood again listening to the silence. Mortimer laid a hand on Jesse's arm and pointed to a small oak a few feet from them. The pheasants roosted on the low spreading branches like hens on a perch.

Mortimer unfastened a sack wrapped round his body under his smock and handed it to Jesse, motioning to him not to move ; he himself advanced towards the tree so slowly that to Jesse, watching, all his nerves taut and listening, it seemed as though he would never reach it. He had watched a lurcher stealing upon its prey in the same way. He reached the tree without disturbing a bird, and then stood motionless. A few seconds later there was a faint, instantly smothered scuffle, as though a wind had sprung up suddenly and disturbed some leaves ; then silence again, followed a few seconds later by another scuffle, and a brace of pheasants lay at the foot of the oak-tree. An owl called, eerily, then dropped down through the moonlight above the tree-tops and moved soundlessly round the copse with a gleam of white breast. There was the sudden commo-tion of a startled bird, and the swift vibration of a bat's wings, and under cover of that rustle of life in the wood Mortimer reached to a higher branch and brought down another sleeping pheasant. It went on for some time ; the listening, the waiting, the imperceptible move-ments, the faint smothered scuffle like a small wind in the leaves. Death moved in a man's hands along the moon-silvered boughs, and it was no more than a wind-stirred scuffle of dead leaves.

They left the copse with the same slow, lurcher-like stealthiness with which they had entered it, but now there was a heavy sack to drag back through the hedge under the nut-bushes and across dew-drenched fields. They walked in silence, taking it in turn to carry the sack, and keeping out of the moonlight.

All the way back to Oldport Mortimer made only one comment. " 'Tis good practice to try taking fowls in the hen-roost that way," he said. " Take them by the feet and clap your other hand over their heads to stop them squawking. With pheasants you wring their necks at the same time. Some bash their heads against the tree-trunk, but it spoils the look of them, and some poulterers object. Same with rabbits and hares. The less they're shot about the better. Better to tidy 'em up a bit before handing 'em over if need be. There's folks don't mind the blood being spilled for the table but don't like seeing it. 'Tis best to take them with a snare."

Back at the outskirts of Oldport they parted company. Morti-mer wanted to get rid of the stuff right away. Jesse was to wait for him at *The Ship's Bell* along the quay. Mortimer gave him five shillings on account. . .

The entering of the tavern cut the night clean in half. Out in the fields, in the cold ' smoky ' dampness of the air, everything had been taut, tense, clear-cut. Once the tavern door had swung to all was confusion ; heat, noise, smoke engulfed ; in the sudden transition from one atmosphere to the other, and the sudden relaxation of strung-up nerves, the strong brown ale went quickly to the head. Then Mortimer came back, rattling silver in his pockets, and ordered bran-dies. He was twenty-two, but life had already bitten lines of bitter-ness and hardship into his young face. He had a thin tight mouth and shifty eyes, and in all his movements the nervous intensity of one perpetually keyed up, always listening, always expecting something to creep up behind him. He was always hunting and always hunted. Tonight, after the successful raid on the copse, his pockets jingling with silver, he was as near to happiness and relaxation as he would ever be. Tonight he would get drunk and sleep with a woman, some painted sailors' Moll who would suit him very well. But if she thought she could take his money whilst he slept she reckoned without his poacher's awareness ; neither alcohol nor consummated lechery could make him more than skim the surface of sleep. Nor did he propose to allow any harpy to strip young Hallard of his share of their night's earnings ; he would do all the necessary payings-out and keep the rest of the money in his own pockets until they were both out of Oldport.

He explained this to Jesse, and Jesse merely nodded and smiled, taking nothing in, his head swimming with the fumes of the brandy, with the heat and noise and smoke, and the excitement of women pressing close to him, offering themselves.

He had no clear recollection of leaving *The Ship's Bell* with Mortimer and two women, and of coming to the tall dark old house in the narrow street where rats slunk amongst the garbage in the gutters running with water. Darkened eyelids and a bright mouth and a hat swirling with feathers ; a painted face seen through a haze—of tobacco smoke, of starlight, of wavering candlelight. He looked round the room, dazedly. There had been another room with a woman and a bed in it. But no children here in the dark corner under the eaves. No marriage bed this. He wanted to laugh at the thought and explain it to the girl, but it was too much trouble to find the words.

The girl took off her flashy feathered hat, ran her hands through her piled-up hair, and came over to him. She had a formula, but for once she did not utter it. He was so young, and he stood looking down at her with a kind of awe and wonder. Something stirred in her ; she put up a hand and brushed back the hair from his forehead as tenderly as a woman in love.

" You're so pretty," he said, wonderingly.

She smiled with quite unprofessional tenderness and led him to the bedraggled bed. But now Jesse was oblivious of squalor, and aware only of the certainty of his blood and the immediacy of release.

IV

A DOUBLE excitement worked in Jesse's veins now ; the excitement of women and the excitement of poaching, and the one was bound up with the other. By day he lived in a dream of moonlight and shadows in still woods, of wild bought kisses, and the hunger and ecstasy of striving flesh. His parents were always telling him, impatiently to ' wake up,' but he had no desire to waken, even if he could. It was enough that his blood was awake.

Every evening, even when he was not planning to go out, he longed for the family supper to be over so that he could escape to his room, to be alone, with nothing to break in on his dream. He would leave his candle unlighted and lean out of the tiny casement sniffing the air like a night animal. There was the domestic inner circle of smells that ringed the farm, the smell of stored apples, the musty smell of old furniture, of burning logs, of stables and byres and rickyard, the cold pungent scent of chrysanthemums in the strip of garden below the window, the rank smell of the duck-pond beyond. Beyond that was the smell of the fields, the earthy smell of fallen leaves, of dead bracken drenched in dew, the cold smoky smell of Autumn dampness and decay; the smell of the woods, the smell of mould, moist and brown and full of moss and fungus, the acrid smell of a dead animal rotting in the undergrowth, the cold, secret, foxy smell of the woods at night. And beyond that still, the smell of the river, the brackish smell of mud, the peppermint smell of wild mint, and the salt seaweed smell of the sea; the smell of harbours and quays, the smell of fish and ropes and tar and bilge-water; the smell of the town that was a smell of horse-dung, and garbage in the gutters, and wood-fire smoke, and an ale and tobacco smell of taverns, and the sweet scent of women's perfumes. And then the final circle that was the strange, subtle, exciting smell of a woman's body.

He remembered her only dimly, the girl in the feathered hat, woman without a name, sailors' woman of the town, but he longed for her with a passion that consumed him night and day, and lived only to get back to her. All the excitement of poaching was bound up with her, the one excitement leading to the other. Stealing pheasants, hares, rabbits, he stole the thing his blood insisted he had a right to, for which his whole tumescent youth clamoured—life. He poached as much from necessity as any man in the valley, since man does not live by bread alone. He ceased to be particular what he poached, so long as there was a market for it. He discovered that there was more money in rabbits than he had supposed. At Mortimer's suggestion he acquired a pair of ferrets of his own and a net. He fixed up a box for the ferrets at the back of the loft above the barn, and kept the net tucked down behind it, under a bale of hay. He arranged with the driver of a mail-van to dispose of the stuff. He was always instinctively on the look-out for the runs of hares and the roosting-places of pheasants, even when they were on his father's land and he knew that he would take none of them. He could never see a bank under a hedge holed with rabbit buries without instantly visualising the net spread across; a pheasant never ran across his path or whirred up from the stubble with a clatter of wings but he knew an instinctive spasm of regret that he was not stalking it. He grew reckless and was prepared to risk a gun on his nocturnal adventures, but dared not take one from his father's rack, and Mortimer refused to lend him one. It was too risky, he always insisted, and if you got caught with a gun as well as a net it meant transportation for sure. Sometimes, in some woods, Jesse would wonder whether transportation was so bad; supposing you were shipped to the other side of the world with no chance of returning—what was so special about this side of the world? There were women to be had at the other side of the world, weren't they? But Mortimer said that a transport ship was hell, with human beings packed down below decks the way they would never dare pack animals. More serious in Jesse's opinion was your gun going off in a skirmish with keepers and wounding one of them, when it meant hanging—and he had a passionate desire to live.

He had several scares. The first time he set out to take pheasants by hand on his own, in taking one bird he disturbed another, and it flew up with a shattering screech and a commotion of wings that seemed to rouse the whole wood to life. The barking of a dog came volleying through the darkness, and he broke out into a sweat, yet dared not move. Nothing happened ; everything subsided into quietness again. It was, he realised, merely a farm watch-dog that had barked, but he lived an eternity of taut-nerved suspense in a few seconds. On another occasion, inside the squire's park, making his way towards the pheasant preserve, he suddenly realised that a keeper was bearing down on him ; he shrank back into a deep pool of shadow by a rhododendron thicket, and the keeper passed so close that the darkness seemed all one with the velvet of his jacket, a corduroy of darkness pressing against his face, blacking out all else. The keeper passed, then paused under an oak-tree. He stood there, peering through the darkness, listening. Jesse felt the darkness pricking with the intensity of his listening, and he himself dared not move. He knew that the keeper knew that there was someone there and was waiting for the trespasser to betray his presence. He knew that the keeper would wait. But he also knew, with a poacher's certainty, that no keeper waits forever. Whereas the poacher, with everything to lose, is prepared to wait indefinitely. He stood staring across at the darkness under the oak-tree and felt the keeper staring back at the darkness of the rhododendrons. In daylight the keeper would touch his cap to him, Farmer Hallard's son, the heir of Valley Farm. Perhaps in a few hours' time. Jesse suddenly wanted to laugh. He grew tired of standing with nothing to lean against, and squatted down under the bushes ; there was a sudden scurry and a badger ran out a few yards from him. Instantly the keeper fired. Jesse remained crouching, waiting, listening. The park darkened as a cloud passed over the moon, and the keeper came out from under the oak and went on up over a rise of the ground towards the faint white glimmer of the mansion. Still Jesse did not move. Keepers had a way of turning abruptly once they had given the impression they were moving off. He did not move until the keeper vanished into the dimness, then he worked his way round the rhododendron enclosure and left the park. It was too risky to stay. The keeper might be going for a dog. The night was not finished ; he had some wires put down for hares outside, on what had once been the common. He never liked being inside preserves and plantations ; even though

34

the common was now enclosed he had a feeling of space and freedom there, instead of being shut in. His snares turned out to be empty ; he should have gone earlier, he reflected, gloomily ; there were some gipsies encamped down by the river, and they had probably got there first. He should have gone at sundown, but had been unable to get away. On such nights of sleeveless errands he would feel that he would go mad with longing and frustration, and be filled with a violent hatred of his father for keeping him without money. He would think then that he could not stand the life of working and living at home ; he would go far away, hire himself out to some other farmer ; or join a ship. But tomorrow was always another day, full of fresh hope, the anticipation of fresh excitement. The day would be taut with the anticipation of the night, the romance of nocturnal adventure, the fascination of danger, the fast-beating heart, the blood pricking with intensity of awareness.

He had another scare on the night when a hare bolted into the wire he had set up at the end of a run, and gave out a piercing scream as it hanged itself. Instantly a keeper's dog came bounding up, barking furiously. Jesse grabbed the hare and the wire and leaping the bank plunged along in the shadow of the other side of the hedge, then headed out across a field of stubble. A bullet whizzed past his shoulder and another grazed his hand. He got out on to the road, broke through another hedge and pelted across Valley Farm fields. Moving warily across the rickyard he felt the blood flowing warmly over his hand. He pushed the hare and the snare into a bed of nettles under the hedge that bounded the rickyard and went on to the house. He felt the need to see to his hand before doing anything more about the hare.

As he approached the house with its long low roof sweeping down over the corn-room, and its attics blinking out high up under the twisted chimneys, there was the click of a latch, and he shrank back instinctively into a clump of elders by some duck-coops. Jessica came out of the store-room carrying a lantern, and he stepped forward.

She started. " You ! " she said, then stated, " I was going to fetch some more wood—there was not enough brought in."

He turned and went back along under the elders and syringas to the wood-pile. She stood holding the lantern whilst he picked out the logs, then noticed his hand.

" What have you done to your hand ? "

He told her, recklessly, " A bullet grazed it."

She accused him coldly, " You were out poaching with Jack Mortimer's gang."

" I was alone." He looked at her. " How did you know I was out after anything ? "

" You leave your traps about. I found some wires in your room one day."

He made no comment and they went back to the house together. At the door of the corn-room he piled the logs up in her arms.

" Will you bring some hot water and some clean rag to my room ? "

" Why should I trouble, pray ? You can run the pump over your hand, can you not ? "

She turned away and went along to the back door of the outer kitchen. Jesse cut in through the corn-room to the dairy and up the back stairs to his room.

He sat down on his bed in the dark. He was certain that despite her words Jessica would come. He could not have said why he was so confident. Any more than Jessica could have said why she came.

She came carrying a pitcher of hot water, a strip of old clean linen, and a candle in a heavy brass holder. She set the candle down on the chest-of-drawers, stood the pitcher on the floor, and came over to him, taking his wounded hand.

" You don't deserve that anyone should care," she said, with prim severity.

He smiled down at her. " Then why do you ? "

She did not answer, but dipped a piece of the cloth into the hot water and began to sponge the wound. Her hair fell forward over his face and he was aware of the familiar smell of it ; a smell of earth and leaves he had always thought it ; leaves lying on wet ground.

Without looking up she asked, in a low voice, " Why do you go out at nights, Jesse ? "

" Adventure, perhaps."

" John thinks you are leading a bad life in the town. Someone he knows saw you coming out of a tavern one night."

He said impatiently, " What does John know about what's good or bad ? What is a bad life ? I am living. 'Tis no life here."

" I have to stay here."

" One day you'll marry—— "

" It will be just the same. I shall only go and live on another farm."

He could only say, helplessly, " 'Tis different for women."

She finished binding the cloth round his hand, then tossed back her hair. She stood very straight, her head tilted back a little ; her whole pose held something defiant—something he used to love in her, but had not seen for a long time and thought never to see again.

" I will tell you something. The other day a gipsy came here selling rush seats for chairs, and rush baskets, and pegs. He was young and tall and brown, and his hair was black as a rook's, and he wore ear-rings, and a ring on his hand. Perhaps 'tis foolish, but when he smiled at me it was as though we had known each other a long time." She looked at him, steadily. " 'Tis foolishness, is it not ? "

" No, Jessica, 'tis not foolish. I think it would always be like that. He smiled at you, and then—— ? "

" Then he said I was pretty, and asked me would I meet him down by the river when the moon was risen."

" What did you say ? " He had the feeling that if he did not prompt her the flow of her confidence would cease, and it was somehow immensely important that it should go on.

" My heart beat very fast and I said yes. But when the moon came up I didn't go. I watched it coming up over the fields very big and the colour of an orange. I leaned out of my window and thought of him waiting, and I was afraid he would come up here."

" You should have gone. You could have slipped out——"

" If I had gone I shouldn't have come back, most likely."

" It would have been an adventure." It was as though he pleaded with her.

The light died out of her face. " I should have been a gipsy girl with a string of coins round my neck and my hair braided in plaits. I should have learned to cut withies and make baskets and clothes-pegs and tell lies."

" You might have been happy."

She moved away from him. " I have no wish to be bad and wild like a gipsy. I want to be good. I pray to God every night to make me good, like John, and to save you from hell-fire, Jesse."

He had the sense of losing her in the very moment in which she had come close, and he called out to her, sharply, " Jessica—don't go ! Stay a little longer. We used to be friends. Now 'tis all John and books and chapel. You are not yourself any more, Jessica. Not truly yourself. 'Tis not wicked to want to be happy. Even in the Bible it says so. You should have met the gipsy, I tell you ! "

" The devil sent him to tempt me."

At that he sprang up and seized her by the shoulders.

" 'Tis all nonsense to say that, and in your heart you know it ! Why not say that God sent the gipsy to bring you happiness ? Why try to make something bad out of it ? 'Tis what people are always trying to do—make a sin of everything ! God meant us to be happy —I'm sure of it ! There are things in the Bible you never learn about at school and in chapel—things that are kept from us. I could show you——"

She jerked herself free of his hands. " Since when did you take to reading the Bible, Jesse Hallard ? "

He said, eagerly, " I found something one day. By chance. A kind of poem. A love poem. I'll show you——"

He went over to the chest-of-drawers and picked up the black-covered Bible and began turning the pages.

She watched him from the doorway, suspiciously, with her old mistrustful woodland-creature look.

He found the place and brought the book over to her. " You read it," he urged. " You read better than I do."

She took the book from him and bent her head over it and her face was hidden in her hair.

She stared a moment at the two pages spread out before her, then read at random.

' *By night on my bed I sought him whom my soul loveth ; I sought him, but I found him not.*'

She looked up, tossing back her hair.

He said, eagerly, " No one can say 'tis wicked. 'Tis the Bible. There's more about it."

" About what ? "

In his eagerness he was not aware of the scorn in her voice.

" About people loving." His own voice was defiant.

She closed the book and put it back on the chest-of-drawers.

" It does not mean what you think it means," she said, curtly, " 'Tis all about the Church and Christ. I am going to bed. I hope your hand will be better by the morning. 'Twould be better not to wear the bandage in case one of the keepers is about. It might look suspicious."

Her hand was on the latch and he made one more effort.

" I heard in Oldport the other evening that if we have severe frosts this winter like last there's to be a fair on the river like the big-frost fair they had in London last year. They are sure to have it. 'Tis going to be a hard winter, for sure. The gulls are already coming in-land, and the berries are thick on the rowans. I thought we might go to it together." He added, smiling, " You might meet your gipsy there."

She said coldly, " That would be a good reason for not going."

She was gone, then, the latch clicking behind her.

He sat down on the bed again, nursing his wounded hand, think-ing that he must go out and hide the snare and the wire in a safe place, thinking, exultantly, that only a part of Jessica had gone over to John after all. That her heart had said yes to the gipsy was something, even though she had not kept the tryst. In her heart she was unchanged; he was sure of it.

Let the hard winter that everyone dreaded come soon ; it could not come too soon. Then whatever happened Jessica should come with him to the fair, and on a tide of gaiety, colour, laughter, be given back to him—fully, finally, and forever.

V

JESSE waited as impatiently for the hard weather as he had for acorn-time. Life seemed to be a series of waiting for something ; you were always living in the future. Today was always something to be got through to reach tomorrow.

After a few adventures in the town he suddenly sickened of it. It was not what he wanted, any more than Anna Holding had been. He spent weeks looking for the girl in the feathered hat, hoping, hungering, for the chance of going with her again. He saw her several times, but always surrounded by sailors, and he knew something like jealousy. Then there was the evening in *The Ship's Bell* when she came up to him, smiling, remembering him, inviting him—and he did not want her. If he had no money, she said, it would not matter ; she liked him. . . . That was the second time a woman had said that to him, and whereas once it would have been gratifying, given him a satisfying sense of power, it suddenly made him angry. All this was not what *The Song of Songs* was about, all these painted sailors' Molls and the squalid beds they offered. Even the animals, who knew nothing of love, were superior to this. "All the girls want to kiss you, Jesse," Jessica had said ; then the thought had excited him ; now it disgusted him, seemed a degradation of his man-hood. Now there seemed a leer in every admiring female glance or smile directed at him, and now that his first youthful curiosity about women was satisfied he recoiled from the desire of women. He wanted a woman all right, but no longer just any woman. Perhaps in his heart he had always been looking for the fairest among women. If Jessica had never gone away from him it might all have been different. He might have been able to wait then for her who was fairest as the moon, clear as the sun.

It came to him with renewed vehemence that night at *The Ship's Bell*, when the girl in the feathered hat offered herself to him for nothing, that he had to get Jessica back. He could not give up poaching now, because it was in his blood, but he no longer wanted the money for women of the town. He needed it so that he might drink with sailors and listen to their talk of ships and foreign places ; he needed it for the independence it represented ; and so that when the frost fair came he would have money to spend on swings and side-shows with Jessica.

39

'*Awake, O north wind . . . and blow upon my garden.*' He carried the invocation in him like a prayer.

In the mornings now the trees stood knee-deep in thick white mists, and hills were islanded in vaporous seas. The valley viewed from above looked like a lake with tiny islands of trees. When the sun got up the day became fresh and crisp and clear, with pale cold sunlight and patches of pale blue sky. There were mauve and purple blurs of Michaelmas daisy in the farm gardens, and visible through the wrought-iron gates of the rectory and the manor, and a wine and scarlet velvet of dahlias. The hovels of the labourers had no gardens ; they had vanished long ago, swallowed up under bills of enclosure. Jessica brought in branches of bronze and yellow beech leaves from the woods, and the pheasants came out along the hedgerows after the berries. The first frosts only rimed the earth, leaving everything drenched when the sun got high into the sky. At midday and in the early afternoons the sun would have almost a summer warmth. There were still pale fingers of honeysuckle in the woods, and a lingering foam of meadow-sweet in the ditches. The sap was running back, but imperceptibly, and the earth offered up its last rich bounty. The plough turned the stubble back into the earth. Mushrooming was as good a pretext for poaching as any. There was a baying of hounds, a thunder of hooves, and the pink coats of the huntsmen charging over the fields, leaping the hedges, flashing along the sky-line of the bare hills. Once it had been an adventure to go out with Jessica, picking up beech-nuts and the shining horse-chestnuts, like polished mahogany, to go mushrooming and black-berrying, and cutting hips and haws. Once they had shared together the excitement of watching the hunt in full cry. Now it seemed to Jesse that everything he did and everything he felt, he did and felt alone.

'*Awake, O north wind . . .*'

Then the ' little summer ' was finished, and a wild west wind sprang up, full of rain, and the leaves began to come down thick and fast, and gardens, fields, woods, became sodden and bedraggled. Now it was no longer possible to take pheasants by hand under cover of the leaves, and poachers grew reckless and took a chance with a gun in broad daylight. The wind changed again, and the frosts began to eat into the ground, hardening it. In November icy winds began to blow in from the sea, destroying the last flowers, stripping the trees of their few remaining leaves, a final sweeping away of summer's last traces. It was winter, cold and biting and unpitying. The first snow fell at the end of the month, and it was a white Christmas. The real hard weather, everyone said, would come with the turn of the year. It was always that way. For Jesse it could not come too soon.

Jack Mortimer was hauled up before the bench on a charge of poaching salmon. The keeper produced a gaff which he said he had found at the spot from which Mortimer had run off. The young man denied that it was his gaff; his was at home in the dresser drawer, he said, recklessly—after all, they had to catch him using it. The magistrates sent round to the Mortimer home and the gaff was eventually produced in court. Jack was discharged—and the Mortimer gang seized the keeper and trundled him in a wheelbarrow out of the valley and nearly into Oldport.

A maid at the rectory was brought to bed of a bastard, attributed to the rector's son, and Mrs. Hallard dismissed the dairymaid lest similar temptation beset Jesse. Jesse had been well enough aware of the girl for a long time; but she was too easy, and he was tired of females ready to fall like ripe fruit into his hand. He was tired of the opposite sex of all ages looking at him dewy-eyed. He wanted Jessica again, Jessica as she used to be, the wild thing peering out of the thicket, sharing things with him without any need of words. When the frost-fair came she would be unable to resist the excitement of it, and once they were sharing something together again all would be well. It had to come, that hard winter.

He was heartened by the fact that the duck-pond at the farm was frozen hard enough to skate on by Christmas, but it was not the same as others years. Christmas was never a very gay affair in the Hallard household; there was a turkey, always, and a plum pudding, and holly behind the pictures, but it also involved extra attendance at chapel, and what had always seemed to Jesse and Jessica as children a series of Sundays in succession. But they were allowed to hang lanterns in the bushes beside the frozen pond and to skate there by their light, and for the two 'wild ones' this was always exciting. This year, however, it was John and Jessica who skated together, and Jesse was left to struggle with two girl cousins who were staying in the house with their parents. One girl was a little younger than Jesse and the other a little older, and both blushed and giggled and whispered together, and thought him the handsomest young man they had ever seen, and flirted with him and simpered and were coy with him until he felt that he could murder the pair of them. He obeyed a malicious impulse and played up to the younger one after a time, and having skated her over to the far side of the pond on Christmas Eve sat her down on the bank and kissed her violently. He had been prepared for her to burst into tears and cry for help; instead of which she flung her arms round his neck and clung to him with a strangulating grip and informed him that she had been longing for him to do that ever since she had set foot in the house.

At which Jesse disentangled himself, got up, pulled her to her feet, and skated her back to the other side of the pond, where he left her, then went off on his own. He spent the rest of the night out under the hedges with his ferrets and a net.

It was a relief when Christmas was over and the visitors departed —the younger sister red-eyed because she did not know when she would see her darling cousin Jesse again, and she was sure her heart was broken and that she would go into a decline. Jesse, who felt that he could afford to be generous now that they were going, gave them both his gentle, charming, meaningless smile.

There were some hard frosts in January, but it was no repetition of 1814, and Jessica told him, triumphantly, " There isn't going to be a frost-fair, and the gipsies have gone."

" There is still February and March," he told her, with a hopefulness he did not feel, " and the gipsies will be back in the Spring."

But February brought only the disappointment of rain and mild days and early primroses, and March howled and lambs were born and then somehow Spring was on the air. In all that time Jesse had been out at night, in the woods and under the hedges, several times a week, taking his stuff into Oldport, drinking in *The Ship's Bell*, talking with sailors, but never going with any of the women. The more they invited him the less they attracted him, whether they offered them-selves for money or what they called 'love.' It was all too easy, when even the whores could be had for nothing, he would reflect bitterly. He frequently wished he were ugly, so that when a woman wanted him it would be for something more than his body. Life seemed all disappointments and hopeless hopes.

On fine nights he liked to stroll about the cobbled streets of the little town and find his way down to the quayside, and leaning against a capstan lose count of time watching the shadowy movements of the ships, with their hulks black against the night, and the lights dipping dimly at their mastheads, swaying in small endlessly repeated circles. Men would come down to the ships and go aboard, some of them lurching perilously on the gang-planks. That was life, he would reflect, to go aboard and roll out of harbour to the open sea, to come after many days to a new place, those far-off coloured places where oranges hung on trees, and green cockatoos lived in jungles instead of in cages. There were the West Indies and the South Seas ; there was Bordeaux, and Marseilles, and Port Said. He was never tired of looking at the things the men in *The Ship's Bell* showed him, brought back from foreign parts, pieces of carved ivory, carved wood, strange leatherwork, strange coins ; a painted fan from China ; an em-broidered shawl from Spain. They drank rum and complained that it was not like the rum you got at sea, not like the rum you drank in the West Indies. Strange, exciting names rolled easily off their

42

tongues—the Azores, the Barbadoes, the Seychelles. Names that blazed with heat and sunshine—Zanzibar, Las Palmas, Buenos Aires, Montevideo. Rio de Janeiro, Hong Kong, they would say, carelessly, as a man might say Bridport or Plymouth. Their talk fascinated him and filled him with restlessness. A farmer's life was a clod's life ; you might as well be a sheep or a bullock or a turnip in a field. But for poaching it would be unbearable. He began to think of the island again, of escape by sea. His first love reasserted itself with a new intensity. No woman, he would think, with a rush of passion, could ever be as beautiful as a four-master with all canvas spread ; no young girl had the grace of a single white sail dipping in the wind. Even the tubs of fishing-boats with their patched russet sails stirred him to something like love. Turning his back on the quays he would have a sense of turning his back on life. One day he too would go aboard and roll out to sea, away from all the frustrations and disappointments.

In the Spring he went with the girl in the feathered hat again. Her name, she said, was Lucy. Lucy Williams. She came from a farm in a Welsh valley ; but it was no life there. You might as well be dead. Then she went to work in a mill, but that was no life either, you might as well be a slave. She came to Oldport with a sailor and spent the rest of his leave with him in a back-street tavern. When he sailed she moved into a room in one of the houses where no questions were asked and lived as best she could. She had a peculiarly sweet smile, and there was something childishly confiding in her manner.

When they left *The Ship's Bell* Jesse walked her along the quays. He was in two minds about going back with her. He wanted someone to talk to. Lucy did not much like being walked over the quays with their rough cobbles in her thin high-heeled shoes and with her trailing skirt, but she was a docile little creature, and she liked Jesse better than anyone she had ever met. If she could have someone like this young farmer, she thought, they could have a litte home and she would cook and clean and there would be no more sailors, and the past would be all forgotten. But the young farmer looked wistfully at tall ships and talked of one day going to sea himself.

He asked her, as they stood looking at the shadowy outlines of moored ships, " Do you never have a great longing to go aboard and sail far away from everything ? "

But Lucy said no, she was mortally afraid she would be sick, and so alarmed when there was a storm. Coming from Cardiff to Oldport in the stage-coach she had been very sick. She had no wish to travel. She gathered her feather-boa round her and shivered in the cold wind.

" Let us go home," she urged, snuggling up to him.

Home ? Was that squalid room home ?

He looked down at her, and the darkness hid the sadness of his smile, but she heard it in his voice.

" You are so small," he said, " like a small soft kitten. Are you not sometimes afraid of what is going to happen to you in the end ?"

She was very often afraid of what would happen to her in the end. She had seen what happened to other women. But she smiled, prettily, and said, " One day I hope I shall find a nice lad like you and marry him. Then I shall settle down."

He wanted to say, " But no ' nice lad ' will ever marry you, Lucy of the town," but what was the use ? Some crazy homesick, lonely sailor might marry her one day, who should say ?

He put an arm round her shoulders. " Let us go home," he said, firmly.

All over again he discovered how lonely a man could be in a woman's arms.

2

At Easter a travelling fair and circus came to Oldport, camping on a piece of unenclosed ground outside the town. Jesse waited for an opportunity to get Jessica alone. He caught her one afternoon in an idle moment leaning on the low red brick wall which divided a strip of garden at the front of the house from the duck-pond. The pond was flanked on one side by the cattle-yard and on the other by a narrow overgrown path which ran between it and a smaller pond, with the orchard and a sheep pasture beyond. Jesse came out of the barn and saw her, across the yard, and crossed over to her. She glanced up without interest, then continued contemplating the ducks on the pond.

He told her about the fair.

" I saw the waggons going along today," he said, eagerly. " There are lions and tigers in cages ; there's an elephant and a camel and swing-boats, and I hear there is going to be fireworks. We could easily slip out tomorrow night after supper."

She regarded him stonily. " John says such places are full of iniquity. There are gin-booths and half-naked women, and there is dancing——"

" We need not see the naked women or drink gin or dance," Jesse urged. " There's no iniquity in animals and in fireworks——"

" We should have to deceive Mamma and Pappa to go, and that would be wrong," she pointed out.

He leaned his back against the wall so that she, on the other side, was looking out over his shoulder. He snapped the head off some tall sorrel and ran the reddish seeds down through his fingers.

"Have you no wish to enjoy life, Jessica? Are you content to stay here forever doing needlework and helping in the dairy and reading the Bible and singing hymns?"

She was silent. After a moment he looked up at her. She looked away and said slowly, "I doubt that a fair is very entertaining——"

He was sure that she was weakening and he swooped immediately.

"Of course it is! Anything we did together would be! You will retire early after supper with a headache. I shall be prowling about and when I see the light in your room I shall go and wait for you beside the wood-pile. You will arrange the bolster in your bed so that if Mamma peeps in she will think you are there——"

She said violently, "You are wicked, Jesse! You have the black heart! And the wicked shall be cast into hell!"

He laughed. "We have always known that, Jessica, but it used not to hinder you when there was anything you had a mind to do."

She straightened herself up from the wall. "I think it unlikely I shall accompany you," she said, sedately.

His heart exulted. He was quite certain, now, that she would.

He strolled back across the yard and re-entered the dusty darkness of the barn. Jessica went slowly along the narrow red-brick path between the house and the pond, forget-me-nots and wallflowers on one side of her, red and yellow tulips on the other, but she saw only Jesse's face looking up at her, eager, pleading—her darling Jesse. Jesse, who was wicked, who went poaching, who drank in taverns, who went with bad women, who kept bad company, like Jack Mortimer. Jesse, whom she loved. Jesse, with whom once she would have been glad to burn in hell-fire.

At the end of the house she hesitated. Turning right she came to the door of the dairy; she had promised to give a hand with the butter-making that afternoon; she no longer went to school; her shadowy female education was complete. She had now only to learn how to run a house and wait for a husband to turn up. She reflected now that turning left she would follow along the overgrown path between the two ponds, and out on to a cart-track. If she went along there she might meet John returning from school. She did neither. Instead she broke through the bushes and scrambled down the bank to the pond and clambered out along a mossy tree-trunk which as long as she could remember had lain across the pond like a bridge. By going to the end of it it was possible to jump across to the other side and the small wood under whose bare trees Jesse had kissed their cousin on Christmas Eve, though this she did not know.

She took the leap from the end of the tree-trunk and landed on the bank and scrambled up into the wood, where she sat amongst the primroses and celandine and wild anemones and wrestled with her soul. Or so she thought of it. On the one hand the gentle, studious, religious John, helping her to save her soul. On the other the wild, wicked, beloved Jesse, tempting her to lose it. But in scrambling through the bushes and plunging into the wood like that she was already a lost soul ; that was the old Jessica, with leaves and twigs caught in her hair, mud on her shoes, the thorns tearing her dress. So that when the devil came forward in person, pressing through the budding branches, it did not seem so very remarkable, though a strange melting started in her blood. He was young and tall and slim and brown ; he wore brass ear-rings, and a red handkerchief knotted at his throat, and his hair was even blacker and wilder than Jesse's.

He smiled at her, his teeth very white and even, as she had remembered them ; his eyes gay. Jesse's smile so often never reached his eyes.

He said, very politely, " Good afternoon, miss. I was in the meadow yonder, and I saw you." He clipped his words with a faintly foreign accent.

Instantly she was the wild thing again, looking out suspiciously from the thicket of her hair.

" What were you doing in our meadow ? " she demanded.

For answer he brought a dead rabbit out from his coat, where it had lain hidden against his body. She was aware, then, of the blood on his hands.

" We needed something for the pot tonight," he said, simply. " What is one rabbit more or less in all these acres ? "

He dropped down beside her, laying the rabbit at the foot of the tree under which she sat.

" I waited for you that night," he told her, and now his eyes lost their gaiety and accused her.

" I am sorry. It was not possible——"

" We have come back here for the fair. Will you come and let a Romany *chi* tell your fortune ? "

" I cannot say. My brother asked me to go with him, but my mind is not yet made up."

" I shall look for you." It was as though he commanded her. He reached out and stroked the fur of the dead rabbit for a moment, then with a sudden abrupt gesture stuffed it back inside his velvet jacket and scrambled to his feet.

" You will come," he said. She was conscious of him standing over her, looking down at her, commanding her, concentrating his will upon her, stinging her own will into resistance. She made no answer and did not look up, and in a moment heard the crackle of twigs and dead leaves under his feet as he left the wood, and still, resolutely, did not look in his direction.

When he had gone the wood seemed curiously empty. She sat a long time, watching a moorhen busy along the edge of the pond, darting into the bank, then out again, with quick scuttling movements. Once a water-rat ploughed along, dark as the shadowed water. The terrible ennui of youth settled down on her. The afternoon stretched endlessly ahead, empty, purposeless. None of the things that could be done were worth doing. Nothing had been worth doing since she had broken away from Jesse. And he who might have kindled the afternoon to life for her she had let go, resisting him with all the strength of her will as she had resisted capitulation to Jesse the night she had bandaged his hand and he had presented the gipsy to her as a symbol of life, vibrant and aflame against the background of the empty days. Now a second time she had let him go, and he had emptied the wood of everything save the aridity of afternoon. And now her heart called after him, wildly, Gipsy, gipsy——

There was a secret which she had never told anyone. Not even God. Now because the gipsy had melted her blood, loosening those strings in which she had laced her spirit's wildness ever since the break with Jesse, she told it to the budding hawthorn tree under which the gipsy had found her. She put her arms round the tree's twisted trunk and leaned her head against it.

" I love Jesse," she whispered into the gnarled bark. " I never stopped loving him. I never minded what he did—that day when we were playing. But I dare not let him think that. I could not allow myself to be so wicked. I was afraid. I thought I could be saved. Then the gipsy came to the door and the bad thoughts and feelings came back. The lovely thoughts and feelings that make you feel happy and glad to be alive."

She sat a little while longer with her head against the tree-trunk and her feet amongst the primroses splashed by the blood of the dead rabbit, and in the relief of confession once again took comfort in the thought that if she went to hell at least Jesse would go with her, and that hell with Jesse would be better than heaven with anyone else.

Besides, in hell there would be the gipsy, who had poached so many rabbits, stolen so many chickens, told so many lies, lived by his wits, and in all probability never been to chapel in his life.

When she returned to the house John was back from school. The first thing he said was, " The gipsies are camped down by the river again. We shall have to lock the fowls up with special care tonight with that dirty thieving lot of vagabonds about."

47

Jessica looked at him curiously, the pale, serious younger brother who never laughed.

"What were they doing?" she asked.

"Oh, they had a fire in the open and were cooking on it. There was a big black kettle and an old iron pot. A woman was spreading rags of washing out on the bushes. A young man was playing a guitar, and there was a young woman suckling a babe with her bosom all bare." He reddened as he said this, but the sight had angered him, in some curious way, and he wanted to tell it—as though he could spit out the memory of it in words. A barefooted girl in a ragged red dress, with numerous bangles on her bare brown arms, and a necklace of coins round her neck, she had smiled at him as he leaned on the bridge; he had scowled back, and she had burst out laughing. He wanted to spit out that memory, too, but there was something a little humiliating in it, and he could not bring himself to tell it. . . .

"They have no shame, those gipsies," his mother murmured.

"They have come to tell fortunes at the fair," Jessica said.

"And to pick pockets, no doubt," Mrs. Hallard supplemented harshly.

Jessica was silent, but there was a low, smouldering fire of resentment in her. In some curious fashion she felt herself allied with the gipsies.

That evening after supper William Hallard brought out the Bible as always, and because he too had seen the painted waggons rumbling along the lanes to the fair-ground, and the gipsies camped beside the river, heard their music and their ribald laughter, seen their earrings, their bangles, their necklaces, their gaudy dresses, their coloured silk handkerchiefs, was full of just wrath concerning the mammon of iniquity, and chose, therefore, a passage from *Ecclesiastes*, which he read in the slow solemn tones of a man pronouncing judgment!

'*A good name is better than precious ointment; and the day of death than the day of one's birth. It is better to go to the house of mourning, than to go to the house of feasting; for that is the end of all men; and the living will lay it to his heart. Sorrow is better than laughter; for by the sadness of the countenance the heart is made better. The heart of the wise is in the house of mourning; but the heart of fools is in the house of mirth.*'

He looked up from the page and let his gaze rest a moment on Jesse as he read this; without looking up Jesse felt his father's eyes on him and kept his own lowered. Jessica saw her father look at Jesse and her heart began to beat fast. Her father read on!

'*It is better to hear the rebuke of the wise than for a man to hear the song of fools. For as the crackling of thorns under a pot, so is the laughter of the fool; this also is vanity.*'

He closed the book, then added, ' *Vanity of vanities, saith the preacher ; all is vanity.*'

Mrs. Hallard sighed. " How true ! " she murmured, lifting the stocking she was darning nearer to the lamp.

Jessica, whose cheeks had become very flushed, suddenly burst out, " But 'tis not true ! How can sorrow be better than laughter ? Who would wish to go to the house of mourning ? 'Tis all lies, lies, lies ! "

She had sprung up and was breathing heavily, as though she had been running, and looked wildly round at her parents and brothers. John stared at her as though she had gone mad, her father as though he would like to beat her, her mother aghast. But Jesse smiled and without knowing that he did so made a little gesture towards her. After that she did not take her eyes from him, but stood there, panting, her wild gaze fixed on him, and he held that gaze with his own, smiling at her and, it seemed to him, all his blood running to meet hers ; the north wind had wakened at last, the south wind risen, and the spices of the garden were blown forth. He was filled with a wild, exultant happiness.

" Who are you to know better than Holy Scripture ? " her father demanded, angrily. " Be off to bed with you, and tomorrow instead of supper you will write out the seventh chapter of *Ecclesiastes*."

" The child is overwrought," Mrs. Hallard cried, distractedly. She could not think what could have come over the girl ; she had been so good and docile ever since she had stopped running wild with Jesse. All this talk of fairs and gipsies must have excited her. To Jessica she said, " You heard what your father said—to bed with you."

The girl turned to go and Jesse came round the table to her, hardly knowing what he did, put an arm round her shoulder, walked with her to the door.

" She needs no help from you," their father said.

" Leave her be, Jesse," Mrs. Hallard murmured. She found the scene ' upsetting.'

" I am going out," Jesse said shortly.

" You will do no such thing," his father informed him.

Jesse turned and faced him. Now it was his own heart which beat fast, and Jessica's quickened for him.

" I would remind you, sir, that I am eighteen years of age and do a man's work," he said. " By the same token I am entitled to a man's freedom."

Before his father could answer he had gone through the door. In the outer kitchen he grabbed Jessica.

" You must go to bed now, as they say," he whispered. " But tomorrow night it will be different. We are free now."

He kissed her forehead, then darted across the kitchen and lifted the latch of the back door and let himself out into the coolness of the April night. He felt light-headed with excited happiness. Jessica and he belonged once more. Whatever else happened now could not matter. Henceforth he would go out openly at nights when he wanted to, instead of slinking out, guiltily. He was free, and it was Jessica who had broken the chains for him. He laughed aloud as he strode through the misty moonlight. His father would probably lock him out; what of it? There were more ways than one into a house.

At *The Ship's Bell* he plunged through the smoke and crowd and found Lucy tentatively eyeing two sailors. He carried her off before they had realised what had happened, bought a drink for her and for himself, then took her outside.

" Let us go straight back," she suggested, anxiously, afraid he would want her to walk along the quays again.

He laughed and pulled out some money. " Take this and go home and sleep alone for once," he said.

She stared at him, bewildered.

" You have some other girl," she accused him.

He laughed again. " If you like—some other girl."

She said wistfully, " For nothing, perhaps ? "

" 'Tis not like that."

" You love her, you mean ? "

" Yes, I love her. I have loved her all my life. For a whole year she went away, but now she has come back. Now go home, little Lucy, go home."

" Some other night, perhaps ? "

" Perhaps."

She sighed, tucking the money in a purse. " You are a strange lad. Why did you come here at all tonight ? "

" You must believe me when I say I do not truly know. It seems I found myself coming here and seeking you. You should be flattered, Lucy."

But it was all too difficult for Lucy's simplicity.

She said, helplessly. " Perhaps some other time, then," and gathered up her skirts, smiling wanly, then turned away up the dark narrow street.

Jesse turned down towards the harbour. A salt wind and a smell of the sea ran up to meet him, and everything in him seemed gathered in a wild shout of joy.

VI

THE Hallards were extremely worried by this outbreak on the part of their ' two wild ones.'

" It must be the spring," Mrs. Hallard sighed.

" 'Tis the original sin coming out ! " her husband snapped.

Mrs. Hallard felt that she could do no more. She had sent the children to Sunday-school and Bible class regularly every Sabbath ; she had had them thrashed, but now you could not thrash a girl of fifteen and a lad of eighteen, however much they might deserve it and your fingers itch to do it. She wondered whether Mr. Meakin, the minister, could do anything, but somehow she could not see the two wild ones listening to anyone so meek and mild ; they would only laugh at him, she felt sure. At the back of her mind, unacknowledged, lodged the traitorous idea that at eighteen Jesse was more of a man than little Mr. Meakin would ever be. Jessica you could put on bread and water and set to write out passages of the Scriptures, but there was nothing to be done about Jesse. William Hallard had also to acknowledge this fact ; he could only heap more work on to him, keep him without money, speak surlily to him, hurl the scriptures at him, and, of course, pray for him. Though prayer helped out with a good flogging was what was needed. Alternately he could turn him out, leave him to fend for himself, alter his will so that John inherited the farm. But this would cause a scandal, and was not a good name better than precious ointment, saith the preacher ? Even if the boy did go out at nights there was nothing he could do without money. That William Hallard's son might turn poacher was as unthinkable as that William Hallard's wife or daughter might turn whore.

He did not lock Jesse out on the night of the scene, and in the morning he made no comment, but set him to work, after the milking, scraping the walls of the cow-sheds preparatory to new white-washing. He hoped that apart from the monotony of doing nothing else all day long, Jesse would feel the degradation of being given this work which the least intelligent of the hired labourers could do. But Jesse was completely indifferent as to how he filled in the working-hours ; his hands did what was required, but he himself was not present in his body. Presently, somehow, it would be evening, it would be night, and he would come alive in a world alight with adventure and romance ; he and Jessica together.

John was aware of his brother's private life, but the same curious loyalty which made it impossible for Jesse to poach so much as a rabbit on the home farm made it impossible for John even to hint at it to their parents. He had discussed it with Jessica, but he knew that she would never betray Jesse. His room was next to Jesse's, and he had often been awakened by the lift of Jesse's latch in the early hours of the morning. Deep down in him, for all his disapproval, he had a kind of admiration for Jesse. It was because he could never be any of the things that Jesse was that he took refuge in learning and in religion. If he could not be handsome and dashing and a success with women he would be clever and pious ; if he could not be loved he would be respected. The only way he could avoid being jealous of Jesse was by being superior to him and he could only be superior to him intellectually and morally. He always smothered the thought that he would have liked to have had his brother's attractiveness and charm, in the same way that he smothered the carnal thoughts that came to him at times. He refused to think about girls in general, but in order to overcome this he had to concentrate on the thought of the one pure, modest maiden whom he would one day make his wife. She would be someone like Mary Byrd, the blacksmith's daughter ; someone neat and quiet and serene ; not plain, but not beautiful either, because beauty and purity did not go together. Mary Byrd was not in the least interested in him, but it was her virtue that she was not interested in any male. And of course it did not have to be Mary ; she was merely the personification of the ideal. Someone who would not giggle and simper like those absurd cousins ; someone not wild like Jessica ; someone of whom his mother would approve ; that was important. He was continually marvelling at Jesse's lack of fear ; he seemed utterly unaware that he was heading for eternal damnation—or not unaware, but indifferent to that dreadful fact. He himself was as full of fear in adolescence as he had been in childhood ; his fears were merely a continuation, an extension, of those fears. He was afraid of the opposite sex, and the temptation and sinfulness they represented. He had no wish for the freedom which was life to Jesse, because he was afraid of it and its terrible potentialities. He had a dread of the open sea booming outside the harbour. Religion and books were a harbour from which he need never sail out into the terrifying and dangerous unknown.

He had no illusions when Jessica abandoned Jesse and came over to him. Jessica, he knew, at heart would always be Jesse's sister, whatever happened.

" Jesse is wicked," Jessica told him at the time, " I want no more to do with him."

It was a triumph of sorts for him, but it left him sad. He knew very well that he could never mean to Jessica what Jesse, however wicked, would always mean to her. She might cease to love Jesse, but she would never love him, John. But he was not sure that Jessica had ceased to love Jesse. She wanted not to, that was all. He and Jessica would never be close. The only person to whom he ever felt any kind of closeness was Mr. Meakin. That lonely, despairing, ineffective little man, he thought, would like to have cut a figure ; not with women, certainly not, but as a fiery evangelist, snatching brands from the burning ; but because of his innate ineffectiveness he could only be scholarly and pious.

" I shall be like him when I am his age "—Mr. Meakin was about thirty—John would think, with a kind of bitterness. " Except," he would add to the dreary thought, " that I shall never be such a good scholar or so good a Christian."

He asked Jessica, the day after the scene, " What made you behave like that last night ? "

She said, " If I told you I doubt you would understand."

She saw the hurt look on his face.

" If I told you that it was because I had met a gipsy and told a secret to a tree you would think I was crazy, would you not ? "

He looked at her uncomfortably, miserably, and on a sudden impulse she flung her arms round his neck.

" Johnny, Johnny, Johnny," she cried, " you will never understand anything, will you ? Never in all the world ! "

Before he could answer she had whirled away from him and out of the room. He heard her singing as she crossed the yard.

He continued standing beside the table where she had left him, staring down at his pile of books. He felt so bewildered and unhappy that only pride, the fear of someone coming in and discovering him, prevented him from weeping. He began to strap his books together, blindly, hating them. He was the clever one of the family, the scholar ; he had all the learning and he knew nothing ; he would never understand anything in all the world, never, never, never.

He picked up the books and went out into the spring sunlight, a thin, pale, awkward-looking lad with unhappy eyes.

He heard Jesse whistling as he scraped the cowshed walls, and Jessica singing as she crossed the yard with pails of milk.

Something damped down within him struggled to the surface of consciousness, refusing to be smothered any longer.

' I also want to be happy ! '

But long ago he had lost the way in the forest of living. He had lain too many nights listening to the weeping of his brother and sister.

2

Jessica laboriously copied out the seventh chapter of *Ecclesiastes* in her best copperplate—her father insisted on that—whilst the family ate their supper of rabbit-pie. At her elbow was a hunk of bread and a glass of water, which she did not touch. Jesse, devouring rabbit-pie with his usual ravenous hunger, was worried about Jessica, thinking that the smell of the food must be torture to her, but she was not hungry and could not have eaten in any case.

When she had finished the task she pushed it across to her father and rose from the table.

" My head aches. I am going to bed," she announced, and Jesse's heart leapt with joy because she was doing as he had suggested.

When she had left the room Mrs. Hallard looked timidly at her husband. " Perhaps I should take the child a glass of hot milk later ? " she said, anxiously.

" I strictly forbid it ! It will not hurt her to fast till tomorrow morning. Let her learn her lesson, the baggage ! Let her soul be chastened with fasting and prayer."

William Hallard fastened his gaze on the unchastened face of his eldest son.

Mrs. Hallard sighed ; it had all been much easier when the children could be thrashed. She did not like the idea of Jessica going without her supper.

Jesse was immensely relieved when his father strictly forbade his mother to take anything to Jessica later. ' Later,' he hoped, Jessica would be at the fair with him.

His father made an effort to keep him at home. He needed some help with accounts, he said.

Jesse said quickly, " I have no head for figures," and added the old formula, " John's the scholar in the family."

" Your brother has his Latin to do," his father said, severely.

John came to the rescue, that innate loyalty at work. " I am well ahead with my work," he said, " I can easily do it."

" Jesse has nothing else to do," Mrs. Hallard protested.

Jesse smiled. " I have made arrangements to go out," he said.

" You have made arrangements ? " His mother was aghast. " With whom, pray ? "

" What does it matter with whom he goes to the devil ? " his father thundered. " Let him go ! ' *Let the sinners be consumed out of the earth, and let the wicked be no more !* ' " He turned his black, fanatic glare on to Jesse. " ' *I will punish the world for their evil, and the wicked for their iniquity, saith the Lord.*' "

Mrs. Hallard gazed with awed admiration at her husband. He was the avenging angel, the messenger of the Lord.

" ' *Let the wicked forsake his way, and the unrighteous man his thoughts, and return unto the Lord,*' " she murmured, in support of her husband.

" The wicked in the meantime will go out," Jesse observed, and went.

All this talk of wickedness that met every attempt at freedom and happiness !

He walked cat-footed along the front of the house, past the lighted, curtained window of the living-room looking out over the duck-pond, and threw a small stone up at Jessica's uncurtained window glowing dimly with candlelight. There was the blur of her face at the casement for a moment, and he crept round the back of the house to wait for her.

She came in a few minutes, breathlessly.

" Supposing we are discovered ? "

" It will be too late to do anything about it."

They left the shelter of the elders and crossed the rickyard silently, hand in hand, closing the gate noiselessly behind them.

But when they came out on to the cart-track they laughed aloud.

" After you had retired the old man tried to keep me in to help with his accounts," Jesse told her, " but John offered to do them."

" Poor Johnny ! "

" Why do you say that ? "

" He never has any fun."

" 'Tis his own fault."

" Not altogether. He cannot help it. He would like a sweetheart, but if a girl smiled at him in a special way he would run a mile."

" He is such a Sunday-school ma'am," Jesse complained. " Let us not talk about him. Look, there's the glow of the gipsies' fire down there below the bridge ! We will cut across that way to Oldport."

They dropped down over the parapet, and there was the crushed-out smell of wild mint, and the moth-like paleness of the blackthorn in the dim starlight, and away across the darkness of the common the lights of the little town.

They skirted the gipsies' camp ; thin dogs chained to the wheels of small carts barked at them, and some children ran together into a group to stand staring at them. There seemed to be only an old man in charge of the camp.

The lights of the fair were not visible from the common because it was at the other side of the town. They climbed up into Oldport, along the cobbled alleyways of streets, under the creaking signs and the flickering street-lamps, past the taverns from which came the sounds of rough male voices raised in laughter and ribald jokes, past the bulging bow-windows of the shop-fronts, across the market-square flanked by old timbered houses.

Jessica kept close to her brother's side and occasionally gripped his hand. She had never been in Oldport, or any other town, at night before. Her heart beat high with adventure. She was a jewelled lady in a coach held up by highwaymen ; she was a smuggler's sweetheart, a gipsy's bride.

Across the town square a narrow road dipped down the other side of the hill on which the town was built, and suddenly the golden glow of the fair lay at their feet, rushlights flaring, bonfires glowing, lanterns glimmering. They gripped each other's hands and smiled at each other, and began to run.

When they reached the fair-ground they seemed instantly engulfed in lights and noise and laughter and crowds. An old man in a dirty smock and carrying a large basket pushed his way forward and they saw that his basket was full of red and blue and yellow silk ribbons and rosettes.

" Buy a fairing for the lady, sir," he cried.

" Of course you must have a fairing, Jessica," Jesse said ; " which will you have ? "

She laughed and picked out a red ribbon, a rosette with streaming ends, which she fastened in her hair. The crowd swept them on down a kind of alleyway between booths—rowdy gin-booths, booths at which you knocked down coconuts, flang darts at a painted figure of Napoleon, shied at Aunt Sally. There were tents with ' Wellington ' inscribed on their flapping portals, other inscribed ' Moscow,' and from within came mysterious beatings of drums. Outside men in high hats invited the crowds to come and see the tattooed lady, the fat lady, the bearded lady, the pygmies. There were ' secret caves ' whose entrances were hung with tinsel and cardboard icicles. There were fortune-telling tents. At the end of the alleyway swing-boats tossed up to the stars.

There were gipsy women with gaudy, long-fringed shawls and flounced dresses, some of them with babies at their breasts. Some offered to tell fortunes, others shamelessly invited anyone whose eye they could catch to cross their palms with silver merely ' for luck.' There were narrow-hipped, insolent-looking gipsy men hawking odd carved wooden figures and hand-wrought copper goods. At any moment Jessica expected to see the young gipsy who had spoken to her. Her heart quickened at the thought.

Then she and Jesse were wandering down an alleyway flanked by caged wild beasts, lethargic-looking tigers, restlessly pacing lions, a mangy bear, an unhappy looking wolf. There was a cageful of monkeys, with a crowd gathered round it, and a prodigious smell, and various cages of birds, some of them for sale. Beyond the menagerie an elephant paced slowly, giving people ' rides.' This small collection was advertised on a gaudy hoarding as ' the world's largest menagerie.'

They rode on the elephant, they were tossed up to the stars on the swings, they dived into the cardboard and tinsel mysteries of the secret cave, they bought bags of confetti and sprinkled passers-by, they ate jellied eels at one stall, hot ginger-bread at another—and Jessica discovered that she was ravenous. In that glittering carnival world the sombre world of thou-shalt-nots and punishments and scriptural threats seemed utterly remote and unreal. It seemed impossible that little more than an hour ago they had been of that world.

When Lucy and another street-woman passed, all sweeping plumes, feather-boas, rustling skirts, décolleté bodices, cheap, glittering jewellery, Jessica thought they were part of the show—strayed from some romantic tent. Lucy saw Jesse and half smiled ; but he looked away, and when Jessica turned back to look after them pulled her round, directing her attention to something else. She was the little sister and must be protected from the corruption of the town. Lucy, he reflected, would suppose that she had seen him with his ' sweetheart.'

But Jessica was interested in the ' beautiful ladies.' If they belonged to any side-show she would like to go and see them.

" They belong to the town," Jesse told her. " They are what John calls ' bad women.' "

Jessica stared at him. " But they looked nice," she said, wonderingly. " The one that looked at you had the sweetest expression imaginable ! "

Jesse smiled. " Bad people are very often nice. Look—they are about to start the fireworks ! "

He pulled her through the crowds just as a rocket burst in the air like a shower of golden rain, and Jessica, utterly enthralled, forgot the pretty ladies. There was a set piece purporting to depict Napoleon surrendering to the English, though when it was all firing away it was a little difficult to make out at all clearly, but it was very exciting, and at least ' Old Bony ' could be distinguished because of his tricorne hat, and it was a fine sight to see him burning so merrily.

But Jessica liked best the showers of golden rain, the bursts of stars, red and blue and green, the strange patterns that seemed like shoals of fishes in the sky, hurtling earthwards. Everything about the fair excited and stirred her ; its flashy gipsy gaudiness ; the smell and feel of it ; the smell of crowded humanity, the smell of the menagerie, the smell of the gin-booths and the ginger-bread stalls, the hot smell of the flares and lanterns, the circus smell of tents. And the feeling of movement, of light and life, of a strong-flowing current in contrast to the still pool that was life at the farm ; she had never known anything remotely like it, never known before this sense of being at the throbbing heart of life itself, so that its pulse became her pulse too, and it was all strange and stirring and exciting.

So that when somebody touched her elbow, and she turned and looked up into the dark insolent face of the young gipsy, it seemed as natural as his appearance in the wood the previous afternoon—in another world, long ago.

" I was looking for you," he said, and now he was not smiling ; his face was intent. She was aware of the fine curve of his nostrils and the proud curve of his mouth.

Before she could speak Jesse bent and murmured in her ear that he would meet her at the swings in half an hour ; then he had shouldered his way through the crowd and was gone. The sky was on fire with gold and blue and green flames, slowly turning over and dissolving into showers of stars, but she saw only the gipsy's dark intent face.

He seized her hand and drew her through the crowds beyond the booths to the outskirts of the fair-ground, where the waggons stood with their empty shafts tilted to the sky, and the tethered horses cropped the grass. The sounds of the fair retreated, and the heat and smell of it. The sea became audible again, and the smell of it was blown on the cool darkness across the meadows. But Jessica still moved in a dream.

He halted her at the back of a waggon, leaning against it and pulling her close against his body, holding her hands against his breast.

" Since the harvesting, when I came to your house, I think of you all the time." He spoke quickly, with a kind of urgency that stirred her blood. Now with the spell of the fair on her there was no resistance in her ; the strings of her spirit were loosened.

" You are not afraid the bad wild gipsies will run off with you ? "

She smiled. " Sometimes I think I should like to live in a tent. It must be fine to be free—to come and go as you please——"

" It is everything." He smiled, and drawing away a hand pushed back the hood of her cloak so that her hair fell loosely about her face and neck.

" Our Romany women do not cover their hair till they are wed," he told her.

He fingered the streaming red rosette. " Now you look like a Romany *chi*," he said. Then his hand was under her chin and his mouth fastened on hers. She had not dreamed that a kiss could be like that, hard and fierce, almost cruel.

" No one has kissed you like that before ? "

She shook her head.

" Then you will remember the Romany *chal*, always."

He kissed her again, then he said, " We are here now only for the fair, then we take to the road again. But we shall come back and camp here for the winter. You will keep the gipsy in your heart till then, little sister ? "

She told him simply, " I could not forget you now if I wished."

" Tell me your name, little sister."

" Jessica. What is yours ? "

" José. My grandparents came from Spain."

He pulled something out of his jacket pocket. " I brought this for you—a gipsy bracelet."

He took her hand and slipped the bangle over her wrist. " Now, little sister, we must go and find your brother."

Wandering on his own between the booths, when the fireworks were over, Jesse encountered Jack Mortimer, with a young man of about his own age, and a girl. The girl and the young man were sufficiently alike to be recognisable as brother and sister ; they had the same pale gold hair and the same discontented mouths. The young man was sturdy, muscular-looking ; Jesse had seen him many times in *The Ship's Bell* and knew him for a fisherman. The girl's attractiveness was spoilt by the sullenness of her expression and manner, and there was something sluttish in her appearance ; the flowers in her bonnet were bedraggled, the ribbons dirty, and her hair escaped untidily from it. Jesse learned that they were Jim and Sally Lane.

After some preliminary chatter Jack and Jim strolled along together, picking their way through the crowds, and Jesse and the girl fell behind.

She told him, without shyness, " I have seen you many a time in the town. In the market on fair-days, and sometimes along the quays. One day I stood quite close to you, but you were looking at a clipper ship as though she were your light o' love ! "

She smiled as she said this, and he suddenly thought her beautiful.

" A ship was my first love," he told her.

" A man is lucky—he can always sail away in one."

" I thought women were always afraid of ships and the sea."

She laughed outright at that. " Not when you are a fisherman's daughter and have five fishermen brothers ! "

" I may go to sea one day, but as a sailor, not a fisherman."

" In a frigate ? "

" Something smaller. A merchant ship."

" 'Tis a hard life, either way."

" I want to get away."

" We have that in common, then."

They bought apples from an old woman with a basket, they threw coins on a game of chance and lost, they rode on the elephant. Then Sally suggested the swings and he remembered Jessica.

"I promised to meet my young sister there in half an hour. It must be past that already, so you must forgive me if I return you to your brother and Jack."

"They will be in the gin-booth," she said. She looked at him steadily. "Ask Jack to bring you to see us. I will spring-clean the house specially. We seldom have visitors—we are not considered respectable. But as to that—neither are Jack Mortimer's friends! Come on Sunday, whilst all the good chapel-goers are digesting their roast beef. We will drink rum and Jim will play his concertina and we will sing songs and tell stories. Perhaps my brothers will tell you about something you may be interested in — as Jack Mortimer's friend."

There was nothing flirtatious in her invitation ; she wanted him to come, he thought, because she was bored, discontented, anything for a change. Perhaps, he told himself hopefully, as he made his way to the swings in search of Jessica, he had at last found a female who was interested in him as a person, not merely as ' handsome Jess Hallard,' that description of himself which had once filled him with pride, but which he had come to loathe.

Leaning against the side of a booth, lost in his thoughts of the golden, untidy, discontented girl, he did not see Jessica leave the gipsy a few yards from him, and he started when she touched his arm.

"Have you waited long ? " she asked, anxiously.

"No. A minute or so only. I met Jack Mortimer and some friends. One was a girl—golden as honey."

"And as sweet ? " she teased.

"No, thank the Lord ! A girl you could make a friend of, not lose your head over for about five minutes and then forget."

"Is that how it is when you lose your head over someone ? "

"I expect so. I've never lost my head over anyone yet. But tell me about the gipsy."

"What can I tell ? It all seems like a dream. But he gave me a bangle. He put it on my arm. If 'tis still there it must all be real."

She stretched her arm out from under her cloak and there was the gleam of beaten silver. She touched it with a kind of wonder.

Jesse was suddenly filled with tenderness. "It was real," he said softly, then pulled up her hood over her head and round her face. "The wind is cold," he said.

They walked back through the crowds and away from the fair and climbed up into the sleeping little town and made their way home, trespassing across the black common, with their arms about each other's waists. Now they belonged, finally and forever.

VII

THE Lanes, in their way, were as disreputable as the Mortimers. All the men drank heavily, and during their time ashore, between tides, when not in the pot-house were to be found betting at the cock-pit. The girl, Sally, was twenty-two and had kept house for her father and brothers ever since the mother had died, when she was fifteen. She was lazy and slatternly, and according to gossip no better than she should be. Certainly no decent respectable lad had ever considered her for a wife, nor, 'twas said, ever would.

Between the drinking and the gambling it might have been supposed that very little money came into the house, but the Lanes, like the Mortimers and many other families, had ways of supplementing their lawful earnings. Because Jesse was Jack Mortimer's friend, and therefore to be trusted, they let him into their secret. It was easy when they were out fishing to meet French fishing-boats that had more than fish on board, they told him, and there was as little difficulty in finding a market for contraband wines and spirits as for poached game. The difficulty was landing the stuff and hiding it till it changed hands ; in that respect poaching was easier.

In the course of a number of Sunday afternoons and evenings with the Lanes in their white-washed cottage, one of a dilapidated row of fishermen's cottages along the quays, Jesse learned a good deal about the ancient craft of smuggling and the ancient sport of cocking, neither of which had interested him till then. The cock-fights he found mildly entertaining ; there were, he conceded, with his appraising farmer's eye, some very fine birds put up, but he objected to fitting them with steel spurs ; it was a pity to see a good bird cut about like that, and, he said in his simplicity, it was unnatural ; the birds should be allowed to fight it out naturally with the spurs with which nature had provided them. Sally told him not to be a simpleton. But he had the same simpleton's criticisms to offer of two other ' pleasures of the town ' to which her brothers introduced him, prize-fighting and bull-baiting. When two men reeled out of a tavern and fought it out in the gutter, full of anger and hate, you understood well enough what it was all about ; but when two men who had no personal animosity battered each other on a platform there was no understanding it at all. Bull-baiting might be all right if the bull, instead of being tied to a stake when the bulldogs were set on it, were allowed free play ; but since the bull was tied up, where was the sport ? It was like a cock-shy—throwing sticks at a tied cock. Added to which it was a monstrous waste of a good bull, and the fact that it had been bred for that purpose did not seem to him, as a farmer, to make it any less of a waste. He was concerned not so much with the cruelty

3

to the bull as with the unfairness of the contest, and the waste. He redeemed himself in the Lanes' sight by his attitude to smuggling. That was something he did understand, though, purely from the point of view of adventure, poaching seemed to him to offer more excitement. At least there were no spring-guns and man-traps on the sea, and if a patrol-ship bore down on you you dropped the stuff overboard and nothing could be proved against you. But the law-lessness of smuggling appealed to him immensely. There were alto-gether too many laws, it seemed to him, and the more that were broken by poor and obscure people, as an expression of revolt, the better. The law served the rich, as he saw it, and the poor served the law, but not all the poor, God be praised, were such fools as to be content to be tied to the parish-cart, humiliated in the poverty to which the rich and the law-makers condemned them, for the sake of a wretched few shillings a week relief from the Poor Rates. He hoped for the day when the poor would revolt and tie the local overseer to the cart and make him drag it out of the parish.

Anger always flamed up in him when he expressed these opinions which he dared not voice at home, but his passion did not stir the Lanes. They went smuggling because it was a fairly easy way of increasing their income, and they needed money for betting at the cock-pit, the bull-ring, the prize-fight, and to spend on good ale; they had no social consciousness, no sense of the injustice with which young Jesse Hallard burned. Cocking was the one subject that could rouse them, whether a main of cocks supplied by the gentlemen of Hampshire was superior or not to a main sent up from Berkshire. At Newmarket and York, they assured Jesse, the stakes were sometimes as much as a thousand guineas a side and forty guineas a battle. But it was no use; Jesse could not visualise such vast sums and had no gambling instinct. A man might gamble his life in a dark wood against a spring-gun or a game-keeper's bullet, for the sake of no more than a brace of pheasants and the few shillings they represented, but in doing so he was defying the injustice of the law, taking back a tiny part of what the government and the landlords had robbed him and his kind. You offered a challenge. You gambled for something you believed in, not merely for greed, like putting money on cocks and bulls and prize-fighters.

He made his points with impassioned earnestness, but the Lanes merely laughed and offered him some more of their contraband cognac or rum. He was a good lad, for all he was no sportsman.

Sally would sit on the window-seat looking out of the unwashed window to the sea, listening to the talk, feeling that her father and brothers were right, yet fascinated by the things Jesse said, but even more by the passion with which he said them. It was, for her, passion misdirected. She took to combing her hair and twisting it into fashionable ringlets, and to tidying herself generally when Jesse was expected. Luck was with her, for there was an evening when, miscalculating the tides, Jesse called when the menfolk were at sea. For the first time he felt the impact of Sally's passion for him. She was clever enough not to fling herself at him even then.

When he left her she had kindled something in his imagination as well as in his blood. She was as unsentimental as a whore ; she did not embarrass him by declaring that she loved him, or demand that he should love her. He recognised that she had her own kind of honesty, her own sullen integrity, and it commanded his respect. She made it clear, as their relationship developed, that she did not want to marry him, that she did not see herself as a farmer's wife. If she married anyone, she declared, it would have to be a seafaring man, so that she was left free for months on end, her husband safely away at sea, beyond any possibility of sudden return. She would cuckold him if she felt like it ; why not ? What man was ever faithful to woman ? In her own way, he thought, she too was a rebel, in revolt against injustice. She too was lawless ; of the outcast world of smugglers, poachers, highwaymen, gipsies. To that extent they were two of a kind. There was someone she could marry if she wished, she said, Peter Vinney, at present on the high seas on his way back from Australia in a grain-ship, but he had a temper, and she was not sure that there was room for two tempers in the family ; also he was inclined to be jealous, and to value his own freedom as much as she valued hers. She was damnably cynical, Jesse thought, but commendably honest.

But after he had capitulated to her he went less often to the Lane cottage. It was a way of restoring his self-respect. It began to afford him as much satisfaction to go into Oldport and not call on the Lanes as it did to go into *The Ship's Bell* and find Lucy free and do no more about her than stand her a drink. He would always have a soft spot for Lucy, he thought ; she had been sweet and tactful when he had been a fuddled, bewildered boy ; he would always be grateful to her for that. Sally invoked neither tenderness nor gratitude in him ; they met on equal ground. When the mood was on him he was attracted by her quality of sullen, smouldering passion, and by her bedraggled golden beauty.

His interest in her ceased abruptly on the summer's morning when he took one of the cart-horses down to Byrd's forge. He had many times taken horses to be reshod, and he had been seeing Mary Byrd for as long as he could remember. Yet in the real sense he never saw her till that morning when she came into the forge whilst he was

63

leading the horse in. Her father was away for a few minutes, she said, he would be back at any moment.

She stood where a shaft of sunlight, alive with dust, came in through a cobwebby window, and he was suddenly aware of her small neat figure, the dark neat dress, the serenity of her face. She looked at him with the candour of a man, the simplicity of a child. It was with almost a shock that he realised that there was no interest in her brown eyes, nothing more than ordinary civility in her manner, that so she would speak to, so she would look at, anyone who came to the forge. Even the careful Sally had shown an interest in him at their first meeting. But Mary Byrd had seen Jesse Hallard many times, at the forge, at the chapel, in the market, and never shown more than a neighbourly civility. Now she merely patted the horse's neck, remarked on the fineness of the day, gave the fire a few puffs with the large dusty bellows, and was for slipping away.

Jesse said involuntarily, " Please don't go."

She stood still and looked at him, puzzled.

" I mean," said Jesse, self-conscious now, " if you would stay and talk to me till your father comes—it would pass the time."

She replied, sedately, " It doth not seem to occur to you men that we women have our own business to attend. This morning we are baking."

" 'Tis a June morning," he told her, smiling. " You are a young and beautiful woman, and a young man invites you to discourse with him, and you speak of baking ! "

She smiled, faintly. " You speak a vast deal of nonsense, Mr. Hallard."

" But I have achieved something—I have made you smile ! "

The smile faded instantly. " I have no doubt that you have no difficulty in provoking smiles in the weaker sex, Mr. Hallard. Unfortunately for you, I have something better to do than to smile attendance upon you ! "

She turned and went out, holding her shoulders very straight, her head high, but unable to prevent the sunlight from touching the brown curls clustered thickly at her neck, or Jesse being aware of the delicate curve of her breast under the severely cut bodice. The low-cut dresses of Lucy and Sally, shamelessly revealing the valley between their breasts, seemed to him far less exciting than that dark, almost aggressively decent gown, fastening high at the throat, with its delicate indication of hidden beauty.

When the blacksmith had the horse's hoof between his knees, Jesse, leaning against the wall turning a straw in his fingers, said casually, " There must be many young fellows come wishing to court your one unmarried daughter, Mr. Byrd."

" Aye, there have been one or two, right enough," the smith told him, " but Mary's not like her sisters. She seems minded to be an old maid. 'Tis a great pity. She's going on five-and-twenty, and 'tis late for a maid to be weddin'."

He looked up at Jesse. " She has the makings of a good farmer's wife in her." he said, " and if a woman hath a few years more than her spouse there be no harm in it, to any sensible way of thinking."

Jesse repressed a smile. " Certainly not," he agreed.

" A man is as old as he feels, and a woman as old as she looks," the old man said, firmly.

If young Jesse Hallard was interested in Mary every encouragement should be given the lad. It would be a fine thing for Mary— who looked like getting left—to become mistress of Valley Farm, and a distinct piece of social advancement for the Byrds. Before he had driven the last nail into the shoe he had resolved to invite young Hallard for supper.

Jesse knew very well what was in old Byrd's mind when he made the invitation. The heir to Valley Farm would be a good ' catch ' for a girl heading for old-maidhood. Jesse smiled inwardly at the thought. It was easier to think of himself as a poacher than as Hallard of Valley Farm. As to whether he wanted Mary for a wife or not he had not, as yet, the slightest idea—having seen her, in the true sense, for the first time only that morning. But she interested him, and the quality of cool serenity which emanated from her was what he needed after Lucy and Sally. He was impatient to see her again to confirm that quality.

He accepted the invitation and was glad that it was no further away than the following evening. He spent the rest of the day scything hay and thinking of her. Of the glint of sunlight on the neat brown curls, of the softness that came into her face when she smiled. Of the coolness and repose of her. She was not beautiful, he reflected, and yet, if she loved, he thought, she might well be the fairest among women.

2

At mid-day Jessica brought bread and cold bacon and a jug of ale to him in the meadow and sat with him a little while under the hedge. The gipsies had remained only the three days of the fair, then had broken camp and followed it, and though Jessica had not seen José since that night the fact that he was no longer in the district left her with a strange feeling of desolation. They would come back for the winter, he had said, but there was all the summer to live through and another harvest, and it was a lifetime.

She was in a state of smouldering revolt. Almost anything seemed preferable to her present life. She had fantasies of running away, of going as a chamber-maid at an inn, as a nursery-maid—anything that would get her out of her present environment. She dreamed of long journeys in stage-coaches ; of London, with its theatres, its gas-lamps, its pleasure-gardens. She had wild dreams of perilous sea-crossings to France, though she never visualised what she would do when she arrived. She wanted something utterly remote from Oldport and the valley. Yet Oldport was better than nothing. There were shops, people, ships, the excitement of stage-coaches and mail-coaches, the feeling of life and movement. At the same time Oldport tantalised too much with its ships and coaches ; it was a gateway through which she never passed, never more than peeped.

She told Jesse, that June morning in the hayfield, " When the gipsies leave here next spring, I may go with them."

Jesse said, " You would be found and brought back."

" They would never find me, because they would never guess. Only you would know."

" You may have been seen with the gipsy at the fair."

She answered confidently, " They would hide me. They would never let me go. Gipsies are clever people. They have always lived outside the law."

" You might be unhappy with the gipsies—had you thought of that ? 'Tis a rough life."

" At least 'tis not a dull one ! What is there for me here ? I can marry, yes, and move from one farm to another ! "

" There are men who are not farmers or farmers' sons, even here."

" I could marry a schoolmaster, or a minister, or a shopkeeper, I suppose ! " She tossed her head. " Thank you ! The man I marry will be a real man ! "

He smiled. " You could marry a sailor, then."

" A sailor spends too much time at sea. 'Twould be too lonely."

She rolled over on to her face and plucked at the white star-flowers on the bank under the hedge, popping the seeds between her fingers.

" You will go away to sea," she said, " and I shall join the gipsies. Then we shall both lead adventurous lives."

" I may not go to sea. I might marry and settle in a cottage. I might marry Mary Byrd."

She stared at him in amazement. " Mary Byrd, who always looks as though she's swallowed a poker ? "

" She's pretty when she smiles."

" But she never smiles ! Jesse, this is foolishness ! Let us both go away with the gipsies in the spring ! "

She sat up, excitedly, seizing his hands. " 'Tis a most wonderful idea, Jesse! Then we shall be together leading adventurous lives! Why did we not think of it before? You will never marry Mary Byrd. If she was ever likely to marry anyone it would be someone like John, not someone like you! Let us make a vow to go away with the gipsies in the spring!"

Jesse shook his head. " 'Tis too far ahead, Jessica. So much has to happen before then. We have only just begun haymaking, then there's the harvest, then the long winter, and Christmas, and winter going on again after that — 'tis nearly a year to the spring!"

"Then we need not wait till the spring. We will tell the gipsies we are ready to join them when they come back for the winter, then we will go away with them to some other place to camp for the winter."

He cried to her with a kind of despair, "Jessica, 'tis impossible to plan! We don't know——"

She snatched her hands away and scrambled to her feet.

" 'Twas you who used to talk about making the most of life, now you talk about settling down! You will end up by being Farmer Hallard of Valley Farm and forget there ever was a time when you went poaching and talked of going to sea, and you will never mention your sister Jessica because she will be the family disgrace!"

Jesse looked up into her dark blazing eyes.

"Just because I am not prepared to run away with the gipsies the moment you say so does not mean that I shall remain here all my life! Supposing we wait until the autumn and see what befalls? People have to do things when they are ready to do them, Jessica——"

He knew that he had failed her, and was filled with misery as she turned away impatiently and hurried back along the path towards the farm. He reflected that but for the encounter with Mary that morning his response to Jessica's plan might have been different. Perhaps he was being foolish about Mary. But that was something he had to find out, and he was impatient to begin the investigation.

VIII

It was clear that the Byrds in their humble way had been at some pains to do honour to Jesse on his first visit. Mrs. Byrd wore the dress usually reserved for chapel, weddings, funerals. She was a tall, thin, gaunt woman with grey hair and a lined face, her expression severe in repose, but curiously sweet and almost girlish when she smiled. She was several years older than her husband and devoted to him. She had found marriage so satisfactory a state herself, in spite of hard work and little money and a large family, that she could not understand Mary's indifference in this respect. When her husband had told her that young Jesse Hallard was obviously interested in Mary she took heart of hope. The best-looking young fellow in the parish, and certainly one of the pleasantest, and the son of the most prosperous farmer—outside of the squire himself, of course—into the bargain—surely Mary would be interested ? It would be fine, Mrs. Byrd thought wistfully, if Mary should make such a good marriage, before it was too late. All the others were happily enough married, but none had had the chance to do well for themselves. Why, if Mary got to marry Jesse Hallard she would have a servant and need never coarsen her hands with rough work, and she would have help in the dairy ; to all intents and purposes she would be a lady— certainly a lady in comparison with her sisters and mother. 'Twas not as though he were not a good, decent lad, too. True, some gossip had said he had been seen leaving the Holdings' cottage one night when Nat was away over at the farm, and there was another story that he had been seen in Oldport in company with a trollop, but you had only to look at the lad's open honest face to know that it was merely gossip of the malicious kind always to be found in small places. Mrs. Byrd prided herself on being superior in this respect, having before her marriage worked as servant in a gentleman's house in London. She felt that she could claim to know the big world and its broader outlook. ' Dadda ' had also worked in London, as groom at a gentleman's stables, so was equally above village and small-town gossip.

When Mary was told that Jesse Hallard was coming to supper the following evening she stared at her father in amazement.

" All the years we have lived here and known the Hallards we have never visited at their house nor had them visit us—what reason have we now, pray, for inviting Jesse ? "

" I was talking with the young fellow this morning," her father told her, " and he was asking about you and if you had never thought of marrying."

The blood beat up into Mary's face. " That young fellow has only to look at a member of the opposite sex to deceive himself that she is ready to marry him ! " she cried, angrily.

" The young woman who gets him in the end will do well for herself," her father said, briefly.

" Aye, she will that," Mrs. Byrd confirmed.

68

" She will be lucky if he does not get arrested for poaching before the wedding-day ! " Mary said, viciously.

" What call have you to say such a thing ? " her mother demanded.

" Oh, 'tis what they say," the smith said, carelessly, " but those who repeat such tales to me get short shrift. Why should Farmer Hallard's son turn poacher ? It makes no sense—except to those who delight in idle gossip."

" I am ashamed of you, Mary, giving ear to such talk," Mrs. Byrd said, warmly.

Mary was silent. She did not know herself whether she believed the stories she heard about Jesse Hallard. 'Twas said there was no smoke without fire, but, when a lad was as handsome as Jesse, spiteful, jealous tongues were sure to wag. Her parents had instilled their own tolerance into her, but anger flamed in her at the suggestion that Jesse assumed she would be only too glad for him to court her. Women were always fools over good-looking men, but Mary Byrd was not prepared to be. Handsome men were always conceited, and not to be tolerated by any woman of spirit. Perhaps it was a good thing that her father had been rash enough to ask Jesse to supper ; the young man would see then that he could not have any girl he liked merely for the asking. Her lips tightened at the thought, and her eyes hardened.

On the evening he was expected she did not follow her mother's example and put on her best dress and a silk apron, and when her mother came back from the market with a chicken she observed caustically that it was a good thing Mr. Jesse Hallard was not a frequent visitor.

" 'Tis well to make a good first impression," her mother said, placidly.

Mary said in her most frigid tone, " I fail to see that it is of the slightest importance what impression we make upon the young man."

Mrs. Byrd continued to spread out her purchases for the feast on the kitchen table and made no answer. Whatever Mary might say, Jesse Hallard's first visit to the Byrd home was of vast importance—as Mary herself would see if she were not so stubborn and prejudiced.

She made no comment when Mary did not change her dress for the evening. She knew by long experience that the only way of handling Mary's stubbornness was by ignoring it. She took down a massive pair of brass candlesticks that had long stood unused on the shelf above the chimney-place and polished them till they were like mirrors and set them on the table. She picked moss-roses from the garden and arranged them in an ornate vase as a centre-piece. She brought out fine white linen napkins which her ' lady ' had given her from her own linen cupboard when she married. No doubt they used napkins up at Valley Farm, anyhow when they had visitors, and Jesse should see that even in a humble blacksmith's home they knew what was correct. The best china was brought out, as though it were Christmas, or a wedding-breakfast. There was no doubt, Mary thought, cynically, that every effort was being made to ensnare the young man.

When Jesse told his parents that he was supping at the Byrds' the following evening they were as startled as he had expected they would be.

" I was not aware that the Byrds were special friends of yours," his father observed.

Jesse replied carelessly that neither was he until that morning, when the smith had invited him.

" Perhaps 'tis Miss Byrd is the attraction ? " his mother said, regarding him keenly.

Jesse smiled. " She's a likely-looking lass, true enough."

" You could do better than that—a blacksmith's daughter," his mother murmured.

" Especially one that has swallowed a poker ! " Jessica said, maliciously.

John looked at her angrily. " Miss Byrd is a gentlewoman ! " he said, violently. " If Jesse achieved such a wife he would indeed be fortunate ! "

He flushed as he said it and his heart beat furiously.

Jessica stared at him in amazement for a moment, then she said, " Have both my brothers lost their wits ? "

Jesse laughed. " Nobody is talking of marriage," he said, and added, " Is a man necessarily courting because he takes supper in the house where there is an unmarried daughter ? "

" If he is himself unattached, yes," his father declared. " Otherwise he has no right to raise false hopes."

" Then if any young fellow comes to supper here, and he neither married nor betrothed, it doth mean he is courting Jessica ? " Jesse demanded.

" Most certainly," his father insisted. " Your mother and I would not encourage his presence here otherwise."

Jesse shrugged and was silent. It had not occurred to any of the Lanes, he reflected, that he was ' courting ' Sally. As to whether he was courting Mary Byrd he did not yet know.

It did not occur to him to change his clothes when he set out to go to the Byrd's, a fact which his mother remarked with some surprise. He brushed his hair, washed his hands, removed the mud from his boots, and considered himself ready. Since he was for once going out at night on a lawful occasion he decided to ride.

Jessica came out and stood beside him in the yard whilst he was saddling the pony.

" You are wasting your time," she told him. " Mary Byrd is not for you."

He told her briefly, " That remains to be seen."

She mocked him, " ' *Fair as the moon, clear as the sun, terrible as an army with banners !* ' "

The look he turned on her was the look John had given her when he had declared that Miss Byrd was a gentlewoman. Before Jesse's look she tossed her head with an insolent smile, then turned away to open the gate for him. She crossed the rickyard and opened that gate for him also, and walked beside him as he rode along the cart-track to open the gate at the end. Neither of them spoke.

At the last gate Jesse said, " Thank you for opening the gates, Jessica. Let us not quarrel—please."

" Quarrel ! " said she. " Why should I wish to quarrel because my brothers have been seized by midsummer madness ? "

Then she turned and walked back along the cart-track through the golden, honeysuckle-scented evening sorrowfully reflecting that she had quarrelled with both of them. She had a sense of having been betrayed by them both, but especially by Jesse. What could Jesse possibly want with a school-ma'am like Miss Byrd ? What would Miss Byrd think of his poacher friends like the Mortimers, his smuggler friends like the Lanes ? And the little sister who only lived for the day when the gipsies would camp once more by the river ?

" Come back," her heart cried wildly, " come back ! "

And turning in at the rickyard gate had the desolate feeling of being far from home.

2

Jesse was completely unaware that Mary had not changed her dress in his honour. He could have wished her to be wearing nothing better than what she wore, which was the dark plain dress in which he had seen her the previous morning. But Mary was immediately aware that Jesse was wearing his working-clothes, and it scored one more point against him. He was so conceited, then, that he believed he need take no trouble to ensure his success ?

She greeted him coldly, unsmilingly, and sat almost in complete silence throughout the meal ; but Jesse was very happy. He felt the warmth of friendly hospitality ; he felt at home, as always

71

in the homes of the poor. He enjoyed the good cooking, and took pleasure in the flowers and candles on the table, and in the softness of the candlelight touching Mary's pale face and smooth brown curls. That she was silent and remote did not trouble him. At last, it seemed to him, he had found a woman who was not preoccupied with his looks, who, if she liked him at all, would do so for some quality in himself as a person, not merely as an attractive male.

All the time he was discussing politics with Mary's father—Mr. Cobbett's flight to America last year, the iniquity of the Corn Laws, the urgent need for Parliamentary Reform, the courage and spirit of the fiery Sir Francis Burdett, that champion of the rights of the common people, the General Election—Jesse was aware of the girl herself, like a backcloth to his thoughts. Thus, it seemed to him, a happily married man might feel reading a newspaper with his cherished wife seated at the other side of the hearth. From contemplation of all the injustices of the social system and the perfidies of politicians, a man might seek the bosom of such a wife with a feeling of home-coming. . . .

He had no opportunity of speaking with Mary alone that evening, but he rode home at a gentle canter through the late dusk feeling a kind of happiness he had never before experienced ; a peaceful happiness. He felt that he had found a new friend in Tom Byrd, a new mother in Mrs. Byrd, and a new hope in Mary.

When Jesse had gone Mary listened in silence to her parents praising him.

" The lad has good sound radical ideas," observed her father.

" The manners of a gentleman," sighed her mother, replacing the festive candlesticks on the mantelshelf with an air of regret.

The bedroom candles were brought forward, the lamps blown out.

" Did you not revise your opinion of the young fellow ? " Mrs. Byrd asked her daughter wistfully, as they went upstairs together, leaving Mr. Byrd below to finish his last pipe.

" He was on his best behaviour, I have no doubt," Mary returned, indifferently.

" You have a cold heart, Mary," said her mother.

" Have I been an unloving daughter, a hard-hearted sister ? " Mary challenged, resentfully.

" No, my pet, no, certainly not. 'Tis what makes it so strange you should be so indifferent when 'tis a matter of securing a husband."

" Women are too easily deceived and men too easily flattered," Mary observed, " and perhaps I have no wish for a husband. Indeed, Mamma dear, 'tis a subject of which I am very weary."

Outside her door she leaned forward and kissed her mother's forehead.

"You're a strange lass," Mrs. Byrd murmured, embracing her, and sighed once more.

Alone in her room, Mary set the candle on the dressing-chest and went across to the window, open to the summer night. She leaned a little while on the sill looking out across meadows softly silvered by a young moon. Somewhere out there Jesse was riding the lanes, Jesse of the gentle smile and the glowing eyes, Jesse full of his passionate feeling for justice, Jesse beloved of women. . . .

She started at the last thought. Was it not precisely because women made so much of him that she must harden her heart against him ? Her parents hardly disguised from her their hope that he would court her and that she would respond ; but what sort of a husband would he make—a man who had always other women after him, and who no doubt, believed he conferred a favour on the woman he married ?

She left the window and began to undress.

"I shall be an old maid," she thought, defiantly ; "no man will ever fool me ! Certainly not Jesse Hallard."

For all that, when she went to bed she lay wakefully a long time thinking about him, the things he had said in talk with her father, the way he had looked, the way the lock of dark hair fell across his forehead, the sudden sweetness of his smile.

When at last she slept she had a strange dream. She dreamed that she was wearing a low-cut dress, such as worn by the women of the town, and that she was walking beside the river with Jesse Hallard, and that he had his arm about her waist, and all the time in her dream she was oppressed by a sense of guilt, and telling herself, ' I mustn't let people see me with his arm round my waist.' Then he bent down and picked some forget-me-nots and tucked them into the bodice of her dress, between her breasts, and she felt his fingers on her skin. ' Now you will remember me,' he said, and stooped to kiss her. She tried to push him away from her . . . and wakened in the grey morning, clutching her pillow and weeping.

IX

JESSE became as frequent a visitor at the Byrds' as he had been at the Lanes', but whereas only the people who lived in the row of fishermen's cottages along the quay knew how often he called at the Lane

cottage, the whole valley knew that he was 'courting' Mary Byrd.
The Byrds themselves proclaimed the fact. It was, they freely admitted,
a feather in their cap. Only Mary kept silent and refused to discuss
the matter. She was deeply embarrassed by all the talk. It was
tiresome enough to be courted by a man you had no intention of
accepting, and to be aware of your parents and the entire countryside
waiting for the announcement of your betrothal.

Jesse's parents raised no objections to the courtship. They
reasoned that whilst on the one hand the heir to Valley Farm might
have done much better, on the other, with that wildness in his blood,
he might have done much worse. The Byrds were decent, respectable chapel-going people, and smithying was an honest trade. It
was not as though Mary were a mere labourer's daughter. There was
a farm cottage empty at Michaelmas, the tenants having decided to go
away and work in the mills, and it would suit a young married couple
very nicely. Marriage would no doubt have a steadying effect on
Jesse.

Altogether, within a few weeks, the stage was set for the announcement of betrothal, and both Mrs. Byrd and Mrs. Hallard played with
the attractive idea of a harvest wedding. Mrs. Byrd was careful
never to let loose a hint of Mary's indifference to Jesse, her utter lack
of encouragement of his suit. Only half acknowledged at the back
of her mind she had an idea that sheer pressure of general assumption
might eventually force Mary to be 'sensible.' As though the assumption that a thing was settled somehow made it so.

Mary's indifference acted upon Jesse as a far more powerful stimu-
lant than the ready response of the other women he had known. He
had a desperate desire that she should see some virtue in him in spite
of his unfortunate charm and good looks. He begged her to tell
him what he could do to prove his sincerity. To which she replied
coldly that she was not interested in having him prove it.

Nothing in her manner betrayed the fact that there were moments
when she knew strange impulses to put her hands on his thick dark
hair and draw his head down to her breast. Times when it took an
almost superhuman strength to maintain her coldness. Times when
it seemed he must surely hear her heart's wild crying, "Jesse, my
love, my dear love!"

But pulling her back all the time was a bearing-rein of resentment. So many women, she was confident, had pillowed his head
on their breasts and called him their dear love. She had never done
this or said this to any man, nor wanted to till now—and fiercely she
wanted not to want to. It was not fair, she would tell herself, resentfully, that with all his experience, he should seek her innocence ;
there could be no equality between them. And she could not be just

74

one more woman to fall in love with him. That she had done so must be her secret and her torment. No one must ever remotely guess.

Her pride rebelled, hotly, against the fact that everyone, her own parents included, had taken it for granted that she would leap at the chance of marrying him ; that assumption that she should feel flattered, honoured, that he had singled her out, the quiet, simple, unexciting Mary Byrd, when he could choose all over the parish. If she married him people would ask each other, no doubt, what did he see in her, and resent it that of all the girls he might have had he should have chosen her, seven years older than himself, and heading for permanent spinsterhood until he came along. It was all quite intolerable, and her pride defeated her passion. For that she did feel passion for him, as the weeks went on, and he visited continually at the house, she could not deny herself. It was her secret humiliation, and the private hell-fire in which she nightly burned.

A good deal of local resentment was caused by Jesse Hallard's interest in Mary Byrd, particularly amongst the daughters of the well-to-do farmers. To pass them all over for the sake of anyone as dull as Mary Byrd . . . it was not even as though he were marrying for money, or as though she were a great beauty.

Jesse himself did not know, in those first few weeks, whether he wanted to marry Mary or not. He could not analyse his feeling for her. Was it love ? Was this what love was, this perpetual hunger to be loved, to have the other person think well of you, to win favour in that person's eyes, to live for a smile, an approving word ? He did not know. He loved Jessica ; and he had desired Sally and Lucy. But he did not feel for Mary either what he felt for his sister or what he had felt for the women he had consorted with. In a curious way he felt for her something of what he had felt for the island when he was thirteen. She represented escape from dissatisfaction. If she would love him it would be a coming to the island, a touching of that remote, dim horizon. It had to be Mary because only she was remote from the common run of women where he was concerned ; only she was fair as the moon, clear as the sun. Only she was immaculate and apart.

By the end of July he felt that it was useless to continue visiting at the Byrds' without coming to an understanding with Mary one way or the other. He was fortunate in finding her alone in the house one evening, her parents having gone out to call on one of their married daughters. The front door was open, as always in fine weather, and he stepped into the stone-floored living-room. There was no sign of her, and he stepped through into the back kitchen and found her sitting on an ancient bench outside the back door, a basket of red-currants beside her, a bowl in her lap to catch the fruit as she stripped it from its stalks. There was a small garden beyond the narrow brick path that ran along behind the house, and tall blue lupins stood up in the mellow evening sunlight like shining spears. Under a huge ancient yew-tree, that reached its flat branches out over the house, was a pile of rusty horseshoes and a grindstone. Jesse had seen it all many times; he had come to know the smithy as intimately as he knew the farm, but because of the importance of the occasion it all impressed itself on him with a curious newness and clarity.

She looked up at him with a faint smile.

" You find me alone," she said.

" I am glad. I want specially to talk to you alone."

He sat down beside her on the bench.

" I have been coming here ever since June in the hope that we might become better acquainted with each other," he told her, " but," he smiled ruefully, " since you will not even walk with me in your own garden we have made no progress. If my presence is distasteful to you it would be better I should remain away."

She turned her calm, clear gaze on him.

" To what end did you hope we might become better acquainted, Mr. Hallard ? "

He reddened slightly, but declared boldly, " I had hoped that we might become betrothed. It would seem that the whole countryside is expecting an announcement——"

" That is hardly of any importance. What is of importance is whether two people love each other or not. If they do not, or if only one loves, then there is no betrothal. I therefore fear the countryside will suffer a disappointment."

The scarlet fruit slipped through her flying fingers ; the neat brown curls rested against her neck and cheek. She was as remote as the morning star.

He sat looking down at his hands clasped between his knees. There was suddenly nothing to say. Why, after all, should a woman like Mary Byrd care for him ? She had probably heard stories of his visits to taverns and bawdy houses, that his friends were poachers, smugglers, and women of the town, that at times he talked wildly of abandoning the farm and going to sea.

He said at last, miserably, " If it makes any difference to you, I have not been into Oldport except on market-days on farm business since that morning I brought the chestnut mare down to be shod."

Against all her instincts something in her insisted, " If you soften towards him now you become one more of Jesse Hallard's triumphs. He must be shown that he cannot get round you as he has got round others."

76

She said quietly, " It makes no difference. I am sorry, but it is best to be frank in such matters."

He got up. " In that case 'tis better I do not come here any more, except a horse needs shoeing ? "

" It might save us both embarrassment," she said, without looking up. To look at him would be to melt with pity and with love. He was so young, and his sincerity wounded her. . . . That treacherous softness he could inspire in women ; oh, harden the heart, the wild, plunging, traitorous thing. . . .

He said, heavily, " I wish it could have been different. It would have meant so much to me. More than I could say. But 'tis not your fault. You had better tell your parents—that we had this talk."

" Yes, I will tell them."

He moved away through the evening sunlight, past the darkness of the yew-tree and the shining blue of the lupins, and round the corner of the house. She heard his boots on the cobbles, and then a few moments later the clatter of his horse's hooves on the high road.

Her heart felt very hard and tight in her breast, and her throat constricted.

' Jesse, my love, my love! One day, perhaps, when you are old and women no longer desire you, and when I am old and no longer a triumph, perhaps then . . . But long before then some other will have wedded you, and you will strut to the end. . . .'

2

On that lambent summer evening when the corn stood up straight and golden and the sky was like stretched silk, Sally Lane leaned against the door of her cottage and watched her menfolk heaving their boat down the dirty beach to the sea, and was suddenly weary of the smell of fish and tar and bilge-water and had an impulse to turn her back on the sea. Hidden away inland, behind Oldport, was a tall, dark, young farmer whom she had not seen for two months, and she did not disguise to herself that she was missing him. During that time fishermen and sailors, her brothers' and father's friends, had passed in and out of the cottage, with much drinking of rum and tellings of yarns and singing of bawdy songs ; life had not been un-amusing. But Jesse Hallard, it seemed, was landlocked somewhere in his valley. Jack Mortimer had told her that he was courting the blacksmith's daughter, and she had laughed . . . and waited for the wind to change. She had been in no hurry ; he would come

77

back when he was ready ; he owed nothing to her any more than she to him.

But that evening something stirred in her, restlessly. She had expected the wind to change before this, and here was a fine summer's evening, and her menfolk at sea, and not even the tight-lipped, shifty-eyed young Jack Mortimer around.

She closed the cottage door, then strolled past the beaches and along the quays, and turned up out of the town and dropped down over the hill and on to the road that curved round heading for the far hills and the valley. She walked slowly, enjoying the country smells, of sweet-briar in the hedges, and meadow-sweet in the ditch, and wild mint along the river, and cattle in the fields. It was good to get a change. And if Jesse was coming out to visit the blacksmith's daughter she might meet him along the road. She walked nearly to the farm without meeting him, and then suddenly, unused to walking any distance, was tired, and turned back.

In this way she met Jesse riding back from his interview with Mary Byrd.

He approached at a smooth canter and did not see her until he was almost on her. Then he reined in and leaned over to speak to her. There was a curious dark strained look on his face, and he did not smile.

Sally smiled up into his sombre face. Round her own her ripe-corn hair formed a halo. Even in his black mood he was aware of her hair and eyes and the curve of her breast.

" You are a stranger these days," she told him.

He said shortly, " Jack probably told you why." Then he demanded, " What are you doing out here at this time of the evening ? "

" I came out hoping to see you." There was a touch of defiance in her voice.

" You must have second-sight, for you chose the right evening, by God ! "

He swung his leg over the pony's back and dropped down beside her.

He said with a kind of smothered violence, " If a man is forbidden one road, he goes another, isn't that so—witch ? "

She put up a hand and touched his face.

" What is it, Jesse ? "

He seized her hand and pressed the fingers to his lips.

" What in hell does it matter ? Come on."

He turned the horse's head and they walked in silence back towards Oldport. Where the road skirted a wood, before dropping down into the town, he stopped in the shadow of the trees and laid a hand on her shoulder, turning her to him. " You still like me, Sally ? "

She laughed, softly, excitedly.

"I came to look for you," she reminded him.

He gathered her to him with a kind of bitter passion.

X

JESSICA was aware of the shadow in Jesse's face and guessed the reason some time before he was forced to admit it to their parents, in explanation of ceasing to visit at the Byrd's, and it brought her back to him. It was not difficult, since it had been only a superficial estrangement at most, impatience on Jessica's part, and preoccupation on Jesse's. They had a great need of each other that summer, Jesse in his disappointment, Jessica in her restless discontent. They began going into Oldport together again, climbing up the steep, narrow cobbled streets to the church at the top, sitting under a lime-tree in the little square in front of the church and looking out over the crazy red roofs of the town to the quays, crowded with tall ships, and beyond the quays the wide sweep of the sea, and the island, dim and blue and merging with the horizon.

They knew the name of the island now, and the name of its principal port, and had been told, but had forgotten, the size of its population ; but it made no difference ; all that was unimportant. What was important was all that the island stood for, and that was unchanged for them both—something remote and unknown, cut off from the mainland, cut off from everyday life ; *escape*. When Jesse murmured, gripping her hand resting beside his on the bench under the lime-tree, "One day we will land on the island," she knew that she was not included in his landing, nor he in hers ; they would land on the island each in their own time and their different ways, and neither could see ahead. Life was all ebb and flow like the tides, and both at that time felt themselves on an ebb-tide. All was a twisting flux, changing and incomplete, perpetually shining with hope and shadowed with disappointment. They were young.

Jessica was required to attend a Bible class on Sunday afternoons at the chapel in Oldport, in addition to chapel in the mornings with her parents. Jesse was also supposed to attend, but had rebelled against it after his declaration of independence and had never gone since. As attendance at the Bible class excused Jessica from chapel in the evening, Jesse urged that she should submit to the tedium of the afternoon ; he walked over to Oldport with her, passed the time she was in chapel along the quays—calling sometimes on the Lanes—

and met her when she came out ; then they had an hour or two together before he need get back for the late-afternoon milking. These few hours on Sunday afternoons became precious to them that summer, and for Jessica lightened the sombreness of the strict non-conformist sabbath. One concession they made to the sabbath—they did not trespass on the enclosed land that had been the common, but went round to Oldport by road ; but this was because Jessica was wearing her best gown and shoes and dared not risk spoiling them by scrambling through hedges and negotiating the ditches that now drained the land.

But sometimes in the long light summer evenings they went joyfully trespassing, and Jesse would show her where he went after rabbits, and the runs of hares, and the squire's coverts where the precious young pheasants and partridges were being hand-reared, until the day when they would be beaten up over the guns for gentlemen's pleasure.

William Hallard was now paying his eldest son a few shillings a week, Jesse having threatened to hire himself out as labourer elsewhere, or go away to sea, but the thought of pheasants running in the stubble, and coming out under the hedges after the berries, and decoyed with handfuls of grain away from their coverts, stirred his blood irresistibly, and once again in the sultry dog-days of August, when the trees were heavy and jaded, he was impatient for acorn-time and the falling of the leaves.

" If you had become betrothed to Mary Byrd you would have given away your nets and wires and ferrets," Jessica told him. " You would have stayed at home at nights and become respectable, and it would have been so dull you would have died of it—or run away to sea ! "

" If I had had Mary it might all have been different. 'Tis not dull to sit at home with someone you love and who loves you. People only go adventuring to fill some other lack in their lives."

Jessica tossed her head. " People deceive themselves, if you ask me—especially when they have been disappointed in love ! To be free, that is the great thing ! To move about and see different things, not to be tied down. Not to be imprisoned in your way of life. People are—look at Mamma and Pappa. They might as well be in the county gaol ! 'Tis no wonder they are so small-minded and prejudiced ! "

Jesse did not know. It was as though he could not think beyond the dream of Mary and her quiet eyes and rare smile. With Mary there would have been no need of escape. As it was, he lived always in the shadow of the island.

On his summer evening strolls with Jessica he was always on the look-out for partridge and pheasant coverts and the roosting-places of

80

the birds. The previous season he had not touched partridges, but now he was more ambitious ; you could only take pheasants one at a time, but you could drive a whole covey of partridges down into a net, and he had been assured that many poulterers preferred netted birds.

Jesse had a revulsion against the harvest-home celebrations that year ; by all means let the labourers get drunk at the expense of the squire and the well-to-do farmers after the toil of getting in the harvest, but watching the procession of laden waggons crossing the fields on the squire's estate one mellow September evening, listening to the cheers and the singing, and aware of the decorations on the horses, and the ' harvest queen,' with her wreath of cornflowers and poppies, seated on the top of the last load, he felt suddenly bitter. For this one night of the year the labourers, the producers, were to be fêted ; for the rest of the year they would be thrown back on less than a living wage, many of them living in hovels inferior to the stables and byres of the horses and cattle they tended ; their well-being certainly less important than that of the squire's pedigree cattle. This was the rural England about which people sentimentalised, and for denouncing which, showing it up in its naked truth, Mr. Cobbett had had to flee to America ! It angered him that the people could not see the mockery of this seasonal feasting, this annual condescension on the part of those who for the rest of the year condemned them to poverty and misery. He longed to run to the head of the procession and cry out to them all to stop, to listen, to ask themselves what was the use of ale and roast beef and cheese-cakes and plum pudding once a year, when the rest of the year their lot was starvation. There were a few who were not fooled, but the rest, Jesse thought, were like children, and treated as such by their employers.

He would have liked to have called at the smithy and aired his opinions with old Byrd, and it was a grief to him that that place which had become a second home for him—his only real home—was now denied him. It gave him acute pleasure to go after the squire's game whilst the merrymaking was going on in the barn, and he absented himself from the Valley Farm celebrations. The picture of his father as the genial, popular, kindly farmer, for one night only, sickened him.

All over the country at this time of the year these charming ' rustic scenes,' which so delighted the gentlemen who wrote for the newspapers, were being enacted, and it was tactfully forgotten that two years ago these same humble rustics had brought the country to the verge of revolution in their demand for work and bread. Had the labouring people themselves forgotten ? Had they sunk back into an apathy of hopelessness ? Tomorrow they would rise at dawn—most of them with headaches from the night's carousal—and the weary round would begin all over again, full of the same injustices, the same bitter class distinctions.

The thought of the sea recurred to him perpetually. There were times when he felt that he could not continue helplessly looking on at the poverty of the countryside, the pitiless injustice meted out to those who were the very source of the land's productiveness. It tormented him, and added to the burden of his own personal inner torment of self-dissatisfaction.

Jack Mortimer, when he had heard that Mary had rejected Jesse, had thought to comfort him with the assurance that he need ' never be short of a woman,' that the women would always ' run after ' him, and all cats were grey in the dark. This easy assurance merely increased Jesse's depression. He did not want these easy women, to whom, it seemed, he was to be condemned all his life. He despised himself for continuing to meet Sally after that chance encounter on the road in July. When her menfolk were at sea he would sometimes spend the greater part of a night with her, but there would be times when lying in her arms he would not hear the beating of her heart against his, or her impassioned endearments, but only the sough of the sea breaking along the beaches, and everything in him would insist, " I must get away! I must get away! "

Then he would raise himself on an elbow and look down at her, fingering her tangled, uncared-for golden hair spread out on the pillow, and she would be oppressed by the sadness in his face. She would round on him, then, demanding why he came there if he found so little pleasure in it. She could not know that he never came so near to loving her as when she was cold to him out of weariness of his melancholy. When he caught himself out deliberately trying to alienate her because only then could he ardently desire her, he stopped seeing her, sick with himself, sick to the bottom of his soul.

The only peace he knew at that time was when he was out at night alone, creeping along under the hedges after pheasants, pegging out his net across a rabbit warren, a couple of ferrets in his jacket pockets. Then in his absorption in stealthy, silent movement everything else vanished. Once poaching had meant for him access to women ; now it offered escape from them.

It was Jessica who held him back from going to sea. He could not leave her. He had the feeling that they were both wandering in a dark, pathless wood, looking for a way out and seeing none. Jessica, he knew, was waiting for the gipsies to return, and lived in a perpetual state of expectancy. When by the end of October there was still no sign of them she began to talk wildly of running away to London. In November she gave up going down to the bridge to see whether the caravan of painted carts was coming inland along the road that skirted the common. Once a tinker pitched his tent beside the river and her heart almost burst with expectancy—and then with the intensity of disappointment.

"They won't come now," Jesse told her. "'Tis too late in the year. They have dug in for the winter somewhere else by now."

"José promised," she cried, and her eyes were wild as the winter woods.

It was the first time he had heard her give the gipsy a name, and it startled him. He had not realised till then that this gipsy obsession was not mere romanticism on Jessica's part, but something real and personal. The gipsy in terms of romantic adventure was one thing, but taken seriously quite another. He was suddenly afraid for her.

"What is a gipsy's promise?" he said.

"If they don't come by the end of the month I shall run away!"

He promised recklessly then, "I will go with you." He would get work in London; with horses, probably, a job such as old Byrd had had. They would take rooms and Jessica would 'keep house.' They would find a way to live. Perhaps they would get rooms overlooking the river, and the ships and the gulls would save them from homesickness. His imagination fastened on the idea and began to develop it. He discussed it with Jessica and it assumed a definite shape. They would make their 'escape' before Christmas, that succession of Sundays invaded by relatives. In time Jessica would meet some decent young fellow she could love and who would love her and look after her, and then he would be free to go away to sea. The more he thought about it the more the plan appealed to him. He had enough money put by for their fares to London; they would get the stage coach outside of Oldport. They would stay at small country inns en route. "Perhaps we shall get held up by highwaymen," Jessica suggested, hopefully. But she never discussed the plan as eagerly as Jesse; she still hoped, and more than half believed, that the gipsies would come back.

Then one mild sunny November morning, ploughing an upland field whose earth was the pinkish-bronze of bracken in late autumn, Jesse looked down into the valley, where the beechwoods still held their copper, and the last leaves spun down from the elms like gold coins, and saw at the base of the white scar of a disused chalk-pit on the far side an encampment of small painted carts, tethered horses with rough coats and shaggy manes and tails, and low tents. There was the flash of a pink shawl, a thin spiral of smoke from a fire, and the barking and yapping of dogs carried across the valley on the thin, still air.

83

When he had halted his horses before turning the plough, and paused to look down into the valley, he had been near to peace, finding pleasure in the rich warm colour of the earth, in the almost springlike mildness of the day, in the black and white flash of the wings of pee-wits over the newly-turned soil, in the late lingering green of an ash-tree at the head of the field. He had always loved that upland field, with its view out over the valley, and the red roofs of the farm build-ings huddled at its foot, and an uprush of love of the familiar scene had swept him. Then suddenly in that very moment of satisfaction it was as though the sun had disappeared behind clouds and the colour was drained out of the earth like the blood from a frightened heart.

It flashed into his mind to go down into the valley and offer the gipsies all his poacher's earnings to go away, but almost immediately came the counter-thought that was more than a thought, that was an inexplicable realisation, that Jessica would already know that they were there.

It was as though they had come for her. He turned back to the plough, calling to the horses, trying to dismiss the thought as absurd, but it persisted.

When he returned to the house at mid-day and saw the light in Jessica's face he had the feeling that she was already gone from him—from them all.

XI

WHEN the horses had been unharnessed and tethered, and the tents pitched, at the bottom of the chalk-pit, José went boldly up to the farm. He was accompanied by his brother's wife, Maria, she of the pink shawl. Maria was very beautiful; she was probably the most beautiful woman in the tribe, and until he had seen Jessica José had been envious of his brother Miguel, a few years older than himself in the possession of Maria. He had never expected to find anyone the least like Maria amongst the *gorgios*, and when he had first seen Jessica he had for a moment thought he was looking at a Romany *chi*. So, it seemed to him, must Maria have looked when she was a young girl, and as Maria looked now so would Jessica look in a few years' time. Since he could not have Maria he must have Jessica, in spite of the fact that she was a *gorgio*, and in spite of the opposition the family would raise to his having her because of that. That he could have Jessica he never for a moment doubted, even that night of the harvest moon when she failed to keep the tryst beside the river. The spring day he had found her in the little wood he was quite sure she would come to the fair ; and after that it seemed to him that she belonged to him. Through hamlets and villages and market-towns and cities he had carried the memory of her for the rest of that spring and the whole of the summer and autumn. His father and brother had opposed the idea of returning to Oldport for the winter and camping in the valley, and he had lied to them with stories of rumours of a winter fair at which the women could tell fortunes and beg silver.

Maria defended him against the family clannishness. She herself had loved a *gorgio* before Miguel. But there had been a little trouble with a gamekeeper one night and he had died of gunshot wounds. If José wanted this girl, where was the harm of it ? It was better that a Romany *chal* should love a *gorgio* than the other way, for the children took the father's name, and whoever José married, be she light-skinned as a lily, the children would bear his name. And this girl was dark enough to be of Romany blood herself, and, José declared, she was *Rome and dree*, gipsy at heart.

Maria loved José. Sometimes she acknowledged the secret hidden within her and admitted that she loved him better than Miguel, who was violent and dominating and almost too lazy to do even a little easy stealing in a crowded market-place. José was only thirteen when she had married his brother five years ago, when she herself was seventeen, and already at sixteen he loved her, but then it was too late. Now José was determined to make this farmer's daughter his *romi*, and if she was prepared to have him for her *rom* and come and live with him in a tent, wandering the country telling fortunes, stealing where possible, living Romanly, why should it not be ? It was a great gipsy triumph to snatch a bride from the *gorgios*. When, therefore, José asked her to come with him to the farm that November morning when they arrived back at the valley, Maria came gladly. The idea was that she should tell the farm maidservant's fortune and cover José and Jessica. If he went alone with his baskets and clothes-pegs he might be sent away without a chance of seeing his Jessica, but a Romany *chi* could coax and wheedle, particularly with a young babe at her breast.

So they came together, the slim, insolent-looking José, and the beautiful queenly Maria with her red flounced dress and the fine pink Spanish shawl with the red flowers that had belonged to Grandbebee, and the green handkerchief on her head, and her long black plaits twisted with coins, and bracelets of coins tinkling at her brown wrists. Mrs. Hallard, shaking a feather-mop from an upper window, saw them crossing the rick-yard together, and frowned at the approaching splendour, the ungodliness of the gaudy clothes filling her with anger. She called to them that she wanted nothing of them, and to be off with them, but they came on, the girl smiling. Then they were under the window looking up at her, and for a moment she was dazzled by the red and pink and green, and the glittering coins, and the fine flashing eyes.

Maria assumed her begging, wheedling tone.

" Spare a sixpence, kind lady, for the poor gipsy and her baby. Three other little children at home, lady. Sweet kind lady—sixpence for the poor gipsy girl——"

" Certainly not ! " Mrs. Hallard said, angrily. " Be off with you this instant ! " and slammed the casement.

But by then the servant had come to the door of the back kitchen and behind her Jessica crowded. She had been helping make the beds, and the moment her mother had murmured ' gipsies ' had sped down the stairs, her heart plunging madly. Maria smiled enticingly at the simple-looking servant.

" Let the gipsy girl tell your fortune, dear," she coaxed. " Cross the gipsy's palm with silver, lady dear, and a little piece of silver at the end for luck, and she will tell you the fine gentleman you are to wed, and those you should beware."

The servant faltered, fascinated, half willing, half afraid, and Maria came closer, boldly, and took her hand.

" Step away from the house a moment, dear," she whispered. " No one must hear."

" My mistress will be angered." Already Mrs. Hallard's voice could be heard calling from upstairs, " Jessica ! Katie ! Send those good-for-nothing gipsies away at once and return to your chores ! "

But Katie was leaning against the wall behind the water-butt with Maria poring over her rough, grimed hand, and Jessica was aware only of her plunging heart and of José's eyes holding hers with their dark fire. She had a sense of all her blood flowing towards him, like a river running out to sea. He did not smile. Even before he spoke she was aware of the compulsion of his will.

" You will meet me tonight—where ? "

She spoke like one mesmerised. " In the lane at the end of the cart-track."

" I shall be there."

Not until he had gone, walking with his shoulders thrown back, his head held high, walking as though he owned the earth and held it in contempt, did she realise that no time had been mentioned. It did not matter ; at whatever time she went he would be there.

She walked on air for the rest of the day. Why had she ever for a moment doubted that he would come back ? She made beds, she dusted, she skimmed the cream from the great shallow pans of milk in the dairy, she stood churning the cream into butter till her arms ached, and all the time it was as though her blood danced. She hummed snatches of song ; all her body seemed to be singing. When Katie, who was plump and red and stupid, chattered about the pretty gipsy and how she had said she would meet a dark man of whom she must beware, and would come into some money, and meet her destiny in the spring, she smiled indulgently. Now she could be patient and sweet with everyone, indulge the whole world, because she alone in all the world had the supreme good fortune to be going to meet José that night. All day her mind held the image of his lean brown face with its proud mouth and compelling eyes.

Jesse had no chance of a word alone with her when he came in at mid-day, and afterwards he went back to the upland field ; but she went to him in the cow-sheds when he came in again for the after-noon milking, and stood beside him. There was no one within ear-shot.

" José was here this morning," she said.

" I saw they had come back. They are camped in the chalk-pit."

" I am meeting him tonight."

He made no comment ; the spurts of milk made a thin music against the bucket.

" Are you not glad for my sake, Jesse ? " she challenged him. " Once you rebuked me for not meeting him."

" I never wanted it to become serious. It makes me afraid for you. They are a wild people, the gipsies. Their ways are not our ways."

" Who would wish them to be ? Did we not talk of running away to London to make a new kind of life because we could not endure any more the life here ? "

" We should have lived in a house, not in a tent," he reminded her.

" So long as one is warm and dry and out of the rain, what does it matter ? "

She turned and left him, and he watched her picking her way jauntily across the muddy yard, and told himself he should be glad she was happy and unafraid of adventure, as he had once urged she should be, but could not shake off the feeling of heaviness. Suddenly an idea struck him. Perhaps these strange, dark, foreign people really could read people's destinies written in their hands ? Perhaps one of the women at the gipsy camp could give him the reassurance he needed concerning Jessica ?

When he went back to the house after the milking he watched for an opportunity to get Jessica alone. He sent Katie out of the dairy on an errand, then said to Jessica, quickly, " I want you to do some-thing to please me. I want you to ask José to take you down to the camp tonight and have one of the women who tell fortunes read your hand."

"But 'tis all lies done for money, all that fortune-telling, surely?"

"There may be something in it."

She laughed. "I would never have thought such foolishness of you, Jesse. But I will ask José."

In her lightness of her heart she would have promised almost anything.

The few hours after the evening meal were sheer torment for Jessica. It seemed as though her parents would never go to bed, though in actual fact they went no later than usual, that is to say at nine o'clock. The Bible reading seemed more than usually dreary and meaningless, her father more than usually pompous and tedious.

'*Yea, the light of the wicked shall be put out,*' she heard him intoning, as she bent her head over her needlework, '*and the spark of his fire shall not shine. The light shall be dark in his tabernacle, and his candle shall be put out with him. The steps of his strength shall be straitened and his own counsel shall cast him down. For he is cast into a net by his own feet, and he walketh upon a snare.*'

She glanced up and met Jesse's eye and their lips curved in a half smile.

'*The gin shall take him by the heel, and the robber shall prevail against him.*'

This reminded Jesse about the snares he had put down, and he wondered whether they would be robbed by the gipsies before he could get to them.

'*The snare is laid for him in the ground, and a trap for him in the way.*'

Spring-guns in the squire's park. Jesse wanted to laugh. For '*terrors shall make him afraid on every side,*' he automatically substituted 'keepers.' But Jessica was no longer even faintly amused by all this reference to traps and snares and nets and gins. It seemed as though her father would never end.

'. . . *brimstone shall be scattered upon his habitation* . . . *his remembrance shall perish from the earth* . . . *he shall be driven from light into darkness* . . .'

It finished at last and the huge black family Bible was replaced on the small table under the window, below the row of geraniums. John's pen resumed its scratching over the paper. Jesse got up and went out without a word. There was the clatter of Mrs. Hallard's scissors as she picked them up and laid them down again, picked them up and laid them down. Jessica yawned and announced her intention of retiring. She kissed her parents on their foreheads and John on the top of his head, took her candle from the table by the door, and went out and up the stairs to her room. It seemed a long time before her parents came up, and still longer before she heard John in his room. Then there was the interminable waiting for the murmur of voices and the creaking of movements to subside. An owl called in the yew tree spreading its ancient branches over the roof. Jessica tip-toed across the sloping floor of the room and took her thick cloak from the closet and wrapped it round her. Out there in the darkness, no more than half a mile away, José waited, but she dared not go to him yet.

When at last she dared to lift the latch of her door the beating of her heart seemed to fill the darkness like a thud of drums, and when a floor-board creaked under her step she stood trembling in the darkness. She waited motionless, holding her breath, but there was no sound, only a scutter of rats in the attic. Surely there had not been so many creaking boards and clicking latches the night she had stolen out to go to the fair ?

A dog stirred when she let herself out at the back door, but she whispered its name and there was a whimper of recognition. Once she was clear of the house, and the stacks of the rick-yard loomed up like the hulls of ships in the darkness, she began to run. There was no moon, but it was not a dense darkness, and she knew every inch of the way.

She was breathless when she reached the end of the cart-track, and the gate had barely fallen to behind her before José stepped out of the deeper darkness under a tree and drew her into his arms.

He kissed her wildly, murmuring words which she did not understand, did not even know to be Romany ; his will closed round her again and everything was a dream.

When he insisted, " You belong to me. You cannot live in a house and marry a *gorgio*," though she had no idea what *gorgio* meant she knew that it must be true because marriage meant José and a tent. ' *Whither thou goest I will go ; and where thou lodgest I will lodge ; thy people shall be my people.*' Marriage meant that.

She said, still in the dream, " My brother wants you to take me to the camp and have my fortune told."

" Tonight ? "

" I promised."

" Come, then."

She showed him the short cut to the chalk-pit, up over the upland field and dropping down into the valley on the other side. From the top of the field they stood looking down at the dull glow of the camp-fire across the valley ; the white scar of the chalk-pit showed dimly in the starlight.

He turned to her then, his hands on her shoulders.

" You are not afraid, little sister ? "

" Why should I be ? "

He replied simply, " You have lived all your life in a house ; I have lived all mine in a tent. Your people are Christians. Mine are thieves and vagabonds."

" Christians also steal," she told him. " They steal the land from the poor."

He laughed excitedly, confidently. " You belong with us, little sister."

He took her hand and they descended the hill together.

Dogs ran out yapping and yelping as they approached the camp, but slank away when José spoke to them. A very old woman crouched over the fire smoking a clay pipe. She stared at Jessica across the flames. José addressed her as ' Grandbebee ' and said words which Jessica did not understand, then he went across to a tent and called softly, ' Maria.'

He explained to Jessica, " Maria is my brother Miguel's wife. She is very beautiful. You are like her."

In a moment the young woman Jessica had seen in the morning—in other worlds long ago, it seemed now—emerged from the tent. She smiled when she saw Jessica. There was nothing of the wheedling, whining ' poor gipsy girl ' about her now ; there was an almost royal condescension in her voice as she said, " Welcome to the tents of the poor people, little sister."

" She comes to you for *dukkerin*, sister," José said.

" *Dukkeripen* is not always wise, brother."

" She promised her brother."

" Come to the fire, then."

They all three went over to the fire and knelt down beside it, opposite the old woman, and Maria took the girl's hand. She studied it intently for some minutes, then looked up and addressed José in their own tongue. He said something back, sharply, frowning, but Maria shook her head, repeating something.

He turned from her to Jessica.

" Maria says she does not wish to read your hand. She says it says too many things."

He got up and pulled Jessica to her feet after him.

" I will take you home," he said.

Maria also rose, her face sombre. The old woman removed her pipe, spat, and muttered. Jessica looked from one to the other of the gipsies, troubled.

" My brother will think there are bad things for the future written in my hand if I tell him what Maria says."

" No matter. Sometimes the future is better hidden." Maria folded her shawl round her and shivered.

José put his arm round Jessica's shoulders. "Come," he said.

Jessica turned to say goodnight to Maria, but she had already turned and walked away.

For a few yards José was silent, then he said, "Maria is right. The future is sometimes better hidden."

There was a kind of hard finality in his voice, and he pulled Jessica closer against his side, as though challenging destiny to separate them.

"Do you believe in—fortune-telling?" Jessica asked, presently.

"I am a gipsy, and the gipsies came originally from the East, and the East has practised this art for thousands of years."

"You still might not believe in it," she persisted.

He did not answer, and again she felt the impact of his will, this time with a kind of stubbornness, resisting questioning.

They crossed the bottom of the valley and began slowly to ascend the hill, pausing occasionally to look at the glow of the camp-fire. At the top they stumbled into a tangle of dead, dry bracken; it made a nest, and he pulled her down into it. He leaned over her, pushing back her hood, fingering her hair, still wrapped in his stubborn silence. Then it seemed to her that he swooped suddenly out of that silence like an owl out of its covering darkness, enveloped her and made her one with his own strangeness and darkness.

3

When he got back to the camp the fire had burned low and the old woman had gone inside. He fetched wood from a pile under an awning of sacking stretched between two poles against the chalk-face of the pit, and when he had started the fire up again sat down beside it, staring into the spurting flames as though he would read the future there.

He did not see Maria leave her tent and did not know she was beside him till she laid a hand on his arm. They spoke together in their own tongue.

She said, "I could not sleep until I had told you—one thing is written in the future, you will not be separated—she will stay with you and none come between you."

"In the spring we go away from here—together?"

"That is what troubles me—I don't see that journey marked in her hand."

"But if none is to come between us?"

"That is so. But the rest is not clear."

91

They sat silent, brooding, staring into the fire, oppressed by a sense of ancient lore beyond their power to refute, because it was in their blood, and had been for thousands of years ; oppressed by a sense of inescapable destiny, irrevocably predetermined.

A horse sneezed in the lean-to against the wall of the pit ; a child whimpered in a tent.

Maria rose. " I must go in." She stood straight and still a moment by the fire, the red light flickering in the coins twisted in her long plaits.

" It is no use worrying, José. We cannot escape our destinies."

He did not answer or look at her, but stayed there, crouching beside the fire, staring into its leaping heart. Maria laid a hand a moment on his bowed dark head, then turned and walked away and was lost in the darkness beyond the outer rim of the fire's light. A heart of fire blazing in darkness, nothing visible beyond its limited circle, but within the fire itself a blaze of splendour—was that how it had seemed to Maria when at his age she too had loved one of these foreigners from that other world, that world of houses and churches and schools and earning your bread by the sweat of your brow—of forcing others to earn it for you ? That world of law and order and living all the time in one place and every day the same. . . . Those who were old and wise said that no good ever came of a Romany wedding a *gringo*. It produced ' half-and-halfs ' who compromised with the *gringo* desire for a house and travelled the roads in caravans and earned their livings more or less honestly, living a life that was neither Roman nor *gringo*. But if you begot children by one who also had this heart of flame, perhaps then the pure wild Romany blood triumphed over the foreign ? The wild dark gipsy blood in which was fused all the century-old mystery of the East, and all the sun-kindled passion of the South. Out of Egypt, out of India, came the gipsies, and wandered the plains of Hungary, and the rocky roads of Spain, and the olive-clad mountains of Italy. *Zigeuners, gitanos, zingaros*. Romans, Romanies ; Egyptians, gipsies . . . horse-stealers, chiromancers, tent-dwellers ; the lawless ones with the heart of flame.

A bridal bed of late autumn bracken, purple-red as the heart of the fire and the new-ploughed fields, but, according to the stars that determined human destiny, no journey into the spring. . . .

He stayed brooding by the fire until it was a heap of grey ash, then went heavy-hearted to his tent.

But morning sunlight found him leaning up against the painted wheel of a cart, strumming a guitar and singing a catch of gipsy song, whilst his grandmother plucked the feathers from a stolen fowl, and his mother fetched water from the spring, and Maria chopped wood and her children ran laughing and shouting between the tents. Whilst his brother carved a piece of wood for his own amusement, and their father lay on his back looking at the pale blue of the sky. For this too was in his blood, part of his gipsy heritage, to sing in the sun whilst the women did their chores, and all of it sufficient unto the day.

XII

IT was impossible for Jesse to avoid seeing Mary Byrd. It was not enough merely to depute others to take the farm horses to the forge when they needed re-shoeing. He always saw her, sooner or later, on market-days in the town square, sometimes with her mother, oftener alone. Sometimes she acknowledged him with a slight nod ; at other times she did not see him, and he was never quite certain whether this was deliberate or not. Occasionally he saw her when he passed the smithy, shaking a mat at the door, or a feather-mop from an upstairs window—a mop of turkey feathers made by the gipsies. Whenever he saw her something ached in him. Marriage with her would have been a coming into harbour. He might, then, he felt, have assumed the responsibility of his heritage of the farm and worked for agrarian reform. His labourers would be the best paid in the parish. He himself was no scholar, but with John's help he might have drafted a petition to Parliament, have followed humbly in the footsteps of Mr. Cobbett. God knows he was not lacking in feeling. But to settle down without Mary seemed to him unthinkable ; he needed her, or someone like her—but was there anyone like her ?— for the wildness in himself to be directed into some useful channel. Without her he was the mill-stream without the mill-wheel, his energies tossing and turning and flowing uselessly away. He had to have peace in himself, the blessedness of sleep after love, before he could be of any use to anyone else ; or so it seemed to him, that winter of his discontent.

In the summer a giant sunflower had burned like a miniature sun against the white-washed wall of the smithy ; now it stood brown and withered, its heavy head hanging like a ship's bell. Whenever he passed it it reminded him that there was a way of escape by sea.

Early on, Mary's parents had expressed their regret to him for what they regarded as their daughter's folly and stubbornness. Mrs. Byrd spoke to him one day in the market-place ; old Mr. Byrd went over to him in the inn. Both declared that nothing would have given them greater happiness than that Mary should have accepted him. Mrs. Byrd even held out the hope that ' she might come round in time,' since there was no one else. Mr. Byrd told him, " She's got an

4

idea into her head that all the women run after you and that you make free with the women of the town, and then her pride steps in. She hath a pride out of all reason, and 'twill be her undoing."

Jesse said bitterly, " I never looked at another woman the time I was courting her, and she knows it. Nor would I if she had become my wife. If I make free with the women of the town 'tis she who condemns me to it ! "

He had black moments of hating her, as he had hated Jessica after their break. Then, full of contempt both for himself and her, he would go to Sally, submit himself to a witchery he despised. Dislocating a rabbit's neck, or cracking a pheasant over the head, he would know a sudden uprush of released hate and cruelty, a kind of vicious satisfaction, and by God, he would tell himself violently, some satisfaction was due to him.

The only tenderness in his life at that time was Jessica, and for her he knew a boundless tenderness. He worried about her because on the nights she stole out to meet José she rose next morning with black rings under her eyes from lack of sleep. It would be past midnight when she went to bed, and she had to be up with the others at five. And he worried because the gipsy girl had refused to read her hand. He did not know whether he believed in ' fortune-telling ' or not ; at the back of his mind he had the feeling that the gipsies had some mysterious occult power that had to do with their " foreignness,' some power to see into the future. He worried because early in December the ground became hard as iron, and the sky a steel grey with flakes of snow drifting on a bitter wind ; how could Jessica go on meeting her gipsy when the bad weather came ? What was to become of her ?

Jessica only laughed at his anxiety. Were there not barns and hayricks, and lofts over cart-sheds, she demanded, gaily. And since when did lovers feel the cold ? All the same, he thought, in spite of her gaiety, Jessica did not look well ; it was not only the black rings under her eyes ; she was thinner in the face, he was sure of it, and he would flood with a fierce aching tenderness ; as in their childhood, she was still the beloved little sister, the one being on earth who came close to him.

Then just before Christmas something happened which broke in on his anxiety over Jessica and his preoccupation with his own dissatisfaction. Jack Mortimer and two of his ' gang ' were surprised by the squire's keepers in the pheasant preserve in the park and hauled up before the Bench, on which sat the squire himself.

Mortimer's entire gang had been in the preserve that night—and so had all the squire's keepers and their underlings. Too many pheasants had been disappearing lately and the bailiff and the head-keeper had organised a drive; they had the wood completely covered before Mortimer and his men entered it. A spring-gun had gone off and wounded the ex-tenant farmer in the leg. It had been the signal for a general flight, but Mortimer and a young labourer had found their way to the wounded man and insisted on trying to get him away, in spite of his urgings to them to leave him and ' run for it.' Mortimer tried to keep two keepers busy whilst his companion made an attempt to get away with the other man. He succeeded in knocking one keeper out and in his fury might have dealt as effectively with the other one had not a third leapt on him from behind. The wood was a tumult of shouting men, clattering, frightened pheasants, and disturbed, screeching owls.

In the morning Mortimer, the wounded man, and the young labourer, appeared before the Bench, Mortimer on the double charge of being unlawfully in the preserve and with assaulting a keeper. With them were three keepers, one with a black eye, at the sight of which a smile curved Mortimer's thin lips.

Jesse heard of the fracas when he went to the inn, after having landed a salmon below the weir that night. With complete disregard for discretion he turned up at the court in the morning, heard the ex-tenant farmer sentenced to six months' hard labour, the young labourer to a year, and Jack Mortimer to transportation for seven years.

His blood rose then and he cried out from the back of the court, " By God, you can't do that! 'Twas a blow struck in self-defence——"

He was still shouting when he was removed from the court and flung head foremost into the passage. He sprawled at the feet of various of the Mortimer family, including the old father who had done a year for poaching rabbits.

" Transportation for seven years the swine have given him! " Jesse cried, wildly, as he picked himself up. Mrs. Mortimer cried out, and the two youngest children, frightened, ran to her, clinging to her skirts, joining in her cries. Behind the Mortimers Jesse saw Jim and Sally.

" There'll be some will pay for this," Jim muttered.

Then Jack was brought out in charge of two constables. He carried his head high and his lips were tight. He laid a hand on his mother's shoulder.

" I'll be back, Mother," he said. " There is no need to take on. 'Tis one way of getting away to sea! "

He looked at Jesse, smiling faintly.

" 'Twas good of you to come," he said, and held out his hand. Jesse gripped it as though he would never let it go.

" 'Twould be better to put the cobwebs away for a while," Mortimer said.

Jesse nodded. He knew that in the presence of the constables he dare say no more, but he understood well enough. When you went to buy a certain kind of net you always asked for a cobweb.

Jesse left Jack with his family and went out with the Lanes. He blinked in the bright cold sunlight of the market-square after the darkness of the passage outside the court-room. He felt dazed with anger and misery. Seven years at the other side of the world for giving a man a black eye in a two-to-one fight ! He could still hear the mother's cries ringing in his head, and the sobbing of the frightened children.

Sally laid a hand on his arm. " Come back with us, lad, and have a tot of rum. Ye look all in ! "

When he got back to the farm at mid-day he found the squire's bailiff, Tom Surridge, sitting nonchalantly on the corner of the kitchen table quaffing ale and recounting with great gusto the story of the affray and the court sequel. He broke off as Jesse came in.

" I was just telling your father I seed ye at the court-house this morning," he said. " Aye, and heard ye, too ! A fine commotion ye made, young man, to be sure ! "

" What are you doing mixed up in this ? " Mr. Hallard demanded of his son.

Jesse said, heavily, " Jack Mortimer was my friend." He turned to the bailiff and glared into his complacent red face.

" As for you, you damned skunk ! "

Surridge set down his mug and sprang to his feet, edging back.

" Get out ! " Jesse shouted at him, bringing up his clenched fists. He could see nothing but the man's red face. The blood hammered in his temples as it had in court.

The bailiff backed to the door, spluttered, fled.

Jesse dropped his fists and turned to his father, his eyes blazing.

" Why do you listen to him, the filthy rat ? Coming here bragging and boasting and crowing because a man is shot in the leg by a spring-gun and the men who stay by him to aid him are convicted ! Jack could have got away—they both could ! Jack takes the pair of keepers on single-handed and——"

" A poacher is a common thief ! " his father broke in on him, violently. " I want no defence of that sort of thing in this house. Men like that should be flogged at the tail of a cart all round the town ! This parish would be a better place if a good many more were transported ! "

The sweat stood out on Jesse's forehead. " And you call yourself a Christian ! " he cried, and then was aware of his mother standing beside his father, her eyes wide and scared, and on John's face the strained look he always assumed when one of the others were being beaten as children. He turned away from them all, despairingly, and then felt Jessica's hand in his, her fingers pressing his. He looked down at her a moment and it was then all he could do not to weep. He muttered something and went out.

He did not return. He spent the afternoon with the Mortimers in their miserable cottage. Various other humble valley folk had gathered there, all discussing Jack's sentence, and the way Jesse Hallard had spoken out in court, and the look of amazement on the squire's face when it happened, and that red fox of a bailie smirking in a corner. . . .

When Jesse entered they crowded round him wanting to shake his hand, stone-breakers, labourers, people with gaunt starved faces and rough hands, more than one of whom had been harnessed to the parish cart for daring to ask relief from the Poor Rates. Someone pushed a mug of ale into his hand. He drank deep, gratefully.

" It was a fair shock to squire when Farmer Hallard's eldest son spoke up for Jack ! " an old man cackled.

" He and the bailie will have it in for 'ee now," another warned him.

" 'Twas a wonder they did not order 'ee to be whipped," old Mr. Mortimer observed, bitterly.

That started them talking of the fifteen-year-old lad who had been publicly whipped at the cart's tail, out of Frome, back in January, for being a rogue and vagrant. Two boys apprehended with him had been transported for seven years. . . .

" Aye, there's no justice for poor folks." Mrs. Mortimer wept afresh.

" What is to happen to us all ? " Jesse cried wildly. " Are things going on like this forever ? "

" Nothing goes on forever, lad, not even life," an old woman muttered.

" There'll be a change sometime," a young man remarked, grimly.

" Not in our time," Jesse said, bitterly.

" Aye, in our time."

Someone said, " There's Sir Francis Burdett campaigning the country for Reform, Truth, Justice. They say he spoke to great crowds in London in the summer, out in Hyde Park, with those words blazed in gold on his chair——"

" But it's we who must make the demand for Reform, Truth, Justice ! " Jesse cried, suddenly, banging his empty mug down on the table. " 'Tis no use leaving it to the politicians ! It must come from us—the common people ! "

He looked round at the ragged company, wildly, and once again in imagination he was heading them up the valley to the manor, pikes glittering in the sunlight, banners demanding 'Bread or blood,' on into the market-place at Oldport, challenging the landlords, and the fat priests who were their toadies, fat with tithes, breaking down the fences, giving the land back to the people. . . .

" 'Twill come," said the young man who had spoken before. " Before God, 'twill come ! "

Jesse left them at dusk and went into the town. He had money in his pocket and a great hole, it seemed to him, burnt in his heart from the day's pain and anger. He was not in the mood for women. If there had been a woman upon whose quiet breast he could have rested his head and slept he would have gone to her gladly ; if there had been Mary . . . but there was not Mary, nor anyone like her, and he did not want the other kind ; they ministered only to the flesh, not the spirit, and it was his spirit that needed ease.

He went into *The Ship's Bell* and drank several brandies. Later Lucy came in, alone, and he smiled at her and went over to her, complimenting her on her bonnet, and bought her gin. He stood a few moments talking with her, then to her astonishment kissed her fingertips and went out.

In the coldness of the night air he felt a good deal more drunk than inside in the heat. He laughed, for no other reason than that being drunk he felt light and free, as though he had sloughed off his body and all anger and pain and anxiety with it. Now nothing in the world mattered except that he, Jesse Hallard, was alive and drunk and free—free of everyone and everything, of the squire's callousness, his father's bigotry, the bailiff's foxiness ; free of pain over Jack and Jessica and Mary. Free of them all and everything they could do to him.

He went swaying along the quays and out beyond the huddled white row of cottages where the Lanes lived, to a wild desolation of rocks beyond, high white cliffs at one side, the white-edged darkness of the sea on the other. He clambered over the rocks and came out to the sea, then began stripping off his clothes. With a careful drunken concentration he folded each garment neatly and tucked it down between two boulders, his boots beside them, and then utterly unaware of the coldness of wind and water waded out into the sea.

He had learned to swim when he was a schoolboy, from those very rocks, and had begun swimming again that summer with Sally's brothers, going out with them in their boat and diving overboard. He swam now with a strong slow precision in the direction of the island, almost invisible in the dim light of a waning moon. He had never swum so far before, and sober would not have dreamed of attempting it ; but now his sense of power carried him on, tirelessly, and oblivious of the cold. He swam until the cliffs became almost invisible in the faint moonlight, and the island began to take shape. He swam until a buoy came bobbing past, then instinctively he grabbed at it, and was suddenly panting for breath and aching in every limb. He knew then that he would never reach the island ; knew it with all the certainty of sobriety. When he looked back at the mainland panic swept him ; it seemed to him impossible he could swim back so far. But the island was even farther.

He dropped off the buoy and began to swim towards the land, and it was not alcoholic elation which carried him along but a desperate effort of will. Now he was remembering everything : Jessica ; the court scene ; the afternoon at the Mortimers' ! even the red silk flowers and curled ostrich feathers in Lucy's new bonnet. He saw the bailiff's sly red face again, the cold anger in his father's eyes, the scared look in his brother's, the dismay in his mother's, the passionate sympathy in Jessica's. . . . To stop making an effort now would be the end of everything. What was the use of swimming back—to all that dissatisfaction ?

He had only to cease making this colossal, exhausting effort and it would all be over. He had always thought of escape by sea, and this was one way, and far easier than joining a ship. It would be infinitely easier to stop making the effort than to go on. Jessica would be all right now ; she had her José. She would understand that in his own way he had at last escaped to the island. She would not grieve for long, and there was no one else, though his mother, no doubt, would make the conventional display of sorrow.

But the will to life carried him on, in spite of the exhaustion, in spite of aching arms and legs that seemed to lose strength with every stroke, and a back that seemed on the point of cracking, and an increasing effort to breathe. Something outside of all reasoning fought desperately with failing strength to reach the dim shore whilst every buffeting wave seemed determined to thrust him back. Something dogged and unaccountable in him held on grimly.

When he finally scrambled out on to the rocks he was completely sober, shivering with cold, exhausted so that he could barely stand, but curiously at peace. He found his clothes, dried himself on his shirt, dressed.

There was the glow of a lamp in the window of the Lanes' cottage as he passed, and he knew that Sally would be alone until daybreak, but he strode past. As he followed the road out of the town it seemed to him all over again that there was everything to live for because, by God, there was everything to fight for.

99

XIII

DECEMBER was a wild month with black nights full of wind and rain, and, despite her easy assurance to Jesse, Jessica began to find it increasingly difficult to keep her trysts with José. On a night when she failed to meet him he came out to the farm and threw small stones up at her casement. She was so frightened by this audacity that after that she began meeting him in the loft over the cart-shed halfway along the lane that led out to the post-road. Then the snow came, in great blinding drifts, and it was difficult even to struggle as far as the cart-shed in the bitter nights, and she agreed to meet him in the barn. The gipsy was completely reckless; he would reach her though hell should bar the way. Jessica, feminine, was full of the dread of discovery. A rat scurrying under the floor-boards of the barn was sufficient to make her cling to him in terror wild visions of her father or John suddenly coming to the barn in the middle of the night seizing her. Sooner or later, it seemed to her, they must surely be discovered, and then her father would use his influence with the squire to have the gipsies sent out of the parish, and José would probably be arrested, and sent to a House of Correction, if not transported. Being a gipsy, it would probably mean transportation, and then she would never see him again. As the weeks went past, too, she became increasingly certain that she could not remain much longer at home. At first the fear that she might be going to have a child frightened her to such an extent that she had even had a wild idea of throwing herself into the mill-pond. José succeeded in calming her; what was there to be frightened about? She would be seventeen by the time the child was born, and there was nothing remarkable in being wed at sixteen. She would be married Romany fashion, and Maria, who had had four children herself, would look after her. His plea was always that she should join them that night, the next night. What was there to wait for? In a few weeks the roads might be impassable, the farm snowbound.

Jessica knew all this, and that there was in fact nothing to wait for. Had not this been her dream, one day to join the gipsies and leave the restraints and the narrowness of the farm forever? But deep down in her she was frightened of the strange dark people who now claimed her because she was bearing their tribe a child. In some moods she was even a little afraid of José, with the feeling that for all their closeness she did not really understand him. He was incalculable. He would be withdrawn from her in his silence. And she was frightened of the completeness of the severance from everything she knew and understood once she had left home. *Thy people shall be my people* assumed a new and terrifying significance. She would become a gipsy wife, she, Jessica Hallard, of Valley Farm. But that was something that nobody of her own world, except Jesse, would ever know. They would know only that she had run away— ostensibly to London. Her parents would be bitterly angry; whether they would grieve she did not know. She could not imagine grief in them, and unable to imagine it could feel no pity for them. Her flight would cause a scandal; it would be a terrible blow to her parents' pride; she realised that; it would be a reflection on their upbringing of her, and on the Hallard home. The farm labourers, who hated her father, would look knowing; they would say, perhaps, that he had driven her from home. Neighbours and relatives would speculate. All this shame she would heap upon them, this bitter blow . . . but there were all the blows at the end of a strap they had heaped on her and Jesse as children to be taken into the reckoning. Yet the thought of cutting off completely from the lovelessness and utter dullness of her home frightened her; it was at least something she knew and understood.

Near Christmas she took Jesse into her confidence. She talked to him in the milking-shed; now that she could not get out to him in the fields it was frequently the only place that offered any privacy. Sometimes she would be alone with him in the loft over the barn when he was giving his ferrets bread-and-milk, but she dared not talk there for fear her father or John or one of the labourers might be down below.

She told him, " Soon I must leave here, Jesse, and marry José."

" Your mind is made up ? 'Tis a serious step."

She made an effort and told him the rest. " I must. I am with child."

To her amazement he replied almost casually, " I was always afraid that might happen. Even so, you could go away and have the child, secretly—there's no need to marry José."

She said with a kind of despair, " 'Tis hard to say what I do want, Jesse. When I am with him everything seems easy—natural. When I get away I become afraid, and everything seems foreign and strange and unnatural."

" 'Tis when you are with him that counts," Jesse reassured her.

He was worried, nevertheless, assailed by the same doubts that troubled Jessica herself. It was one thing to talk romantically of going off with the gipsies; quite another to take the revolutionary step of doing it. But Jessica was committed now to leave home, and that being so, he reflected, trying to dismiss his misgivings, it was probably better she should go to José. Perhaps she was truly at heart a gipsy. He tried to reason with himself. What was there against the gipsy life ? They lived well enough; they raised healthy children, they contrived to eat well ; they had a healthy contempt for the law ; their lives were full of colour and movement. Did it make so much difference whether one lived in a house or in a tent ? Why should not the gipsy José make Jessica as good a husband as anyone from her own world—and what could she hope for from that world but some red-faced farmer or bailiff ? The gipsies were out-casts from society ; but then, at heart, so were he and Jessica, and all who were not wealthy and powerful. And the gipsies at least were not a starved, defeated people like the farm-labourers, toiling from dawn till dusk for a few shillings a week, and imprisoned or trans-ported, or even hanged, when they dared to fight for their right to something better than slavery. The gipsies were a free and an arro-gant people, the slaves of none, and despising the circumscribed lives of the *gorgios*. ' Gorgeous ' for them meant stifling, imprisoning. And if everything seemed well to Jessica when she was with her gipsy, was it not her blood speaking with an older, deeper, surer wisdom than any that came from the mind, twisted by upbringing, beaten upon by prejudice ? If you were not to be stifled and imprisoned within the walls that environment built up round you from childhood, you had to have the courage to take risks, face adventure, turn your back upon the security of the mainland and in a north wind face the open sea. You had somehow to reach that dim island on the horizon, and you had to go alone. You had to find your own way.

In the end it was Jesse himself who organised Jessica's flight a few days before Christmas. It was impossible to wait any longer, with the state of the roads worsening ; they had to go, too, when the moon was right ; to have waited any longer would have meant being overtaken by the moon ; even a young moon reflecting on the snow gave too much light for runaway purposes. It was Jesse who com-posed the letter she left for her parents asking their forgiveness, bid-ding them not to worry on her account, and promising to write from London. ' I have long contemplated this step,' she wrote, at Jesse's dictation, ' owing to the exceeding dullness and emptiness of my life at home and wishing for a broader experience than is possible here.' They were very proud of this letter, flattering themselves that even the scholarly John could not have composed a better—though his spelling, no doubt, would have been more accurate, and his handwriting a copperplate perfection which Jessica's did not even remotely resemble.

It would have been unwise, Jesse decided, for Jessica to have gone straight to the gipsy encampment. It was important to lay a trail that would put everyone completely off the scent. She would spend the night at a decent inn in Oldport, to which Jesse would take her, and in the morning would board the stage-coach for London. If a number of people who knew her by sight saw her do so, so much the better. She would leave the coach at the market-town of Broom, several hours' journey away, and should the guard observe her, and point out that they had not yet reached London, she would explain that she was feeling travel-sick and proposed to rest for a few hours and go on by the next coach. She would make her way to the market-place and wait by the horses' drinking-trough, where the carriages and gigs and traps were lined up to take passengers from the coaches to places outside of the town. A muffled figure would approach her and take her straw basket from her. It would be José, who would drive her in a light cart back along the road she had come. When they were well away from the town she would hide under the bales of hay in the cart. José at that point would abandon his disguise, and all that would be seen along the road would be a gipsy driving a light cart with a load of hay. If any strangers ever came to the camp she would keep out of the way, but with the deep snow no one was likely to make their way out along the lonely valley road to the chalk-pit. Only Jesse himself would come sometimes—if he might be allowed. At this she flung her arms round his neck and cried that of course, of course he would be allowed, her darling Jesse, and then, for no reason that she could define, began to cry, burying her face in her apron. They were together in his room, as on the night when she had first told him about the gipsy. Under cover of opening his bed and taking him hot water they made opportunities for intimate talks.

She wept only for a moment or two, but the childish, pitiful sound filled Jesse with anguish. He had never known her to cry except wildly, in terror, as a child, when he had been beaten, and that had been quite different from this soft, curiously heart-broken weeping.

"Jessica," he pleaded, his arms round her, "there's nought to be frightened of."

"'Tis not that I am frightened," she said, when she had mastered her tears, "but it doth come easy to me to weep these days, and I am sad because we shall not share the adventurous life together."

Suddenly, it seemed to him, they were back in childhood, standing on the quayside at Oldport, or at the top of the hill above the town, under the lime-trees in front of the church, looking out across the forest of ships to the dim blue island, her hand in his, the little sister like a small wild animal peeping out from the thicket of her hair, and pity in him, and remorse, and the feeling of a betrayal he could not help, because secretly he planned to go to the island alone, because she had no part in his own dreams of escape. He felt helpless now as then, and could only mutter, awkwardly, "I shall be seeing you from time to time—nights when I'm out with my nets maybe."

"But when we break camp in the spring—after that we shall never see each other again."

"Who knows? One day you may camp in the valley again. Or contrive to send word to me where I may find you. What is written in the future is hid—'tis better to leave it so."

That night was the last she slept in the narrow four-poster bed under the sloping roof of Valley Farm, for the night after she stole out and met Jesse in the dark little path that ran between the ponds and they set out together for Oldport for the last time.

2

When Mrs. Hallard found the letter in Jessica's room she read it with an accelerating heart, and then ran out of the room calling hysterically for Katie. When the girl came running up the stairs in alarm she collapsed in her arms. After that all was stir and commotion. Smelling-salts had to be brought, and sal volatile, and the master fetched, and the house seemed full of hurrying feet, scared whispers, and cries of lamentation. William Hallard stormed about declaring that the ungrateful wench should be brought back at once, and was furious with John for the mild suggestion that London was a great city, and 'twould be like looking for a needle in a haystack.

Mrs. Hallard wept endlessly, clinging to John, the darling child who had never given trouble, never disappointed her. He did his best to comfort her.

"The letter says she will write," he reminded her. "'Tis not as though we shall never hear of her more."

"'Twould be best we should never hear of her more," William Hallard thundered, suddenly changing his line. "'Twould be best her name should never be mentioned more in this house! Let her be cast with the wicked into hell!"

"Oh, William, William," Mrs. Hallard moaned, "the scandal, how shall we face the scandal?"

John suggested, "We can give out that she has gone to stay with relatives in London."

"Katie will tell the whole valley! The whole of Oldport will know! We shall be the laughing-stock of the parish!"

William Hallard turned and strode out of the room. He found Katie weeping in the back kitchen. She was weeping because her mistress was weeping, and because of the general upset. She dried her tears quickly on her apron as the master came in.

He said severely, "Your mistress is distressed because I have sent Miss Jessica to stay with relatives in London. If any other story is circulated I shall hold you responsible, and you will be dismissed without a character. I trust I make myself clear?"

" Yes, master."

He went out in search of Jesse and found him in the yard.

" 'Twas you who put Jessica up to running away ! " he roared at him.

Jesse regarded him mildly. " Jessica—running away ? On a moonless night, with the roads like glass ? "

" She has gone," his father roared at him, " and 'tis your devil's work. You will travel to London by the next coach and fetch her back ! "

" Have you her address, then ? If so I will go with pleasure. I have long had a wish to see the big city."

" 'Twas you who gave Jessica the coach-fare. What money had she for going to London ? "

This was a point which Jesse had omitted to cover in his carefully-laid plot, and he knew a moment's confusion, then said, blandly,

" What money have I to give her ? Such pittance as I have is spent in *The Ship's Bell*—'tis well known ! I was there last night, and this morning am without a groat ! "

" No doubt from the company you keep you are well acquainted with ways of acquiring money other than by earning it."

" I was never lucky at the cock-pit," Jesse said, simply.

His father scowled and turned away. At the back of his mind he was convinced that his elder son had had a hand in Jessica's flight, but the devil was in those two, and there was no penetrating to the depths of their black souls. Why had he to be afflicted by such children, he who had always lived an upright, God-fearing life? Wherein had he sinned against the Lord in their upbringing? Never had he spared the rod, or failed in the teaching of Holy Scripture. Yet his elder son and his only daughter had grown up to be an abomination in his sight and before the Lord.

Mrs. Hallard had retired to bed at five in the afternoon with a megrim, due, she said, to shock. Katie, looking awed, served the evening meal to the master and the two young gentlemen. The table looked strangely empty without Miss Jessica ; the place would not be the same without her. She was the only one with any life in her ; the only one who ever laughed in the dark old house. She wondered where she had gone. The mistress would never have had such vapours and hysterics if 'twas merely to London, as the master gave out. Deeply she envied the young mistress whatever romance lay behind her mysterious disappearance from the farm. At this very moment she might be dashing with some fine young gentleman post haste to Gretna Green. . . .

In the absence of his wife and daughter, and in the bitterness of his heart, Mr. Hallard did not read aloud from the Bible that evening.

After supper he sat for some time and read in silence, and then, taking the Bible with him, went upstairs to where Mrs. Hallard sat propped up, invalid-wise, in the huge wooden bed weakly sipping a bowl of gruel by candlelight. He regarded her sternly. They would pray together, he said, for courage to face the adversity with which the Lord had seen fit to afflict them. He observed with displeasure that there were fresh tears on his wife's face. What was there to weep about, he demanded. The heart should be hard in the face of sin.

Mrs. Hallard dutifully removed the traces of tears, but she said in a low, shaken voice, " Forgive me, I beg of you. 'Tis that I keep wondering where she is sleeping tonight. She was always such a wild thing. Perhaps there is some man she has gone off with. Perhaps 'twas he who gave her the money to go—to him, maybe? " Her voice quavered, weakly, as her fears took hold of her, the old deep fears of the flesh.

" Where she sleeps tonight or any other night is no concern of ours," her husband informed her, and seating himself on a chair beside the bed began turning the pages of the Bible. He found a place and began to read :

' This I say, then, Walk in the Spirit, and ye shall not fulfil the lust of the flesh.'

Mrs. Hallard clutched her gruel basin and felt the words burn into her own flesh. That terrible lust of the flesh into which years ago William had initiated her, and the shame of which even now was almost too much to contemplate. That lust which had produced those two wild ones, Jesse and Jessica, and her darling John. Surely he had been sent to her to compensate for all the shame and humiliation. If it had only been John who had come upstairs to sit with her ! She struggled to concentrate on the words which were filling the cold room.

' Now the works of the flesh are manifest, which are these : Adultery, fornication, uncleanness, lasciviousness. . . .

' Envyings, murders, drunkenness, revellings, and such like . . . they that are Christ's have crucified the flesh with the affections and lusts. If we live in the Spirit, let us also walk in the Spirit.'

The words seemed to her to roll terribly off her husband's tongue— as though he relished them ; shameful words, adultery, fornication, uncleanness, lasciviousness, lusts. Terrible words representing terrible acts.

William closed the book and carried it over to the chest-of-drawers, then began to undress. She stared at him, dismayed.

" 'Tis early yet to be thinking of bed," she ventured, tremulously.

" It hath been a wearisome day," he said curtly.

Mrs. Hallard felt herself begin to tremble under the bed-clothes.

"I was thinking of getting up for a little," she murmured.

"Save your breath to blow out the candle," he commanded her.

When in the darkness she felt his beard against her face and his hands begin to move stealthily over her she wanted to scream out; the shameful words beat in the darkness like sin; the terrible crucifixion of the flesh. . . . But she dared not scream; her two sons were in the room below; and silence made no acknowledgment of the deeds of darkness. And she was nothing if not dutiful.

3

When they were alone John looked up from his books and demanded of Jesse, in a low voice, "You know where our sister is, do you not?"

Jesse met his brother's eyes. John would never betray him; he knew that.

"Of course."

"She hasn't gone to London?"

"What do you think?"

"I think she would be unlikely to go to London alone, and I know of no one she would go with."

Jesse said, "She hasn't gone to London, but I cannot tell you where she has gone. Some secrets are too heavy to carry."

His fear was that if he knew John might go after her and try to persuade her to return; it would make Jessica angry, and perhaps anger the gipsies, and also John might be indiscreet and be seen visiting at the camp, and suspicion might be aroused.

"Will she be happy where she's gone?"

"Happier than here. She had to get away."

"Other people have to live here."

"We are not all the same. I may go myself eventually."

"I thought you had such a feeling for the land!" There was a sneer in John's voice.

Jesse tried to explain. "Staying here you just watch it being swallowed up—taken away from its rightful owners."

"There's our own land—have you no feeling for that?"

"The land without the flesh and blood that cultivates it is nothing. I am one of Farmer Hallard's labourers myself, and thank God every day that I have not to support a wife and babes on my earnings!"

"You do nothing to help these downtrodden people you profess to care so much about."

"I'm not a Cobbett or a Burdett—what can a rough, ignorant sort of fellow like me do?"

John said acidly, "I suppose it was rough, ignorant fellows who organised the risings in 1816, wasn't it?"

"'Twould be no use organising merely a local rising. It has to be the whole countryside—and even when it is, look what happens, men get transported, imprisoned, hanged—and after 'tis all over everything goes on the same."

"Then you have no solution to offer for our agricultural problems?" No counsel for the prosecution ever adopted a more withering tone.

John's thin lips were twisted in a sarcastic smile; he was paler than usual because his heart was beating fast with his hostility to his brother. Now as they sat facing each other across the table John could afford to hate his brother, because now it was he, John, who came out on top, John, the scholar, the intellectual; now Jesse was merely an inarticulate, groping labourer.

Jesse looked at John's thin face, his supercilious smile, his scornful eyes, and he was troubled. It was true he had no solution, only a vague hope that in Parliament something would be done, through people like Sir Francis Burdett, who cared about what was happening to the land, and the flesh and blood that made it bring forth. Yet it was he himself who had maintained that reform must come from the people themselves, that it was no use leaving it to the politicians. At the back of his mind was a hazy, confused idea that sometime there must be something that was more than a rising, more than a revolt, something that approximated to a revolution, too strong to be swept away by the terrorism of imprisonment, transportation, hanging. But confronted by John's scornful eyes and sarcastic smile, and his cold clear mind that might be full of learning but had no real understanding, he could find no words to explain all this. He could only mumble, hopelessly, "No, I have no solution."

"In that case, as a farmer's son, I suggest you might sometimes consider the landowner's point of view."

"There should be no landowners," Jesse muttered. "'Tis the whole trouble—the land should belong to the people—them that produce——"

"You think they could keep the price of corn up better than the experienced farmers, I suppose?"

"I don't want to keep the price of corn up—I want to bring it down low enough to give the common people a cheap loaf."

"Then the farmers would be ruined and unable to pay the higher wages you radicals are always clamouring for—in fact they would have to lower wages, and nobody would be any better off, the poor people least of all."

"If to get cheaper food you've got to pay lower wages, then 'tis he whole way of doing things is at fault," Jesse said, despairingly, " and maybe the common people could take over and do better. Now 'tis always the poor that make sacrifices—maybe there could be some sacrifices made at the top."

John said, quoting their father, " 'Tis always the farmer who is called upon to make the sacrifices. We shall see what Farmer Jesse Hallard makes of Valley Farm one day."

" I shall never own Valley Farm—or any other ! "

Jesse got up abruptly and stood looking down at his brother.

" 'Tis your farm, John. I could never stay here long enough to inherit it. Besides, I have no wish to become an employer and land-owner."

" You don't want the responsibility," John sneered. " 'Tis pro-digious easy to tell others how things should be run, but 'tis another matter to do it oneself."

Jesse shrugged. " If you like." He had the feeling that even if he had the words to express himself properly it would be useless to try to make John anything less than their father's son.

He went over to the table beside the wall, where the candlesticks always stood, ready for bedtime, and had a momentary pang because Jessica's candle stood there. It flashed to him that she would never again light a candle and ascend stairs to bed. From now on the stars were her candle and her bed a gipsy's palliasse.

As he passed the door of his parents' room he heard a low, half-smothered sound of weeping between the vibrations of heavy snoring. His mother lay weeping whilst his father slept. Did she weep for Jessica? He felt no pity for her, the tormented woman lying wake-ful in the darkness. Why should he pity her who had never pitied the pitiful weeping of her children? It was too late now to weep for Jessica. Now she was beyond need of pity. She was the wild thing escaped from the cage at last. Tonight Jessica was a gipsy's bride and lay in his arms. Who should weep for Jessica? In her own fashion she had braved the north wind and the open sea and landed on the island. But that was something the woman weeping in the dark to the accompaniment of her husband's snores would never under-stand, because for her there was no island.

XIV

CHRISTMAS passed almost unnoticed at Valley Farm that year, marked only by extra attendance at chapel, and the usual annual distribution of clothes to the thriftless and undeserving poor. Mrs. Hallard made a mild, tearful protest when ordered by her husband to give away everything of Jessica's she had left behind. The finality of such a gesture frightened her. Until then Jessica had been merely the errant daughter who would one day return, covered with shame, perhaps, but also with penitence. That she might never see Jessica again had not occurred to her, and when it did she was stricken not so much with grief as with dismay and bewilderment. And if Jessica had merely gone on a visit to friends or relatives in London, how account for the giving away of her clothes? Folk would talk, she pleaded, piteously, and Jessica's sudden departure was likely to cause scandal enough.

"Let folks say what they will!" was all the satisfaction she got from her husband.

It was John who suggested to his mother, privately, that she could give out that Jessica was having fashionable new London clothes, and had no further use for her old things. 'Twould be a lie, but surely one the Lord would forgive? He was filled with pity for his mother in her humiliation and distress, and his heart hardened towards Jessica and Jesse, yet there was that deep, curious loyalty which forbade him betray them, and, questioned by his mother, made him insist that he was sure Jesse knew nothing about Jessica's flight.

Jesse visited the Lanes at Christmas, depressed by the gloom of the farm, and Sally put her old spell on him, and he surrendered to it with his old bitterness. He did not visit Jessica until the turn of the year. He was convinced that if she were unhappy she would somehow contrive to get a message to him, and lacking such a message he was diffident about intruding on a world in which he had no part. But the desire to see her and confirm that all was well with her turned in him restlessly; he felt that if he could see her just once, for a few minutes, he would be satisfied. He resisted the idea for a few weeks, but it nagged at him as in the beginning the desire to be out poaching and the desire for women had nagged at him, and one fine dry starry night when the roads rang like iron under his horse's hooves he rode out to the chalk-pit.

He saw the glow of the camp-fire from some distance away, lighting up the whole face of the pit, and as he drew near heard the sound of music and singing. His horse began to show signs of nervousness as they approached, and he reined in and dismounted and tied up under a hedge, then went on on foot.

He had been gone only a few minutes before Tom Surridge broke through the hedge on the opposite side of the road. It was a fine night and he was doing a little hedgerow and covert strolling for the pure pleasure of hoping to catch a fellow-human in wrong-doing. He had taken to this nocturnal exercise ever since the day Jack Mortimer and the other two had been brought up before the Bench ; he had been convinced since that day that young Jesse Hallard was one of Mortimer's ' gang.' That being so, it would be great satisfaction to catch him ; but doubly so in view of the incident at Valley Farm. One of these fine nights, he was confident, he would catch the young scoundrel pegging out a net along a bank, taking up the wires at the end of a hare's run, or trespassing in a game preserve. Sooner or later they all got careless. A fine scandal it would be when Farmer Hallard's son was brought up before the Bench under the Game Laws—and a fine piece of work on the part of the squire's bailiff.

He had been thinking these pleasant thoughts as he had moved quietly along the hedges that starry night, and been absorbed in them until he had become aware of the sound of a horse's hooves. He wondered who might be riding that lonely road after dark, and his curiosity was intensified when the sound ceased close at hand. He abandoned the hedgerow then and took a short cut across the rock-like ridges of a ploughed field, but by the time he had finally blundered over to the hedge which divided the field from the road, and had found a place to break through the hazel-nuts and hawthorns, the rider was out of sight.

He scrambled down the bank, jumped the ditch and crossed the road, making a soft clicking noise to the horse. Something pricked in his blood when he saw that it was Jesse Hallard's. He stood stroking the horse's muzzle and asking himself what Jesse Hallard might be doing along that road after dark. Was he perhaps courting a girl behind a hedge? But young Hallard did not do that—to the great disappointment of the valley wenches. There was no inn or ale-house along that road for miles—nothing but the gipsy encampment. Perhaps he was fascinated by a gipsy girl. Farmer Hallard, that good chapel-goer, would be interested to know he had found his son's horse tied up by the gipsy camp.

He smiled to himself in the darkness, untied the reins, and hoisted himself up into the saddle, turning the horse's head back in the direction of Valley Farm.

2

Jesse's arrival at the chalk-pit was greeted by a great barking and yapping of mongrels, who ran out to meet him, menacingly. An old man emerged from the smoke and addressed him, civilly enough, but there was suspicion in his manner.

" Good-evening, brother."

Jesse said, " Good-evening. I am Jesse Hallard. I have come to see my sister."

But even as he spoke Jessica came running towards him, crying his name in a tone in which tears and laughter fought together.

For a few moments Jesse was aware of nothing but the fact that he was holding her against his heart, Jessica, the beloved little sister ; then he realised that her hair was covered by a gipsy handkerchief and her body wrapped in a gipsy shawl, that there was a string of coins round her neck, and that heavy ear-rings hung from her ears. Then he was aware of the wild dark faces watching him from the fire's edge, watching him intently, mistrustfully, with a kind of latent hostility.

José detached himself from the group. He stepped forward and stood beside Jessica, who clung now to Jesse's arm, gazing up into his face as though she could never look at him enough.

" It is unwise for you to come here, brother," José said, quietly. " If you were to be seen the *gorgios* might come for our sister."

Jesse said urgently, " I had to know that she was well and happy." His eyes searched her face. " Tell me, Jessica—you have no regrets? "

She smiled and reached out a hand to José. " We are very happy," she said, and drew him close to her, then turned to Jesse again.

" Tell me," she said, " what happened at home when they found I had gone? "

" Mamma had the vapours, as might be expected. Our father is convinced that I helped you get away. John is aware that I hold your secret, but he is also aware that it is useless to ask me. It is given out that you have gone to relatives in London."

Jessica laughed, softly. " And Christmas," she said, " what happened at Christmas? Did our cousins come again? "

" No, no one. Mamma gave your clothes away to the poor—not without a few tears. I fear you are cast out, Jessica."

" She has no wish but to be with her *rom*," José said, firmly. He added, " We were married, Romanly, the evening of the day I brought her back. We are *rom* and *romi*."

Jesse said, with sudden despair, " How are we ever to meet again, if you are roaming the country, and I go to sea? "

Jessica said quickly, " I can send a letter from time to time, to wait for you at *The Ship's Bell*, or to the Mortimers."

There was a sudden clatter of horse's hooves receding into the distance. Jesse spun round and ran across the road ; he could see nothing in the dimness, but it was clear that his horse had gone from where he had tied it. He ran back to Jessica and José.

" Someone has stolen my horse ! I must go." He seized Jessica and embraced her hurriedly.

" Pappa will make a dreadful scene—he will want to know where you were ! " Jessica cried, dismayed.

" He will not be told," Jesse said briefly. He pressed José's hand. " Be good to her always," he said.

The gipsy said, simply, his head high, " We are not like the *gorgios* ; we do not ill-treat our women or go off with others."

When he reached the road Jesse turned to look back. Jessica stood with José's arm round her shoulders watching his departure. She waved to him till he was out of sight, lost in the darkness where the trees closed over the round road, shutting out the sky.

All the way back Jesse pondered the problem of the stolen horse. It must surely have been some wandering vagabond ; no one in the valley would think of taking Jesse Hallard's horse ; how would he dispose of it? His anxiety over the impending scene with his father crowded out his thoughts of Jessica.

Seeing a light still burning in the farm living-room he decided to speak to his father that night over the loss, rather than defer the unpleasant matter till the morning. He strode in, determinedly, then stopped short at the sight of Tom Surridge sitting opposite his father in the chimney-place.

The bailiff grinned. " I brought yer horse back for yer, boy. Wandering along the chalk-pit road I found her. 'Twas a mercy the gipsies did not go off with it."

Anger blazed up in Jesse. " 'Tis a damned lie ! My horse was not wandering. I tied her up securely enough. What right have you to take her ? "

" She was wandering loose," the bailiff insisted, and turned to William Hallard. " 'Tis fine thanks for bringing the beast back safe, when the gipsies might have taken her ! "

" What were you doing out along that road at this time of night? " Jesse's father demanded.

Surridge suggested with a sly smile, " Perhaps he was after a pretty gipsy wench—'twas hard by the camp I found the mare wandering as I was telling you. Or maybe he was looking for his little sister there ! "

" My daughter is safely in London with relatives," Hallard snapped, but in that moment a great fear was born in him that perhaps that was what had in fact happened, not so much that the gipsies had run off with Jessica, as that she, the wild thing, had run off to join the gipsies. He would not put it past her. How could she have got the money for London—or Jesse got it for her? And what was Jesse doing riding along the gipsies' road after dark?

" Very glad I am to hear it," Surridge murmured, and got up. He leered at Jesse, " Another time you be courtin' the gipsy wench 'twould be best not to leave your horse loose."

In a rush of rage and hate at the man's impudence Jesse's right fist swung up and landed on the bailiff's jaw, sending him reeling across the room. Before he could recover himself Jesse had swooped after him and had him by the shoulders and spun him round.

" Get out of here, you dirty sneaking rat! " he roared at him, and reached out and grabbed the string of the latch, then propelled the bailiff through into the back kitchen with the toe of his boot.

" You'll pay for this! " Surridge shouted, but when Jesse bounded out into the back kitchen after him he bolted through the door into the yard.

Jesse came back into the living-room and faced his father.

" I should have thrown that rat out the last time he was here," he said violently. " Any more of his damned interfering and I'll kick him into the next parish! What right had he to ride off with my horse? "

" What business had you out with the mare along that road? " his father demanded.

" Am I a child that I must answer for my every movement? " Jesse demanded in return.

His father asked bitterly, " Isn't it enough that you degrade the name of Hallard by consorting with poachers and smugglers and common labourers without you must be running after gipsy thieves? "

" I was running after no gipsies," Jesse said.

" Then what business takes you out on that lonely road at this hour? "

Jesse was silent. His father glared at him. " If those gipsies know anything about your sister, afore God I will have every man-jack of them whipped out of the parish at the tail of a cart! "

He reached a taper down from the mantelshelf and thrust it angrily into the fire. Jesse watched him carry it across to the table where the candlesticks and tinder-box stood. His mind revolved with only one thought—I must warn Jessica and José tonight.

He said, " That the gipsies should know anything about Jessica is a most fantastic idea, sir. Does a gently nurtured girl go off from her comfortable home to dwell in a tent with gipsies? "

" Jessica would go off with the Devil himself and live in a sty if it suited her wickedness! " his father declared, and went out.

Jesse remained leaning against the table, listening to his father's heavy tread, the lift of the latch of the bedroom door, the creek of the floor-boards overhead, the thud of his father's boots dropped one after the other, then he turned down the lamp and went out for the second time that night.

It infuriated him to find that the bailiff had brought in his horse sweating, and not even thrown a piece of old sacking over her. She stood in the yard, tied to a post, steaming in the cold air. He rode her gently back in the direction of the chalk-pit. Surridge, he supposed, was out to cause trouble between him and his father, but that was less important than the extent to which he suspected that Jessica might be with the gipsies and had sowed this doubt in his father's mind.

The fire had burned low by the time he got back to the chalk-pit and he saw no one about. He dismounted and walked the horse past the smouldering ashes of the fire, and the barking of the dogs announced his arrival as before. He called " José," and in a moment the gipsy emerged from a tent.

Jesse said, " I came back to warn you that my father suspects that Jessica might be here He will probably come here tomorrow to search. You had better get Jessica away for a few days. If you all go it will look suspicious. Tell her 'twas the squire's bailiff took the mare and started this idea in our father's mind."

" I knew it was unwise for you to come here, brother."

Jesse ignored this. He insisted, " My father must not find Jessica here. He threatens to have all of you whipped at a cart's tail if he finds you know anything about her disappearance."

José laughed, shortly. " Will he bring a troop of yeomanry with him, brother, or does he believe he can do it single-handed? "

" It is serious, José."

" Certainly it is serious, brother. Thank you for warning us. But remember—you must not come here again, brother."

Jesse promised, " I shall not come again, have no fear."

" Farewell, brother."

" Farewell, José."

He rode back slowly, and now he could let his thoughts dwell on Jessica. She was happy ; he was sure of that. That gesture with which she had turned to José was evidence enough. Nothing now must spoil that happiness. It would be a relief when the spring came and the gipsies broke camp. So long as they remained there there was always the risk of Jessica's presence amongst them being discovered. He had the feeling that when the gipsies broke camp it would be time for him, too, to go. The perpetual undercurrent of hostility between himself and his father had not been helped by that night's events ; it had been aggravated before that by Jessica's flight. What was there to remain for with Jessica gone and Mary denied him? Nothing but the monotony of the farm-days, and the prospect of seeing the chimneys of mills invade the quiet valley, and one by one the country people disappear into the maw of the ever-expanding machine of this new industrialism. Perhaps in time the valley would become a manufacturing town, and people would forget that it had ever known grazing sheep and cattle, hayfields and wheatfields and orchards, known the scent of bean-flowers and clover and meadow-sweet. It was not a prospect to wait for, yet in one sense the sooner it happened the better, for the countryside was like a wounded animal with no hope of recovery, and the sooner it was put out of its misery the better. People like his father and the squire believed that they could lord it over the common people forever, lowering their wretched wages when the price of corn fell, and making all manner of excuses for not putting them up when the price of corn rose ; living out their completely selfish lives unchanged to the end. But the face of the world was changing, and that rapidly, and they were doomed with the doomed countryside, did they but realise it.

Until the gipsies left he would remain ; even if he did not see Jessica there was the feeling of her presence, and that he was there if she should need him. In the spring he would find a ship. Beyond that he could not think ; but now he knew finally that for him the old life was already finished.

XV

WILLIAM HALLARD said nothing to his wife of the suspicion that was turning in his mind, placed there by the bailiff. If he were proved wrong he would look a fool. But his deep conviction that Jesse knew something about Jessica's disappearance, added to the fact that Surridge had found his horse by the gipsy encampment, looked as though it might add up to something, and he was determined to find out. If any one gipsy were found responsible the fellow would have a beating from which he would not quickly recover. The thought gave him acute pleasure. If he could prove that Jesse had had a hand in the matter he would turn him out, lock, stock and barrel. Jessica he would take to his brother's farm in the Scottish highlands, ten miles across the moors to the nearest post-road, and he would see to it that Jesse did not know where she had gone. To curb her spirit before the journey she would be shut up in her room on bread and water.

These thoughts were strong in his mind as he rode out to the chalk-pit the morning after Surridge had brought back Jesse's horse. At first they gave him pleasure, then he began to reflect on the tragedy of a man whose only daughter runs away from home, perhaps to disgrace herself with a mob of gipsies, and whose eldest son was little but a wastrel. He recalled his gratification when his wife had produced a daughter. He had had a picture of her growing up in modesty and grace and the fear of the Lord ; she would take the Bible class and be a model of Christian womanhood to the whole valley. It would be said of him that he was blessed in his children, but doubly blessed in the ownership of a pious wife and daughter. He would be proud to be seen at chapel with his womenfolk on his arm. Instead of which his only daughter, and his son and heir, had grown up like a couple of young gipsies, wild, strong-willed, lacking in all sense of duty and obedience. For a little while it had seemed as though Jessica had settled down into a maidenly piety, but she had broken out again, and he was convinced that that damned scoundrel of a Jesse was at the bottom of it. He could think of his eldest son with nothing but a black anger. It was a thousand pities the press-gangs no longer operated since the war ended ; Jesse pressed into service in the Navy would have meant his father spared the painful duty of disowning him—as he was sworn to do, afore God, if his visit to the gipsy camp proved what he expected it to prove.

As he rode along on that steel-grey January day he found himself envying that lowly person the blacksmith, because for all the lowliness of his estate he had a daughter of whom he could be proud. If Mary had accepted Jesse he would at least have had a dutiful daughter-in-law, to compensate him for the waywardness and wickedness of his own daughter. He could not but respect her for refusing Jesse, though it grieved him sorely. 'Handsome Jess Hallard' he was called throughout the valley, but at least one young woman had had more sense than to be infatuated by the good looks that were nothing but a source of sinfulness. He admired her for this strength of character, but regretted that she could not have devoted herself to reforming him.

When he reached the chalk-pit he saw a middle-aged woman bending over a cauldron on the fire and stirring its contents. An old woman smoking a clay pipe sat on the ground with her back against a light cart and her feet stretched out to the fire. A young man and an elderly man appeared to be cleaning out the lean-to in which the horses were stalled, behind the tents. They all looked up at the sound of horse's hooves and remained staring whilst the rider dismounted and, leading his horse, approached the camp. The woman straightened herself up from the cauldron, and the men came out of the lean-to and stood beside her. They all looked to Mr. Hallard extremely wild and hostile, but he continued towards them until he was within a few feet of them. The old woman said something in a language he did not understand, and spat. The elderly man separated himself from the others and came forward.

" Good-day to you, brother."

Mr. Hallard was not prepared to be cordial with such riff-raff.

He said boldly, " I wish to speak with my daughter."

The gipsy looked at him steadily. " Why do you seek your daughter here, brother? "

Mr. Hallard chanced another throw. " My son who visited you last night told me that she was here."

The gipsy's eyes did not falter. " We know no son o. yours, brother. None has been here last night nor any other."

" Why should I take your word for it? "

" No reason at all, brother. Would you like to examine the tents of this poor person's camp ? "

" I intend to do so ! "

The gipsy smiled and bowed, then turned back to the others, talking Romany. The middle-aged woman shrugged. The young man scowled. A swarm of mongrels came yapping round the farmer's heels as he stepped forward, still leading his horse. The man who had addressed himself to him touched the horse's reins.

" I will take your horse, brother."

" You will keep your damned thieving hands to yourself ! " Hallard commanded, violently.

The gipsy dropped his hand, still smiling his strange, dark, hostile smile.

" As you wish, brother."

Then they stood watching the stranger whilst he peered into each tent. Occasionally they made brief remarks to each other in what he thought of as their damned lingo. He was about to lift the flap of a closed tent when it suddenly opened from within and a young woman whom he had to admit to himself was ' uncommonly handsome ' emerged with a great flash of pink shawl and green kerchief. A child clung to her soiled flounced skirt, and there was the flash of gold coins at her throat and wrists.

She smiled at him, and he stared at her, fascinated, because he had never seen such fine white even teeth.

" Will you come into the poor gipsy girl's tent, brother, and let her tell your *dukkerin*? Will the pretty gentleman cross the gipsy's palm with silver, for the sake of her little ones? "

Mr. Hallard recovered from the hypnotism of her ravishing smile and stepped back as before the Scarlet Woman incarnate.

" I want none of your lying and thieving, wench. I am here looking for my daughter. Kindly allow me to examine your tent."

" If you will cross the poor gipsy girl's hand with silver, sweet gentleman."

" I should not think of giving you a groat ! Out of my way ! "

He attempted to brush past her, and immediately a hand gripped his shoulder and he looked into the blazing eyes of the young man who had been standing by the fire.

"We permit no *gorgios* to speak in that wise to our women! If you wish to see into this tent, which is mine, you will cross the *rani's* hand with silver."

"You are a lot of damned rascals! I will have you turned out of the parish!" But he pulled out his purse—only to find, to his disgust, that the smallest coin it contained was a crown. He flung it at Maria's feet. Neither she nor Miguel moved. Maria smiled faintly, her head tilting a little higher.

Miguel said, quietly, "You must cross her palm with it."

There was nothing for it but to stoop and pick it up and place it in the girl's brown hand.

"Thank you, sweet gentleman," said she, stepping aside that he might inspect the tent behind her, the sole occupant of which was a year-old child seated stark naked on a heap of rags. It waved its hands at the bearded face which peered in at it, and made crowing noises.

Mr. Hallard withdrew his head indignantly. He had now seen into all the tents, and that no one was hiding in the lean-to was obvious. It suddenly seemed ridiculous that he should have for a moment imagined that Jessica had joined the gipsies.

He straightened himself, scowling, and immediately Maria began to laugh, at first softly, then in a crescendo of malicious amusement.

Ha-ha. Ha-ha. Ha-ha-ha-ha-ha!

Then Miguel began to laugh, a low, derisive chuckle that became a rising tide of mockery.

Ha-ha-ha. Ha-ha. Ah, ha-ha, ha-ha, ha-ha-ha-ha-ha!

It was taken up by his parents.

Ha-ha! Ha-ha! Ha-ha-ha! Ha-ha, ha-ha. . . .

And then the old grandmother began to cackle.

He-he, he-he, he-he-he-he! Te-he-he, he-he-hee-hee!

Seeing all the adults laughing, the children began to jump about, screeching and shouting excitedly. Maria's tall straight body leaned backwards like a reed in the wind before the force of her laughter.

Ha-ha-ha! Ah, ha-ha, ha-ha, ha-ha-ha-ha!

Her mother-in-law clasped her belly with the pain of so much mirth.

Ha, ha-ha, ha-ha-ha, ha-ha, ha! Ah-ha!

Miguel stood with his head thrown back laughing as though he would never stop, as though it gushed up in an endless fount from the very core of his being, and the dogs added their noises to that of the children and the black torrent of laughter.

Ha-ha, ha-ha! Ha-ha-ha-ha-ha-ha-ha!

119

Hallard gazed from one wild dark face to another as though he thought they had all gone mad, but as he looked at each one the laughter increased, each started off again in a fresh paroxysm.

Ha, ha-ha, ha-ha, ha-ha, ha!

And all the time the old woman sat by the fire cackling like a witch *He-he-he! Te-he-he-he-he-hee!*

" Are you all out of your minds? " Hallard shouted, and then, as the laughter only intensified, a curious panic seized him, and he sprang into the saddle and urged his horse out of the chalk-pit and on to the road, the wild dark laughter seeming to follow him in mounting black waves.

Ha-ha, ha-ha, ha-ha-ha-ha-ha! Ha, ha-ha, ha-ha, ha-ha, ha!

The last he saw of the gipsies they stood huddled together in a group, the dogs and children still leaping round them, their eyes following him, their bodies still bending and shaking with laughter.

Ha-ha, ha-ha, ha-ha!

It was not any kind of laughter that he understood. He had the feeling of it being a conspiracy of laughter, the laughter of people who finger knives in the folds of their gaudy rags. A black laughter of people without principles or shame or pity. The laughter of a bottomless mockery.

Ha-ha, ha-ha-ha-ha. . . .

Riding as though the devil were at his heels he heard that laughter when there was a mile and more between him and the gipsy encampment.

Ha-ha-ha . . .

It rang in his ears for the rest of the day, and its evil was only exorcised at night by the reading of Holy Scripture promising the eternal damnation of the wicked.

XVI

WITH the turn of the year Jesse gave up going into Oldport except when he had ' business ' there, that is to say a few rabbits or a hare. Then he would visit *The Ship's Bell* when he had disposed of the game, and if he saw Lucy alone would buy her a gin, but he never went home with her or visited the Lanes. He had a sense of marking time, of waiting. When the earth was released from the grey grip of winter, when the ice melted on the ponds and in the ditches, when the frozen furrows thawed out, and the sap began to rise in the trees, and the grass to take on a new green after its winter dullness, he had the feeling that then something would thaw out in himself, that he would feel the sap of life in himself rising once more, releasing him into new activity. Then the gipsies would take to the road again, and with the knowledge that Jessica was gone he would be free to go—where he did not yet know; but that he would know when the time came he was convinced.

In the meantime it amused him to tantalise Tom Surridge over his nocturnal activities. The bailiff now talked openly of Jesse Hallard as ' the biggest poacher of the lot,' boasting that one of these days he would have the pleasure of bringing him up before the Bench, and there were plenty to report the boast back to Jesse. For his part, Jesse was grateful to Surridge for supplying a little excitement just when life was at its dullest. But for him he might have given up poaching at that time. Now the outwitting of the bailiff became his one satisfaction, and laying false trails for him a game of which he never tired. He began to look out for him as carefully as a few months ago he had searched for the roosting-places of pheasants. He made as careful a study of Surridge's movements as of the movements of game. He discovered that the bailiff appeared to have a fixed idea that he would eventually catch him along the hedgerows with nets and ferrets on him. Therefore on several occasions he allowed himself direct encounters with Surridge and the two assistants with whom he had taken to going about at night since he had begun the Hallard hunt. The two assistants would hold him up at the points of their guns whilst Surridge searched him for incriminating evidence. Once Surridge, diving into Jesse's jacket pocket, and encountering something warm and furry and alive, was convinced that he had found ferrets, but the living furriness when yanked out and held up in the moonlight for inspection proved to be merely two newly-born kittens. Jesse laughed in his face and walked off—to the disused shepherd's hut where he had hidden nets and ferrets before setting out for a little preliminary fooling. A few nights later when Surridge and his men encountered him they passed him by, and it happened that on that occasion, not seeking an encounter, Jesse had everything on him. He knew after the kittens episode that Surridge would not risk being made a fool of again, and would not search him, but rely on catching him red-handed one night, in the actual process of netting rabbits or setting or taking up a snare. Scoring against Surridge became to him a game far more exciting than the actual poaching.

William Hallard appealed to the squire to turn the gipsies off his land, but the squire was not predisposed to oblige Farmer Hallard. For one thing there was every reason to suppose that young Jesse Hallard could account for some of the pheasants that had disappeared in the autumn, and for another he had not forgotten the scene when Mortimer and two of his gang had been charged. He had no reason at all for obliging William Hallard, and if ' that damned Calvinist,' as he called him, objected to the gipsies being in the district it was a very good reason for seeing that they stayed there. For himself he had no objection to gipsies and every objection to non-conformity. So the smoke from the gipsy fire continued to curl up from the chalk-pit, and almost every day Jesse went up to the ridge of the upland meadow and looked down at it and the low white huddle of tents, longing for a glimpse of Jessica, yet always terrified that she would appear and that others beside himself would recognise her. Once on a morning of pale February sunshine a sound of singing carried across the valley on the cold still air ; he recognised the tune as the one he had heard on the night he had ridden out to the camp, a song of a few notes endlessly repeated, a strange, reedy, Oriental melody, peculiarly haunting, and under the notes of the song the twang and strum of a guitar. He liked the romanticism of the singing, but no less he liked to hear the dogs barking and to see the smoke rising from the camp-fire ; these things offered a reassurance of warmth and domesticity, an illusion of stability and security. He knew that when the gipsies had gone from the chalk-pit he would avoid the ridge of the upland meadow ; the valley would have become intolerably empty. But so long as they were there he knew the continually renewed compulsion to go and look down on the place that held her, the little sister, his heart's love, no longer a garden enclosed, but the springs of her youth open and flowing.

Then one gale-racked night early in March, when Jesse was in *The Ship's Bell* after doing business with the guard of the stage-coach due to leave early in the morning, the door opened and Miguel entered. For a moment the smoke and glitter and babble of the place seemed to bewilder him and he stood with his back to the door peering through the smoke, searchingly, then seeing Jesse came over to him. Jesse detached himself from the two sailors with whom he had been drinking and Miguel with a jerk of his head motioned him away from the bar counter.

" José sent me to find you," he said, quickly. " You must come at once. Our sister is asking for you."

Jesse had the sensation of his heart turning over and all the saliva leaving his mouth.

" Jessica? She is ill? "

" Yes, brother. The women are with her, but she is like a mad woman, knowing no one and all the time calling for you."

Jesse gripped the gipsy's arm. " Come outside," he urged.

Outside the inn, in the black darkness full of the roar of the wind and the fury of the sea, he demanded, wildly, " What is it? What is wrong? When did it happen? "

"It is woman's trouble, brother. The day before yesterday the baby comes that should not come till the summer. Then it is all over and everything seems well, except that our sister cannot sleep. Then this evening comes fever and pains and she is asking for you all the time."

"We must get a doctor!" Jesse cried.

"I have horses in the yard, brother."

Jesse grabbed the gipsy's arm and they plunged through the darkness together and round to the side of the inn.

"You can ride bareback, brother?"

"Of course." He had no idea how much money he pushed into the hands of the ostler who untied the horses.

When they were half-way to the doctor's he suddenly reached out and caught at Miguel's arm and they reined in.

"There is only one doctor in Oldport," Jesse said, "and he knows all of us. We must get a doctor from Broom, but I will stop and see Jessica first—I can go that way, by the valley road."

As they turned the horse he asked, "How did you know where to find me?"

Miguel told him, "We first sent Maria to the farm to look for you. She was to say she had come to tell the young master's *dukkerin*. But she could not see you. She hid behind a haystack, and when it became darker went up to the house, and when the servant came to the windows to close the curtains made a sign to her to come outside. Then she asked for you and the servant told her she thought you had gone into the town, as you did not come in for the milking."

Jesse groaned. "I was up at the sheep-fold with a ewe that could not deliver herself of her lamb. But how did you know where to look in Oldport?"

"José knew from our sister that it is your custom to frequent the inn, brother."

Then they were plunging through the darkness again, heading for the valley, leaning low over their horses' necks and riding like the wind. Once they were clear of the town and could give their horses their heads they did not speak again.

The glow of the camp fire was visible from some distance away and Jesse was aware of nothing else. When they finally reached the chalk-pit Jesse left his horse to Miguel and went running and stumbling over the stones to the tents. The sound of Jessica's voice crying his name over and over again pierced his heart like a knife. He was vaguely aware of the old grandmother, and of the father of José and Miguel, crouching beside the fire, and of Maria emerging from the tent from whence came Jessica's cries. Then he was in the tent, and saw Jessica lying on a mattress with José's arm under her head and his

123

mother at the foot of the bed, and a terrible cry burst from him, as it were from the very pit of his belly.

" Jessica, my darling ! "

At that cry she raised her head and opened her eyes and looked at him with recognition.

" Jesse—I knew you would come ! "

She sat up, falling forward over his arms as they went round her. She clung to him, laughing and crying together, as on that evening when he had ridden out under the compulsion to see her. He laid her back on the pillow, brushing back her hair from her hot forehead. Her hands burned on his. Her eyes fastened on him were like black fires.

Jesse looked at José. " We must get a doctor to come out from Broom," he said.

José nodded. " Miguel will go," he said. " Tell him, Maria."

Jessica cried out at that. " No, no, Maria. A doctor will say I must go to a hospital. Don't let them send for a doctor, Jesse, I beg of you ! I have no pain now—in the morning I shall be well——"

José bent down and laid his cheek against hers.

" No one shall take you away from me," he murmured.

Then he lifted his head and looked at Jesse and his eyes held the utmost agony. He said with a curious slow deliberation, " A doctor can do nothing." Jesse felt the impact of the gipsy's will forcing him to understand, driving each word like a spike into his brain. Almost as though it had been said aloud he received the unspoken message, " This is what Maria read in Jessica's hand and why she would not tell." The agony in José's eyes seemed to Jesse to enter his own flesh then, draining the blood from his heart. When he cried out, " 'Tis not true ! " it was the unspoken statement he answered.

Jessica closed her eyes and murmured, wearily, " José is right."

José laid a hand on her forehead. " Sleep," he whispered.

She moved restlessly under his hand, and there was a tinkle of gold coins at her neck and wrists. She looked terribly neglected, Jesse thought suddenly, with her black hair matted on the grimy, coarse-covered pillow, and wrapped in a bright dirty shawl. Her hands looked as he had always remembered her hands in childhood, as though she had been grubbing in the earth.

" My eyes ache with tiredness," she said, " but my mind is wide awake. 'Tis full of all the fireworks we saw at the fair that night, fountains of stars and showers of fishes. My brain is all afire with them. Golden rain, so pretty . . . And such pretty ladies . . ."

Her voice trailed away and for a few moments it seemed as though she would sleep, then she murmured, drowsily, " Tell Miguel to bring his guitar and sing the song about the *rye* and the *rawnie*. I would like Jesse to hear it."

" 'Tis better you should try to sleep," Jesse urged.

She opened her eyes and smiled at him. " My mind is wide open," she insisted, " 'tis only my eyes that keep closing. Tell Miguel, José."

José spoke to Maria in Romany and she got up and went out of the tent.

" He will come in a minute," José promised, gently.

" Tell Jesse about the song," she murmured, closing her eyes again.

José said, quietly, " It is springtime in the song. There are two doves in a greenwood tree. Below there is the lover and his lady. The doves make love, and the lover and his lady. That is all. They are very simple, our Romany songs. Miguel played and sang this song the night I fetched our sister from Broom and we were married Romanly."

" 'Tis a happy song," Jessica whispered, and smiled at Miguel, who had entered with his guitar, then folding her two hands on Jesse's closed her eyes again, urging Miguel to sing, ' Romanly'.

" It is better you should sleep, little sister," Miguel said in a low voice.

José spoke to him in their own tongue, tersely. Miguel shrugged and began to strum the guitar and to sing the song whose notes had floated across the valley to Jesse that cold bright morning a few weeks ago, but he sang it now without zest, in a voice that sounded as though it might break at any moment, and the strings of the guitar seemed to Jesse to twang listlessly, and he was aware of the wind rattling the flap of the tent and howling like a pack of wolves along the valley.

At first Jessica smiled as he sang, but before he had finished she seemed to have fallen asleep. When he had finished Miguel went out, and Maria and the mother with him, leaving only José and Jesse crouching beside the mattress.

She died in the early morning, without recovering consciousness, but only José knew. Jesse had fallen asleep with one arm flung out over her body. He was wakened by José's wild despairing cries as he sought to call the dead back to life.

After that all was confusion, a babel of Romany, and people crowding into the tent, dogs barking, disturbed children crying. Then Miguel brought horses and Jesse found himself stumbling away through the darkness, himself leading one horse, Miguel the other.

Cocks were crowing when at last, utterly exhausted, he dismounted at the gate that led off the post-road and on to the cart-track, and Miguel went back with the horses. Dazed with shock and misery, his mind held only one endlessly reiterated thought, that he had slept whilst Jessica was dying.

" We will bury her in the evening," Miguel had said, when they had parted. He remembered it, but the words had no meaning because his brain could not reach to that finality in which the thin darkly brilliant flame that had been Jessica's life had not merely faded into the horizon along a gipsy trail, but suddenly ceased to be, in a world in which nothing else was changed.

2

At breakfast, and again at dinner that day, Jesse looked at his parents and wondered what they would say and feel if he suddenly announced, " Your daughter is lying dead down at the gipsy camp ! " And to what extent grief and pity would fight with moral indignation if he went on to tell them of what she had died. Would they bring her back in order that she might be buried in hallowed ground? Would their father, having sworn she should not set foot in the house again and ordered her clothes to be disposed of, have received her back dead? But she would not have wished to have been brought back, could she have chosen, he was sure of that ; she had chosen José in life and she had been his in death, for he had had her last moments, he and none other, not even the brother to whom she had been so close since childhood—there was no bitterness in that thought, but a deep pain, a passion of remorse.

He was tormented, too, by the thought that if he had not taken her to the fair at which she had met José again everything would have been different and she would still be alive. He recalled that she had declared at the time that the fact that she might meet José again at the fair was a good reason for not going, but he had urged the gipsy on her as a symbol of life and he had brought her death. He should have left her to John and prayers and Bible-reading and chapel-going and hymn-singing . . . but at that thought something in him protested that she had never really belonged to John and that half-life ; that it had only been a phase of her adolescence ; that she had always been ' Rome and dree ', as the gipsies called it, gipsy at heart. If it had not been José some other wild passion would have swept her. Perhaps the gipsies were right in their belief in inevitable destiny.

He had a great longing to talk to someone, but there was no one. His only friend had been Jack Mortimer, and he was in Australia, God help him. He could not think of the Lanes as friends ; there were times when he had been glad of Sally's unsentimental hardness, but it was not what he wanted now. As to Lucy, the only comfort she understood was gin and the bed. There was Mary of the quiet eyes and gentle heart—surely she could at least give him friendship

126

w when he needed it so much? The thought of her was like a
ht at the end of a long dark tunnel. He resolved to call at the
rds' on his way back from the gipsy camp.

He did not stay for the evening meal, at which his mother pro-
sted that he had eaten practically nothing all day, and his father
owned and muttered something about 'the pleasures of the town'.
t that he turned upon his father such an utterly stricken look that his
other was startled and demanded to know if he were well.

" You have not looked well all day," she said, " and your manner
strange—as though you had something on your mind."

" I am well," he told her, " but 'tis true I have something on my
ind."

" You are not in any trouble? " she pleaded, anxiously.

" Not as you understand it," he assured her.

" Gambling debts, no doubt," observed his father.

" On a farm labourer's wage? " Jesse inquired.

" Supplemented by the proceeds from various infringements of the
ame Laws, I have reason to believe."

" You don't mean poaching? " Mrs. Hallard exclaimed, startled.

Jesse was forced to smile in spite of his unhappiness.

" That was clever of you, Mamma, to put it so briefly ! "

" You would never descend to that, Jesse? "

" Better men than I have done so."

John said quickly, " Jesse likes to be thought daring and the friend
of the common people." He looked curiously at Jesse and there was
flash of understanding between them. John had deliberately put an
nd to the discussion.

He followed Jesse out into the back kitchen.

" Is anything amiss? " he inquired.

Jesse had a momentary impulse to tell him, but cheked it ; it
would be unfair to burden his brother with so weighty a secret, he
effected.

" Someone I loved deeply died last night," he told him.

John stared at him. " I'm sorry," he said, helplessly. He stood
or a moment beside Jesse, who was washing his hands in the stone
sink. All day the look on his brother's face had made him want to
reach out to him across the gulf that had divided them since childhood. There was that only deep loyalty stronger than all jealousy
and difference. But what was there to say, except out of his heart,
' I am sorry ', and that he had said. He obeyed an impulse and laid
a hand on his brother's arm for a moment, then turned away, abruptly.
Jesse, he knew, must be very lonely since Jessica had gone ; but he
himself had been lonely for as long as he could remember, even at that
time when outwardly Jessica had come over to him. He filled with

self-pity at the thought, and after that momentary outward gestu[re] retreated once more within himself, closing the shutters after him.

Jesse was touched by John's gesture of sympathy, but nothing himself went out to John; it was as though they were not of the sam[e] clay. Only he and Jessica had ' belonged '.

He rode out to the chalk-pit with the same sense of unreali[ty] as he had ridden out from it in the early morning with Miguel at h[is] side.

He found the entire gipsy family sitting round the fire in silenc[e.] José got up as Jesse approached, and took the reins from him whe[n] he dismounted.

" I will tie her up with our horses," he said.

Jesse went with him to the lean-to.

" What has happened? " he asked.

" We buried her in the beech-wood just above us," he said. " W[e] waited for you, but it began to get dark and we could not wait longer[.]

" I couldn't get away earlier," Jesse told him, and then, as they le[ft] the lean-to, " Will you take me to the place? "

José nodded, and they went along the back of the chalk-pit togeth[er] and began to scramble up into the woods above its face.

They moved cautiously between the trees by the light of t[he] lantern José carried and descended a hollow. Halfway down t[he] gipsy halted.

" It is full of bluebells in here in May," he said. " We came he[re] one evening together when it was getting dusk and she told me. Sh[e] said you and she came here together as children."

" Yes." Jesse felt as though his heart and throat must burst.

" We found some primroses under the leaves when we were diggin[g] and Maria put them in her hands. We buried her with her neckla[ce] of gold coins that was the wedding gift from us all, and the silver gips[y] bangle I gave her that night at the fair." José's voice was complete[ly] flat.

Jesse was silent a moment, then he said, with difficulty, " I am gla[d] you buried her here."

They turned and climbed up out of the hollow. At the top Jo[sé] said, " We are leaving here tomorrow, as soon as it is light. We sha[ll] never return."

Jesse made no comment, and as they descended into the chalk-p[it] José said, " Maria saw all this written in her hand. She told me tha[t] no one should come between us but that she saw no journey into th[e] spring together, and she feared the Ides of March for us, but this sh[e] did not say. We had only the winter together, though I dreamed [of] her all one spring and summer and autumn. But it was not to be."

Jesse said, painfully, " You are young, and in time you will marr[y]

128

someone else, but you will always remember her—the little *gorgio* who loved you? "

" What do you think? " He spoke almost contemptuously. He added, " If I held a thousand women to my heart *she* would still be here ! "

Back at the camp Jesse said, " I will go now. 'Tis best."

Without a word José went over to where the horses were tethered. Jesse was about to follow him when Maria came forward and laid a hand on his arm.

" I took a lock of her hair for you," she said in a low voice, " I thought you would like to have it."

She brought it out from under her gaudy shawl, wrapped in a scrap of red silk.

He tried to thank her, but the words choked in his throat. He could only press her hand.

José brought his horse and Miguel rose from the fire and joined them. They all three, José, Miguel, Maria, walked with him out on to the road. He shook hands with each of them, without speaking. Just as he was about to mount his horse Maria stepped forward and taking his head between her brown hands kissed his forehead.

" A gipsy's blessing on you, brother, wherever you go may fortune follow you ! "

He found words then. " And you too, sister ! "

He looked back when he was in the saddle and waved to them. It seemed strange that he would never see them again.

XVII

WHEN he knocked at the door of the blacksmith's house that evening Jesse felt his heart, which until then had been like a stone in his breast, begin to beat heavily.

Mrs. Byrd opened to him, and when she recognised him her voice rang with welcome.

" Come in, come in," she cried, " stranger that ye are ! " and then as he followed her into the warm, lighted living-room, " Look who's here ! " she announced triumphantly.

The blacksmith was sitting in the chimney-place, spectacles pushed up on to his forehead, a paper discarded across his knees. Jesse noticed that the spinet was open, and from where she stood, beside it, he had the impression that until he had knocked Mary had been playing. He saw the colour rise up into her face as he looked at her. She smiled faintly, and curtsied. Her father sprang up and gripped Jesse's hand. Mrs. Byrd bustled about bringing ale, cheese, and a loaf fresh from the oven. Mary brought a candelabra from the spine and placed it in the centre of the long table, beside a bowl of early primroses. To Jesse the whole room glowed with warmth and light and that peculiar quality of simple comfort and ease he never found in his own home. He knew that he had been right to come here ; that this was a place in which to relax his taut nerves. He threw off his heavy coat and went over to the fire, where a log hissed greenly amongst leaping flames and gave out its pungent smell of wet woods. He held his hands to the blaze and felt an inward thaw from the numbness of pain. This was home ; there was no other place. He looked up at Mrs. Byrd gratefully as she set the ale in a pewter mug down beside him on the settle. She smiled at him, her eyes soft, tenderness welling in her, succumbing as always to his looks and charm, and marvelling all over again that Mary could be so unnatural as to be indifferent.

" You are very good to me, Mrs. Byrd," he told her.

" What woman wouldn't be? " she demanded, gaily.

He sighed. " Mary, I'm sure, thinks 'tis all a sad mistake." He smiled at her, ruefully, but she went over to a work-basket on the table by the window, with its row of geraniums, turning her back on him. Her heart beat painfully.

Jesse drew a long heartening draught of the ale, then told them, " I came here tonight because I have just lost someone who was everything to me. I felt the need to be with friends."

The blacksmith said, " You were right to come here, lad."

" We heard your sister had gone away to London," Mrs. Byrd murmured.

" 'Tis not that. The loss I speak of is death. I have just come from the grave. 'Tis a terrible thing when everything you care for is under the earth."

He sat staring into the fire, and not knowing how else to express the deep sympathy she felt, Mrs. Byrd replenished his mug. Mary came back from the table by the window and stood leaning against the tall straight-backed chair in which her father sat.

" I am sorry," she said, in a low voice, " I am very sorry." All her blood yearned to put her arms round him, draw his head to her breast, comforting him with love and pity, but she stood by her father's chair, spinsterish in a severe grey dress, her face as impassive as a nun's.

" We are all very sorry," Mrs. Byrd affirmed, " and proud it was us humble folk you came to in time of trouble."

She went over to the door that led out to the little hall and the stairs, and winked at her husband, jerking her head towards the hall.

130

"I must go and open the beds," she said, "and you might bring in some more wood, Jim."

"Aye, I was meaning to do that." Mr. Byrd rose obediently.

When they were both out of the room Mary sat down in her father's chair.

"That is Mamma's idea of tact," she observed, drily.

Jesse said, "I am grateful to her. It was you I came to see, Mary. I felt the need of you."

She said, primly, "You have my friendship—if you wish it."

He smiled, sadly. "Friendship carries a certain amount of affection, I believe?"

"I suppose so—yes."

He got up and came over to her, kneeling before her. She shrank back into the chair, away from him, but he took her hands, holding them firmly and compelling her to look at him.

"This evening, riding here, I thought that if I might rest my head on your breast I would forget the pain and misery in me. May I—for one moment?"

"Mamma and Pappa will be back any moment!" she protested.

He made no answer, but released her hands and laid his own on her shoulders, his head on her breast. Until that moment her whole body was strained away from him, then suddenly it was as though everything in her relaxed. Involuntarily a hand went up and hovered over his hair, but so lightly that he was unaware of it.

He closed his eyes for a moment. "I can hear your heart," he told her. "It beats like a frightened bird." He rested there a moment more, then rose.

"Will you do something for me?" he asked. "'Tis only a small thing, and I promise never to ask anything more of you. No need to look so anxiously! 'Tis only that you will put on your cloak and walk a little way along the road with me when I go. 'Tis not much to ask of friendship—and affection!"

She promised a little breathlessly. She could still feel the weight of his head on her breast and his gipsy black hair brushing her chin, so lightly, yet stirring such tumults in her blood.

When her parents returned they found Jesse still sitting looking into the fire, and Mary at the spinet, a thin light melody escaping under her fingers. She felt a certain shyness in playing with Jesse there, but it was less embarrassing than continuing the conversation with him. Jesse knew nothing of music, but he found the spinet's high thin notes soothing to his spirit and pleasing to his senses. He had the feeling that if he might not spend the rest of his life with his head on Mary's breast he would like to sit by a fire and listen to her playing the spinet by candlelight.

131

Mary ceased playing as her mother entered, but Mrs. Byrd said, briskly, " 'Tis a pretty enough air, but it needs the words to it. Let us have the words, pray ! "

To Jesse she added, " She hath a pleasing voice, but she is loth to sing when company is present."

Jesse smiled. " I am not company, and I should like very much to hear the words. I can assure you I shall prove the most appreciative and the least critical audience in the world ! "

" I cannot do justice to the song," Mary protested, " and I would beg to be excused."

" Sing it, sing it ! " her father insisted, coming in to the room. " All this false modesty ! "

Her colour high, Mary returned to the spinet, singing in a voice as thin and sweet as the instrument itself.

> ' Weep you no more sad fountains ;
> What need you flow so fast ?
> Look how the snowy mountains
> Heaven's sun doth gently waste ! '

At the end of the first verse she took her hands from the keys.

" The second verse is too sad."

" I would like to hear it," Jesse said, simply. The music and the words and Mary's voice stirred him deeply. He had the excited sense of new vistas opening up, as when he had discovered by chance *The Song of Songs*.

Mary sang the second verse with more confidence.

> ' Sleep is a reconciling,
> A rest that peace begets ;
> Doth not the sun rise smiling
> When fair at even he sets ?
> Rest you then, rest, sad eyes !
> Melt not in weeping,
> While she lies sleeping
> Softly, now softly lies
>   Sleeping.'

When she had finished Jesse turned to her, his eyes alight for the first time that day.

" Thank you," he cried, fervently, " thank you. I know nothing of such things—poetry and music and the like. 'Tis a famous piece, no doubt ? "

" 'Tis from a book of seventeenth-century songs and airs," she told him.

"Perhaps there are many more such, if one but knew them?" he asked, wistfully.

"Yes." She checked the impulse to add, "Sometime I will play and sing some more for you."

He got up from the settle. "I am glad I came here tonight," he said, "and I thank you all for everything—the good ale, the music and singing and 'the rest that peace begets,' as it says in the song."

"There is always a welcome for ye here, lad," the blacksmith assured him.

Mrs. Byrd murmured, "Come again soon."

"I will get my cloak," Mary said quickly, and then in reply to her mother's questioning look, added, reddening, "I promised Jesse I would walk a little way along the road with him."

Whilst she was gone Jesse went out and untied his horse. She joined him a moment later.

They walked for a few minutes in silence, then Jesse said, "I can never thank you enough for this evening, Mary. I shall remember it always."

Her heart answered him, "My darling! My darling!" but she said, only, sedately, "I trust that one day you will find a lasting peace."

"'Sleep is a reconciling'," he murmured, then added boldly, "but it must be the sleep after love for lasting peace, I think."

She was silent, fighting the thought of night-long sleep with his head pillowed on her breast. When they had gone a little farther she turned to him.

"I must go back," she said, "'Tis far enough."

He stopped immediately. "'Twas good of you to come so far."

She held out her hand to him. "Goodnight, then."

He took her hand and raised it to his lips. "Goodnight, Mary, and thank you for everything."

She was gone then, running down the road, back to the warm red glow of light from the house, and Jesse hoisted himself up into the saddle.

As he rode on through the darkness he felt a deep aching sadness, but the wild pain which had racked him during the day, and as he stood in the hollow that was Jessica's grave, had gone. It was as though he had come to terms with grief. Now he was able to think of Jessica as sleeping in the beech-wood, under the dead leaves through which as children they had gone shuffling together; of Jessica sleeping after her wild love, round her neck the bridal necklace of gold coins, and in her hands the year's first primroses.

He felt that he had come to terms with Mary also, and there was blessedness in that thought. Now at least he had her friendship; he would never be as lonely again. One of these days, he liked to think, he would come to terms with life itself, and out of all the chaos of living some sort of intelligible pattern evolve, and the deep peace, the supreme reconciliation, of sleep after love. It was a thought which was more than a thought; it was that impassioned beseeching of life which is prayer.

XVIII

SEVERAL people remarked that the gipsies had gone early that year, that they did not usually break camp until April. Jesse made no comment, even when he heard his father boasting that he had had something to do with the gipsies' early departure, through his influence with the squire. He had never realised how deeply he hated his father until that time. For his mother he had only contempt; she was a poor thing, hysterical, full of the fear of her husband and of God. He felt pity, sometimes, for John, but never closeness. He pitied him but felt powerless to help him, because fundamentally, he knew, John was his father's son, narrow, religion-bound, and a land-owner. He would live out his joyless life at the farm, the price of corn always uppermost in his mind, and the fear of God in his heart. Valley Farm would prosper under his management as it had under his father's, and he would be hated as his father was hated, and be contemptuous of that hatred.

Ever since Jack Mortimer had roused him to anger and revolt with his stories of the persecution of men under the Game Laws, and he had seen, nakedly, the bitterness and defeat of the countryside, he had known that he did not 'belong' to the house of Hallard, and that the time must come when he would leave the place that had never been in any real sense 'home' to him. If he had any home it was at the Byrds', but though his last visit had done much to ease his spirit he did not go back. He was determined that the next time he went it should be to say 'goodbye'. He had made his peace with Mary, but he knew well enough that she was not for him and that only pain and frustration could come of continually seeing her. He had to get away; right away. For a long time, now, it seemed to him, he had lived in the shadow of a ship, and now, with Jessica gone, it was time to go.

The clipper, *Baltimore Girl*, was lying at Oldport, just back from the West Indies. She had the fine, lithe, greyhound lines of her breed, and a certain romance attached to her because of a dashing career as privateer during the war. Sometimes Jesse thought her the most beautiful ship he had ever seen—or for that matter the most beautiful thing he had ever set eyes on at all. He had struck up acquaintanceship with the bo'sun the previous Easter, and had been taken over the ship and felt that he loved every rope and spar and timber of her. Now, just when he needed her, she was back in port, and there seemed to him significance in the fact. The more he thought about it the more significant it became, and within a week of Jessica's death he decided to go into Oldport and have a word with the bo'sun concerning the chances of signing on for the next voyage.

He could always be sure of finding the bo'sun in the inn in the evenings, and he set out with as much eagerness as he had once gone after the adventure of women.

When he looked in on that particular evening the bo'sun was not yet there, and he decided to stroll along the quays and look for him aboard ship. He was not in the mood to drink by himself, and he had not seen anyone in the inn that he knew. It was early yet ; later the place would fill up.

It was a wild night of scudding clouds, an angry-looking moon occasionally emerging, and a black pool of stars. Jesse strolled along with his eyes on the ships, and had come almost to the end of the quays, to where the *Baltimore Girl* was berthed, when a female figure suddenly stepped out of the dark shadow of a net-shop and laid a hand on his arm, speaking his name. He thought for a moment it was Lucy, then caught the gleam of bright hair from a pushed-back hood and realised with a sensation of dismay that it was Sally. He felt that he did not in the least want to see her at that moment, but he smiled, involuntarily, the old charming, meaningless, indulgent smile.

" Sally ! I was coming to see you one of these evenings."

She accused him, unsmiling, " You've not been near since Christmas —you were glad enough to come then ! "

The bitterness in her voice astonished him. One of her good points was the casualness, almost indifference, with which she had always accepted his own casualness, making no demands on him in their relationship, leaving him free to come and go as he pleased.

" I intended coming out to the farm if I didn't see you soon," she informed him, adding, after a moment, " I very specially wanted to see you."

He said, a little stiffly, " I am sorry if I have offended you, Sally. What did you want to see me about ? "

Three drunken sailors, arm in arm, lurched past them, singing discordantly, and there was the ribald laughter of street-women seeking to attract their attention. A spatter of rain was flung up by the wind.

Sally said, impatiently, " We can't talk here. Walk out to the rocks with me. We can't go home—they're all there."

Jesse suppressed a sigh, and took her arm. He had not been out to the rocks since the night he had had the crazy impulse to try to swim out to the island. It seemed a lifetime ago now, the day that Jack Mortimer had been brought up before the bench, and he had had his first encounter with Tom Surridge. He eyed the *Baltimore Girl* wistfully as they passed her, the fitful stars caught in her rigging. How beautiful she was in her nakedness, without a stitch of canvas. all her lovely lines laid bare! He drew Sally's attention to her, halting her a moment to look at her.

" I came down here tonight to look for the bo'sun," he told her " If possible I want to get signed on for her next voyage. She's due to sail again at the end of the week."

Sally asked, contemptuously, " What will they take you on as— cabin-boy? "

He told her, simply, " I'd go as that, to get away. 'Tis nothing but loneliness since Jessica went."

She made no comment and they walked on, beyond the harbour to the stony wilderness of rocks and boulders under the high white cliffs. He had more than once made love to Sally in that wild place, in secret sandy places between the rocks ; it seemed strange to be going there with her now, utterly without desire, wanting only that she should say what she had to say to him and be gone . . . so that he might return to an earlier love, a lovely ship.

Now they went only a little distance in amongst the rocks, and then she stood with her back against a tall boulder and faced him.

" Well? " he demanded, smiling.

" I suppose you have forgotten that we ever came here together? " Her voice was bitter.

He answered patiently, " Why should I forget? You were sweet to me, Sally. Did you bring me here to reproach me with neglecting you of late—is that it? "

She said violently, " I brought you here to tell you that you've got to marry me, Jesse Hallard! You can go to sea if you like, but you'll marry me first—I'll not stay here and bring up a bastard in disgrace and on parish relief! "

Jesse said, bewildered, " Do you mean that you are—with child? "

" What did you think I meant, pray? "

" Why should you hold me responsible? There were others, always. You told me so yourself. Peter Vinney's ship was in at Christmas. Why not ask Peter to marry you? You always said you would marry a sailor ! "

He was suddenly very angry. He felt himself being trapped. She was probably lying about her condition ; and if she were not she probably had no idea who was responsible. He felt strongly that he would far rather marry Lucy Williams than Sally Lane ; Lucy would at least be faithful to him, he thought, grimly.

" You dare to say that to me ! " Sally cried, and let loose on him such a flood of invective that it seemed to beat about his ears like spume from the sea. She accused him of being a clumsy and inadequate lover, of whom she had never had pleasure, to whom she had never at any time given herself except from pity, and he in turn had used her like a street-woman. Now he was going to betray her as he had betrayed his friend to the squire's men. . . .

That was too much. He could afford to be indifferent to her insults concerning his relations with her, but to accuse him of betraying Jack, whose arrest and trial had been such agony to him, was intolerable. He realised in that moment of soaring rage how utterly outside of everything he cared for she was ; if there had been any betrayal it was she who had betrayed him with her squalid carnality devoid of all tenderness.

He did not know what he said to her ; he only knew that he had to stop that torrent of abuse and fantastic lies. He sprang forward and gripped her, pressing his hand over her mouth. She struggled wildly —like a rabbit in a net was how he thought of it—and her teeth bit into his hand. He let her go then and turned away, wanting only to have done with her, but by then she was hysterical with rage and clung to him screaming that he should not get away from her so easily, that she was not to be shaken off just when it suited him. Disgust rose in him then, and in a final fury he gripped her wrists, tearing her hands away and flinging her off with such force that she fell backwards on to the rocks.

He did not know that she had fallen ; he only knew that at last he had freed himself of her frenzied clinging and clawing, that at last he had silenced her. He strode away through the darkness with a darkness blacker than the night in his blood and brain ; he had a sense of that darkness beating in him like the beat of the sea.

In that black fury he strode unheeding past the *Baltimore Girl*, past *The Ship's Bell*, and away out of the town. He wanted only to walk and walk until he could walk down the rage and disgust in him. In his desire to avoid people he climbed up through the back streets of the town, stumbling over cobbles, splashing through the water running in the gutters, and cut through an alley which brought him out at the back of the smithy. There was a light in an upstairs window, the curtains undrawn. Something in his brain registered, ' Mary's room,' and he came to himself.

He leaned against a fence with a sudden sense of exhaustion, and clung to the fence, breathing heavily, the sweat wet on his face, and looked up at the window. He saw Mary move across the room, carrying a candle. He saw her shadow moving with her across the room, the silhouette emphasising the neat fall of her curls, the soft swell of her breast. She came to the window, raising one hand to the curtains, then stood a moment looking out, and it seemed to him that she looked straight down into his face. He strained upwards to her through the darkness in an agony of yearning.

" Mary! My love! My love! "

Then she drew the curtains and the window was as black as his despair.

He had an inward vision of the light and warmth that waited behind the drawn curtains of that house under the ancient yew, but he could not go in, there was such blackness in his soul. He could still feel the imprint of Sally's teeth in his hand, and her hands clinging to him, and the obscenity of her words beating down on him. Some sort of purification was necessary before he could come into that blessed place again, and for that purification he felt a need of the wind-swept sky and the wide dark fields and solitude.

2

He was out in the darkness of early morning bringing in the cows by lantern-light, when he felt a hand pluck at his sleeve. He turned and looked down into the lined face of old Mortimer.

The old man lowered the lantern Jesse had lifted to see who had accosted him and jerked his head towards the darkness behind them. Jesse left the cattle to plod on down towards the farm and stepped aside with the old man.

" What are you doing up this way so early in the morning? " Jesse inquired cheerfully.

" I had business with the mail-coach, and a good thing, as it turned out, for I heard summat, lad. It seems the night-watchman found a young woman dead on the rocks this morning, and that you was the last person seen with her. Tom Surridge has told how he seed you meet her down by th' 'arbour, and others seed you leavin' the town by the back way. The constable's on his way up here now with Surridge and two others. If ye want to make a get-away ye ain't got a minute to spare. I cut away across the fields, poacher's way, and got here ahead of 'em."

For a few moments Jesse stood silent, dazed with shock, and the old man stood peering up into his face.

" Ye got no time to spare if ye want to make a get-away, lad," he repeated, urgently, and bent down and blew out the lantern.

Jesse said at last, slowly, on an indrawn breath, " Is it possible to kill someone and not know it? "

" Seems like it is," the old man muttered, " Point is can ye prove ye had no intent? Or that ye was elsewhere and Surridge lyin'? "

" No. I met her, and we went down to the rocks and we quarrelled. She kept screaming at me and clinging to me and I shook her off, but God's truth I didn't strike her—I couldn't have killed her——"

" Maybe she fell and caught her head against a rock. They might not bring it in wilful murder——"

" But it might be a life-sentence! God! " The sweat broke out on his face. " What am I to do? " he demanded wildly.

" Get away, lad. You was talkin' of clearin' off to sea—maybe ye could stow away. Maybe there's someone in the town could hide ye till ye could fix it. One o' them women you and Jack used to go with. They know what it is to be 'unted——"

Jesse's brain began to work rapidly as he recovered from the first shock. Lucy! Lucy would hide him till he could fix up something. He had some money, and as good luck would have it he had it on him, because when he had got in last night he had flung himself down on his bed without undressing.

He gripped the old man's arm. " Do I stand a chance of getting into Oldport without being caught? "

" If ye go now, yes, for they're lookin' for ye up here—keep off the roads and drop down to Oldport on the common side and worm yer way up through the back alleys——"

" I know—I know. It's goodbye then, Joe, and bless you——"

" Good luck, lad. Keep under cover, and not a word 'twas me as warned ye——"

Then Jesse was racing away over the fields through the lifting darkness, his heart plunging like a hunted hare's.

From the top of the hill above the valley he crouched in a beech-wood where he had gone many a night after pheasants, and looked down on to the road, his whole body tense with listening as on that night when a keeper had stood motionless under an oak tree a few yards away. All his poacher's training came into play now as he listened to the sound of horses' hooves on the road below. He could just make out the figures of men and their riders ; there were four of them—Surridge and the constable and two others, as old Mortimer had said, heading for Valley Farm. In about ten or fifteen mintues, he esti-mated, they would be there, and it would only be a matter of minutes before they would discover that he was not at the farm, then they would be thundering back down the road to Oldport, having lost the scent.

When they had gone he scrambled down through the beech-woods into the valley, and cut away across the common. The light was grey when he came into the narrow back-streets of Oldport. A lamplighter was putting out the street-lamps; Jesse dodged into an alley-way until he had passed. A couple of sailors came out of a shabby house and headed for the quays. A rat stirred the garbage in the gutter.

Jesse made his way to the disreputable street in which Lucy lodged. Like most of the houses in that street the front door was unlocked, and he slipped in and mounted the dark stairs to Lucy's room, praying that he would find her alone. It was a relief to find the door of her room unlocked. He went in and spoke her name, softly.

After he had spoken a second time she started up in bed.

" It's Jesse," he whispered. " Light a candle."

He heard her groping for the tinder-box that was always beside her bed, and in a moment she had struck a light. The candle flame sputtered and settled down. Jesse turned the key in the lock and went over to her.

She smiled at him. " 'Tis not many I'd be glad to see at this time of the morning," she told him.

He sat down on the bed beside her. " Listen, Lucy. I want to hide here for a day or two. The police are after me. It's hanging or a life-sentence if they get me."

She stared at him in amazement.

" You'll let me stay, Lucy? " he pleaded. " I want to get away in a ship. There's a bo'sun I know who may help me. I have some money, Lucy—you won't lose anything by having me here a day or two."

" I don't want money for helping someone in trouble."

She put out a hand and touched his. All over again she thought how young he looked, but now his good-looking face was haggard, and the old tenderness flowed in her.

" You look worn out," she said softly, " lie down beside me."

He lay down beside her gladly on the squalid bed and she put her arms round him, and put up a hand and brushed back the hair from his face as on that first occasion.

He rested his face against her breast and closed his eyes and he imagined that it was Mary's breast, and Mary's hand caressing his head, and Mary's lips in his hair, and peace filled him. Here was sanctuary.

Presently he slept a little from sheer exhaustion, and all the time Lucy sat with her arms round him, looking down at him. He was hunted and had come to her to hide. He had thought of her as a friend. She was proud for the first time in her life, and so happy that tears of happiness melted the mascara round her eyes and ran in black rivulets down her rouged cheeks.

140

Jesse stayed three days and three nights with Lucy. During that time she went out each morning to buy food, and each evening to drink gin in *The Ship's Bell* and pick up the gossip. She brought back to Jesse the news that the disappearance of Jesse Hallard was the talk of the town, and that it was in all the papers. A watch-out was being kept at London lodging-houses, as it was thought he might have joined his sister there. A description of Jessica was circulated because it was possible that if she could be traced the ' wanted man ' might be traced. Mr. and Mrs. Hallard had admitted that their daughter had disappeared before Christmas and that they did not know her where-abouts, though they had given out that she had joined relatives in order to avoid a scandal.

Now, Jesse thought bitterly, they were up to their necks in scandal, and a kind of black bitter laughter rose in him. He wondered how much horror and dismay there was in John, and what hell-fire passages from the Bible their father read out at nights in the farm living-room now, in the tribulation his children had heaped on him. He tried to think of Sally dead, and he could not make it real ; it was as unreal as that he could have killed her. He wondered what the Byrds were thinking, and Mary especially. The old people might try to defend him, he thought, give him the benefit of the doubt, but Mary, he felt sure, would condemn him, asserting that this was the sort of disaster which overtook people who led dissolute lives in taverns and with street-women.

It seemed that his friends, as always, were among the poor and the outcast, poor old Joe Mortimer, and little painted Lucy. Surridge had thought to get even with him, but he had cheated him, by God, thanks to the loyalty of these humble friends.

Lucy's devotion touched him deeply. It was a passion of devotion. For the time being she lived only to serve him, utterly. When she came in from marketing in the mornings, and from *The Ship's Bell* at night, locking the door behind her, her face would be radiant with happiness, because she had come back to him. She had loved him from the first time he had come to her, a shy, clumsy boy, and now she was privileged to serve him, to cook for him, eat with him, sink into sleep at nights with his head on her breast, waken him in the mornings with her kisses—and a heart swelling with love. For three days and three nights she was happier than she had ever dreamed possible. Now he was not merely the good-looking well-to-do farmer's son who took her because he wanted a woman and liked her better than the others ; now he was wanted by the police on a capital charge, and because of that he was her guest, and her lover.

That he would be her lover whilst he sheltered with her had no occurred to her, and had certainly not occurred to Jesse during the first panic-stricken, horrified twenty-four hours. But waking beside her in the half-light on the second day he saw her curled up beside him in a curiously childish attitude, and he was filled with tenderness and gratitude. He took her into his arms then with something very like love in his heart—a tenderness he had never at any time felt for Sally. He felt for the first time, then, that he was making love to a woman, and not merely possessing her, and because he kissed her lips and murmured soft endearments to her Lucy was deliriously happy.

"Why didn't I find you before?" he cried to her. "Everything might have been different then!"

But that was too deep for Lucy's simplicity; after all, she had been his 'first'; he found her as soon as he had found a woman at all. It was not her fault if he had not loved her sooner; God knows she had loved him, in her foolish, wanton, hopeless fashion.

For three days and three nights there was this fusion of passionate tenderness and an anxiety in which every step on the stair could set the hearts of them both beating with apprehension. And for Jesse, behind it all, a sense of nightmare unreality such as he had known when he had been wakened by wild cries and looked down on the dead face of Jessica. Nothing, it seemed to him, had been quite real since the night he had taken Jessica into Oldport for the last time and left her at the inn. Paradoxically, the moments of forgetfulness with Lucy were the moments of reality. Amidst all the horror and squalor and dread, the gentleness and devotion of Lucy, and his own impassioned gratitude, shone out like a star in a wild dark sky. All this, he deeply felt, he would remember, long after the nightmare of the rest had faded. Their love-making was heightened in intensity by the sense of ecstasy trembling all the time on the brink of disaster; because at any moment there might come the fatal step on the stair, and because of the imminence of separation.

Lucy knew the bo'sun of the *Baltimore Girl* well enough—he had been her 'guest' on several occasions, and would have been during those three days had she not insisted to him that she was 'engaged'. He made a ribald joke and suggested that if she was 'too busy' at home she should come aboard ship one evening. He was a short, thickset, sensual, good-natured man with a ready laugh and an open purse. On the night before the *Baltimore Girl* sailed Lucy took him at his word and went aboard ship, and into his cabin. To his surprise she warded off his embraces and announced that she wanted to talk to him about a serious matter. A friend of hers, she said, was in trouble with the police and had to get away. She wanted him to help her.

142

He said at once, " Don't tell me that 'tis you who are sheltering young Jess Hallard, ma'am? "

She turned her childishly innocent gaze on him. " Him that's wanted for the murder of that poor girl? What a dreadful idea, Mr. Kendrick! La!"

" That young feller never murdered anyone, not of malice prepense," Mr. Kendrick observed, drily. " The police seem to think 'tis his sister who's sheltering him somewhere in London," he added, " but I would wager a whole trip's pay 'tis some pretty wench like yourself. You're surely not going to deny to an old friend, now, Miss Lucy, that you never took him to bed yourself—no offence meant, I'm sure."

Lucy smiled her sweet smile. " Oh, to be sure, Mr. Kendrick, I've nothing against Mr. Hallard *personally*. I always found him a very pleasant young gentleman, but after all he was the last person seen with that poor girl. La, it makes one feel all goose-flesh to think of it!"

" All right, my pretty. What about this friend of yours, then— what's his trouble? "

She said boldly, " He deserted from the Navy."

" Did he, indeed? " Mr. Kendrick looked disapproving, and she reached out her gloved hand and laid it on his wrist.

" Please, Mr. Kendrick, he's only young. Give him a chance to get away. If he smuggles aboard ship and you don't discover him till you're well out to sea, you could put in a word for him to the captain. He has a little money, too——"

The bo'sun's eyes twinkled. " Are you trying to bribe me, ma'am? "

" Money hath power sometimes," she said.

" So hath a pretty wench! " He leaned across the table to her. " If I make it possible for your friend to get away aboard this ship will you come to me before we sail? Is that a bargain, ma'am? "

She smiled at him, resolutely. " 'Tis a bargain," she said, quietly.

" Good. We sail at six tomorrow morning. If you will bring your friend here in the early hours, say about three, there will be no passengers arriving as early as that, and I will see that he is stowed away safely. I will meet you at the top of the gangway and take your friend below. You will wait for me here."

" Thank you. You are a good friend." She got up.

" You are welcome, ma'am." He smiled and bowed, then rose and opened the door for her.

When she got back Lucy said nothing to Jesse about the terms of her agreement with Mr. Kendrick. She herself attached no importance to them ; but she feared that Jesse might ; gentlemen were apt to be a little strange about such delicate matters. Jesse must not feel that she was ' sacrificing ' herself in any way for him—and indeed 'twas no sacrifice, for Mr. Kendrick was a very pleasant gentleman and the offer he had made was fair enough. For such a favour as he was granting 'twas a small favour to grant in return. What was the frail body of Lucy Williams? Nothing, except in the service of Jesse Hallard, and in a few hours now he would be gone from her—perhaps forever. When the clipper had sailed everything would be as it was before: the street-corner, the quayside, *The Ship's Bell*, the endless succession of sailors, furtive tradesmen, married men for the most part, these seeking an excitement not to be found in the heavy respectability of their marriage-beds—uncouth farm-labourers making merry on market days. Sometimes a rakish squire's son, or an officer from a ship. But mostly sailors and tradesmen and farm-hands. But always, now, the memory of these three days and nights with Jesse Hallard, and the dream of seeing him again, or the forlorn hope of meeting someone like him—someone she could love and serve faithfully all her life, if only she might be allowed to do so.

On their last night together they talked, for the first time, as friends do, telling each other about their childhoods. Jesse had forgotten that she came from a farm, and was astonished to discover that they also had the same narrow non-conformist background, that where their childhood was concerned they had much in common, the same story of religious fanaticism and beatings.

Lucy had many times as a child felt the end of her father's belt whipping round her thin body for some trivial childish offence, and known the excitement and terror of seeing her brothers and sisters punished in the same way, lain shivering and weeping, and listening to their cries and sobbing. And all the time, Sunday-school and Bible class and the chapel services, and the grim sabbaths, and the everlasting talk of damnation and sin, and the rabid insistence that the greatest sin of all was attraction to the opposite sex, however innocent. She ran away from the drudgery and deadliness of farm-life and worked in the mill newly opened in the valley ; in due course a girl with whom she formed a friendship there introduced her to the sailor with whom she went to Oldport, spending the time with him till his ship sailed.

" He would have married me, but that he had a wife already," Lucy sighed.

" When I have gone you must try to find someone who will marry you," Jesse urged. " I don't want to think of you going on with this life. 'Tis a bad life, Lucy. I don't mean it the way the ministers mean it, but bad living, as I see it, no real happiness to it. With someone who really cared for you it could be for you always like it's been these few days together."

She smiled, sadly. " Indeed I might find someone to care for me," she said, " but to be as it has been with us 'twould have to be someone I cared for in the same way, and difficult it is."

144

It amused and pleased him when she relapsed into the sing-song Welsh accent and its phraseology. She endeared herself to him almost hour by hour during those three days ; at times she seemed to him like a small, bright bird ; at others like a child, or a kitten, and he would be filled with a kind of indulgent affection and enjoy the sense of her happily yielding to it, softly relaxed. At other times it was from her that all tenderness flowed, and he would be aware of her gentleness and devotion flowing like a soothing balm over the pain and grief and dread in him. Then he would know an abatement of the agony over Jessica's death, and the horror over Sally's.

He could tell her now that it was Jessica, his sister, whom he had loved all his life, and who had gone away from him for a whole year ; he recalled to her the night when he had given her money and told her to go home and sleep alone. He showed her the lock of hair he carried in a purse fastened to his heavily studded belt, and told her that Jessica had died just over a week ago, but he could not bring himself to tell her the whole wild romantic tragic story. It was not that he did not trust Lucy, or that he did not wish her to know, but simply that he was still too close to it all and could not bring himself to speak of it. When he spoke of Jessica at all it was with such evident distress that Lucy forbore to question him. He told her of his hopeless love for Mary Byrd and of the spell that Sally Lane put on him. Lucy had known Sally by sight and reputation and strongly disapproved of her. Girls like Sally represented a real menace to girls like Lucy—a point of view which had not occurred to Jesse before, and which interested him. Lucy, he realised, never gave herself lightly, because she never gave herself at all unless she loved, as in the case of her first sailor-lover, and as in his own case ; for the rest, she had her price, and in that lay her self-respect. Sally gave herself promiscuously and freely and loved no one and had no self-esteem except the unjustified one of considering herself superior to the whore who sold herself. To Jesse, just then, Lucy seemed not only fundamentally respectable, but an angel of goodness.

On that last night he fought sleep like a man in a condemned cell, in a wild attempt to hold back the dawn. He had the despairing feeling of being unable to face the darkness and the unknown that waited outside. He wanted the life in the squalid little room at the top of the tall shabby old house in the disreputable back street to go on indefinitely, with its inexpressible blessedness of sanctuary for flesh and spirit alike. Strange, he reflected, that now that he was being hunted like a fox, and had gone to earth in a house that was nothing but a lodging-house for whores, he should have found such peace, and a kind of beauty. The thought came to him that perhaps there was too much making love in the world and not enough loving.

145

People looked at each other with too much heat in their eyes and not enough warmth in their hearts, so that passion became merely lust, devoid of tenderness, a surface, frictional thing, a titillation of the senses, instead of something deep in the blood, profoundly emotional, touched by strangeness and wonder, a little awed by its own power.

Whereas once he had only been able to think of Lucy as a pretty, gentle whore, now he found it impossible to think of harlotry in connection with her. Now it seemed to him that however many men she might have taken to her bed she was utterly without harlotry, that in some strange fashion her innocence had been preserved. She was his refuge, but she was Jessica, too, evoking his protectiveness. Intellectually he was aware that she knew more of the realities of life than he, probably, would ever know, but it made no difference. And in a tense, keyed-up, hunted fashion he was happier than he had ever been. But it had to end ; the smell and sound of the sea that came in, night and day, through the broken window was an unceasing reminder of the darkness and uncertainty that waited outside, and in their last few hours together he faced the realisation that the time had come to face the north wind and the open sea and make the journey to the island, alone.

Lucy had never lost sight of the fact that their time together was nothing but an interlude, and to get Jesse safely stowed away in the *Baltimore Girl* seemed to her part of her devotional service. That Jesse Hallard could have no permanence in her life she had accepted, in her simple fashion, from the first. She counted herself lucky to have had that brief happy time with him ; she would derive happiness merely from the memory of it for the rest of her life.

To comfort him she said, " Perhaps one day you will be able to come back," but in her heart she did not believe it, any more than he did.

She was all ostrich-feathers and feather-boa and long gloves and rustling silk, and perfume and cosmetics, the night they left the little room together and crept down the dark stairs. At the last moment she had taken the parma violets he had insisted she bought with his money in the market-place that morning, and which had stood all day in a chipped china mug on the table at which they had had their meals, and tucked them into her waist-belt. Somehow it seemed to him that that bunch of wilting flowers cancelled out the whorish flashiness of her finery, reducing a quality of brittle brilliance to something softer, a kind of radiance, such as a bride might wear, or a woman deeply loved and walking proudly with her lover.

In the street he wanted to hurry ; but she urged 'twas better they should stroll, and he recognised the wisdom of that, though it was torment to act on it. He kept his hat pulled down over his eyes and his chin sunk in the collar of his coat. It had been agreed between them that if possible his anonymity should be preserved until the ship sailed, lest at the last moment the bo'sun had qualms about allowing a man wanted by the police to stow away.

He had a moment's dismay as they came up the gang-plank and saw Kendrick waiting at the top, but the bo'sun did not recognise him in the darkness ; with a jerk of his head he indicated to Jesse to follow him and turned away, moving off along the deck.

"Allow me, pray, to bid farewell to my friend ! " Lucy protested, and catching at Jesse flung her arms round his neck and pressed her lips to his, then as she drew away from him pressed his hands against her breast and whispered, " Good-bye and good luck, my darling ! "

He wanted to thank her for her goodness to him in his need, but at the last there were no words. He could only murmur, " Bless you, Lucy, I shall never forget you," and then with a final pressure of her hands on his she was gone, with a flurry of feathers and a swish of silks and a patter of thin, high-heeled shoes along the deck, and he was following the bo'sun down an iron ladder into the seemingly bottomless pit of the ship's hold.

XIX

WHEN the *Baltimore Girl* was well out to sea, rolling and creaking, rhythmically, with an easy confidence, her long sharp bow nosing the waves like a hound on the scent, and some of the passengers were already being sick, Mr. Kendrick went below to interview the stow-away.

Jesse was still crouching behind the enormous pile of rubble being carried as ballast which the bo'sun had indicated to him as a hiding-place before he had hurried back to Lucy. Jesse stepped forward boldly into the light now as the bo'sun approached, no longer attempting to conceal his identity.

" We know each other, Mr. Kendrick," he said. " I am Jesse Hallard—very much at your service, sir, and asking your pardon for the deception."

Mr. Kendrick peered at him through the gloom. " Young Jess Hallard? Bless my soul, so it is! Why didn't the little baggage tell me? I asked her if 'twas she was shielding you, and she denied it—came to me with some yarn about a friend of hers who had deserted from the Navy ! "

" You must forgive her, sir. We needed your co-operation too much

147

to take any chances. You might well have refused to turn a blind eye to a stowaway you knew to be wanted by the police "—he hesitated a moment, then added, resolutely, " for the murder of a woman ! "

The bo'sun observed drily, " 'Twas a wonder Sally Lane was not murdered years ago ! "

" If she died by my hand 'twas an accident, as God is my witness ! " Jesse declared violently. " She was clutching and clawing at me like a mad woman ! I shook her off, but I swear I never struck her ! "

Mr. Kendrick laid a hand on his shoulder. " Easy, lad, easy ! 'Tis a pity that more like her that infest the ports don't come to sudden ends and never mind now. What we've got to consider is your position aboard this ship. I'll have to take you along to the skipper, and I warn you he'll not be pleased to see you ! Likely as not he'll be for turning you over to a British captain when we reach Baltimore and having you shipped back home."

" Perhaps I could slip away when we dock? " Jesse suggested.

" We had a stowaway last voyage—climbed the anchor-chain ! Then got away when we reached port and cheated the skipper of the free passage home he'd planned for him ! The old man swore he'd have the next stowaway put in irons before we berthed."

" I could go over the side before then and swim for it. I'm a strong swimmer."

" I was going to suggest you went overboard before then. Off the south-west coast of Ireland, off Mullen Point, we keep close in to pick up our bearings from the Point beacon, and there are a number of small islands off Mullen Bay. Inishmullen is the largest and the nearest. Of course if we run into bad weather you'll have to take your chance when we reach America——"

" When shall we be off the Point? "

" We should make it by this time tomorrow, unless the wind changes. We're doing fifteen knots at the moment." He added, proudly, " She's done eighteen, before now. This is the fastest clipper that ever came out of Baltimore ! "

" How close in to Inishmullen shall we be? "

" About five miles."

" 'Tis a goodish swim in cold weather. If the tide is right, though ——"

" Aye, it will be. Now we'd best go along and see the old man."

The skipper had truculent-looking moustaches and small fierce blue eyes and an aggressive manner, and as Mr. Kendrick had prophesied, he was not disposed to be lenient with stowaways. He demanded to know how this one had got aboard, and Jesse, recalling his predecessor, replied promptly, " By the anchor-chain, sir."

" What was the watch doing? " He glared at the bo'sun.

Mr. Kendrick said he would inquire into the matter.

"Why did you stow away?" the captain demanded next.

"I wanted to get to Baltimore, sir," Jesse replied. "I hoped that once I was aboard I should be given a chance to work my passage——"

"You will certainly work," the captain informed him, "but you will be transferred to an English home-bound ship at the other end. Take him away, bo'sun."

Mr. Kendrick took him away, to the crew's quarters. He indicated a bunk.

"You had better get a bit of sleep," he said. "You'll be turning out in an hour or two."

Jesse rolled into the bunk, but he did not sleep. He lay listening to the creaking of the ship and the thud of the waves against her sides and the unfamiliar sounds of the ship's bell timing the watches and the scurry of feet along the deck. A man in the berth above him snored heavily. A lantern swung from the ceiling above a long table with benches on either side. There was a smell of grease and bilge-water and feet. The air was stale and sour. Cockroaches wandered up the wooden wall-side of the bunk.

Jesse watched them abstractedly. America, or an island off Mullen Point? If he failed to get away at Baltimore he would be sent home, and that meant arrest as he stepped off the ship. The alternative was a five-mile swim off a wild, rocky coast. Once in a crazy exhilaration he had tried to swim out to an island and had failed; but this time if he failed there would be nothing to swim back to—nothing but a white wake left by a ship. But if it was a question of death by the hangman's rope, or of a life-sentence, or even ten years, he preferred death by drowning in an attempt to reach the sanctuary of an island off a wild coast.

On this thought, which was a resolve, he finally slept.

2

If he had any lingering doubt as to which course he would pursue it was disposed of by his day in the ship. He discovered that a ship ceased to be a thing of beauty below deck; then she becomes merely a stinking black hole. And his time on deck was limited to the time it took to do his share of the scrubbing. After that he was sent below to shovel the ballast.

He worked with the man who had snored in the berth above him, an enormous Swede, and a Scotsman who recognised him from having seen him in *The Ship's Bell* but who did not know his name. In reply to their questionings as to why he had stowed away, he told them, briefly, that he had been working on a farm and had tired of it and wanted to see 'the new world.' He had tried to get signed on in a ship, he said, but having failed resolved to stow away and hope for the best. They assured him that a few weeks below deck, even in the smartest clipper afloat, would find him wishing himself back on the farm. After a few hours in the hold he was prepared to agree with them, in principle.

He discovered that men did not go to sea from any romantic motive, neither sea-fever nor the spirit of adventure, except in the case of youths. But in the *Baltimore Girl* even the cabin-boy was at sea for no more romantic reason than that he preferred it to being an under-paid farm labourer or working in a mill or going down a pit; he did not enjoy life at sea, but it was a lesser evil. So far as Jesse could make out, none of the clipper's crew shared the bo'sun's pride in her, and were quite unaware of her beauty. The magnificent array of sails on her backward raking masts, which gave her such an imperious look, for them merely represented so much work and an intricacy spared them in ships that carried fewer sails. They regarded her speed as her only virtue, because the time spent at sea was a period of frustration, cutting them off from women and taverns.

Jesse had listened to a good deal of sailors' talk on the subject of women in *The Ship's Bell*, but he discovered that at sea the topic was discussed from a considerably more brutal angle. It dealt in per-versities and had a lewdness which did not colour it ashore. In his mood of tenderness and gratitude where Lucy was concerned, the talk jarred on him, and when half a dozen of them were sitting round the table together in the evening over their ration of rum he asked them, " Do you never talk of anything but women when at sea? "

One of them, a Cockney, mocked him. " 'Ark at 'im! 'E'd like us to talk poetry!"

The Swede tried to explain. " It is like this, you see. If we dis-cuss politics, then we quarrel. Nobody agrees. With religion the same. But when we talk of women, then we all agree! "

The wind held and they went rolling and plunging down the Irish coast at a good fifteen knots, and something stirred in Jesse's heart when he heard one of the men observe that they would be 'off Mullen Point' by morning. Ireland from the sea looked like one large flat green field, but 'twas very different down off the Munster coast, they assured him; then 'twas wildness itself, nothing but rocks and gulls, and the last place God made, and the people wild as gipsies, as unfit to rule themselves as blacks.

In the small hours of the morning as great a restlessness seized Jesse as during his last few hours with Lucy. He hung about the poop straining his eyes through the darkness for the landfall of Mullen

Point. It was a good clear night and a moderate sea, and the wind was in his favour. He felt eager and alive and confident. He had the urgent feeling of ' What thou hast to do, do quickly'. He preferred a longer swim to going overboard when it was getting light. He wanted to escape into the darkness and see the daybreak from the sanctuary of the island.

The bo'sun brought him an extra ration of rum, and the ship's position. He, too, was anxious for Jesse to be gone.

" The wind and the tide are in your favour," he told him, peering anxiously first at the black sea and then at Jesse.

Jesse swallowed the generous tot of neat rum and felt it like fire in his body. He laughed, nervously excited.

" I'll go now," he said, recklessly.

" You could bide till we were off the Swallow Rock and then make for it," Mr. Kendrick suggested.

" And risk being dashed against the Rock? No, thanks ! " He held out his hand.

" Goodbye. Thank you for helping me."

The bo'sun gripped his hand. " Good luck," he said. " Maybe you could get a message to me sometime—just to let me know you reached shore. No need to give your whereabouts if you didn't wish. Maybe Lucy would like to know, too. You could write to Baltimore, Maryland, care of the company."

Jesse promised, and the bo'sun said, " Give me time to get back forrard."

He hurried away, and Jesse pulled off his boots and dropped them over the side, and his jacket followed them.

He took a last look at the wind-filled beauty of the *Baltimore Girl's* great spread of sails, then dived overboard as confidently as though he were merely going off Oldport jetty into the harbour.

He and the ship seemed to part company with astonishing rapidity. He seemed to have been in the water only a few minutes before she became a grey phantom melting at the head of a wide white wake. He thought of the bo'sun's proud claim, " The fastest clipper that ever came out of Baltimore ! " All day and all night she had seemed to crawl.

He swam steadily, conserving his energy. His great fear was cramp from the coldness of the water ; at present the neat rum gave him at least the illusion of warmth.

When the ship had finally faded into the darkness, and not even her wake was left on the water, he had an intense feeling of loneliness. One dim distant light on shore or on a fishing-boat would have made all the difference, but the sea was empty and the grey hulk of the land offered nothing but its remoteness. Then time played tricks on him.

He seemed to have been swimming for a long time without getting any nearer land or picking up the glow of Mullen Point beacon. It was a heavier sea than he had anticipated, and he had to swim through each large wave as it rose to avoid being buffeted. He felt that he was making slow progress, and he was beginning to get cold.

The growing numbness in his body seemed to reach to his mind. He swam mechanically from the simple instinct of self-preservation, then, as he began to tire, there was the insidious suggestion that cessation of effort would be blessedly peaceful, the complete and final escape.

The stars paled and the blackness melted into grey, and the greyness of the island became more clearly defined, and he picked up the beacon at last, but the land seemed as distant as ever, always separated from him by an endless expanse of rough steel-coloured water that was stealing his strength from him with every stroke. He wondered, vaguely, how long the will could triumph over physical exhaustion. He tried to think of a world in which rushlights shone in cottage windows and in which there were taverns full of brightness and warmth and laughter. He tried to think of the Byrd's living-room, full of warmth and light, of hissing logs and lighted candles and the thin sweet notes of the spinet. He tried to recall Lucy's room, that had nothing to commend it except the refuge it offered. He tried to think of Lucy curled up like a child or a kitten in the big ugly bedraggled bed. But it all seemed utterly remote, as though there was not and never had been any reality but this of heaving grey water and cold fading stars and unattainable land.

When he had made a supreme effort of will and swam back to Oldport after failing to reach the island he had been buoyed up by the will to life ; life had been heavy with dissatisfaction, but there had been Jessica, and a resurgent revolt against the injustice of life for the poor and powerless. Now there was no Jessica, and he had deliberately turned his back on the fight, and his own life was forfeit for a wanton's. What point now to struggle?

The wind and the tide are with you, the bo'sun had said. Very well, then, let them do the work ; let them wash him up where they willed ; he himself was beyond further effort and his ebbing strength craved only the blessedness of oblivion. Life was too difficult ; it called for too much struggle.

His last thought as a mountainous wave took him and engulfed him was that it was at least something to have cheated the hangman. . . .

PART II

ESCAPE

'In the language beyond learning's reach
  Passion can teach,
  Speak in the speech beyond reproach,
  The body's speech.'

Donal MacCarthy (translated from the Irish by Frank O'Connor).

I

FULL consciousness of his surroundings came very slowly—though how slowly, that it was a matter of days, he did not know till later.

At first he was aware only that faces came and peered at him through mists of smoke, and one face in particular, a woman's face, neither young nor old, and with thick braids of dark hair. Old, lined faces came and looked at him, and sometimes the faces of children, but there was no other face which regarded him so intently and so often through the wreathing smoke as the face that was neither young nor old. One day he thought the face came close, hovered over his, and that lips touched his, but he could not be sure, nor make the effort to determine whether it was reality or fantasy. He lived in a world of shadow and dream.

Then there was the day when the face smiled at him ; there was that moment of conscious realisation, and it was like sunlight coming suddenly into a room. He smiled back, and it was the beginning of return to the conscious world. The return was gradual, beginning with small things. He became aware of the smoke-blackened ceiling, and the strong sweet smell of peat on the smoke ; of the earth floor and the few rough sticks of furniture ; of a long dresser with rough bowls and platters ; of an old woman wrapped in a black shawl sitting by a fire on the hearth ; of the bright colours woven into the shawl crossed on the young woman's breast ; of the curve of her breast when the shawl slipped away or was discarded, a curve fine and full and proud . . . like the sails of a ship before the wind, a three-master with long lithe lines and backward tilting masts. 'The fastest clipper that ever came out of Baltimore.' Somebody had said that. He made an effort and remembered. Mr. Kendrick had said it. He had also said, 'The wind and the tide are in your favour.' That must be why he was here. But where was he? Was this island or main land?

153

He raised himself on an elbow and demanded, "Tell me, someone, where am I?"

The young woman got up from the fireside and came over to him and stood beside his bed, smiling down at him.

"You have come to yourself," she said, and her accent was its own kind of music. "I am called Ria Rooney, and herself there is my mother. This is the island of Rull."

"How did I get here? I remember only being in the sea."

"Two who were pickin' up seaweed found ye on the beach and brought ye up here, and sure weren't we thinkin' the last gasp had gone from ye, when Paddy and Festy O'Shea began workin' the two arms of ye, like 'twas a pump, and wasn't it the ocean itself they were after pumpin' out of ye so that ye could breathe again, and all Rull lookin' on with a great wonder like 'twas a holy miracle?"

The old woman who had come up behind her daughter looked down at him and crossed herself. "Aye, and a holy miracle it was," she affirmed solemnly.

"Amen to that," said Ria.

"Rull?" Jesse repeated, confusedly. "Where is Rull? I was heading for the nearest island off Mullen Point—Inishmullen I thought 'twas called."

"Ah, sure, 'tis further along the coast altogether, on the Sound. Rull is in Blackrock Bay. Maybe the strong current of the Sound swept ye through into the Bay itself."

"How long have I been here?"

"This is the third day. 'Tis English you are?"

"Yes." Then with a sudden realisation of what that might mean to these people, he added, "But England has no use for me except to put a rope round my neck. I stowed away in a clipper ship and went overboard off Mullen Point. The captain would have given me up when we reached America and I should have been sent back. I preferred to take a chance with the sea."

"God is merciful to those who put their trust in Him," the old woman observed.

Jesse sank back on the bed with a sudden feeling of weakness. As he did so a sharp pain stabbed through his head and he raised his hand to the centre of the hurt.

"'Twould seem you struck your head on a rock," Ria said. "Ye were bleedin' like a stuck pig when the O'Sheas brought ye in. They said a blow on the head would likely account for ye not comin' to yerself this long time." She regarded him intently, then asked, "And why would the English wish to be hangin' ye?"

Before he could reply the old woman had rapped out, "Ah, and why would they wish to be hangin' anyone at all, but for the great blackness that is in their hearts, God forgive them!"

She hobbled back to the fireplace, and Ria said gently, "Rest aisy now, and I'll be after bringin' ye a sup of broth."

He closed his eyes. He felt dizzy with weakness. The smoke seemed to be swirling in his head. It was an effort to think, and somehow there was no need to.

Then arms strong as a man's were lifting him, and Ria had an arm round his shoulder, and with her free hand was holding a shallow bowl of a pale steaming liquid to his lips.

"Sup this," she urged, "'twill put life into ye."

He obeyed her, and the liquid tasted of smoke and faintly of potato, and he felt the warmth of it in his body and it gave him an illusion of returned strength. He felt a stirring in his belly and it came to him that he must go outside and that he was wearing only some kind of a rough homespun shirt.

"I need my clothes," he said, "I must go out."

She brought them to him and helped him into them, throwing back the coarse grey blankets that had covered him and accepting his nakedness as though he were a child. When he stood he leaned heavily on her shoulder. The old woman came and helped him shuffle his feet into rough cowhide shoes. Still leaning on Ria, he moved giddily towards the door.

The intensity of the light outside dazzled him for a few moments after the smoky darkness of the interior. Then as his eyes accustomed themselves to the brightness he was aware of a distant coast-line that seemed composed of misty purplish hills full of deep shadows, across a stretch of blue water flecked with white under a stiff breeze. In the foreground there was grass, and black and white goats graz-ing, and grey boulders, and brown rocks covered with golden seaweed. And there was a smell of the sea and of salted fish and burning turf.

He was taking in the colours and the smell of it when a ragged barefoot youth with a hunched back rose up from some hidden place amongst the boulders and limped over to him, and without a word Ria transferred Jesse's arm from her shoulder to the boy's, then went back into the house.

The boy was not tall enough for Jesse to put his arm round his shoulder; he could only rest his right hand on the boy's left shoulder, using him as a human crutch.

He looked down at him, smiling faintly. "I've no strength," he apologised. "But I need go no further than decency permits from the house."

"Sure," said the boy.

When Jesse emerged from behind the boulder to which the boy

had conducted him he was aware of a change in his weakness; it wa
no longer the dragging feeling of the weakness of sickness, but had
become the light, slightly exalted weakness of convalescence, as though
his body had stirred in response to this new land and given itself
up, eager to be made whole again. He stood looking at the house
It was a low white-washed cabin, its thatch secured against gale,
by large stones laid on it. There was a black peat stack at one side
of it, and chickens wandered in and out of the open door. The
house was so much part of the landscape, Jesse thought, that it looked
as though it had been thrown up like some kind of fungi from the
earth itself. To right and left of it, and behind it, at some distance,
were similar cabins, crouched amongst boulders and peat-stacks, and
everywhere were low walls that were merely large stones piled one
upon another. So much grey stone gave an impression of great wildness and bareness, but some curious quality of light and colour saved
it from desolation. Small black cattle grazed amongst the boulders,
and there were clumps of wild yellow iris here and there, and everywhere a white fluff of bog-cotton and the reddish ears of bog-asphodel.
The only trees were a group of gaunt thorns beside a toy-like church
with a large bell in an open tower; the branches of the thorns were
twisted and distorted by the great gales that had swept them. Two
donkeys, grey as the boulders, sheltered sadly from the wind between
the peat-stack and the house.

Jesse took it all in with a curious deep satisfaction. It was as though
he had always known that it would be like this.

He turned away from his long contemplation of it to look at his
companion, who regarded him from under a flurry of straight uncombed
fair hair, and from a pair of eyes which Jesse saw suddenly were almost
dazzlingly blue. He had high cheek-bones and a wide mouth and
outstanding ears, and a remote, lost look. Jesse smiled.

" What is your name? " he inquired.

" Seamus Byrne."

" How old are you? "

The boy shrugged and looked away. " Goin' on sixteen, maybe."

" Which is your house? "

" Over fornint." He jerked his head in the direction.

Jesse lifted his weight from the boy's shoulder and leaned back
against a boulder. The boy leaned with him, and they stared at
nothing and everything, and there was the sound of the sea, and the
sudden sobbing bray of a donkey, and the lost cry of a sea-bird, and
the wail of a child, and the rattle of a donkey-cart along a bog-road out
of sight between its walls, and all these sounds part of a quietness
that seemed to go deep down into the earth, into the blood, as though
earth and sea and sky, bog and boulder and rock, were saturated in

his hush, and man himself become part of it. It was the landscape
of a dream, through which one might walk forever and never wake.
Sleep lay over the squat houses, the silent cattle, the thin bright sunlight.
The strewn grey stones as old as God.

Jesse had the feeling of the past dropping away, fading into unreality. He had made his landing on the island. He had come
home.

The primordial strength of sea and bog poured into him, seeping
through his skin and into his blood, and he slept that night the deep
healing sleep of a man in whom the forces of wholeness, of flesh and
spirit, for a little while disintegrated, knit together again in a strong
new rhythm.

II

THE 'man of the house' in the Rooney home was Martin, Ria's
brother, a tall, gaunt, silent man of about twenty-eight or thirty.
A younger brother, Willie, Jesse learned, had been drowned at sea
one wild winter, and he only in his teens. Another brother, Brian,
was in America. There was a sister married and living in Cork, in
a house with stairs, and windows back and front. The father of the
family had died of a chill some years back, he having a terrible weak
chest, the way it was always afflicting him in the months of winter, the
old woman said. Now Ria and Martin worked the bit of land, and
the mother looked after the house and, in the summer, between potato
crops, made bread occasionally, as a change from oatmeal. Martin
went out in the curagh, fishing, and took his catches on market-days
to Burra, on the mainland, bringing back flour and yeast, or a bag
of oatmeal, but seldom anything more ; when there were seed potatoes
to buy, flour and oatmeal had to be dispensed with.

Having known the homes of the English farm labourers Jesse believed he had seen the lowest level of subsistence possible for human
beings ; in Rull, he discovered, with amazement, that there was an
even lower level ; that people could and did subsist mainly on potatoes,
salt fish and milk. In the Rooney home the milk was goats' milk,
but even in homes where there was a cow or two only buttermilk was
drunk by the family ; milk which could be turned into butter and
sold on market-days was too valuable a substance to be squandered on
the family. Similarly with the eggs and lobsters, they were too
precious for home consumption. No one in the island—not even his
reverence—ate fresh meat. There would be an occasional rabbit

poached on the mainland, or a hen past laying put into the pot, but even when such were available they were sold whenever possible. A hen for the pot could generally be sold to his reverence; you took it along alive, in a bit of sacking, and if he wasn't wanting it that day you took it home and brought it back a day or two later. If somebody else had just been to his reverence with an old hen you saved it and took it over to Burra on market-day. But generally speaking you sold very little and bought even less; when things went not too badly—they never went well—you somehow managed to make ends meet; when they went badly you starved, and this, Jesse gathered, was true of the Irish peasantry everywhere, though life was hardest in the west and south-west and the outlying islands.

The Rooneys lived rather better than some of their neighbours because they were a family of adults; to feed a large family of young children from the uncertain yield of the sea and the niggardly land, half rock, half bog, was an endless struggle. 'God will provide,' the priest always said of every new-born child and every child on the way, and inasmuch as the child usually survived and somehow straggled up into a gaunt adult, God may be said to have done so, though He sent no more food to the table.

The priest himself lived in what the islanders called a two-storey house, that is to say a house that was not a mere mud-and-wattle cabin, but made of brick, and with an upstairs. It also had windows, as befitted such a 'fine large handsome house' that had the whole of five rooms to it, though what one man could be wanting with so many rooms, and he a celibate, none could tell, except for the great grandeur of it. 'Twas said that in the Vatican there were hundreds of rooms, and if His Holiness needed that many to keep up his position, why wouldn't Father Conneely need five? To be sure the gate of Father Conneely's house swung by one hinge, and an upstairs window was broken and boarded up, and on the roof a bucket with a hole knocked through served for a chimney, and when the wind was in a certain direction his reverence's living-room was as full of smoke as any cabin kitchen, but none but a fool would deny it was a fine house, for all that, a residence worthy of a man of God. Now would any wish to deny his reverence his occasional pinch of tea—which 'twas said cost as much as six shillings the pound—or the hens that came to his table, or the eggs he had no need of selling.

For a time Jesse was nervous of the priest. Here was an educated man who might be curious about this Englishman who, according to the Rooneys, had fallen overboard from a clipper-ship bound for America; who might even have heard of the wanted Jesse Hallard; but he discovered, to his relief, that Father Conneely had been too long on the island to be much interested in the outside world. His

...e apart from the Church was centred in ancient Celtic literature, ...nd he was accounted a great scholar, it being known that he possessed ...number of books. When he was not studying his books or attending ...is professional duties he was to be seen contemplating the sea—or ...ternity, maybe—through one of his uncleaned windows, or striding ...riskly round the island, his head thrown back, the wind lifting his ...rey hair, his blue-grey eyes misty with Celtic poetry and legend and ...istory. Rull had nothing to complain of in Father Conneely. He ...vas a mild, kindly, comfortable man, convinced of the holiness of ...reland, and the dispensation of a special grace to her people.

Jesse was at first grateful to him for his incurious acceptance of ...is presence in the island, and then impatient of him. Couldn't he ...ee that his flock lived on the border-line of starvation whilst he ate ...heir hens and indulged in his occasional pinches of tea and dreamed ...f ancient monks and saints and their learning? Was it nothing to ...im that these people were illiterate and ignorant and bound body and ...oul by superstition and the inertia of hopelessness? Did it never ...ccur to him that out of his great store of wisdom and learning he ...wed them something more than the Church's sacraments and con-...ession? That they too were human and might like to eat chicken ...nd drink tea occasionally, and read and write their own language, ...nd know something beyond the struggle for existence?

"But what could his reverence do, at all?" Ria protested, when he ...aid all this to her.

Jesse insisted that his reverence could appeal to the authorities for ...a school in the island; he could teach some of the children himself; ...e could assist the people in securing relief in the bad times, as their ...right, and discourage begging; and he could ally himself with the ...people against the landlords and tithe-collectors.

But Ria thought all that none of a priest's business, and indeed ...vouldn't it be a terrible thing, now, if one of these days a landlord's ...agent should be found hit over the head, the way it had happened ...before now, and his reverence mixed up in it?

At times Jesse was impatient with the people themselves, with Ria and Martin and all of them, for asking so little of life, for their humble acceptance of their meagre lot, their complete lack of any attempt to improve upon it. The first time he watched a man taking down part of a wall in order to let a cow through he was amazed; surely it would be simpler to make a gate than to be continually taking down and replacing the stones?

"But wouldn't it be a terrible lot of work, now, to be makin' a gate?" Ria said, when he discussed the matter with her, "and sure 'tis no trouble at all to take down a few stones and put them back. Knockin' the wall, 'tis called, and for why would anyone be after changin' the ancient ways and labourin' to no purpose? Isn't it very English you are, with such ideas?"

He thought that was probably true; he was of good English yeoman stock, used to the good living and the neat, efficient ways of his class. He was constantly comparing the solid, well-fed comfort of Valley Farm, with the bacon hung in the chimney, the fresh-baked bread, the good home-brewed ale, the well-housed cattle, the clean cool dairy, the candles in their polished holders, with the poverty of the life he now lived, where bacon was an undreamed-of luxury, like tea or sugar, and candles as unknown as crockery. Rushlights, made from rushes gathered in the island, took the place of candles; but as often as not no grease was available to soak them in, and then, when night fell, there was no light but what came from the dim glow of the fire. Not that there was any need of light once the day was done, since there were no books or papers to read, and talk could be conducted as well by firelight, and for story-telling, indeed, there was no better light. If it was a question of a wake or a wedding a few candles would be forthcoming as well as rushlights, for the sake of respect or gaiety as the case might be; but for general purposes firelight served well enough until the time came when the daylight lasted till bedtime.

At first the smell of the burning turf would seem to Jesse at times almost overpowering in the strong sweetness it gave out, like a kind of incense, yet he loved it with a curious intensity, as though it were the breath of the beloved. Similarly, when he handled the rough wooden bowls which served for practically all purposes, in place of crockery, he would experience something akin to tenderness, because their fashioning had a primitive childish simplicity. There was something touching in that simplicity, and in the fact that these rough utensils had served for generations, some of them for hundreds of years, fulfilling their purposes with a perfection somehow lacking in more sophisticated articles, and which gave them individuality and even a kind of beauty.

It seemed to Jesse that there was nothing squalid, as there was in the wretched lives of the English labourers, in the poverty of these islanders, that they brought distinction even to the border-line of starvation. There was nothing makeshift in the rough simplicity of their home-made bowls and platters, benches, tables, stools; everything perfectly fulfilled its functions. They were down to the bare essentials of living; they had no learning, no books, no newspapers, no amusements—not even that of a harvest-home or a fair; for them a fair meant a sheep and cattle and pig market. On the rare occasions when a letter came—from a relative in far-away America it might be—they took it to the priest to read for them. He would even on occasion write a letter for them, but the sending of letters was even rarer than the receiving of them. In some respects their primitive way of living reminded him of the gipsies; they had a gipsy inconsequentiality and fatalism, and the natural poise and pride of the gipsies, but none of the underlying gipsy hardness and worldliness; there was no guile in them. They were utterly without ambition; utterly unconcerned with the thing called progress.

And if a cow died, or the wind blew the smoke down the chimney, or someone was drowned at sea, it was all ' the will of God.' There was the priest to give them absolution for their sins, the blessed Virgin to intercede for them, and the hope of heaven hereafter to reconcile them to hardship and sorrow and suffering on earth. The lives of the women were dedicated to the children; the lives of the men to wresting a living from the earth and the sea that all of them might eat and keep a roof over their heads. They had none of the English craving for respectability, none of the English shame over poverty. Like the gipsies they could beg, when they had need to, without losing dignity. They had the natural dignity of animals, and, Jesse discovered, a wit and humour all their own.

2

For a while he was intensely aware of his ' foreignness ' amongst these people. He was alien to their language, thought, and religion. At times he found it difficult to realise that they worshipped the same God as his parents worshipped and shared the same hope of heaven hereafter. For as long as he could remember religion had been associated with fear, punishment, and the threat of hell. These people seemed not at all concerned with these things, but perpetually hopeful of forgiveness and heaven, and to regard the Blessed Virgin and the holy saints as friendly neighbours whom they had known all their lives, and through whom they might expect to get round the Almighty. Certainly the Virgin and the saints were as real to them as their neighbours, and as intimately involved in their daily lives. It bewildered him at first, and a little embarrassed him. In nearly every house in Rull there was above the doorway, within, the crimson emblem of the Sacred Heart. Every time he encountered it Jesse was reminded of his ' foreignness ', as acutely as every time he heard the Gaelic tongue.

There were families in the island who spoke only Gaelic—for, as Ria said, why should they be speaking anything else when they had never been further than Burra? On the roads, and when the men were launching their curaghs, he heard only that strange tongue, and everything in him so freely given out to the place and the people would recoil in on himself again in sudden loneliness. He was aware of his foreignness every time a child bobbed up from behind a rock to stare at him, or a woman came to the door of the cabin to watch him pass. Young girls talking and laughing together as they approached him would break off suddenly at sight of him and become silent, staring gravely, as at some strange animal, or lowering their eyes and glancing at him furtively. He was aware of the eyes of the men and youths who lounged against walls and along the pier, waiting for tides, following him long after he had passed, and to approach them, their eyes all turned fixedly on him, was always an ordeal.

He had unhappy moments of feeling that the very island itself stared at him in its deep silence and waited for him to go. He was always telling himself that he must go, but the thought was always countered by the question—where? He had the sensation of moving all the time in a dream from which he could not wake—because he could not sufficiently exert himself. He was held in a deep inertia, and had a sense of his mind and spirit having become a part of the grey rains and mists that swept the island for days on end, a greyness that obliterated all his past life, as the mists obliterated the mainland and sometimes the island itself; in this greyness thought crystallised itself into one endlessly repeated sentence in his mind, ' *Sleep is reconciling*', and he would be filled with a deep melancholy that flowed in him like unshed tears, and the face of Jessica, both wild and tender, would wreathe itself in the driving clouds.

When he had been in the island a few days he had no idea what day of the week it was, still less what day of the month, and on sunless days, which were frequent, no idea of the time. On sunny days the open door of the cottage acted as a sundial; there were no windows, and the day could be measured by the passage and retreat of the sunlight across the earth floor. There was, after all, no need to mark the hours more precisely than that. There was no point, that anyone could see, in doing today what might be put off till tomorrow—which was why the hinge on Father Conneely's gate was never mended; for what could not be postponed indefinitely there was seldom any immediacy; you had to learn, said Ria, to take life ' aisy ', and ' not to be so English ', and then you found that for most things there was ' time enough '.

To any suggestion of Jesse's that a certain piece of ground should be dug up ready for the spring sowing and planting, one or another would answer with easy carelessness, " Ah, sure, there's time enough ! " Only when it was a matter of a she-goat or a sow ' in season' , it seemed to Jesse, was there any immediacy. He alternately admired the islanders and was exasperated by them.

As his strength returned he tried to help about the place ; Martin showed him how to cut turf ; Ria taught him to spin wool from the island sheep. He learned how to run up a sail in a curagh, how to set a spoon-bait and troll for pollock, how to set a lobster-pot, how to make the rough shoes called *pampooties* out of a strip of cowhide. He helped Martin to dig the shallow soil ready for planting the potatoes on Good Friday ; he carried soil from one part to another ; he went down to the shore and fetched up loads of seaweed for manure, balancing the load on the donkey's back ; he took the sow to the island boar. Whatever he found to do about the place he did, and still it seemed to him he was an outsider, surrounded by kindness and friendliness but full of inner loneliness. He never met people on the road, going to Mass or returning from it, but he would be oppressed by this feeling of being shut out, of doors closed to him. He knew no devotion to the Sacred Heart ; he spoke no word of Gaelic ; at the core of these people's lives all was strangeness.

Had Jessica felt like this amongst the Romany people in the beginning, kept at a distance by the strangeness and foreignness of their lives? But Jessica at least had had José's love to wrap round her like a cloak, he reflected, and the fact that she carried a Romany child within her made her one of themselves. If Ria should love him he might be absorbed in the same way into the life of the island. The thought startled him, as though it had come on him unawares, yet he knew that from the beginning he had been aware of Ria, of the curve of her breast and the fall of her hair, with its smell of peat and the sea, and that she walked straight and proudly like a gipsy.

As the weeks passed and the soft insidious excitement of spring began to stir the air, the thought of her crept between him and sleep at nights. He would lie on his straw mattress in a corner of the kitchen, Martin asleep in a wooden cot built in beside the fireplace, thinking of Ria with the old woman in the adjoining room. He wondered if she lay staring at the dark thinking of him ; and if it had indeed been only in his own imagination that she had pressed her lips to his one night before retiring to the inner room. He wondered how old she was ; sometimes, when she laughed, she seemed like a girl ; at other times she seemed older. Then he discovered that she was younger than Martin, and guessed her age at about twenty-five or twenty-six. There was in her the stillness he had loved in Mary, but whereas Mary was all soft femininity and gentleness, Ria had rather more than a streak of masculine strength in her. She had the hardihood of all the island women. She could handle a spade or a boat as well as a man ; for all the soft swell of her breast her body was muscular and strong, and he was aware of a quality of strength in her personality.

That he began to desire her was part of his regeneration, but out
side of his physical impulse towards her was the reassertion of tha
deep longing for personal integration through inner peace which had
been at the core of his dream of marriage with Mary. What she
thought and felt about him he had no idea. Sometimes, without her
speaking to him or even looking at him, he felt her close to him ; as
though something in her flowed out to him, unbidden. Sometimes
her dark gaze rested on him as though she would draw him to herself,
make him her lover, and there would be a quickening of his own blood
in response before their gaze fell apart. At other times she would
seem indifferent to him and leave him wondering as to whether he had
merely imagined the rest.

There was a fine mild Sunday, the first spring day of the year,
when it seemed to him the entire island was at Mass, and he had a
feeling of intense loneliness, of having lost all identity. He went out
of the house and walked some distance along the sea-shore, and then
sat down on one of the upturned curaghs that lay along the strand like
sleeping black seals. The sun came diffused from a sky banked with
cloud, yet the island was held in a curiously intense light that seemed
to come up out of the sea. On the mainland, across the blue-grey
waste of the bay, the mountains were mistily purple, full of shadow,
and there were long shadows on the sea. Some geese straggled past
behind him, stretching out their long necks and hissing ; gulls wheeled
over with fretful, quarrelsome cries, and there was the incessant crash
of waves on the shore ; yet the stillness seemed untouched, to be a
part of the strange, strong light. Ria was like that, the thought came
to him, full of an action that left untouched an inner stillness. He
knew now that he was in love with her and that his whole future was
bound up with her ; accepting him she made him part of the island,
and only she could do this ; rejecting him she sent him away into the
darkness of the unknown ; either way she determined his destiny, as
surely as the gipsy had determined Jessica's the day he had come to
the door with his baskets fashioned of rushes and his brushes of tur-
keys' feathers. Of all that other world now only Jessica, lying in the
beech-wood above the chalk-pit, with the bluebells pushing up shining
green blades through the dead leaves—only she seemed living and
real. He fumbled in the purse at his belt and took out the lock of
her hair, and with the feel of its silk on his fingers knew a loosening
of the strings of the heart. The fever that was Ria subsided and he
sank into a reverie that was all Jessica.

Back again in Oldport, sitting on the bench under the lime trees
and looking out over the huddled red roofs of the little town to the
masts of ships, Jessica at his side, her wild hair restrained under the
Sunday bonnet, he did not hear steps on the road behind as the chapel

emptied. He was only aware of Ria when a hand touched his shoulder, and, starting, he looked up into her face framed in the multi-coloured shawl. He rose, replacing the lock of hair in his belt, a little confusedly.

" I am glad you are back," he said, " I was lonely."

She watched him fumbling with the purse. " You were brooding on the past, maybe? " She added, " There does be a power of sadness in thinking on such things."

He told her, simply, " I was thinking of my sister. She died just before I left England. She was very dear to me."

He saw the instant compassion in Ria's face, and, to his surprise, her eyes filled with tears.

" She is in heaven," she cried. " 'Tis how you want to think of it—that she is in heaven ! "

She lifted a corner of her shawl and wiped her eyes.

" Was she young then, the poor thing? "

" Sixteen."

" Ah, God help us all, wasn't Willie no more than that when the curagh capsized ! "

He drew her hand through his arm. " Let us walk along by the sea," he said, " I want to talk to you."

They went down over the strand that was all fine, smooth crushed shell, and small, perfect cowrie shells, and limestone coral, white and grey, to the sea's edge. They walked a few yards, and then he said, " You have never asked why I went overboard off Mullen Point——"

" 'Tis on account of some crime, surely. You said the English were only wanting you for hanging——"

" Does it not occur to you that perhaps I might be wanted for something very serious—for murder, for example? "

" It does, then. But in the heat of anger anyone might be strikin' an unlucky blow, with no killin' intended at all, and no decent Christian person holding it against him." She smiled up at him. " Sure, it might be happenin' to anyone ! "

He stared at her in amazement and saw that she was quite serious.

She continued, " Accidents do be happenin' all the time. There was a quiet, decent lad here at one time, that was over in Burra drownin' his shamrock on St. Patrick's night, and not knowin' what he was after doin' with the drink in him. Then a black Protestant from the North starts pickin' a quarrel with him, and this poor young feller as fightin' drunk as the other one, and a knife handy, God help him. But not a thing does he be knowin' of any killin' till a boatload of police is out here from Burra, with the sheriff and enough rifles to put down a riot. We've come to arrest Michael Byrne for the murder of a man, says they, and Mike is out fishin' in the bay, and everyone along the pier can see his boat with the sail up as plain as the light of day, but not a livin' soul is breathin' a word. And when the police have gone on up over the beach several go out in their boats to warn Mike and help him get away. That's the way it is."

" And did he succeed in getting clear away? " Jesse asked.

" He did, then."

Jesse was silent for a minute or two, reflecting on this story, then he said, " If I did any killing I swear to God it was not intentional! 'Tis a terrible thing, all the same, for a man to think perhaps he has the blood of another human being on his hands, and a woman at that." It brought the sweat out on his forehead to speak of it even now, and aware of his distress she pressed his hand and said gently :

" 'Tis the intention not the deed that does be countin' in the sight of God."

He said with sudden bitterness, " Where I come from God is a God of punishment, not of understanding and forgiveness. I was brought up to believe that the wicked shall be cast into hell."

" Ah, now, did ye ever hear the like of that? If 'twere true, who would be in heaven at all? "

Jesse did not know the answer to that and they walked on in silence, and when they reached the point where a way led up over the rocks to the cabin he stopped and regarded Ria intently.

" Could you ever bring yourself to marry a black Protestant, Ria? "

She looked at him and saw the intentness in his face and told him, the colour beating up in her own, " If I loved him, and if he loved me, and if he would give a solemn promise that our children should be brought up in the Catholic faith——"

He answered, wildly, " I do love you, Ria, and I would give such a solemn promise. If you will marry me I can stay here and become a real part of the life here. If not I must go away—at once."

He did not know that he held her hands, that he drew her towards him as he spoke, that he was trembling. He only knew that he had never known any desire as intense as this, that she should say yes ; that the whole of life seemed balanced on the slender thread of her decision, a thread which she could snap and drop him into the void, utterly without direction, or take up and weave into the pattern of her own life, and the life of the island. All the old pain of Mary's refusal throbbed in him.

" I need you, Ria," he urged, finally, and she felt in her blood the desperation of that need, that it was as though she had power to grant him life or death. His intensity was like a light, blinding her spirit. She closed her eyes against it and said in a low, shaken voice, " We will be wed at Easter."

III

FATHER CONNEELY married them in the tiny white-washed chapel in the presence of the entire population of the island ; those who could not get in knelt on the ground outside. The ponies and donkeys of those who had come from the other side of the island were tethered to iron rings in the surrounding low wall. Some children had placed small bunches of wild daffodils at the foot of the crucifix by the gate in honour of the occasion. The red petticoats of the women were brilliant against the day's flat colours of blue and grey and white and brown.

Ria had plaited her hair and twisted the braids round her head ; she wore the shawl with the bright colours in the border and the fine long fringe, and there were shoes on her feet. Jesse had gone into Burra to find a wedding-ring for her, but there was no such thing in the place, and he had journeyed all the way to Cork ; it had taken him two days, but he had come back with a fine broad gold ring that was the wonder of the place, and only he knew how many stealthy nights along the hedges and in the dark woods under a poacher's moon that ring represented. In Cork, too, he had bought a fine coloured silk handkerchief from a seaman he had talked with in a chandler's shop with a counter at one end for the sale of ale ; the seaman had come by it in foreign parts and parted with it for the price of a drink. This handkerchief Ria wore proudly folded over her bosom, its secret splendour hidden under her shawl, to be revealed when she had left church. She conducted herself altogether proudly, holding herself very straight, a touch of defiance in her manner, because she was marrying a black Protestant, and an Englishman at that, and a stranger, and she was well enough aware that there were those who found cause for criticism in this.

Jesse had still the feeling of everything happening in a dream. The lighted candles on the tiny altar, the wild daffodils in little gold vases, the blue and gold painted figure of the Virgin, the priest's robes, the musky smell of incense that shut out the smell of the sea, the dark-shawled kneeling figures, the strange prayers and invocations—he had the feeling of looking on at some ritual in which, though he stood there in the flesh, he had no part. All that was real was the proud straight figure of Ria at his side, her strong, rough hand in his, and the ring on it shining brighter than the Virgin's crown or the altar ornaments.

Then it was over and there was the smell and sound of the sea again, and the strange light that was both bright and soft, and the hills on the mainland standing out with a purple-blue brilliance because of the rain in the air, and there was a great babble of Gaelic, and a great shaking of hands, and now that she was no longer in church Ria allowed the shawl to slip back from her head and breast, and the fine-coloured silk handkerchief was displayed for the amazement and wonder of all beholders. Her wild dark beauty was accentuated by the gipsy colours, and by the flash of excitement in her eyes, darkly blue as the hills at evening.

Looking at her, Jesse's heart filled with pride and love and desire, but he could not shake off an underlying sadness. He longed for the moment when he would be alone with her at last, unbraiding her hair and forgetting everything in its shadows. Only as Ria made him a part of herself, it seemed to him, could he become part of the island and its people, close the door upon the past and give himself completely to the new life.

He untied the donkey from the wall, helped the old woman on to its back, and then with Martin walking beside the donkey, and he and Ria behind, and a large procession of the islanders following, they made their way back to the cabin.

He had his first taste of poteen, and learned that there was a still in the island, and that many of the innocent-looking barrels that went over in the curaghs to Burra ostensibly for water—of which there was none in the island—were full of the illicit liquor. Ah, sure, the police had their suspicions, they told him, but weren't the police always after suspecting everyone of everything? Wasn't that the way they made their living, entirely? Something of the old poaching spirit stirred in Jesse's blood, the excitement of adventurously breaking the law. The poteen itself seemed to him to have a singularly unpleasant taste, but its liquid fire burned away his melancholy so effectively that he who did not speak a word of Gaelic had fantastic conversations with gaunt old men and women who did not speak a word of English, with the utmost satisfaction on both sides, expressed in winks, nudges, nods, and a riot of laughter ; he who could no more dance an Irish jig or reel than he could fly, jigged and reeled with complete satisfaction, anyhow to himself, and to the immense merriment of the company. Gaelic or Romany, fiddles or guitars, what did it matter so long as you escaped the hounds that were on your traces? He did not know it, but amongst a wild people of centuries-old untamed blood, he was the wildest in the island that night. A white fire burned in his brain, obliterating everything but the crazy present. Then in an interval between dances a young man with a flame of red hair leaned his shoulders against a wall and began to sing, a wild sad song that had curlews in it, and sea-gulls, and the wind on a March night, and a curious haunting melody emerging from the wildness. He sang in Gaelic, but Ria came over to Jesse and murmured the translation to him.

" The poet tells him that the one he loves is not young. He answers her that neither are the hills ; neither is the sea, yet both have their beauty, their secret sources of joy. Then the poet says to the woman that one day he will desert her, because he is young, and a girl will beckon to his youth, and the woman replies that one day she will be dead, and so will he, that one day is tomorrow and belongs to the future, like death, but today belongs to the present, and today he is her lover, and she says, ' What is the rest to me? ' "

" In the Gaelic," she said, " our songs are always drinking-songs or love-songs, full of wild sport, or great sadness and longing."

There were a number of songs after that, some with a strange keening quality to them, others rollicking as a jig, but what they were about Jessie did not know, because Ria was lost to him in the crowd that filled the small dimly-lit cabin, full of peat smoke and the dust raised by feet dancing on the earth floor.

After a while he felt a need for air and went out into the starry darkness that held the strong smell of seaweed and the crash of waves on shingle. He walked away from the house and sat down on the wall that bounded its patch of land. He felt a little dizzy from the impact of the cold air against a head on fire with poteen. The earth seemed suddenly to behave like the deck of a ship. He had a sense of preserving a precarious balance between sea and stars, and it seemed to him he was back in the *Baltimore Girl* ploughing her way through the darkness to an unknown destiny. When Seamus came limping out carrying a rough, home-spun blanket, Jesse asked him, confusedly, " Is it time to be going? "

" Where would ye be after goin'? " the boy inquired, mildly.

" To the island. Where else? "

" Sure, and weren't ye washed up half drownded at this very island weeks ago? And isn't it the great chill ye'll be after takin' if ye don't take care? " He made an attempt to wrap the blanket shawl-wise round Jesse's shoulders, but he was pushed aside as Jesse staggered to his feet, standing upright, swaying, but filled with a sense of power.

" Does a man who is accustomed to being out under the hedges in all weathers take a chill like a woman? " he demanded, impatiently, and vaulted the low wall, to demonstrate that though drunk he could do it.

" If anyone asks for me I am in the sea," he announced, and swayed away seawards through the darkness.

Seamus hurled himself after him. " It's drownded ye'll be entirely ! " he cried, stumbling over the rocks and stones.

Jesse merely laughed and quickened his pace. The sea's edge quivered like quicksilver in the uncertain moonlight. This time, by God, he would reach the island. . . .

Seamus stood staring after him a few moments, despairingly, then turned and limped back to the house, where he burst in upon the party with the news that himself was drownded in the bay.

Everyone crowded out on to the beach with cries of dismay and excitement, and Jesse could be made out swimming strongly for the open sea. Someone said something about him being swept away by the current if he got beyond the bay, and with shouts of ' By Jases, so he will ! ' and ' Mother of God ! ' Martin and another man ran to the nearest curagh and proceeded to launch it down the slipway. Ria stood staring at the bobbing head on the water, her arms folded on her breast, her head high.

One and another cried to her to take it aisy and not be worryin', but to them all she insisted, ' No harm will come to him,' and in the dimness no one could see that her fingers clasping her arms were driving their nails into her flesh.

Completely unconscious of the consternation he had caused, Jesse suddenly turned and began swimming back to the shore before the curagh reached him. As on the previous occasion, the swim had cleared his brain of the fumes and given his sense of power a new direction. He was oblivious of the crowd gathered on the beach ; when the moon was freed of cloud he saw Ria waiting, straight and tall and confident ; everything else was merely so much background for her. Seamus stood shivering at her side, still clutching the blanket. She took it from him, and as Jesse came up out of the sea went down the shingle to meet him.

" Isn't it the bold one ye are? " she demanded, but he saw that she was smiling in spite of the severity of her tone. He allowed her to wrap the blanket round his shoulders, and they went up over the beach with their arms about each other's waists.

" I came to you the first time out of the sea," he told her, and in a confused way he felt that it had significance.

The crowd began to break up and straggle away, telling each other —those of them who were sober enough—that it was morning already, and that it had been a grand wedding, with himself after drownding himself a second time. There had not been so much excitement in the island since the last eviction party had come ashore amid a hail of stones. The wedding of Ria Rooney would be talked of for many a day—in fact until there was something else to replace it in interest, which, as nobody else was due to get married or to die just yet, so far as was known, might be for some time. A fine couple they had made in the church that morning, and no doubt a fine couple they would make in the bed that night, God's blessing on them, and on the child they would by the grace of God beget. . . .

IV

As there was no empty cabin available, and no money to build with, the young couple occupied the inner room of the Rooney cabin and the old woman slept in the corner of the big room, where Jesse had slept, but with a rough screen knocked up by Martin to give her privacy. Martin was courting a girl over at Burra and would soon be leaving the island and starting a small place of his own. Her father was a small farmer, wealthy compared with the islanders—he had both sheep and cows—and everyone was agreed that Martin was marrying her for her money, but they bore him no ill-will on that account, for wouldn't any man who had the chance do the same?

Jesse quickly discovered that they all slandered each other with the utmost goodwill. Their gossip was frequently witty in its scurrilousness, but there was no real malice. When they said of Jesse that he was probably a deserter from a ship, or possibly even wanted for 'slaying', no criticism of him was implied. Any man might desert a ship, or strike an unlucky blow, and by God there were plenty crying aloud to be murdered. They enjoyed a little scandalous gossip, and even when there was a barb in it it was all informed by an amused tolerance. A scandal that made a good story was worth repeating for its own sake, not with any intention of maligning the person concerned. To slander a man very often was to make a hero of him ; a man might, for example, be reputed to be so mean he grudged the breath he spoke with, and then a kind of fascinated awe would attach to him, and to clear his name of that slander would be to detract from his interest, and rob him, even, of a certain admiration.

Everyone ' knew ' that Michael Flaherty had married a woman old enough to be his mother for no other reason than that he wanted a woman about the place and no one else would look at him ; and that on the morning after his wedding he was so indifferent to his bride that he got up early and went out fishing. Everyone ' knew ' that the priest had refused to marry pretty young Kitty Finnigan to old Patrick Flaherty, ' that decaying mountain of flesh ' as he was said to have called him, and the two had had to go to the mainland to be married ; a great scandal it was—but they said it with their faces lit with laughter. They liked talking ; it was their only pastime, and they were full of the simple romantic stories of Gaelic lore. The men got drunk at wakes and weddings, but at other times they were strictly temperate. Once a week, on market-day, they went over to Burra with whatever they had to offer, with pollock, lobsters, eggs, a young pig, a hen past laying and now offered for the pot. On fair-days they would go over to sell a calf or to buy one. When they had nothing to buy or sell they went for the adventure of the thing, to see different faces, talk with men from other parts of the country. They lived in hovels, on salt fish and bread for the most part, and their language was full of an unconscious poetry, and their faces were wild and dark and humorous and sad. Temperamentally lazy, they were forced by their conditions of life to work hard in order to survive ; temperamentally thriftless, circumstances forced a rigid economy on them. They were at once lawless and God-fearing, superstitious and fatalistic. At times they seemed to Jesse as callous where suffering was concerned, and as indifferent to hardship, as animals ; at other times full of warmth and compassion. In time he realized that both was true of them.

He found in them a poetry and imaginativeness and fire lacking in their English counterparts ; they were a passionate people, and he loved them. They accepted him now as one of them and his home-coming was complete. It was sanctuary, but it was not peace. When he could forget the past he was happy, but it always reasserted itself. He was endlessly tormented by the memory of the episode with Sally amongst the rocks. It seemed clear to him, now that he was able to think about it free of the first panic and hysteria, that in flinging her away from him she had fallen and caught her head on a rock or boulder ; which meant that he had killed her. Was there so much difference between killing a person of intent and by accident? There was a difference in law, but what moral difference was there? He had treated Sally violently, she who at one time had given him all the peace he had known. He did not sentimentalize over her ; their relationship had never called for that ; there had been no tenderness between them ; but the fact remained that he had at one time been glad of her—and her wantonness, and that in a fit of anger he had treated her so brutally that she had died of it. What right had he to refuse to accept that she was with child by him? His sense of guilt insisted that he had no right. His whole relationship with her had been despicable, and in the end it had been cowardly and ugly. What right had he to happiness, he who walked about with the blood of another human being on his hands?

He would have days of such black brooding, particularly when the great gales swept the island, blotting out the mainland, driving the rain in in grey mists from the sea, blowing the smoke back down the chimney, streams of water in under the door. There would be no daylight in the cabin then, and nothing but darkness in his mind. He would become silent and morose, and when he was alone with Ria, his head against her breast, would cry to her wildly for the reassurance she could not give, that he was not responsible for Sally's death.

She would alternately try to convince him that the past was dead, that nothing mattered now except their life together, and to see Father Conneely, to enter the Church and seek its comfort of confession and absolution. She failed in both directions. He could not be persuaded that it did not matter whether or not you had killed another human being ; and he could not feel that his salvation lay through the Catholic or any other Church. He had strongly the feeling that salvation lay within himself—if only it could be given a direction. He knew that Ria prayed for him and had others do so, but it was all outside of himself ; no amount of divine forgiveness of sins, he felt, could give his spirit ease. There had to be either the complete wiping out of the charge his conscience—and the world—made against him, or some profound act of expiation. If the one did not come—and he did not see how it could—he must await guidance for the other, but he was convinced that it must come from within himself ; the Catholic way of confession and absolution seemed to him too easy. ' Go thou and sin no more ' did not expiate the past ; or so it seemed to him, in his troubled broodings.

On days when the sun shone he would forget for a little while. Then he would be absorbed by the beauty of the island, feel that he could stand for ever on a headland with the grass blowing in the wind and the hills deeply blue and long shadows on the blue-grey sea, and the smell of peat and kelp and gorse-flowers on the air, and gulls wheeling and geese straggling, and over all the strange, diffused yet luminous, light. Then every stone in that wilderness of stones would seem blessed, and the sobbing cry of a donkey something to break the heart with pity and love. Then the drone of a bee and the soft surge of the sea, that were a part of the deep, dreaming stillness of the island, would assume a quality of sacrament. Then he would feel that he understood the meaning of prayer, and that his spirit went down on its knees before the blessed stones of Ireland as before an altar. On those, his good days, he would find pride and satisfaction in the hard work demanded by the struggle for existence. He took a pride in the improvements he made about the place, and in his good English farming knowledge and experience. Soon what became known as ' Hallard's place ' became the neatest in the island, and the most productive.

Because there were no trees except the stunted twisted thorns round the chapel, spring made no spectacular arrival in the island. Superficially there was no change in the landscape of rock and stone, and brown and green bog, and distant blue hills ; but the grass became greener, a shining green, and the gorse put out more and fuller blossom, and all manner of small flowers sprang up in the bog ; primroses appeared amongst the grass on the drier ground, and under the stone walls, and clusters of tiny violets. There was a patch of snowdrops in the priest's garden, and every cabin had a few daffodils springing up beside the peat-stack, or along the unmade, muddy path up to the front door. A new growth of reddish shiny leaves appeared at the base

of the dead-looking twigs of the fuchsia bushes; across the bay ther
were fires on the hills at evening where the furze was being burnt dow
on the cultivated land. There was a running of water everywhere
and ditches overflowing, and a new, disturbing softness in the air,
quickening of life and desire. The stony, brown and green landscap
looked much the same all the year round, Jesse thought, until yo
looked into it, and then in spring you found that it was all excitingl
changed, and you felt the change in your blood.

He planned to get trees planted about the cabin in the autumn t
protect the place from the fierce winds that swept in from the Atlantic
and because, too, he had a great longing to see trees again; in May
there should be apple-blossom, and there should be evergreens, fir
and spruces and such, to remind in winter of spring and summer
Everyone told him that it was impossible to grow trees, because of the
gales; but in Burra an old man assured him that trees could be grow
if he persevered and had patience; he must plant them in the shelte
of the house, and he must plant a great number in order to raise a few
those that survived doing so from the protection afforded by those tha
would die. There were forests enough in Ireland at one time, he said
but the English used them all up. Everyone laughed at Jesse, including
Ria, over his ambition to grow trees, but he planted them, doggedly,
and interested Martin in the draining of the land and the more extensive
use of animal manure. Everyone spread seaweed for manure, but
Jesse insisted that whilst it was good the earth needed something
more; more cattle needed to be introduced into the island. Slowly
he began to interest Martin and a few of the others in the elements of
more scientific agriculture, pointing out that it was no use complaining
year in and year out of the poorness of the soil without any attempt at
improving it, that you could not be continually taking from the earth
and returning nothing, and that a good deal of rich, naturally fertile
soil was allowed to waste from lack of drainage.

" Ah, he'd be after drainin' the bog itself! " they mocked him, but
he urged that they should save their breath till they'd seen what kind
of a potato crop would result from his labours, and how he would raise
plenty of swede-turnips for taking to market, and green vegetables that
would save them from outbreaks on their skin from salt fish and potatoes
every day and week and month of the year.

That first spring and summer he was full of enthusiasm and energy
and initiative, impatient of the inertia, as it seemed to him, which
helped to keep the people so desperately poor. He had to come by
bitter experience to the realization of the disaster represented by a
bad potato crop, or the failure to rear a litter of pigs, or the death of a
cow calving, and by the winter storms which frequently made fishing
impossible. Then he was still measuring everything by English

174

onditions and standards. Because everything was new it was full of potentialities ; he had still to discover what was and was not possible, and the strange, lost, summer beauty of the island laid a spell on him, so that the wild spring weather was forgotten, and autumn and winter remaind unimagined. Then the fuchsia flamed along the stone walls, 'red as the blood of the blessed martyrs who died to save the Holy Catholic Church from the destruction of the English ', as the old woman said. The distant hills assumed a purple grape-bloom which enhanced their mystery, so that it was easy to believe, as the people said, that they were the home of the fairy ones, the Shee. The bay subsided into a summer dream in which the waves merely lipped the shore, and the shining bodies and gentle faces of seals flashed up sometimes between the rocks. The island seemed to lie in a pool of diffused sunlight, only the cries of the gulls, and the sweep and dip of their wings, and the swish of scythes in the long grass, breaking the stillness. The air was drenched, then, with the pungency of drying seaweed and the strong almond-sweetness of gorse blossom in hot sunshine. The turf on the bog-land became springy underfoot, and there was a fluff of bog-cotton and the rust of bog-asphodel everywhere. Yellow irises thrust up out of the brownish bog-pools and made fairy-rings in the marshy places, so perfectly circular that it was difficult to believe they had not been planted there. Though some said that they had—by the Little People.

Father Conneely rewhitened the stones that bordered the path up to his crumbling porch, where an uncared-for rose-bush put forth clusters of cream roses, and though the weeds were everywhere his garden was much admired.

Ria was with child, expecting to be delivered early in the New Year, and she and the old woman were very happy about it. Jesse was torn between pride and dread. If anything happened to Ria such as had happened to Jessica he felt that he would be unable to face it ; but these fears he kept to himself, thereby intensifying their torment.

In August of that year, 1819, something happened which took his mind off his broodings on the past and his fears for the future. He was in Burra one day when an English newspaper was being handed round to those who could read it ; it had been brought by a sailor off a ship which had berthed at Cork. Jesse took it eagerly. It was the first newspaper he had seen since he had left England. It seemed there had been more labour troubles in England. Sir Francis Burdett was in the picture again, agitating for Parliamentary Reform, but without success. Huge protest meetings had been held all over the country by dissatisfied workers. At St. Peter's Field, Manchester, 60,000 had marched with banners bearing the reformist slogans, ' No Corn Laws',

' Universal Suffrage ', ' Annual Parliaments ', ' Vote by Ballot ', and the yeomanry had been called out to dispel this huge demonstration. They had charged, Jesse read, with drawn swords, and several people had been killed ; those who had not been sabred had been trampled to death by the horses' hooves and the panicking crowds, and hundreds had been injured. Various of the leaders had been arrested and imprisoned.

Jesse read the account with all the old anger rising in him ; once again the common people had been cheated of their rights, and this time a right as elementary as the right to bread, the right to assemble freely to discuss their wrongs. He had a sudden sick vision of the flashing sabres, the rearing horses, the plunging hooves, the panic-stricken crowds, and a realization of the bitter sense of defeat afterwards. Were the people always to seek justice in vain?

The only person he felt he could discuss it all with was old Mrs. Rooney, in whom the passion for justice burned fiercely. He described to her the conditions of the agricultural workers in England, explained their dispossession under the Enclosure Acts, and told her of the bread-or-blood riots and the tragic results, and of Mr. Cobbett and Sir Francis Burdett, and all her rebel blood rose in sympathy. She gave him in turn Irish history, the ruthlessness of ' the butcher, Cromwell ', the brutality of his son-in-law, General Ireton, who died of the sweating sickness caught during the siege of Limerick, thus proving that God is just, the persecution of the Catholics, the tyranny of the English land-lords, the mockery of Irish ' independence'. . . .

She rocked herself to and fro before the fire as she spoke.

" Those who rob and persecute the poor people of Ireland are the same who deny bread and freedom and justice to their own people," she declared. " 'Tis all part of the same black wickedness. But one day Ireland will be free—when Palm Sunday and St. Patrick's Day do be fallin' on the same day, that year will Ireland shake off the English yoke. Aye, when the palm and the shamrock do be meetin'. . . . But as to your own people there does be no tellin ', God help them, and 'tis a terrible thing, so it is. But 'tis men the like of yourself they do be needin', to be leadin' them and givin' them courage ! Maybe one day by the grace of God yourself will be fightin' the great cause of freedom. Aye. The English poor or the Irish, 'tis all one fight I'm thinkin'. . . ."

Jesse began to realise that the problem of existence for the Irish smallholder and agricultural worker was very much the same as for the English. Agriculture flourished, but not for those who did the actual work of tilling the soil. As in England, the landlords lived in mansions and their tenants in hovels. Common lands were annexed and enclosed by the land-owners, so that the poor were not merely robbed of free pasturage for their one or two cows or sheep, so that it became impossible to keep them, but lost in addition their rights to gather firewood and cut turf. Small farmers and small-holders were reduced, as in England, to becoming labourers, paid at the rate of sixpence a day. In many instances the ' cottier ', as he was called, to rent a potato patch and grassland for one or two cows had to pay for them in labour. He and his family subsisted on potatoes and milk, and if the potato crop failed or the cow went dry he had nothing to fall back upon, since he earned no money by his labour, with the result that he was, to use the common expression, ' never a ha'penny above a beggar ', and frequently begging became an unavoidable part of his existence.

The landed gentry, for the most part, were indifferent to the hardships of the poor, whom they regarded as lazy and thriftless. In very many instances they were absentee landlords, who knew nothing of the conditions under which their tenants struggled for existence ; or they were ' middlemen ' who rented the land from the gentry and sublet it to the peasantry, and these were the hardest and most hated landlords of all. Out of an average total annual income of six pounds ten shillings, Jesse learned, the labourer would have to pay four pounds for his potato patch and two pounds for the rent of his cabin. Where the rent was demanded in money it was usually raised by the sale of a pig, which was fed on the potatoes left over after the family had been fed. Tithes for the support of a church patronised by less than a tenth of the population had also to be paid, but they were only forthcoming with great bitterness, and also, as in England, there were periodic outbreaks of revolt against the imposition of these tithes, and against high rents and low wages.

From old Mrs. Rooney Jesse learned of the Whiteboys and the Steelboys and the Blackfeet, of ' Moll Doyle and her Children ', of the Caravets and Shanavests, Ribbon men and Rockites, and other secret societies organised to fight the landlords and the tithe-collectors. Armed bands would go out at nights and tear down the fences of enclosed land, kill or hamstring cattle, and dig up the grassland in order to force the landlord to let it for tillage. Occasionally a tithe-farmer or tithe-proctor or landlord's agent would come to grief on a dark night at the hands of these armed bands. Savage repression and persecution always followed these outbreaks, which were most frequent in the South and the West, where the people were both poorest and wildest, but ' Whiteboyism ' was never completely suppressed, but remained a smouldering fire, a persistent guerilla warfare between landlords and their tenants and labourers, like the guerilla warfare in England between gamekeepers and poachers. As in England, too, the agrarian unrest was intensified after Waterloo, when prices soared and wages fell ; blood flowed and lives were lost, and there were imprisonments and deportations. Those who could, emigrated to America, where food was supposed to be plentiful and there was said to be work for all ; many of the unmarried young men joined the British Army, and there was an annual migration to England and Scotland for the harvesting.

The Rull islanders, Jesse discovered, had the reputation of being a wild and intractable people ; eviction parties always came ashore armed, and the landlord's agent was always accompanied by a constable from Burra. There was nothing the people dreaded or resented more than eviction ; it was the utmost calamity, and brought out a wild grief and anger. The lamentations of the evicted family and its sympathisers would rise up like the keening at a wake, in it the suffering of a whole people. The island belonged to a Lady Bannerdown, Anglo-Irish and Protestant ; she was said to live in great style in Dublin, and to have a castle on an island off the Kerry peninsula ; she had never set foot in Rull, but there were stories of cottiers' carts being whipped off the road by her servants to make room for her carriage passing through Burra. After the last eviction her agent had been found bound and gagged and clubbed in a wood on her Kerry estate, and it could not be fastened on to the evicted family, for they had never stirred out of Rull, where they were sheltered by neighbours. It was never fastened on to anyone, said old Mrs. Rooney, for who would tell of strong young men putting out in curaghs after dark and heading for the mainland and returning before 'twas dawn?

In Rull every family lived off its potato patch and fishing, and in each case the pig was ' the gentleman that paid the rent '. A few families had cattle, black bullocks for the most part that were sold on fair-days at Burra or Cork and sent inland to be fattened up, since there was not enough pasturage in the island ; a few had cows, and most had goats. It did not take Jesse long to realise that his fine ideas for the improvement of the land were impracticable, for the simple reason that there was no money to spare for the introduction of more cattle into the island, and not enough grass even had the money been forthcoming, and the potato patch which had to feed the family and fatten the pig left no room for the cultivation of roots for winter fodder. His ambition to grow swede-turnips and green vegetables, and to drain the land, collapsed before the realisation of the number of potatoes he needed to grow, and the impossibility of sparing what little money he handled for anything but the sheerest necessities. His theories were all sound enough, but there was no surplus, either of land or money, for carrying them out. He realised that what had at first seemed to him the inertia of the people was merely acceptance of the natural conditions and the system of land tenure under which they lived. Periodic outbreaks of ' Whiteboyism ' after a bad winter

elieved the pressure of resentment, but solved nothing, and Jesse was
driven back upon the bitter reflection that, for Ireland as for England,
o long as there was landlordism there would be poverty, and starvation
in the midst of plenty. The land-owners were the enemies of the
people, and the people lived out their lives between smouldering revolt
on the one hand and a half-superstitious, half-religious, fatalism on the
other. It was the fatalism of a people who had for generations expected
nothing of life on this earth, but who hoped for heaven at the end.
It was ' a black iniquity ', but it was also ' the will of God ' that things
should be as they were.

Jesse brooded upon it all as he had brooded upon the slow defeat of
the English countryside, but he did not see himself in the role old Mrs.
Rooney suggested might be his. As a boy, he remembered, he had had
romantic fantasies of leading bread-or-blood marchers out of the valley,
with banners bearing defiant slogans and pikes glittering in the brave
sunshine, but after the sense of defeat that held the countryside entered
into him and the lack of peace within himself conspired with it ; he had
to liberate himself before he could hope even to assist with the liberation
of others. He had come to the island, and he had found love, but
there was still no reconciliation with life, none of the rest that peace
begets ; there was the daily physical struggle with earth and sea, and
always, behind everything else, the unlifted darkness of that night with
Sally on the rocks.

It did not occur to him, any more than to Ria or the others, that a
better living might be made on the mainland, where there was water,
and where it was possible to dig a few feet without coming to the bare
rock. For hundreds of years people had lived in Rull, grappling with
its deficiencies, accepting the hardships of life there as inevitable,
taking what comfort they could from the reflection that for the poor
life was much the same everywhere, and quite unable to think of
anywhere else as ' home '. Jesse accepted Rull as part of his destiny ;
had not fate washed him up on its rocky shore? And was it not Ria's
home? The Rooneys had been born and lived and died there for
generations ; they were not to be uprooted now. Bound up with the
fatalism of the islanders, too, was a kind of stubborn pride ; they were
not to be defeated either by the landlord or by natural conditions.
They did not belong to the mainland ; they were island folk, born and
bred, and if it was your nature to live on a rock in the ocean you were
never really happy anywhere else, and it was generally believed that
if you went away sooner or later you would come back. People sometimes went from Rull to the mainland, or all the way to America, but
in the end the homesickness became too much for them. They had
' the strong nature in them ', and had to return to where they belonged.
That was the way it was. And in Rull at least you were your own

master ; you were not required to give your services for the leaking roof over your head and the patch of ground by which you lived. Not to be a mere labourer was a great thing. It gave you leave to call your soul—if nothing else—your own.

In short, as old Mrs. Rooney pointed out, and as Jesse soon discovered for himself, you had to learn to be grateful for small mercies and not fret about tomorrow. Tomorrow, in any case, never came ; there was always only today, and you could, after all, only live one day at a time, and sooner or later, by the grace of God, there would be a wake or a wedding, or a landlord's agent found with his head bashed in, to take your mind off your troubles. . . .

V

As it turned out, the next event of importance to Rull was not the death of George III in January of the following year, but the death of old Mrs. Rooney in the early spring. She had lived to assist with the birth of her first grandson—the other married daughter having produced only girls to date—and was looking forward to Easter and the anniversary of the wedding, but she caught a chill whilst helping with the potato-planting, and died within a few days of being confined to bed.

With her passing Jesse felt that he had lost the only person he could talk to in the island. He had found with the fiery little old woman, with her bitter tongue and rebel spirit, a mental companionship impossible with Ria, and to which she made no pretences. All Ria's non-physical life, he quickly realized, was centred in her religion ; at the core of her life was the Mass on the one hand, and on the other, the physical plane, the hearth and the bed she shared with Jesse, and all that gravitated round those things. The old woman had been in America as a young girl ; her vision was not bounded by the wave-washed rock that was the island. With her it had been possible to discuss such abstractions as justice and freedom and the rights of man. Ria's innate fatalism made any such discussion with her impossible, even if she had been interested in the world beyond Rull, which she was not. She had been deeply devoted to her mother in spite of this temperamental difference between them, and mourned her with a wild grief which at first seemed to Jesse, unaccustomed as yet to such emotional display, inconsolable. He had been at first startled and then a little shocked by the wake ; in spite of the wailing and lamentations it seemed to him almost as much of a merrymaking as a wedding ;

certainly as much poteen was consumed. The silence and stillness of the little old woman in her rough coffin seemed to him to rebuke so much noisy mourning. He was impatient of the chatter and the morbid curiosity, and the women wrapped in their black shawls seemed to him like so many carrion crows hovering over the dead. He could not understand why people who had had no special affection for the old woman during her lifetime should so readily weep over her death; he mistook for insincerity what was in fact a child-like simplicity. Death was always sad, even though the deceased was as sure of heaven as old Mrs. Rooney. He was glad when the coffin was finally screwed down and taken away on a donkey-cart to the churchyard, the entire population of the island following, as they had followed the wedding procession a year ago.

He was startled, and a little shocked, too, when Ria's grief after the funeral, when all the guests had finally departed, turned to passion in his arms which had sought only to comfort her. He experienced a sense of shame in responding to that passion, but on that tide of emotion their second child was conceived. Ria's sister, Nora, who had come from Cork with her husband for the funeral, and who was accommodated with her man at the priest's house, also conceived that night, a fact which, when he was acquainted of it some months later, Jesse found inexpressibly shocking, though he said nothing to Ria.

It was some time before he was able to accept the emotionalism of these people in all its primitive simplicity. They were as excitable as children, equally easily moved to tears or laughter; the wildness of their griefs was compensated for by the facility with which they recovered from them, so that to an outsider they seemed, confusingly, both tender-hearted and heartless. A wild grief transmuted to a no less wild passion was a perfectly natural transmutation, since it was all part of the same roused emotionalism, the same excitability; but Jesse had to shed much more of his English reserve and his innate non-conformist moral pretences before he was capable of comprehending this simplicity and lack of pretence.

He was fulfilled in his hope that this second child, born at the end of the same year as the first, should be a girl. At his request she was called Mary, Ria and her mother having had their own way in calling the first child Patrick. In calling her Mary he had the feeling of wiping out some of the guilt of her conception. Ria was pleased to call the child Mary because it was a holy name; it was holy for Jesse too, but for a reason which had nothing to do with religion. Deep down in him Mary Byrd was still enthroned as the remote, impossible ideal of the fairest among women, his love for her a morning-star, for ever poised above an incorporeal, visionary dawn. But of this, Ria, who knew all about Lucy and Sally, knew nothing.

181

The following spring Martin left the island to begin his own married life in Burra, and Ria's third child, another son, whom they called John, was begotten of that festivity.

As his family increased Jesse had less time in which to think about improving living conditions and the land, and in any case no money to spare for any such plans. 'Hallard's place' was still the best-kept and the most productive in the island, but at best it only yielded a bare living, and for all its neatness of whitened stones and well-kept thatch remained a hovel with an earth floor and no windows. At first he had missed the comforts of Valley Farm and the good food, and even more the efficient farming and domestic implements, but as the children arrived in quick succession he accepted the hand-to-mouth, day-to-day existence the island demanded, and by the time he had been there a year or two had almost forgotten a better-fed, better-ordered, less strenuous existence. He did a little poaching on the mainland from time to time, with Clancy Byrne, an older brother of Seamus'; but for the market always, never for the pot, in order to be able to buy the next sack of seed potatoes, or a young pig on fair-day, and always at the back of his mind was the anxiety to keep the rent going.

In his preoccupation with the struggle for existence for himself and his family the past receded from him as though it had been no more than a dream. The time when he had been 'handsome Jess Hallard' of Valley Farm seemed remote to the point of unreality. He would try to remind himself, sometimes, that he had parents and a brother still living; that there were people who remembered him and perhaps spoke of him sometimes and speculated as to what might have happened to him, and as to whether he was or was not responsible for the death of Sally Lane. But always the figure he saw in that dead life seemed to bear no relation to this self that was married to Ria and was the father of her children; there was no reality but the present, yet that too assumed at times the quality of a dream. He had repeatedly that feeling of the mists and rains that so frequently swept the island having got into him, filling him with their greyness, like a sleep, and the stillness seemed to enter into him so that he became part of it, speaking but little, smiling sometimes, absently, at a child, his eyes full of a grey distance. They said of him in the island that he was 'kind of silent', but many of them were that, since unless there was a fight, a wedding, or a death, there was little to talk about, unless you were full of poteen, or the mood for story-telling was on you. They said of him, too, that he was 'a fine figure of a man', but this roused no special interest amongst a people where physical beauty was the rule rather than the exception; Jesse Hallard was tall and dark and wild-looking, with fine eyes and a smile to melt your heart, and he walked as though he owned the earth, but most of the young men were like that, and why wouldn't they be, since they were all descended from kings and queens, and if a man was young and proud and lusty why wouldn't he be aisy on the eye? Only the old were ugly, but by then it was no matter, since you were about to finish with the flesh for good.

With nothing to mark the days, Jesse lost count ; there were Holy Days, and there were seasons ; there was a time for planting potatoes and a time for taking them up ; there were autumn gales, and the days growing shorter and colder, and a powder of snow on the distant hills ; there were months of driving rain and the whole island running with water ; there was the gradual reassertion of spring ; there was the fuchsia rioting in crimson showers along the stone walls once more, and the bogs starred with flowers ; there was the lobster season, and money a little more plentiful ; by such things was time measured, and the days of the week and the names of the months were as unimportant as the hours measured by clocks.

For the rest, there were births and deaths, wakes and weddings, and the consumption of poteen was equally great at both. There were the sad wild songs and the endless story-telling, and the wild keening for the dead, as though the living would release their souls to join the departed. There was the smoke blown down the chimneys and the rain under the doors and the patches of damp coming out in the walls. There was summer and the yellow roses blooming once more by his reverence's door. There were the sweet, melancholy long light nights and all the stones giving back at sundown the warmth they had held all day. There were the cries of the curlews, full of loneliness, and the island floating like a mirage in a colourless sea. And at all times the sense of isolation, of being beyond the world.

2

Jesse was popular in Rull, as he had always been amongst poor and humble and simple people. The first instinctive mistrust of him as an Englishman was readily dispelled by his friendly easy manner, and the charm which he knew how to exploit when it suited him. They discovered that he was a man after their own hearts ; a darlin' man. . . .

The Byrnes were his first friends in the island. They were the nearest neighbours, living in what was really two cabins, the family having ' built on ' as it increased. Mrs. Byrne had had ten children and raised eight, of whom Seamus was the youngest, not counting a little girl she had adopted from a poverty-stricken family on the mainland. The little girl had flaming red hair and was always referred to in conse-

183

quence as Red Bridie, her name being Bride. Mrs. Byrne had adopted
her shortly after her husband had been drowned when out fishing in
the sound in wild weather. She would be nice company for Seamus,
she said, and you could never have too many children in a house. That
anyone as poor as Mrs. Byrne, and who already had eight children,
should wish to adopt another seemed astonishing to Jesse, but no one
in Rull thought it in the least extraordinary ; one more mouth to feed
made no difference when there were a number of you. Mrs. Byrne
declared that she liked young people about her ; Patrick had been
like that, too, God rest his memory. She was never happier than
when the entire family crowded into the cabin kitchen and raised the
dust with their dancing feet. They were obliged to prop up the ceiling
with posts when they danced because there was a loft over the cabin
and vibration was like to bring it down. There were so many of
them, counting the husbands and wives of the married ones, that a
gathering of the Byrne family was a party in itself, with no need of
outsiders. " Isn't it the great advantage of a fine large family the like
of ours? " Mrs. Byrne demanded. She liked to sit by the fire, a massive
elderly woman with faded fair hair and brilliant blue eyes, wrapped in
her black shawl, watching the young people dancing jigs and reels and
joining in their wild songs. She drank poteen and smoked a clay pipe,
and when she laughed, which she did frequently, threw back her head
and slapped her thighs like a man. It was one of her boasts that she
could spit as far as any man.

Living with her were, besides Seamus and Red Bridie, two girls,
Moira and Sheila, aged seventeen and eighteen, two sons, Angus aged
twenty, and Clancy aged twenty-one. The two eldest daughters,
Frances aged twenty-three, and Louie a year older, were both married
and living in Rull, as also was the eldest son, Patrick, aged twenty-four.
Sheila flirted mildly with Jesse, and Clancy liked to go with him on
poaching expeditions on the mainland. He wanted to go to America,
but that would leave only Angus and the girls to manage the place,
and they had three cows. He was a restless, eager, good-looking youth,
and Jesse formed a great affection for him.

The Byrnes occupied somewhat the same position in Jesse's life
as the Mortimers had at one time ; their cabin was a place in which he
always felt at home, sure of a welcome, and their perpetual gaiety
lifted him out of his black moods. Ria was just a little disapproving
of them. They were too ' riotous ', she said, and also she was a little
jealous of the fact that they had three cows. And Patrick had married
that fat plain Mary Reilly instead of herself . . . though now that she
had Jesse she could afford to forgive him this, since Jesse was easily
the handsomest man in Rull, and it was a good thing, entirely, he had
been washed up at Rull, for the Byrne boys were becoming altogether

too conceited, the way it made you want to take them down a peg or two, particularly young Clancy, with his flashing eyes bluer than the summer sea, and a smile like the sun itself. . . .

The Byrnes represented warmth and friendship, but not even Clancy could satisfy his need for someone to talk to. Clancy was gay, fatalistic, indifferent.

" Ah, sure, 'twill all be the same a hundred years hence ! " was his invariable reply to any attempts Jesse made to discuss English oppression and the evils of the social systems in general and landlordism in particular.

" A hundred years hence 'twill all be very different ! " Jesse would declare, passionately, but young Clancy was not interested, and suddenly Jesse, a few months younger, would feel very old, and a great weariness fill him. At such times he longed for the companionship he had known with Jack Mortimer, in whom resentment of injustice, and revolt against it, had produced a bitter, flame-like anger. He found relaxation with the Byrnes, but not stimulus. Part of the relaxation he felt with them lay in his awareness of their family unity. His own family life had been all conflict, alliances of parents against children and children against parents, with John torn between loyalty to his mother and his feeling for his brother and sister. There had been all the hate and resentment roused by the beatings, and all the fear in the religious teaching. Home had always been a place to escape from. But the Byrnes flowed with completely mutual love and goodwill ; they liked each other and were amused by each other, and the mother instead of being a source of conflict was the centre of all this goodwill and affection and happiness. They called her by her name, Maureen, as though she were of their generation ; the fact that she was their mother seemed to them purely incidental. They did not dutifully love her ; they liked her as a person, and they all found each other good company and played up to each other, and laughed till the tears ran down their faces, and cried on each other's shoulders when the poteen worked in them, or when they told each other sad stories, as they sometimes did, till one of them would think of or invent something amusing, and they would all laugh again, ' fit to blow the roof off entirely '.

Moira married and went to live in another part of the island ; Angus married and brought his bride to live there ; Bridie of the flaming hair grew up and flirted a little with Jesse in place of Sheila, who was by then interested in someone who might marry her, though it was well known that the men of Rull were long a-courting and slow of marrying, and middle-aged marriages were common in those parts, all on the principle of ' there's time enough'. It was vaguely understood that Clancy had a girl in Burra, but Jesse suspected that he liked too many girls to settle down with one. There were times when Jesse felt more companionship with the silent young Seamus than with the irresponsible Clancy, despite his affection for him.

" Ah, they've no more brains than the back of me foot, and that sees nothing but mud ! " Ria would exclaim of the whole family, impatiently, though she was inclined to mother Seamus and Bridie, and had a secret soft spot in her heart for the good-looking, happy-go-lucky Clancy.

Another family with whom Jesse formed an easy, intimate friendship was the weaver's, Tim Reilly, the brother of ' that one ', as Ria always referred to her, disdainfully, that Patrick had had the bad taste to marry. When Jesse first came to Rull Reilly was a gaunt, starved-looking man of about thirty, with a young wife and two young children. One room of their cabin was entirely given over to the loom, and here was woven the material of most of the clothing worn in the island. The women spun the yarn themselves at home and brought it to Reilly to weave for them. He wove them a strong coarse flannel from which they made waistcoats and shirts for their menfolk, and, dyed a bright warm red, petticoats for themselves. For coats and trousers for the men he gave them à closely woven frieze that kept out the weather. He worked at his loom day and night but remained one of the poorest men in Rull. He could not charge more than a few pence a yard for the material he wove, because no one could have afforded to pay more. His home was more neglected than most because his wife was too busy looking after the potato patch and the chickens and the children to have time for much sweeping and cleaning. She was very pale and delicate-looking, which, in a community of brown, sturdy, robust women, made her conspicuous ; she even had very pale-blue eyes, and very pale fair hair, and she produced pale delicate children whose noses were always running and who cried more than most children when they were teething. She was very thin, and her shoulders were rounded and drooping, though when Jesse first met her she could not have been more than twenty-two or twenty-three. It seemed to him almost a miracle that anyone so frail should have been born and bred amongst that wilderness of stones and survived its wild weather.

She was silent and withdrawn, and at first Jesse had been inclined to disregard her curiously tentative presence ; then one day as he leaned in the doorway talking to Reilly he surprised a look of extraordinary tenderness on her face as she crooned over a whimpering child, and suddenly realized that she had beauty. It gave him a sensation almost of shock. After that he was sensitively aware of her. Her unobtrusiveness was such that her personality was always suggested rather than stated, and after the definiteness that was Ria, and the assertiveness of the Byrnes, Jesse found this curiously appealing. When he addressed himself to her, and turned his charming smile on to her, deliberately exerting his charm, it gave him pleasure to see the faint colour come up into her pale cheeks, delicate as a wild-rose in an English hedge. She stirred his imagination as no one else in Rull did, though he never came closer to her in friendship than that tremulous response, never ventured to call her by her name, which was Clare, in all the years, though quite easily he slipped into calling Reilly by his Christian name.

He realised, quite early on, the devotion between those two. He had the feeling that Reilly treasured his pale, delicate young wife, as something rare in those wild parts where the women were strong and hard in physique as the men. And that her husband's love and devotion was the fire which kept her thin shivering body warm, and the flame which kept alive the spirit in it. Without such a protective, cherishing love it seemed to Jesse she could not have lived.

Reilly himself was a sombre, silent man, endlessly preoccupied with the struggle for existence. He was deeply religious, full of humility and resignation ; to complain of his lot would have been to reproach the Almighty, and that he could not do. Jesse made no attempt to challenge this attitude to life. Of what use to rouse discontent where you had no solution to offer? And he had none. That one day there would be an upsurge that would sweep the country to the point of revolution he was convinced ; the fires of resentment could not smoulder for ever ; not for ever would the poor submit to the seizure of part of their crops to pay tithes not merely for a Church in which they had no part but which they actively hated ; not for ever would they sweat out their lives in order to put rents into the pockets of absentee landlords, whose only use for the land was to make it produce money. But in the meantime, until there was that great upsurge of revolt, tearing down fences, digging up grasslands, laying a tithe- or rent-collector by the heels and knocking him on the head ilke a roosting pheasant, exciting as it was, as exciting as any adventure under the poacher's moon, was merely to risk your freedom, and it might well be your life, to no purpose. Whenever it came to a clash between peasants and military or police, the armed forces of the Crown—the hated foreign Crown—always won. When a man had a wife and children dependent on him, like weaver Reilly, or Jesse Hallard, they did better to remain at home, biding their time. Jesse did not have to live long in Rull before he lost his impatience with the islanders in their fatalistic resignation. It was their way of coming to terms with life ; behind them was always the vast comforting illusion of the Church with its promise of heaven when the struggle on earth was done. The poor had to believe that theirs was the Kingdom of Heaven ; they had nothing else to believe in. They had to look to the Church for comfort, for there was nowhere else to look.

To the full realisation of all this Jesse came gradually as his Englishness fell away from him and he became more and more part of the life of the island ; as the struggle that was that life laid hold of him, moulding him to the island shape as the gales bent and moulded the few stunted trees, so that no other shape was possible for them.

They left him spiritually lonely, the boisterous, happy Byrnes, the silent, withdrawn Reillys, but they gave him something, too ; from the Byrnes he gained another and happier conception of home life, from the Reillys a quietness he needed, a resignation that was its own kind of reconciling. The flame of Bridie's red hair lit something in his heart, something that had to do with gipsy fires and his love for Jessica. If Clancy failed him in some respects he was his salvation in others, for showing him how to set a wire for a rabbit the strain of his responsibilities as a husband and father would be lifted from him ; he needed that reassertion of youthful adventurousness. He needed to laugh till his sides ached with preposterous old Mrs. Byrne, as much as he needed to sit silently with the Reillys, or lean up against a wall with Seamus, staring at nothing in particular, spitting occasionally, and letting life flow over for a little—as a respite from the daily swimming against the tide.

All his life, it seemed to him, he had been doing that—swimming against the tide, first in his conflict with his parents and their jealous, punishing, anti-life God, and then in his revolt against the injustices of the social system and its slow, insidious destruction of the land ; and now in the relentless daily struggle for existence that was life in Rull.

Jessica, he would reflect, had swum against the tide, too, and been washed up in a gipsy encampment, known her brief rapture, and died without waiting for the spring. He had been washed up on this wild wet rock in the Atlantic, and known a feeling of home-coming, found love and begotten children. But sleep after love, the inner peace that held on waking, and which was the supreme reconciliation with life, he had still to find. Little pools of peace he found in the shadows of Ria's loosened hair, but the winds and rains of the spirit still beat upon him, like waves upon rock, when he emerged from that tender shadow. His spirit was still troubled by his failure to achieve the dream of Mary, by the sense of violation over Jessica's death, and by the doubts over Sally's. Jessica's death had taken meaning from life and his marriage had failed to restore it—which also troubled him. He worried about his children, and the children as yet to be born to him. They would grow up Catholic and Irish—that is to say damned, unless something rather more than sporadic outbreaks of ' Whiteboyism ' happened. It seemed to him that he had given them nothing except life, and that life would give them only the struggle for existence, their share of the same struggle going on all round them.

But when he said this to Ria she was a little angry. "Isn't it the greatest nonsense you're after talkin'?" she demanded. "Won't they be fallin' in love, at all, and havin' the great and grand time with the courtin' and kissin' and marryin', their hearts as merry as a lark at mornin', God's blessin' on them? Isn't it any pleasure ye've had at all of our wedded life, all these years, Jesse Hallard, we two with our arms about each other in the darkness, and you after sayin' the fine poetic things that do be goin' to me heart like a sheet o' lightnin'?"

It was in his mind to answer her that once the courting and the kissing, and the poteen-drinking and the dancing and singing at the wedding, were over, and the first excitement of exploring the kingdom of the flesh together, the net of daily struggle closed round, tightening its meshes, it seemed, every year, as each new child arrived. There were the moments of blessed forgetfulness, the moments of sweetness and wild beauty and healing tenderness, but they were moments pitted against years. It was in his mind to say this to her, but since the old woman had died he seemed to have got out of the habit of talking about anything except the potato crop and the fishing and the children. Silence became for him not a matter of mood but of habit. There had never been anyone much to talk to. For a while there had been Jack Mortimer, but they had not met often; and for an even shorter while there had been Jessica, the Jessica who had turned to him after the Easter Fair. Then for a year old Mrs. Rooney. After that he had hoped for a time that there might be Father Conneely, with whom he had talked after the funeral, but it had come to nothing.

The priest was willing enough to talk, but not of the things uppermost in Jesse's mind. He was prepared to talk for days and nights on end of Celtic literature, legend, poetry, and the fine beautiful Gaelic tongue. He considered it little less than blasphemy that anyone who 'had the Irish' should speak anything else, except for the purpose of making themselves understood to strangers. He invited Jesse to his house to see his books.

Jesse was dismayed by the comfortlessness of the priest's house, for all it was the grandest house in Rull. He had always pictured it as warm and snug, full of books and old shabby comfort. Full of books it certainly was, in untidy heaps everywhere, many of them with a thin film of mildew on their covers and their pages mottled with damp. Jesse had not known a house could be as damp as Father Conneely's. On wet days the water ran down the blue-washed walls in rivulets, like rain on windows, and slid down the handrail of the banisters of the famous stairs. There were great mouldering patches of damp on the walls under the windows, and on the landing a bucket to catch the water dripping from the roof.

" 'Twould be a good thing to put a new slate or two into that roof, Father," Jesse suggested.

" Ah, sure 'tis well enough as 'tis," said his reverence, and brought out for Jesse's inspection the crumbling parchment of a centuries-old manuscript in the Gaelic. " Isn't this a beautiful thing now?" he demanded, his eyes alight with pleasure.

Jesse stared at the brown brittle page and the strange hieroglyphics and listened to the drip-drip of the rain in the bucket and the scurry of rats in the skirting and under the floor-boards. The rooms were large and bare and incredibly cold. Even the living-room, in which there was a fire, was cold. This room was considered very grand in Rull because it contained a tall, straight-backed chair which was said to be like the papal throne, a writing-desk, a table covered by a grey-white cloth off which Father Conneely ate his meals, a special chair at which to sit at this table, and another chair at which to sit at the desk, and a number of shelves upon which there were nothing but books, if you ever heard the like of it. The papal throne usually had a wet coat steaming on its back before the fire, and the remains of the last meal were usually standing on the grey-white cloth. When Father Conneely had been over in Burra there would also be a bottle of whiskey—only poteen was distilled in the island—*usquebaugh*, he called it, ' water of life', and referred Jesse to the Annals of Loch Cé. . . .

He never offered Jesse any of the precious *usquebaugh*, not from greed or discourtesy, but simply because he himself was not present in his body, but wandering about in the dust of long-dead ages ; his guest became merely a receptacle into which to throw ideas, or pour a stream of knowledge released by handling a book, letting fall a comment, following up a suggestion. Jesse was a vaguely sympathetic presence a little more intelligent than the general run of people he met nowadays ; he was literate, and not entirely absorbed in corporal things, and that was sufficient.

After his first visit to the priest's cold, damp, book-filled house Jesse had no illusions as to any satisfying friendship in that direction. He could have gained Father Conneely's attention by addressing him as a priest, but he did not want to make that appeal, and did not feel entitled to make it. He did not seek confession, though his spirit was troubled enough. He felt a need to discuss the social problems of suffering humanity which were always impinging on his consciousness, and all the spiritual problems of good and bad living, in the broadest sense, which impinged on those social problems. He was concerned with the whole problem of reconciling the grunt and sweat of the struggle for existence with a full rich life of emotional and spiritual experience. Father Conneely, it seemed to him, had great wisdom, but the wisdom of a scholar, not of experience. The sort of wisdom his brother John would acquire. He would know everything—and nothing. He would know everything that was written in books, and nothing of what was written in the heart and blood of man himself, who must always be greater than books. Jesse had a deep distrust of books, other than the Bible, in which he had found, by chance, a human wisdom of yearning flesh and spirit.

He ceased going to the priest's house in search of friendship, and went only when he had a few eggs, or an old hen for the pot, or a rabbit to sell. The house seemed to him like a shell, or a hollow ruin ; there was no warmth in it, neither physical nor any other kind ; it was womanless and childless, and a woman was needed to bring a house to life, and children to keep it vital. A woman imparted something of her own life to a house ; he was sure of it ; it was as though she put a kind of warmth and livingness into everything she touched ; as though the atmosphere itself took something from her warm body with its rich living promise of children. But the only woman who had anything to do with the priest's house was old Mrs. Byrne ; she swept and straightened and dusted, but a woman needed to live in a house for it to take from her presence, and Mrs. Byrne only came in for an hour each morning to tidy his reverence up, as she expressed it, and make a meal for him.

In the famine year of 1823, however, something happened which took Jesse back to the priest with renewed hope. There arose the leader for which the country had long waited, rallying the poor and oppressed, the homeless and hungry, behind him and the newly-founded Catholic Association. Here was the wind long awaited to fan the smouldering flame ; here was a leadership to which the humblest could respond, since every parish had its priest, and every priest was behind ' the Liberator '. All the hopes and dreams of a suffering—in many cases starving—people were concentrated in this young barrister, through the medium they best understood, the local priest and the Church, so that in spite of the misery, as the bad harvest followed the bad potato crop, excitement swept the country from end to end. This, it seemed to Jesse, marvelling, was the great upsurge for which he had waited, and which alone could liberate a people from the yoke of poverty and oppression. O'Connell's name was on every tongue, and eyes sunken with hunger flashed with excitement and hope, and the gnawing in the pit of the stomach lessened a little in the eager exchange of heartening stories, a great many of them exaggerated or entirely fictitious, of what O'Connell had said here, what he had said there, what ' the boys ' of this or that county had done—a story of burnt ricks,

191

fired farms, bludgeoned landlords and their agents, of a dashing and mysterious ' Captain Moonlight ' who rode by night with a band of followers, terrorising the oppressors who exported the corn the people needed, and turned starving families out into the ditch because with nothing to fatten the pig on they could not find the rent, and extorted tithes for a foreign Church, and how the English Parliament was at its wits' end. . . .

In spite of the pitiless evictions and the hunger, ' The old country is coming to itself again ! ' they said—out in their curaghs, in their cabins, in the market-place and along the quayside of the mainland. Stories were told of tithe-collectors thrown into the sea, or left bound and gagged amongst the rocks of the sea-shore, or in ' a nice small handy bit of a wood ', and the priests giving God's blessing on it all, and preaching in their churches that it was right to refuse to pay, and up Catholic Ireland and Daniel O'Connell. . . .

The Byrne boys went over to Burra night after night to join some gang intent on adding its share of terrorism to the general agitation. This was something a good deal more exciting than poaching, or making and disposing of illicit spirit, and it took your mind off your belly for a while. They were joined by the O'Sheas and other of the unmarried young men of the island. The married ones were less adventurous and were to a great extent held back by their womenfolk, but in the blood of every man and woman there leapt an eager excitement, a sense of triumphant assertion.

Father Conneely gave O'Connell his blessing, but preached against secret societies and recourse to violence. He was deeply distressed by the outbreaks of rick-burning and hooliganism all over the country, and by the fact that the young men of Rull were taking part in these disturbances. Not by such means was Catholic Ireland to be liberated, he declared. Mr. O'Connell himself did not call for such action, but only that the people should resist paying the tithes and press for the Catholic Emancipation Act. He pointed out that Rull was not one of those areas where the owners of potato patches were called upon to pay tithes, and as tithes were not payable on pasture-land not even the Byrnes, who could be considered small farmers, paid. There was no excuse for the young men of Rull participating in the disorder. He himself strongly supported the Association, and was prepared to work for it in every way open to him as a priest, but individual acts of violence could only bring calamity without helping the holy cause.

Jesse was at first dismayed and then furious when he was informed of the priest's pronouncement in chapel, and he called at the damp book-filled house once more.

" Everyone is saying you are not behind the people, Father, and there is bitter disappointment. I have had your sermon in chapel today translated to me, and it makes no kind of sense. This is the revolt we have waited for—are the people not to accept it? "

Father Conneely brought his gaze back from eternity and his mind back from the past and turned his eyes, the colour of the sea, upon the young man.

" It is the duty of every Irish Catholic to support the Association. Let the people refuse to pay tithes, let the priesthood make clear its opposition to every party opposing Catholic emancipation—what has this to do with Captain Moonlight, and Moll Doyle and her Children, and all such ruffianism? "

Jesse cried, passionately, " For years the people have submitted to the ruffianism of the landlords and their henchmen. Now 'tis the turn of the people ! Before the people were organised individual acts were useless. Now every individual act is part of an organised whole. 'Tis the expression of organised revolt——"

" 'Tis the expression of Original Sin ! " the priest retorted, adding : " What good does it do when fine young men are sent to the gallows, or cast into prison or transported overseas? In this island no one pays tithes——"

" But we pay rent, by God, almost the whole of our earnings ! And if we don't pay tithes ourselves are we not to stand by others that do? Is that your Christian spirit, Father? "

" Destroying property and assaulting persons is standing by no one but the Devil ! " Father Conneely sighed. " For the young men who go gallivantin' to the mainland every night seeking their Captain Moonlight 'tis nothing but a grand adventure, I'm thinking, and little they're caring for the Emancipation Act or any other ! What thought has Clancy Byrne or Festy O'Shea or any of them ever given to the evils of the times that now their blood should be so hot for justice? "

Jesse left the priest unconvinced. He told himself bitterly that it was what might have been expected from a man who loved books and stones more than men and women, who listened to the confessions of men and women yet had himself no real contact with the living world. But for Ria and the babes he would have been out with Clancy and Festy and the others on their nocturnal adventures. This was the ancient guerilla warfare between the possessing classes and the dispossessed, and all his poacher's blood leapt up in response to it ; but now it was something a thousand times more important than the war between gamekeepers and labourers turned poachers ; this was a war which had to have a culminating point, and upon its outcome depended the life of a whole people.

Old Mrs. Byrne was full of the exploits of her sons, Angus and Clancy, and continually lamenting the fact that she was old and fat and a woman and unable to take a hand herself. Tim Reilly was inclined to take the priest's point of view that no good would come of hitting a few tithe-proctors over the head, though, mind you, 'twas always a good thing to be doing ' for the principle of the thing '. His wife merely hoped that the fine brave boys would not be after landing themselves in trouble with the military and the police, and she crossed herself as she said it. Ria's attitude was similar, except that her heart quickened with a thrill of triumph every time she heard of a tithe-collector being thrown into the sea, and with a fine sense of pride when she heard of families who had refused to pay the tithes and were being distrained upon barricading themselves in their house and stoning the distraining parties from the loft as they approached.

It went on for some months before the authorities got the upper hand completely and restored something like order in the country, then, before the severity of the measures taken to suppress it, and the people's realisation of the ineffectiveness—apart from personal satisfaction and the settlement of personal grudges—of such tactics, the terrorist campaign subsided, though O'Connell's went on as vehemently as ever, the whole country tingling with pride and expectancy before the impact of his mighty rhetoric. Resistance to the payment of tithes went on, and there were sporadic outbreaks of violence. ' Captain Moonlight ' still rode with his band of followers in different parts of the country—a legendary figure who had yet enough of reality to leave a fair amount of arson and destruction in his wake.

Rull survived the famine without deaths or evictions. There was the fishing and there was the goats' milk. Jesse, with English persistence, had managed to raise a few green vegetables and was able through them to ward off the skin disease which affected most of the islanders as the year went on. It tormented him more than hunger to see the dark circles round Ria's eyes developing into hollows as starvation got a grip on her. But they were all hollow-eyed, and all the adults were sacrificing themselves for the children ; at all costs the milk had to be saved for the children. Father Conneely did what he could, bringing out such meagre reserves as he had and distributing them, and making persistent efforts on the mainland to secure the relief from England that was always expected but never seemed to arrive. It was through his personal influence with Lady Bannerdown that there were no evictions, though the Byrnes were the only ones who were able to meet the rent when it fell due, and they did that only by the sale of a cow in calf. He sent letters to America, and later in the year parcels of food began to arrive. The island survived, but it was a terrible year, some said as bad as 1811 ; others said it was worse. They prayed with Father Conneely, and they pinned their faith to Daniel O'Connell, and thanked God they were still alive. Things might be worse, they said. Though how much worse they had yet to earn ; they lived of necessity one difficult day at a time, and 1833 was a decade ahead, and she who was to be the ' famine queen ' of 1847 till a child at Kensington Palace. . . .

VI

THE following year Rull paid the price of its part in the general insurgence. Clancy Byrne was brought back dead, shot in an affray with the soldiery. Angus and the O'Sheas carried his body up over the beach in the pale soft light of summer dawn. There was that mistiness and stillness in the air which promised a grand day. Angus' wife Rosaleen was standing in the doorway looking out over the bay and saw the curaghs come in. She looked fine and beautiful with her night-dark hair and her red petticoat, and her strong bare brown legs, and her breasts lifted to drink in the clean cool sweetness of the morning air. And fine and beautiful were the purple-blue mountains with the plumes of thin cloud on them that morning, and the brown rocks with the golden seaweed that seemed luminous in the soft clear light. Fine and proud Angus looked, standing up in the curagh with his fair hair lifted by the breeze, then bending his strong slender young body as the boat beached. Fine and proud the dark O'Sheas with their fierce eyebrows and wild melancholy dark eyes. And proud and pitiful Clancy Byrne at the bottom of the boat with the blood congealed on his face, and his blue eyes fixed and staring, and his fair hair matted with mud and blood, and mud and blood upon his good rough shirt put on clean for this last mad disastrous adventure.

The light went out of Rosaleen's face as they lifted him up out of the curagh, and the cry that she sent up roused the whole house, roused the Hallards, roused everyone in the cabins round about, set the dogs barking and the children crying, brought the whole island to life. The young came running, the old hobbling and limping ; they came barefoot and wearing flapping *pampooties*, the women with their hair loosened on their shoulders, disordered from the night, the men tousled and hardly awake. They crowded into the kitchen where there had been so much dancing and singing and laughing, and they crossed themselves, and called upon the Mother of God, and there was wild heart-rending sobbing, and an undercurrent of persistent moaning, and every now and then a wailing like the wind in the chimney on a stormy night.

Someone went for the priest ; someone else brought candles. Old Mrs. Byrne threw her petticoat over her head and rocked to and fro with a low moaning ; Bridie clung to her, weeping, begging her to be comforted, assuring her that Clancy was happy and in heaven. In all that weeping, moaning crowd only Jesse stood silently looking down at the dead boy. He knew then that he had loved Clancy, with his irresponsibility and gaiety and his reckless courage. Clancy had kept his own youth alive. Now looking at his dead body he felt old; old and tired. He knew again the anguish of spirit he had felt when he had said good-bye to Jack Mortimer at the court-house. Then, too, he remembered, there had been a sound of weeping. He was fated, it seemed, to lose the few friends he made; first Jack, then old Mrs. Rooney, and now Clancy.

He put an arm round Ria's shoulders and led her weeping out of the cottage. She was heavy with child.

" Mother of God, why did it have to be him? " she cried, over and over again.

Later in that still, golden summer day she was seized with pains, and in the dawn of the following day, after protracted and agonising labour, and with a swarm of women round her bed, was finally delivered of a male child that died almost in the moment of its birth . . . she who until then had born fine healthy children with a natural, animal ease.

Listening to her cries and moans, and to her bitter weeping when she knew that the child was dead, Jesse felt that his own cup of bitterness was full. Why had there to be such suffering, such futility? Was this agony what Jessica had known that wild March day? What purpose was there in bringing the seed to life in the womb only to destroy it? It was like planting crops and allowing the weeds to choke them.

Father Conneely offered what comfort he could, reminding him that ' the Lord giveth and the Lord taketh away ', and that ' as our days so shall our strength be ', and speaking of Divine Purpose hidden from human comprehension. The gentle, earnest words flowed over Jesse like water over a rock, leaving him sullen and resentful. What was this monster of a God who had destroyed the life in Jessica's womb, and Jessica with it, and destroyed this latest child of his and Ria's in the very moment of its birth, and caused Ria to cry aloud with the agony of tortured flesh? Was there truly any Divine Purpose behind the confused pattern of living? It was difficult to believe. Why must Clancy, who was young and full of laughter and warmth and courage, be taken when brutes and bullies and tricksters remained? It made no kind of sense that he could see, and drained life of all meaning.

At Clancy's funeral next day the keen went to his heart like a knife. The very gulls wheeling and dipping and crying overhead seemed to take part in it ; their querulousness and the wail of the keen became fused in a great despairing protest against the ultimate calamity of death. He and Augus Byrne and Paddy and Festy O'Shea carried the rough home-made coffin on their shoulders, and the entire population of the island followed, a straggling procession winding its way along between the stone walls and crimson fuchsia hedges, a moving train of black shawls and red petticoats and grey-white frieze coats, a raggle-taggle of men and women, young and old, those who walked straight as gipsies, and those whose shoulders were bent with age, and with years of toil, and with them solemn-eyed children, and grey morose donkeys, all moving slowly through the sunlight, across the green and brown landscape, between the translucent blue of the sky and the deep summer blue of the sea. Bare feet and feet shuffling in *pampooties* made a flurry of white dust along the bog-road ; wild flowers and clusters of yellow roses from Father Conneely's garden wilted on the coffin. A child darted out of the procession to pick a spray of meadow-sweet from the side of the road ; a donkey sent up suddenly its own sobbing keen. The squat white cabins huddled close to the earth under their thatch, staring out sightlessly at the sea across the wilderness of stones lit by the summer flame of fuchsia ; they looked drowsy and contented and full of siesta, their whiteness brilliant in the sunlight. On the undersides of the gulls' wings as they wheeled there seemed flashes of pale green, the colour of ice, so luminous was their whiteness against the blue. The air was full of the almond scent of gorse and the green smell of grass with the sun on it. The island was no longer a wave-beaten rock, a heap of stones grey as the wind and rain ; it lay in the almost motionless blue of the sea laved in summer serenity. In that serenity the drone of a bee was commotion, and a sudden movement of cattle or sheep amongst the boulders disturbance. The sea was tinselled by the sunshine, and the mountains on the mainland were darkly purple and distant and folded in shadow.

Jesse felt his heart swell with love and grief and pity. Such beauty, and such pain.

Then they were at the little stone-built chapel, and there was a lingering smear of creamy blossom on the stunted thorns, and children's bunches of wild flowers at the foot of the great crucifix by the entrance, and a tying-up of donkeys to the rings in the white-washed wall, and the procession wound on up to the incense-smelling dusk beyond the sunlight.

Afterwards Jesse walked back with the priest, but there was nothing to say. The Lord giveth and the Lord taketh away—what was there to add to that? It was the Will of God.

The fatalism of the island was beginning to lay hold on him.

VII

THREE more live, healthy children were born to Ria and Jesse. A year after the premature birth there was another girl, whom they called Ria, and their next child was also a girl and at Jesse's wish they called her Lucy. By 1827 this child was the youngest of five.

The following year O'Connell carried the day in the County Clare and it was a foregone conclusion that with his brilliantly triumphant election the Catholic Emancipation Act would be passed. It was passed the next year and the country was wild with joy. The triumph, however, was short-lived, for a few months later a vicious second Act was passed which reduced the electorate from 200,000 to 26,000 since by it only those paying an annual rent of ten pounds were eligible for a vote. Those who had risked eviction and victimisation by voting for O'Connell, their contribution to the great ideal of the Catholic Association, that is to say the great mass of forty-shillings-a-year tenants, were left voiceless. It had taken great courage for the very poor, their lives dominated by Protestant landlords, to vote for O'Connell, but they had had that courage, and on it the 'Liberator' had swept to victory. Theirs was the brief glory of Catholic emancipation, and theirs the bitter aftermath of its betrayal.

Black hatred filled Jesse's heart; it seemed to him a miracle that the very stones of Ireland did not cry out to God. Truly, as old Mrs. Rooney had said, the same ruling class persecuted both its own people at home and the Irish poor. As when he had been a shocked and bewildered boy, he asked himself then as a man, was there no justice anywhere for the common people? And if men like Mr. Cobbett and Sir Francis Burdett at home, and Daniel O'Connell in Ireland, could not find a way to lead the suffering masses to justice and freedom, who in God's name could? Still, within himself he felt that in the end it did not rest with politicians and leaders, however gifted, however passionately sincere, but with the people themselves. What he himself had cried wildly in the Mortimers' kitchen the day Jack had been sentenced to transportation, that it was no use leaving the fight for Reform, Justice, Truth, to the politicians, that it must come 'from us, the common people', that, he was more convinced than ever, in the face of the betrayal of Catholic emancipation, was the only way.

The reflection took his mind back to Oldport and the valley. He wondered whether there had been any more arrests for poaching in the parish, and that set him wondering about his parents, the farm, John; about the Byrds, and if Mary had married, and Lucy still haunted *The Ship's Bell*, and if José still mourned Jessica, or whether his wild young blood had found another young *gorgio* who looked like a Romany *chi*. . . .

Sometimes he would ask himself why he should care about what happened in England, since there was nothing he could do there to help the poor and dispossessed, any more than in Ireland, and since his family and friends must long ago have ceased expecting ever to set eyes on him again, and probably had no wish to. His life was rooted now in this remote wild Irish island ; he had his wife and his children ; for all its hardship and poverty it had become ' home ' in a way that Valley Farm with all its comfort had never been. England did not want him except to imprison him and perhaps even put a rope round his neck. He had finished with England, but it was as though England had not finished with him, and this had something to do with the fact of Jessica buried in the beech-wood above the chalk-pit ; and with music and candlelight and warmth at the Byrds ', and Mary's quiet face ; and in some curious inexplicable fashion with the fact that he did not know for certain whether or not he was responsible for Sally Lane's death ; England held the answer to that dark question-mark which had encircled his life since that night. There would be times when he would feel the combination of these forces, his love for Jessica, his idealisation of Mary, his torment over Sally, drawing him back as though they had thrown invisible cords around him. Then he would find himself staring at the stunted thorns round the chapel, and the few scrawny trees he had with difficulty persuaded to grow round the cabin, and the wilderness of stones spreading in all directions, and find himself thinking of English orchards in rosy bloom and green English fields and English woods full of bluebells, and a sweetness of primroses sprawling over grassy banks under English hedges, and the cottage smell of pinks in June. With a kind of sweet pain he would remember the dark red velvet of the wallflowers along the brick path in the strip of garden at the front of Valley Farm, with the duck-pond in front of it, and the cattle-yard flanked by the barn at the side, and the syringa trees at the back of the house with their white waxen load of blossom and perfume. And of the tall blue lupins shining like spears in the mellow summer evening sunlight at the smithy, and the ancient yew-tree spreading its arms protectively over the roof. He would recall the bracken-covered hills above the valley, and the beech-woods in their delicate spring green and autumn gold, and the crazy red roofs of Oldport, and the overhanging casements that seemed to lean across the narrow alleyways of streets to gossip to each other like old women, and the excitement of the coaches clattering over the cobbles. In the summer the common would be a green sea of bracken flowing away to the pyramid of the town perched up on its hill, with the masts of ships like a thin winter forest at its base. In the days when he had walked there with Jessica, before the fences went up and it ceased to be common land, it seemed to have been perpetual summer, the surrounding

199

fields always golden with buttercups, the air always drowsy with the scent of meadow-sweet and the hum of bees. All childhood was in the memory, the scene drenched in sunshine, pouring rich and clear from cloudless blue skies. Here the sunlight, even on the brightest days, came diffused through a thin veiling of mist, the sky low and heavy with cloud ; there was a kind of twilight even at noon, a wild, sad light, and with it the timelessness of wilderness without trees to mark the seasons. He never ceased to love that strange, ' lost ' landscape steeped in its unearthly light, but he would have moods of increasing nostalgia for English hedges with their riot of nut-trees and hawthorn and wild rose and brambles, for English fields in June, and the scent of honeysuckle on the air, for the stubble-fields of autumn, and the pheasants coming out along the hedgerows after the berries ; for the excitement of starting up a hare, and the satisfaction of the crick of a rabbit's neck under his hands, with a soft rustling of hazel trees overhead and a soft crackle of dry bracken underfoot. For the authentic thrill of poaching you needed the English setting. There was, also, no thrill in breaking the law in a naturally lawless country.

He would fall into reveries of life as he had once known it as he sat beside the turf fire in the dark, primitive cabin, or when he was out alone in the curagh after pollock, or inspecting his lobster-pots. Sometimes the song Mary had sung would run through his head, and he would hear again the thin sweet notes of the spinet, and see her face with its remote drawn look. New vistas had opened up for him that night when, as a boy, he had discovered *The Song of Songs*. He had glimpsed a world of poetry and music of which he knew nothing, but whose beauty stirred him deeply and in some curious fashion reconciled him to the pain and ugliness in life. He had so greatly needed at that time ' the rest that peace begets ', the sleep that reconciled—but it had to be sleep after love, he had insisted, in a sudden flash of insight which music and poetry and Mary's presence had kindled in him. He would remind himself that now he had a woman who passionately loved him, his wife and the mother of his children, and whom he dearly and passionately loved ; that he had come to the island of his dreams at last, and found sanctuary there, and struck roots into its soil ; but when the nostalgia was on him such reminders would avail him nothing ; then he would feel imprisoned in the island, and in Ria's arms, and become moody and silent, and go off alone to the other side of the island, straining his eyes out to sea after England-bound ships, and envying the gulls their freedom. At such times he would believe that if only he could see Mary again even at a distance he could be content. The past threw invisible cords around him and drew him back. It was as though he had to be reassured that the old world was still there, that this wave-washed rock on which he lived out his life was not the prison it sometimes seemed, but that he could go out from it to the wider world. Then he would remind himself that it could be nothing but folly to go back ; that he was wanted by the police, that he had a woman's death on his hands, that it was crazy even to think of it. But the desire worked in him with the relentlessness of a fever. He became obsessed by the idea that just to return to Oldport anonymously, tread its cobbled streets once more, enter *The Ship's Bell*, see the giant sunflowers outside the smithy, and the post-road running out from the town through the valley, would allay his restlessness, afford him satisfaction. He was like a child needing the reassurance of its mother's presence.

For five years he knew this recurrent homesickness which was always intensified by visits to the mainland, because the mainland was the road back. He never spoke to Ria of this restlessness, but she sensed it in him as time went on, and tried to bind him closer in the only way she knew, through the physical bonds of his need for her, and her need for him, their marriedness, and the children ; she came to recognise the significance of the dark look on his face on the days he returned from Burra, and when he leaned against the gable of the house staring out at passing ships outside the bay, following the flight of a gull with a curious yearning look. She would be troubled, then, and pray for him, that he might be given the grace to remain contentedly with her and the children, that she might be given the power to hold him through her love.

In the spring of 1830 she bore another son, whom they called Clancy. By that time the two eldest children, Patrick and Mary, were so like the children who had been Jesse and Jessica Hallard that their father would gaze at them in wonderment, and when Mary looked out under a tangle of dark hair like a wild creature from a thicket he would turn aside with a sudden intolerable pain.

Patrick was always watching the ships crossing the bay ; always asking questions of what lay beyond, bringing Jesse up against the limitations of his own knowledge. At those times he envied John his book-learning so that he could answer the innumerable questions more adequately. The boy liked to go with his father into Burra and mix with the crowd along the jetty and in the market-place. He was excited by the feeling of life and movement in the little town, as the boy Jesse had been in Oldport, twenty years or so ago. When his mother told him about America and ' Uncle Brian ' he announced his intention of going there one day himself. When his father told him about England he wanted to go there too. Then Mary would declare that wherever Patrick went she would go too, but Patrick would shake his dark head at that ; such adventures were not for girls—and Jesse would have an almost anguished realisation of the little sister shut out from her brother's dreams.

An old deep pain would stir in him watching his children. He envied Ria her casual, easy acceptance of them; she loved them dearly, but he had the feeling that she knew nothing about them once they had ceased to be babies; she was always, he felt, preoccupied with the youngest child, or with the unborn child. After the child who died she was not happy again till she was with child once more. She never worried about the additional burden each child represented; she accepted implicitly the priest's easy assurance that God would provide, and, whatever Jesse might think about it, it seemed to her that God did provide, since with the one exception the children thrived, and somehow they managed to find the rent, and there was always goats' milk and potatoes if nothing else. Jesse seemed to her to worry needlessly. He was still too English, after all the years, she often thought, too careful, too full of anxiety for the morrow.

It was not easy at first for Jesse to see his children running about barefoot, and to know that they ate little but potatoes and milk and salted fish. That Jesse Hallard's children should be ragged and shoeless was an affront to his pride; he had moments of misgiving in which he asked himself if he had any right to bring them into the world if this was the best he could do for them. As a mother Ria seemed to him astonishingly and alarmingly casual on occasion. He and Jessica and John had been so carefully brought up, with woollen stockings and underwear in winter, and never allowed to sit on damp grass or get their feet wet, and their chests rubbed with warm oil when they had colds, and steaming balsams to inhale, and mugs of hot milk at bedtime, and a vigorous washing of hands and faces night and morning, and the tall-backed hip-bath filled with hot water every Saturday night; all had been so methodical and careful, and, he supposed, in the light of the new life, so English. His own children knew nothing of all this; they sprang up from the straw mattresses in the clothes in which they had lain down at night and they raced out into the wind and rain and mist like young animals newly let out of byres and stalls. The only bath they ever knew was the sea. In the summer they were very clean because they were always in and out of the sea; in the winter they were only clean on Sundays, so that they could go decently to church. They got colds and fevers, and sweated and coughed and shivered and vomited, and somehow recovered from their ills. Their faces and limbs were very brown and their hair was always in their eyes, and they were always bounding about amongst the rocks and boulders like young mountain goats. They had the slender grace of young wild animals. In the presence of strangers, as when Nora and her husband came visiting from Cork, or when they were over in

202

Burra, they huddled together, shy and wild and staring ; at other times they gave an impression of their young souls being wide open to the sky, with a wild joy washing over like sunlight.

Sometimes as they swarmed about him Jesse's heart would swell with love, only to contract again with pain at the realisation of how little he could do for them. It was not as though they had been born to Jesse Hallard of Valley Farm ; they had been born to Jesse Hallard, fugitive from society . . . .

During the first few years in Rull he had thought comparatively little of the life from which he was exiled. Everything had been submerged in the strangeness of the new life, and the process of adjustment to it. He had had to learn to adapt himself not merely to a new and very much harder way of living, but to a new attitude to life, because the island was a world in which neither progress nor ambition had any part.

His world at that time was all physical. There was the physical daytime world of wresting a living from earth and sea, a world of strenuous physical labour, of struggle and sweat ; a world that was all wind and rain and driving mists, rocks and stones, turf and kelp, market-days and trampling sheep and cattle, and squawking pigs and hens, and an ever-present anxiety. And there was the physical night-time world of the inner room, of Ria's warm breasts and streaming hair, and the wild dark journeys they made together. That kingdom of the flesh he explored with her was all darkness and fire and an ecstasy he had known with none of the others, or even remotely imagined. It was all the passion of *The Song of Songs* made living in the flesh. Through Ria he lived again all the storm that was Sally, all the tender-ness that was Lucy, and in some strange, indefinable fashion much that had entered into his love for Jessica. Ria had all Jessica's gipsy quality of wildness and lostness, but beyond that a quality of vitality and strength that was peculiarly her own. On the physical plane she gave him all that he needed, but there was a point at which they went apart, in spite of love and tenderness and the common interests of children and the struggle for existence ; it was as though, ultimately, their world was bounded by the physical. Which meant that for Jesse Mary still remained the morning-star, remote and unattainable, undesiring and ever to be desired.

The greater part of Ria's non-physical life was centred in the Church ; its candles and flowers and incense and ritual, its comfort of confession and absolution, its prayers and holy mysteries and blessed saints, were for her what *The Song of Songs* had been to Jesse in his groping adolescence, and his dream of ships and far-off and foreign places and ultimate escape as he grew older, and his idealisation of Mary Byrd as he came to manhood. That is to say it was revelation and reassurance, and escape, and faith, and the road to heaven. On

Sundays and holy days she left the world of hardship and struggle and bare rock and comfortlessness, and entered a world of gentleness and beauty and peace, from which she returned refreshed and comforted in body and spirit.

Jesse had no such outlet for the non-physical part of himself. For a few years his absorption in Ria, and the new life generally, was such that it did not matter; then, gradually, as he became increasingly a part of the island life, and increasingly familiar with the kingdom of the flesh he explored with Ria, the old unrest began to stir in him again, and he began to be aware of the ships crossing the bay, to speculate upon their destinations, and as to what was happening in England—whether the flare-up of Peterloo had had any sequel, whether industry had yet invaded the valley, and what was happening to the agricultural workers. On his visits to the mainland he saw an Irish paper occasionally, but never an English one. The English sailors he sometimes met appeared to know nothing of England except the ports; the Irish who went over for seasonal work were quite useless so far as bringing information went. It was by the merest chance that he heard in 1824 of the passing of the Combination Act legalising the hitherto unlawful trade unions. This news excited him so much that he prowled hungrily round every tavern patronised by English seamen in the hope of English newspapers and first-hand information. He learned that the passing of the Act had resulted in a wave of strikes all over the country for higher wages. Something in him quickened at the news, as over Peterloo. Five years between the bread-or-blood riots and Peterloo, and four between Peterloo and the first Combination Act—things moved slowly, but they moved, proof that all the time the fire was alive and smouldering. . . . .

By 1830 the dissatisfaction throughout Ireland was acute. The emasculated Catholic Emancipation Act had not removed the hated tithes, eased the poverty of the cottiers, or made their tenure of the land more secure. The peasants still saw their crops and cattle seized to maintain a Church in which they had no part, and which was an abomination to them. Resistance hardened, and the military raided the farms and turned the people out on to the roads at the point of the bayonet. Farmers, cottiers, labourers, small-holders, armed with only sticks and reaping-hooks, faced the soldiery and the armed police unflinchingly, with a stubborn, desperate courage. At Rathcormack twelve men were killed in a struggle with a considerable armed force in an attempt to save the few poor possessions of a widow who was being distrained upon for the sum of forty shillings due for tithes. At Newtownbarry twelve peasants were shot, and twenty died of their wounds. When a raid by the military and police was expected the people erected barricades of turf and thorn and stones. They gathered at night and collected the cattle from farms where an order for distraint had been made and drove them out of the county. They attended the markets where the distrained goods and cattle were being sold and when possible pulled the auctioneer down from his box, and would-be purchasers dared not buy for fear of what would happen to them if they did. It was insurrection on a far larger scale than anything that had preceded O'Connell's election. The secret societies were ceaselessly active in spite of the savage attempts to suppress them. Captain Moonlight rode harder than ever by night, and many a fine, smiling young man, the like of young Clancy Byrne, was carried home in the morning with his eyes staring and his hair matted with blood and his decent homespun shirt torn to ribbons.

Jesse felt his heart sick within him. Would it never end, the sacrifice of these splendid, stubborn, passionate people? And what was the 'Liberator' doing in the English Parliament, what were all the politicians doing, all the champions of Catholic emancipation? Side by side with the tithes war was the agitation for the repeal of the Union. Suddenly it came to Jesse that even full Catholic emancipation, down to the re-enfranchising of the forty-shillings-a-year tenants, would not be enough; the country had to be altogether free of the English yoke, free to work out its own destiny.

He brooded on all this, and on what was happening at home, and the hunger to discover how it was with his own country worked in him like a fever. Then on a fair-day in Cork, when he was over selling a pig to raise the rent, an English sailor from one of the new coasting steamers that put in there told him that 'things were happening in England'. Four labourers had been found dead under a hedge, of starvation, and Lord Winchilsea, mentioning the matter in the House of Lords, said that this was not an exceptional case; whole families were living on roots and sorrel; they would be unable to keep body and soul together were it not for smuggling, poaching, thieving. Their fathers had lived on the fat of the land, meat, bacon, cheese, eggs a-plenty, but they lived like the Irish peasantry, on bread and potatoes. They no longer had gardens in which to grow their own produce and keep a few hens; they had no common lands on which to graze cattle; they no longer brewed their own beer; when they had any money despair drove them to the ale-houses. Four hundred labourers in Kent had just destroyed some threshing-machines, and a hundred constables and some soldiers had been sent to restore order. A farmer who had said that he would be well pleased if a plague broke out amongst the rabble, as he called them, when their carcases would at least make good manure for his hops, got his ricks fired for his pains. The destruction of the new threshing-machines that put men out of employment was going on everywhere, and big rewards were offered for informers, but there had been none. The people were not to be bribed. Farmers were receiving threatening letters with a drawing of a knife at the end, and the words, ' Beware the fatal dagger '. They were signed ' Swing '. There was an officer who had fought in the French war and who rode the countryside with a band of followers ; he was known as ' Captain Swing ', but no one rightly knew who he was. . . .

" The brother of Captain Moonlight," Jesse suggested, grimly, and gripped the sailor's arm.

" I've got to get back to England. What chances of stowing away aboard your ship? "

" No need to stow away," the sailor told him, " you could work your passage. We're a man short—a man fell down the hold and broke his neck when we were unloading."

Jesse thought rapidly. He knew that the steamer sailed at noon. There would be no time to get back and tell Ria. And, all things considered, it was better not to go back ; it was easier to go without saying goodbye. He had to go ; this was a chance which might never happen again. It was a God-sent opportunity.

He sent the rent money back to her with the message that he had gone to England and by the grace of God would be back within a few weeks ; he prayed that she would forgive him, and that she would not worry, but he had this chance to see his own country once more, and something in himself that he could not account for insisted that he must take it. . . .

When Ria received this message from Tim Reilly, who had gone over to Cork with a few rugs he had found time to weave, she stood very straight and faintly smiling, though her fingers gripping her elbows drove the nails into her flesh, as on her wedding night when she had stood on the shore watching Jesse swimming out towards the dangerous currents of the bay, and all she said was, " He had to go. 'Tis the strong nature in him sends a man back to his own people in the end."

" He'll be comin' back, ma'am, before harvestin' does be over," the weaver said, to comfort her, " there be a power o' love in him for his wife and children, I'm thinkin'."

She smiled, proudly, though her eyes blinded with tears.

" 'Tis all in the hands of God," she said, simply, and turned back into the house, where the afternoon sunlight lay in a long pool across the floor.

She did not see the steamer that carried her man away from her crossing the bay because she sat within, her petticoat thrown over her head as she rocked herself to and fro crying to the Blessed Virgin to have pity, to send him back, her dear one, the father of her little ones, her love and her darling. How should she sleep at nights without her breast pillowing the dear dark head? How should she live by day without his shadow thrown across the floor, but lying instead across her heart ?

PART III

RETURN

'Sleep after toyle, port after stormie seas . . .'

I

THAT the steamer, having called first at Plymouth, should make Oldport its next call was more than Jesse had dared hope. His heart beat heavily as they chugged up the coast, under the green and white cliffs. He was down below when the ship put into Oldport Harbour, and when he was free to come up on deck knew a sudden feeling of panic which had nothing to do with fear. He had no fear of being recognised ; he knew well enough that the gaunt, bearded islander he had become was not to be recognised as ' Handsome Jess Hallard ' who had disappeared over ten years ago. Even his voice had changed and was full of Irish inflections. His panic was a shrinking from contact with the old life again, the dread of finding it changed, the dread of finding that he himself had changed so much he could make no contact with it, and with all this the dread of that contact as an experience which might prove too much for his keyed-up nerves.

When at last he forced himself to come up on deck, blackened from shovelling coal, his clothes covered with grease and dirt, some of the quayside loungers laughed. He was like a blackamoor from a fair, they declared, or an old scarecrow beaten black by the weather. But Jesse was quite unaware of the attention he attracted. He stood staring across the quay, at the gables of *The Ship's Bell*, at the crazy-looking red roofs piled up behind. He crossed the gang-plank wonderingly, moving across the quayside as though in a dream. He was back in Oldport. He said it to himself, but he could not make it seem real. At the door of the tavern he looked back. More than one ship with funnels lay along the quayside, strange-looking ships with the lines of sailing-ships, but with paddle-wheels and funnels, and belching smoke. Graceless things they seemed to him, and his spirit was troubled.

The tavern was full of sailors, as always, but there were different faces behind the bar, and the English voices all round him had a curiously foreign sound. He had the feeling of being a stranger. He longed for, yet dreaded, the sight of a familiar face. If old Byrd should come in, or Lucy, he did not know whether he would rush forward to grasp their hands or shrink back into a corner. But there were no familiar faces and something ached in him. His memory threw up something it had absorbed years ago in the long tedium of chapel hours—' *He shall return no more to his house, neither shall his place know him any more* '. He felt the cold breath of the old teachings blow over him from the past, and shivered and ordered himself a rum, though it was high summer and the sun blazing outside.

He was served by a bar-maid in a very low-cut bodice and with a fringe curling on her forehead. He stared at her, fascinated. It was a very long time since he had seen a fashionable young woman. She smiled at him.

" 'Tis strange to be drinking rum and shivering on such a fine summer's day," she observed.

" 'Tis some sort of ague I'm after takin' in foreign parts," he told her.

" You're Irish—come over on one of the new steamships I suppose? "

" Yes," he added, eagerly, " but I used to work as labourer here. I know these parts, though it's years since I was here. I suppose there have been great changes? "

" I'd not know ; I only came here this year." She turned aside, indifferently, to serve another customer. His eyes followed her, wistfully. . . .

A man at his elbow said, " Once a man could return to a place after years and find everything as he had last known it. But not now, sailor, not now ! Once people were born and wedded and raised up families and died, and that was about all there was to it. But 'tis all different now. 'Tis a different kind of living."

Jesse turned and looked into a lined face that was both familiar and strange. It was no face that he knew, yet it was also a face he had known since he was a boy ; the face of the English farm labourer, mapped as much by hunger and anxiety as by weather and the years.

" Aye, everything is changing all the time," he went on, and sighed, and stared thoughtfully into his ale-mug. " You're off one of these new ships. You know how it is. Once it was a clean life at sea. Now you come off a ship black as a sweep. 'Tis the same with the land. 'Twas a good life once, even for poor folks. Now there are machines. Every threshing-machine a farmer puts into a barn puts fifteen men out of work from harvest till May. Did you know that, sailor? No, being a seafaring man you wouldn't. But that's how 'tis. Once the labourer's wages were helped out by common rights—free grazing, free firing. Now there are no common rights, so cows are not for poor folks, and they must go mug in hand to the farmers for a drop of butter-milk for the children. And the money buys less all round, because everything costs more. Everything goes up but the wages, and they stay the same. The farmers say 'tis impossible to pay higher wages

208

or lower the rents because of the tithes, and the rectors refuse to lower the tithes, so the farmers refuse to pay the half-crown a day most people are asking now, and the country is in a ferment."

" 'Twill be worse afore 'tis better," another man said, grimly, and there were murmurs of assent from those standing round.

" Some districts are asking only two shillings a day," said one.

" Arundel wants two-and-three," said another.

Jesse inquired, " What is the rate in this district? "

The man who had first spoken said fiercely, " We're demandin' half-a-crown, and by God we're going to get it if we have to burn down every rick and smash every threshing-machine in the parish ! "

There were murmurs of approval, and, " Aye, that's right," and, " That we are, Joe ! "

" Are the farmers coming to heel? " Jesse asked.

" Some have, but most are holding out. The biggest farmer here, John Hallard over at Valley Farm, is holding out for the Arundel rate —and what means threepence a day to him? "

" Takes after his Bible-punchin' skinflint of a father ! " someone said, viciously.

Jesse's heart quickened. " Is he dead—the old man? "

" Aye—a few years back. His heart had been troublin' him for some time, by all accounts."

" It never troubled him on account of those who toiled for him," one man observed, drily, and Jesse suddenly realised that he knew that man. His name, he remembered, was Wainwright, and he had worked at Valley Farm ; but he was bearded now and changed in ten years, like himself.

" Aye, 'twas a great pity the eldest son was not there to inherit," an old man murmured, and instantly Jesse knew that it was old Mortimer, frailer than he had remembered him, more bowed, and almost smothered now, it seemed, in ragged whiskers and a kind of scarecrow's straw hat. But the voice was the same.

In his excitement it was an effort to keep his own voice steady, but he asked with careful carelessness, " I seem to remember there was some scandal about him——"

" Aye. On account of some wench found dead on the rocks. He was the last person she was seen alive with, and that and the fact that he cleared out made it look black against him, but there's plenty never believed ill of him, for all that ! He was a good one for knockin' a hare or a pheasant over, but not a woman ! "

There was some laughter, and when it subsided Jesse asked, " What happened to him? "

" 'Tis thought he got away to sea. 'Twas a terrible disgrace to fall on a family like the Hallards."

" And comin' on top of the daughter runnin' off to London a while before," the man they addressed as Joe added, and chuckled.

A ragged dirty tramp of a man with an unkempt black beard, and heavy eyebrows coming down over wild eyes, spat suddenly and made his first contribution to the conversation.

" Whoever killed her, she was a bad one, that one found on the rocks! Played fast and loose with all the men around the town, she did, a proper Jezebel! "

There was a little winking and nudging amongst the men, and one of them patted the tramp on the shoulders, laughing.

" All right, Dad, we all know she was your light o' love and betrayed you with every tar that came ashore, not to mention Handsome Jess, but let the dead rest! "

Above the titters of laughter Jesse forced himself to ask, " Mrs. Hallard—is she still living? "

" The old lady, you mean? She survived the old man only by a year. 'Twas said she didn't get along with her daughter-in-law. She was mistress so long as the old man was alive, but when he was gone and young John took over there were two mistresses, like, and you know how 'tis, there can't be two mistresses in one house. They say she was jealous, too, Master John being the favourite son and the apple of her eye. . . . Taken all in all, she hadn't much to live for with him married and the old man gone——"

" 'Tis hard to think of John married," Jesse said, with an effort. " As I remember him he seemed a lad not likely to prove the marrying kind. Bookish, he was, and never an eye for a wench——"

" That may be, but once his handsome brother was out o' the way young John came to life, sudden like, and went courtin' Mary Byrd good and hard for the best part o' three years, and in the end she said him yea."

Jesse stared at old Mortimer and tried to give meaning to the words his ears had just heard but which his mind refused to accept.

" John Hallard married Mary Byrd, you say? "

" Aye. Love's a rare funny thing. 'Twill make a wench refuse a fine-looking man like Jess Hallard, with vigour and spirit, and accept a brother that can't hold a candle to him in any way."

Jesse asked, still full of the sense of unreality, " Have they any children? "

" Aye. A boy and a girl, and another on the way. They called the boy Jesse and the girl Jessica—she's the youngest."

Jesse felt that he had heard about as much as he could stand for the present. He had a great need to go and sit down quietly, alone, and sort everything out. There were two more questions he wanted to ask—if there was any news of Jack Mortimer, if he had returned from

Australia, and if any of them knew what had happened to a girl called Lucy Williams. But he could not bring himself to ask old Mortimer for news of Jack; to admit to the father that he had known the son might lead to too many questions; and none of the men with whom he had been talking, he felt, would know anything of Lucy; that was something he must find out from the women who would come into the tavern in the evening. She herself might come in, even, though he doubted that; she would hardly remain in the same small town for ten years. Probably it was useless to make inquiries. She would be over thirty now, he reflected. She might have found someone to marry her. Or she might be dead.

He bought beer for old Mortimer, and for Wainwright and the man who had first spoken to him, and another rum for himself, and when he had swallowed his drink gave the others ' Good-day ' and went out. Everything they had told him seemed to be going round in his head. Instinctively his feet took the road out of the town and he found himself heading for the valley.

II

As he approached the smithy panic overtook him again. He suddenly realised that he was neither prepared to meet the Byrds nor to find strangers living in the old house under the giant yew. He turned into a cornfield where the sheaves stood like golden-brown tents and worked his way along the hedge, moving with his old poacher's lightness, and instinctively on the look-out for pheasants. There were plenty of young oaks and ash-trees in which they might roost at nights . . . it was a hedge he knew of old. When a golden cock pheasant whirred up a few yards ahead of him his heart leapt with pleasure. It was a fine plump beautiful bird, and it seemed a terrible waste to be walking there with the thing within such easy range and no gun handy.

He skirted several fields golden with harvest, climbing steadily up to the ridge that flanked the Oldport side of the valley. A rough road ran along the top, and there was a belt of trees. He stopped in the shade of the trees to rest and look down on the familiar scene, then was aware that he was not alone. A tall straight-backed man, whose riding-coat somehow fitted him like a uniform, was seated on a chestnut horse and gazing intently at the valley; when he turned his head for a moment Jesse had the feeling of looking into the face of a gipsy disguised as a gentleman. It was a dark, proud, challenging face, with something wild about the eyes.

Jesse gave him 'Good-day'. The horseman regarded him for a moment, then demanded, "Are you a labourer in this parish?"

"I came off a ship this morning," Jesse told him. "'Tis ten years since I was in these parts."

"You have returned to find the whole country in the melting-pot, my good man! A child ten years old has been sent to prison for taking part in a machine-smashing riot! That is what this country has come to! Labourers are sent to prison for two years for picking up dead partridges, and the parsons take a poor man's only cow for the tithe of his cabbage garden! Small farmers are turned off their lands to make room for foxes! The children struggle with the pigs for food and sleep o' nights on damp straw under rotten thatch!"

The man's eyes blazed with a fanatic light.

"Then they call us criminals when we burn down the ricks and plunder the homes of those who grow fat on the sufferings of the poor!"

"Might I ask who you are, sir," Jesse inquired, "that you dress and speak like a gentleman and ride a blood horse, if I mistake not, yet are on the side of the common people?"

The stranger replied, with dignity, "I served as an officer in the French wars. I came home to find the peace worse than the war. In 1816 I was merely an onlooker. I had my own affairs to attend to. Now I am a free man, and ready to swing for justice if needs be!"

Jesse started. "You wouldn't be Captain Swing himself, sir, by any chance? I have heard talk of that gentleman——"

The man laughed, a short, bitter laugh that was more like a bark.

"Who is Captain Swing? Some say he is Captain Hunt. Others that he is a one-time agricultural worker who served with the artillery in the French war and that he has no just claim to a military title. Perchance Captain Swing is nought but the spirit of revolt moving the common people at last?"

Jesse sat down on a fallen tree-trunk and chewed at a stem of sorrel.

"It takes more than a spirit to send threatening letters with a drawing of a dagger at the end," he observed, "but whoever it is sends the letters signed 'Swing', God's blessing on his work, say I!"

The stranger laughed his short bitter laugh again and bowed in the saddle, then wheeled his horse and cantered away down the road in the direction of Oldport.

Jesse remained seated on the tree-trunk brooding. What the wild-eyed stranger had told him confirmed what the English sailor at Cork had said, and all he had learned on the steamer coming over, and all that he had heard in *The Ship's Bell*. When in Burra two months ago he had heard that George IV had died he had been indifferent; on the steamer they had told him that the new King,

William IV, was in favour of Reform, but that the Duke of Wellington was stubbornly resisting concessions—not for nothing was he called the Iron Duke. Not from kings and statesmen was help to be expected for the common people; 'God save the King', the people cried; it was time they cried 'God save the people', and it seemed they were beginning to realise it, but were they going the right way about it to secure their ends? Ricks and barns had been fired all over the country before now, back in 1816, and in Ireland after the betrayal of the Catholic Emancipation Act, but none of that terrorism had achieved anything—except imprisonment or transportation or death for those who took part in it. Perhaps Father Conneely had been right after all when he had urged the futility of violence? He had put his faith in God and O'Connell. But the English had not this deep belief in prayer, and there was no 'Liberator' risen up in their midst; when petitions to Parliament, and the speeches of politicians, failed they saw no alternative to violence. And they were fools, fools! They held power in their hands—if they would but realise it, a power far beyond that of kings or statesmen. They it was who by their toil made the earth bring forth; they were the producers; they it was who made the wheels go round in the factories; they even made the machines they turned upon! Why did they not withhold their labour, both in the factories and in the fields, till they were conceded a living wage? But what had happened in the countryside? In the very midst of their revolt the fools had gathered in the harvest, instead of leaving it standing in the fields; now the farmers could afford to bargain. If workers in mills and factories could strike, as they had shown they could in 1824, so could workers on the land. But instead they went rioting and plundering, burning and destroying, and it all achieved nothing except additional misery. . . .

He got up abruptly, full of a kind of angry impatience. Presently he would go back to *The Ship's Bell* and try to make old Mortimer and Wainwright and the others see the madness of their campaign and how they were squandering the precious power that was theirs. But first he had a pilgrimage to make and a confusion of personal matters to sort out.

2

He followed the ridge road along till it dropped down into the valley, which he crossed well away from the houses and then picked up the road to the chalk-pit. People passed him on the road and gave him 'Good-day' without recognising him, nor did he recognise any who addressed him, though occasionally there was a familiar inflection in a voice.

When he reached the chalk-pit he looked for the ashes of recent fires, but there were none. Had that particular tribe of gipsies ever been back during the ten years? He thought it unlikely; José had said, emphatically, with bitter passion, 'We shall never return.' But he had also said, 'If I held a thousand women to my heart *she* would still be there!' When the first wild grief had subsided he might have felt Jessica's spirit drawing him back sometimes. Ten years ago, Jesse reflected, he would have sworn that he himself would never tread that road again, traverse the chalk-pit and climb up into the woods behind.

Now those woods were deep and green with high summer, and the bluebell leaves were a thick dark grass, with a million seeded stalks to show where their flowers had been. 'They must have been a fine sight in May,' Jesse found himself thinking. He made his way through the wood and dipped down into the little hollow where the bluebell leaves were still thicker, and there were clumps of primrose leaves. The wood seemed full of bird-song and sunlight, and stillness, and the memory of spring.

At the bottom of the hollow he knelt and touched the cool damp earth.

"Jessica," he whispered, "Jessica," and his heart swelled with love and pain.

> '*Sleep is a reconciling*
> *A rest that peace begets——*'

Jessica the night of the Easter fair, with the fairing ribbons in her hair; Jessica alight and alive for the first time for months; Jessica given back to him, finally and forever. Jessica touching the silver bangle with the look of wonder in her eyes; Jessica wrapped in a gipsy shawl running to him across the chalk-pit, flinging her arms round him, assuring him of her happiness; Jessica carrying the gipsy child in her young body. Then Jessica lying on the mattress in the tent, feverish, her hair matted and neglected, gipsy coins round her neck, gipsy bracelets on her arms, babbling deliriously to him of the *rye* and the *rawnie* who loved beneath a tree in springtime, and bidding Miguel sing. . . .

He stretched himself out on the bluebell leaves, his arms flung out, his fingers dug deep into the dead leaves, as though he would reach down through the earth to embrace her, the little sister, a garden enclosed once more, a spring shut up, a fountain sealed.

> '*Sleep is a reconciling——*'

his brain repeated, and he was back again in the house under the yew-tree with his head resting a moment on Mary's breast and hearing her

214

heart beating like a trapped bird. Ten years ago he had gone from this wood to her, and found a kind of peace, a sense of reconciliation with life. Now she belonged to John, and the strangeness of that was something he could not as yet comprehend. Mary was Mrs. John Hallard of Valley Farm, and there were two children, Jesse and Jessica. Jesse and Jessica Hallard of Valley Farm. Why had John and Mary called their children Jesse and Jessica? Was it a token of forgiveness for the disgrace the first Jesse and Jessica had brought upon the house of Hallard? Was there love as well as forgiveness in that remembering? He was filled suddenly with an intense desire to see this other child who was Jessica Hallard.

He sat up, brushing the dead leaves from his sleeves, and then it was that he saw the little cross of twisted willow driven into the ground where the patch of bluebell leaves ended—as it might be at the head of a grave.

He pulled it out and fingered it, wonderingly. It was clean, not yet weather-stained, and there was sap in it still. Only the gipsies knew that Jessica was buried there. There were no signs of encampment in the chalk-pit, but one of them at least had come back, and who should that one be but José?

He replaced the cross and got up. Jessica was not forgotten, and she lived again, perhaps, in a child at Valley Farm. Now he knew for certain that he could not return to Rull without having seen this other Jessica, his brother's child, and Mary's.

'Weep you no more, sad fountains!' The melody and the words ran in him now exultingly, as he followed the road above the valley in the direction of the farm.

III

WHEN he was above the river he left the road and plunged through the bracken and heather of the hillside to the lower road and the bridge, where he dropped down over the parapet and knew again the familiar crushed-out pungency of wild mint. He washed the coal-dust and grease of the ship from his face and hands in the river, then climbed back on to the road. He began to feel hungry and wondered whether he might call at the cottage he had always known as Jordan's, lying back in a field a little further along. The cottage belonged to Valley Farm, and Jordan had been one of its labourers. Jordan's had been one of the cottages in which he had made himself at home in the old days, but they would be unlikely to recognise him now, he felt confident, and Mrs. Jordan was not one to turn away a hungry stranger on the road.

The cottage stood up in the field like a rock in the sea; there was no surrounding garden as he had remembered it. As he approached a bedraggled-looking youngish woman came to the front door to shake a piece of sacking.

He gave her 'Good-day', with his pleasant smile, and told her that he had expected to find a family called Jordan living there.

She said, "We've been here the last five years. Jordans went away to work in the new mill over at Broom. We'll be goin' ourselves likely, if the half-crown a day they're all askin' in these parts isn't forthcoming." Her voice was sullen. She added, "'Tis no life, livin' worse than pigs. The pigs at least get enough to eat."

"Are you likely to get the new rate?"

"Mr Hallard is offering the Arundel rate—two-and-three, and he's got all his father's stubbornness. How would he like to raise up his children on less than half-a-crown a day?"

Jesse sighed. "Those who have never known poverty have no understanding. 'Tis the same everywhere, ma'am."

He became aware of a number of small barefoot children clinging to her skirts. He smiled at them, then said, "But I mustn't keep you from your work——"

"Are you going far, pray?"

He said quickly, "To Broom—I have relatives there."

She eyed him a moment, then said a little diffidently, "I could spare ye a drop of buttermilk and a piece of bread if 'twould help ye along the road——"

"If 'tis not robbing the children 'twould be most welcome, ma'am, but I must be allowed to pay for it."

"There's no need," she said, briefly. She brought the food to the door, and he drank down the buttermilk and thrust the bread into his pocket, then pressed a florin into her hand 'for luck.'

She laughed then. "Do you mistake me for a gipsy?" she demanded.

"Take it for the children," he insisted, then asked, "D'you get gipsies in these parts?"

"Some passed through here the other day, but without camping or coming to the doors. I believe they used to camp here regularly every year, but that was before our time."

He had not doubted that José had come back recently and placed the cross at the head of the secret grave in the wood, but it was satisfactory to have it confirmed.

He continued along the road with a spring in his step, but when he came within sight of the Valley Farm lands he slackened his pace, uncertain still as to whether he should go up to the farm and make himself known to John and Mary or content himself with secret

216

limpses of them and their children. The wheat on the upland mea-ow, he noticed, was still awaiting the sickle. In the broad fields ehind the house labourers were tying and stacking the sheaves.

He went on towards the house and it was as though he had left nly yesterday. Not a hedgerow flower seemed changed. Two oung children were playing at the gate which led down the rough art-track to the rick-yard—that gate, he reflected, at which José ad so often waited for Jessica. The boy, he judged, was about eight ears old, the girl five. They were playing a game he and Jessica ad liked to play—pushing the gate as far back as it would go climbing n to it, and then letting it swing back. When it banged against the ost they laughed and jumped off to repeat the exciting performance. Even at a distance Jesse was aware of their darkness.

Then he was almost on them and it was as though he were looking t his own two eldest children, except that his Jessica was now as old s this young Jesse. He hardly looked at the boy. The girl's likeness o his own child, and to the child Jessica who lay in the beech-wood ad been, fascinated him.

At the sight of the trampish-looking stranger the children stopped laying and the girl drew close to her brother and stood looking out under her tangle of thick dark hair like a wild creature from a thicket, uspiciously, ready to dart away at the slightest alarm.

The boy said, a little truculently, " This road's private. It leads o my father's farm. If our bailiff sees you he will put the dogs on to you—he doesn't like tramps and gipsies."

So Valley Farm had come to that, had it—a bailiff who turned the dogs on to wanderers of the road.

Jesse said, " I used to work here years ago, boy. I knew your father when he was a little boy, and your mother when she was a little girl and lived at the smithy."

" On Sundays we have tea there," the little girl informed him, triumphantly. She took a step forward, throwing back her head like a young colt.

" You can't guess my name? " she challenged.

" Jessica," he told her, smiling.

The light went out of her face. " You cheated ! " she accused him. " Someone told you ! " and withdrew to her brother's side again.

The boy, who had been regarding Jesse gravely, inquired, " Where do you live? "

" Far away from here on an island off the coast of Ireland."

" I'd like to live on an island. There's an island you can see from Oldport. I'm going there one day. I want to go all over the whole world. My father says that now there are steamships it will be easy for folks to travel about."

217

"I came from Ireland in a steamship," Jesse told him.

The boy's eyes sparkled with interest. "What was it like? Wa it very fast?"

Jesse did not reply; he was no longer looking at the children someone was coming up the track, a man wearing the leather breeche of a farmer, and with a gun under his arm—a man who could only b John, the same slight stoop of the scholar, the same cold remote look . . . Jesse was amazed at how little his brother had changed; h had been a boy when Jesse had gone away, and now he was a mai nearing thirty, but a young man, his face unlined, and he looked, i came to Jesse suddenly, very much the gentleman-farmer, very mucl John Hallard of Valley Farm, and he was conscious of his own wor and stained homespun, and the ravages that ten years of hard living had wrought in his face. He was a man who had lived all that time near the starvation level, and had survived a famine; John was ob viously a young man who had always lived well, and never known any great worry or hardship. Something very like jealousy twisted in Jesse watching his brother's approach, and it came to him that tha was strange, because once it was John who had been jealous of him . . . A spaniel ran at John's heels, and it too had a comfortable well-fed look.

"'Tis my father," the boy cried, and ran down the track towards him, followed by his sister. John came on with the children on either side of him, and Jesse waited, leaning against the gate.

John frowned at the unkempt figure which showed no sign of respect fully moving aside as he approached.

"What do you want, my good man?" he demanded, as he came up.

Jesse said quietly, "I came to see my niece and nephew, and my brother John and his wife."

John stared at him and then came closer, still staring.

"You're not—Jesse?" He almost breathed the words.

Jesse smiled, grimly. "Yes, John, 'tis your long-lost brother all right—a little the worse for wear, unlike yourself, but the bad coin turned up again."

"We thought you must have gone to America."

"I was going, but thought better of it and went to Ireland instead."

"There's been a lot of trouble over Ireland—those damned Papists!"

Jesse's blood rose. "'Tis the English who starve them who are damned—or should be! You seem to be having the same old troubles over here, too—those damned labourers still demanding the right to live!"

"We are having some labour disputes at the moment—unpro-

218

ressive hooligan elements have been going up and down the country smashing machines."

Jesse was aware of the old familiar cold hostility. He laughed, bitterly. "You don't change, John. Have you still no solution to offer beyond keeping up the price of corn?"

John retorted. "'Twould be more to the point if *I* asked *you* questions!"

He turned to the children. "Run on ahead, I wish to speak to this gentleman alone."

The boy hesitated, staring, full of curiosity.

John commanded, "Did you hear what I said, son? Be off with you, but wait for me at the rick-yard gate. Mind now, you are not to go on to the house without me."

"Yes, Pappa." The boy took his sister's hand and they ran on ahead.

"I wish to avoid startling Mary," John explained. "She is expecting another child before the end of the year, and the news of some mysterious stranger brought her by the children might throw her into a fluster. She miscarried last year; she is not as strong as one could wish. As I was saying—'tis surely for *me* to ask questions of *you*! You are aware, I presume, that to all intents and purposes you are still wanted for murder?"

"I suppose so. But since my own brother failed to recognise me it seems I have little to fear."

"Might one inquire why, if you were innocent, you ran away?"

"I was in a panic. And I did not know if I was indeed innocent, nor do I now."

"You mean that you struck that unfortunate young woman?" There was horror in John's voice.

"Certainly not. We quarrelled and she clawed at me and clung and I threw her off. If she struck her head on the rocks in falling I am responsible for her death—murder in the second degree 'tis called, I believe."

John was silent a moment, then he said, "They might have given the verdict 'Unproven' at the trial, had you stayed."

"They might have, but I had only one life to lose, and I happened to value it."

"'Twas a terrible shock for our parents—coming on top of Jessica's disappearance. You admitted that you knew where our sister had gone—where is she now? Don't tell me you brought her back with you—that she's at the end of the lane waiting to be restored to the family fold!"

Jesse was aware of the rising anger in his brother's voice.

He said, quietly. "Jessica died ten years ago, a week before I went away."

"Jessica's dead? You knew that our sister was dead and you neve[r] let any of us know? What right had you to keep it secret?"

John's pale face was flushed with anger. Jesse had never heard hir[m] speak so violently.

He told him, "I had every right. She joined the gipsies and die[d] of a miscarriage—puerperal fever, isn't it, that sets in? Would it hav[e] comforted our parents to have known that?"

"She joined the gipsies? Was she mad? Gipsies! Dirty, thievin[g] ruffians!"

"Not dirty," Jesse corrected, drily, "and not more thieving tha[n] landlords and parsons who rob the poor with their rents and tithes[.] As to whether she was mad or not—by your standards, yes. At leas[t] she had the wisdom not to stay to become imprisoned in her life lik[e] poor Mamma."

John was silent for a few moments, too profoundly shocked fo[r] immediate words. He said at last, "Was she given Christian burial, might I ask?"

"She was buried as she loved and as she was wed, that is to say Romanly."

Jesse looked at his brother and saw that he was deeply distressed. All this, he realised, was very terrible to his narrow orthodox soul, and he suffered on his sister's account, as he had at the time when he had watched her going over to Jesse after her brief spell of piety with him. Jesse felt himself softening.

"People have to get satisfaction out of life in their own way, Johnny," he urged.

John faced him, angrily. "What satisfaction did Jessica get— dying at sixteen? She threw her life away, and 'twas all your influence I doubt not, you and your wild living and your godlessness!"

"'Tis not how long people live, but how much," Jesse murmured.

They had reached the rick-yard, where the children were amusing themselves on the gate. The brothers had covered the last few yards in silence.

"When did you arrive?" John asked, forcing himself to make conventional conversation because of the presence of the children.

"This morning—off a steamer from Cork."

"How long do you propose to stay?"

"The steamer returns in two days' time. I was thinking of rejoining her tomorrow—there is always work to do in port."

"You could stay here——" John felt himself obliged to say.

"If I could stay tonight I would be grateful, if Mary has no objection, but I would like to go tomorrow—there are some inquiries I want to make in Oldport concerning someone I knew there."

John was barely listening, his mind preoccupied with the thought

220

of Mary and her reaction to the news of Jesse's return. Unacknowledged at the back of his mind was always the thought that Mary had
turned to him after Jesse had gone in much the same way that for a
little while Jessica had turned to him after her break with Jesse. He
had loved Jessica but she had never really belonged to him ; he loved
Mary, but was always fighting the thought, the feeling, that she was
constantly seeking Jesse in him. That she had refused Jesse and had
married him, John, the younger and less attractive brother, proved
nothing except that women were queer cattle. . . . He had moments
of intense bitterness in which it seemed to him that it was always Jesse
who was loved, and himself always nothing more than the substitute
for Jesse.

He said, rousing himself from this brooding, " Perhaps 'twould
interest you to examine the threshing-machine whilst I go on and
acquaint my wife "—he used the term deliberately, to remind his
brother that any question of competition where Mary was concerned
was now finished—" of your arrival. The children can go with
you."

" Are you not afraid of the labourers coming and smashing up the
fine new machine? " Jesse inquired.

" Only let them try ! " John's hand tightened on his gun, and Jesse
was a boy again, in the farm kitchen, listening to his mother anxiously
inquiring of his father as to whether there was likely to be trouble at
the farm, because of the rioting, and his father replying that they
would know how to deal with it if there was, and glancing at the
gun-rack. . . .

The boy stepped up to Jesse. " I'll show you the machine," he
said, eagerly.

" Me too ! " Jessica cried.

Jesse took her hand. " Yes, you too, little one," he said, smiling,
and it was his own child's hand he took, and the hand of the little
sister, long ago.

2

When John returned a few minutes later he found Jesse not absorbed in the wonders of the machine but sliding down the chute from
the loft with the children, and the barn was full of happy shrieks and
cries.

" He's got a little girl just like me ! " Jessica shrilled excitedly as her
father entered.

John was startled. " I was not aware that you were married,
Jesse."

"These ten years. I have six children—the two eldest are Patrick and Mary, then there's John, Ria, Lucy and Clancy, who was born last spring."

"Is your wife Irish?"

"Yes—Catholic."

John frowned. "The children, I trust, will not be brought up as Papists?"

"Of course. 'Tis a condition of Catholic marriage to a non-Catholic. I see no objection. At least the Catholic Church offers love—not fear!"

For a moment he was irritated, then he smiled. It was as futile as ever to quarrel with John and his ideas—ideas fixed since boyhood and only strengthened as the years went on.

"'Tis all one to me what church they go to," he added, "or whether they go to none at all; all I care about is that they should be happy. But I promised Ria before we married, and I promised the priest at our marriage, and at least there's nothing to terrify a child about Our Lady."

John said stiffly, "I would prefer not to discuss such things in front of the children. Let us go to the house. I thought it best, by the way, to warn Mary that you are somewhat changed."

Jesse said, with sudden humility, "Thank you, John." Until that moment he had been glad that he had changed out of all recognition; now, about to meet Mary, the idea that he would present himself to her as a stranger—a rough uncouth stranger at that—unmanned him a little.

He asked John, as they left the barn, "Has Mary changed much?"

"Is any woman the same at thirty-five as at twenty-five?" John demanded. "She still hath beauty, if that's what you mean."

As they crossed the rick-yard from the barn a tremendous scent assailed them.

"The syringas still bloom, then," Jesse observed.

"I would have cut them down but for Mary. I had intended to clear all that bit of land. What did you think of the threshing-machine?"

"Until I'd seen it in action I couldn't say. At the moment I cannot imagine feeding the sheaves into a machine. But then I couldn't imagine a ship going without sails before I saw a steamship in Cork harbour."

John said firmly, "Machinery has come to stay, and the country-side has to accept the threshing-machine as the towns have had to accept the spinning jenny! One day, I doubt not, we shall both sow and reap by machinery, and all coaches will travel by steam instead of horse-power. Over in Ireland did you hear about Mr. Stephenson's 'Rocket' last year? A remarkable performance, by all accounts. Soon people will be travelling everywhere by railway at twenty miles an hour or more. A start was made with the Stockton and Darlington Railway five years ago. Mr. Stephenson was the engineer for that, too. . . . We live in stirring times, I assure you, my dear brother!"

But Jesse was more interested in the Valley Farm ricks; they were as good as ever, he thought, standing up like firm golden cliffs with their tarpaulins like layers of blue-green grass. A man was thatching one with rushes.

"We had a good hay harvest," John said, briefly, eyeing the thatcher critically.

"A pity for it all to burn," Jesse murmured, then turned to his brother. "I hear you're standing out for the Arundel rate? Surely the labourer's worthy of his hire. . . ."

"In our father's time they were paid a shilling a day, or less."

"Progress isn't merely a matter of machinery," Jesse suggested.

John demanded, angrily, "Is one to be dictated to by a pack of saucy rascals?"

Again Jesse had the sense of the futility of attempting to argue with his brother—in whom William Hallard, with all his social and religious bigotry, lived again.

He stood a moment watching the cows coming into the stockyard from the meadow, moving slowly, heavily, with full udders, and suddenly realised how much better was their condition than that of any cattle he had seen in the last ten years. They seemed very big, too, after the small Irish cattle.

John said, "They have good cattle in Ireland, I suppose?"

"We have to send them inland to be fattened—we've not much grass out in the west."

"How d'you manage, pray?"

"Those who have cows ship them over to the mainland in the winter for the grazing. But I have only a potato patch."

John stared at him as they leaned together on the stockyard gate.

"Can you support a large family on that?"

"Aye. By living as we do. The fishing helps out, in season."

"You look half-starved."

Jesse smiled ruefully and touched the dark head of the child swarming up the gate beside him.

"Where I live we thank God if we're not starved entirely."

"As a man sows, so shall he reap!" John said, drily. He looked steadily at his brother. "What sort of harvest did you expect from that crop of wild oats you were sowing before you ran away?" he demanded.

Jesse met that accusing gaze. "You should have been a parson, Johnny."

John made no comment, and they walked along the back of the house, the children running ahead. Nothing had changed, Jesse noted; still the long bench with the wooden milk-buckets and stools upturned on it along the wall, still the grindstone by the orchard gate, the dog-kennel made from the old cider-barrel, the hens huddled in dusty hollows under the elder-trees and perching on the wood-pile. . . . Sadness and happiness fused in him. Nothing was changed, yet everything was changed. John was now the master of Valley Farm, and Mary was his wife, and Jessica would never return.

At the door of the back kitchen he was suddenly conscious of his rough clothes, his unkempt hair and beard.

He looked at John, anxiously. "My clothes," he said. "She knows what to expect?"

"I told her you had become an Irish peasant," John replied, curtly, and led the way in.

Jesse followed with his heart beating heavily. John lifted the latch and Jesse heard him saying, with a heartiness that sounded not quite true, "'Tis your turn to welcome home the prodigal son, Mary!"

He stood aside for Jesse to enter. The blood rushed to Jesse's head; he had a confused impression of the familiar room, the ingle-nook, the tall wooden settle, the bench along the wall opposite the fireplace, but there were books in the room now, and a bowl of roses on the table, and a spinet by the window, and at the heart of all this a woman heavy with child, a woman with a grave pointed face and brown curls in neat clusters about her neck, a woman who might once have been Mary Byrd. He stood gazing at her with his pulses hammering, and she came forward, smiling faintly. She was very pale, he noticed, as she came close, and ten years had drawn a network of lines under her eyes, and lines beside her mouth.

She gave him her hand and a little curtsey.

"'Tis good to see you at Valley Farm again, Jesse," she said. "Be seated, pray. I will bring you food—you must be famished. John says you came off a ship this morning. . . ."

She spoke rapidly, nervously, a little at random.

He sat, awkwardly, on the edge of the settle, as though he were a stranger, whilst she moved about, assembling crockery, opening cupboards and drawers.

"'Tis all so strange," he said, wonderingly. "This room—all those books, the flowers, the spinet—like it was at the smithy. 'Tis pretty. . . . And you wedded to John, and living here at Valley Farm. And this room, the same yet not the same. . . . 'Tis all so strange. . . ."

She set home-made bread and cheese and cold rabbit-pie and seed cake, and a mug of home-brewed ale, beside him on the settle, and he was reminded, vividly, of his last visit to the smithy.

"Ale is better than tea on a summer's day," she said. "I suppose in Ireland, as here, everyone drinks tea nowadays, even the poor people?"

He shook his head. "No, ma'am—'tis too poor a country for that."

He lifted his mug and drank deeply. The good English home-brewed ale, there was nothing like it. . . .

She sat looking at him, her heart aching. Was this gaunt, starved-looking man really 'Handsome Jess Hallard'? What had life done to him in ten years to change him so much? He was a fine-looking man still, but he had lost that quality of *panache* that had both fascinated and infuriated her. He no longer strutted, she thought, and it was not every woman, now, who would turn her head to look at him a second time—though many would, still. . . .

John broke in on her reverie, addressing Jesse. "There's no call to say ma'am to her—she's your sister now." He put his gun up in the rack and went out, followed by the children, for whom the novelty of the stranger had already worn off.

"Does John seem changed to you?" she demanded, when they were alone.

"Yes and no. In himself, no. He is our father all over again, as I thought he would be, narrow and bigoted and intolerant. He's filled out—one would take him for what he is these days, a prosperous farmer, not a scholar——"

He broke off in dismay. "You must pardon me! I forgot he was your husband—'tis hard to realise——"

She smiled, a small, bitter smile. "'Tis no matter. I too know that he is your father all over again. Every night he reads from the Bible, and he is very strict with the children."

Jesse asked sharply, "Does he beat the children?"

"We quarrel most about that."

"Not Jessica—he doesn't beat little Jessica?" It was as though he pleaded with her.

She said in a low voice, "Wasn't your sister Jessica beaten at that age?"

"Yes. It was terrible. But John was never beaten. He was a good child——"

"These children are wild—high-spirited. John says they are young colts that must be broken in or they will go the same road as the first Jesse and Jessica Hallard."

Jesse said, grimly, "They will go that road *because* they are beaten! Tell me—what else do you quarrel about?" He had a sense of his whole being vibrant with a quivering anger.

"The labour troubles. My father is of the opinion that John should

225

fall into line and pay the demanded rate, and I share his opinion. John tells me 'tis no affair of mine and that I am tainted with my father's radical views." She hesitated a moment, then added with a kind of recklessness, " He says sometimes that I should have married you—then he says we could have let Valley Farm run to rack and ruin together ! "

Jesse said, sadly, " If you had married me, Mary, 'twould all have been very different—but 'tis to no purpose to talk of that. You had no love for me and there was no more to be said."

She could tell him now, " I did love you, Jesse. But I couldn't be one more woman captivated by ' Handsome Jess Hallard '. . . . 'Twas pride got in the way—if something had happened to you and you had ceased to be handsome I could have said yes. . . ." Her voice trembled and faded into silence.

He said, bitterly, " And now that I come back unrecognisable as Jess Hallard, the way no woman would be looking at me twice, you can tell me——"

She said without looking at him, and almost in a whisper, " Had you met me for the first time today you also would not have looked a second time at me—even had I not been with child."

Was it true? He didn't know. Did one love only the shell of a person? All these years he had loved the memory of Mary as she had been ; there had been no bitterness in that woman, neither in her face nor in her soul. Pity filled him suddenly.

" Mary—life hath done a lot to us both—'tis not only our faces that have changed. . . ."

He got up and went over to the window, fingering a scented geranium on the sill. His mother, he remembered, had always been, as she expressed it, ' very partial to' a scented geranium and pressed leaves of it in her prayer- and hymn-books. In the little garden below the window were sweet peas, like a multi-coloured swarm of butterflies, and a tea-rose straggled up the wall. A moor-hen darted in and out under the confusion of willows and brambles and hawthorns that hedged the duck-pond. From the open casement came the familiar farm smells of hay and cattle, and summer garden scents of lavender and roses and cloves. Against that wall, he remembered, he and Jessica had leaned discussing the Easter fair. . . .

He said suddenly, " If 'twould not tire you I'd like to walk outside for a little——"

She rose immediately and they went out together, through the little door of the tiny hall that separated the farm living-room from the parlour, used only on Sundays. The hall, he noticed, was different. There was a grandfather clock, and a glass case full of stuffed birds, owls, jays, a sea-gull, and a number of small bright-coloured birds.

He stopped a moment to look at them. " John shot them," she told him, adding, " We quarrelled over the sea-gull. I cried—it was so beautiful. Why should anyone wish to shoot a sea-gull? Why did it have to come inland that day to be shot down in a field like a pheasant? "

" Perhaps John was jealous of its freedom," Jesse said, and she looked at him, puzzled.

" Why do you say that? Does John wish to be free—of me, of the children, of Valley Farm? "

" No. But he does not wish others to be free, either. Like our father, he has never believed in freedom. He believes in things like discipline and punishment and fear."

She smiled, sadly, stepping out through the front porch into the afternoon sunshine. " What sort of things do you believe in, Jesse? "

For a moment there was a flash of the old charming smile.

" Oh, stupid things like love and freedom and being happy and living one day at a time. I don't care about progress and machines —I want people to have enough to eat and a roof that doesn't leak and good ale sufficient to make the heart merry."

They began to pace up and down the red-brick path in the narrow strip of garden, and he told her about Rull, and Ria and his children. He told her about the struggle for existence, ' Captain Moonlight ', the famine, and after a while they leaned on the wall and looked at the water and watched the cows being driven out after the milking, and he asked her, " Did you believe that I killed Sally Lane—that I ran away because I was guilty? "

She said, simply, " I believed at the time what I still believe, and what my parents and many others also believe, that if 'twas at your hand she died, then 'twas an accident and that you are innocent in the sight of God."

He pressed her hand a moment. " Bless you for that, Mary."

They were silent, watching the cows crossing the lane into the meadow. Labourers were going home in twos and threes.

" Are the men here very discontented? " Jesse inquired.

" They come to work late and they leave early, and they are sullen and surly. There have been two deputations about the wages, but John refused to see the second. Yesterday he received a letter signed ' Swing ' and with a knife drawn at the end. All the farmers are getting them."

" I had heard about it. Who is this Captain Swing? "

" Nobody knows. Some say his wife ran off with a lover a few months ago, taking all his money with her, and that he drinks and is reckless because his heart is broken and he doesn't care whether he lives or dies. There are all manner of stories."

"Do the farmers come to terms when they get these letters?"

"Some do. They even put the threshing-machines outside to be destroyed. But Mr. Johnson over by Broom refused to bargain with the men or give up the machine, and next night his barn and ricks were ablaze."

"Doesn't John realise what he's risking for the sake of threepence a day?"

"He's stubborn. He won't give in on principle, he says. Last night he and Mr. Surridge sat up till dawn with their guns in case anyone should come and try to fire the place. Tonight the squire is sending two of the assistant keepers over."

Jesse said quickly, "He can send the squire's men back tonight— I will sit up—but not with a gun."

"And how do you propose to defend the place unarmed against a mob?" John had come through the porch and overheard Jesse's last remark.

They both straightened up from the wall and turned to face him.

"I've seen enough bloodshed and murder to no purpose in Ireland," Jesse said. "Men don't have to murder each other to get justice——"

John laughed, unpleasantly. "I'd be mighty obliged if you would be good enough to tell that to the rascally mob when it arrives—led, no doubt, by the dashing Captain Swing flourishing a pistol! Personally I propose to meet them as our father would have met them, with a gun!"

"If you shoot, so will they. Are you anxious to make Mary a widow, and she with a child on the way?"

John said, coldly, "'Tis not necessary to have been a poacher to be a good shot!"

Mary's voice trembled as she said, "I wish you would be reasonable, John."

"I am so reasonable, madam, that I refuse to be dictated to by a mob of ruffians!"

John remained leaning against the porch, his arms folded, frowning angrily.

The afternoon was melting into evening; there was an evening mellowness in the sunlight, and gnats spiralled above the pond. The sky's blue was dissolving into amber, and stillness settled down like dusk. The slam of the rick-yard gate emphasised the silence that followed, and the moan of a cow in a near-by field was full of a sadness that took Jesse back to Rull and the cries of sea-birds and the sobbing of a donkey, and he thought of Ria sitting outside the cabin at this hour and looking at the sea, and the children playing on the coral strand below, leaping barefoot along the sea's white edge. In a few days he would be back and all this seem like a dream, the merest glimpse of a

228

world he had once known. He thought of Ria's wonderment if she could see even the back kitchen of Valley Farm, and the old pain touched him again, the sense of his own inadequacy, because he had thrown away his heritage and would never be able to give those dear to him even the smallest measure of comfort or security. He sighed.

Mary looked up at him, questioningly.

He smiled. " I was thinking of the difference between this life and life in Rull."

" You deliberately turned your back on this life," John said, sharply, adding, " 'Twas only natural after you ran away and there was all that scandal that our father should alter the will and make me his heir."

" I never wanted or intended to become master of Valley Farm," Jesse told him. " I want something much less—three acres would do if there was an acre of good pasture—and to own that bit of land, not to be beholden to any landlord unless the state itself was landlord——"

" Still the revolutionary, eh? " John mocked him.

Jesse sighed again. " No, Johnny, still the dreamer, that's all. At least no landlord or government may seize a man's dreams for rent or tithes. . . ."

He turned to Mary. " May I fetch you a wrap? The sun is going down."

" I think we should go in. . . . 'Tis so still and silent, as if everything were waiting for something to happen. . . . Let's go in and light the candles and I will play for you on the spinet. ' *Weep you no more, sad fountains* '—or have you forgotten? "

" It hath remained with me all these years," Jesse assured her, fervently. " Only today I was recalling it——"

She said with a sudden flash of gaiety, " Then you shall have another to take back with you ! "

John said dourly, preceding them into the house, " There are songs enough in Ireland, I doubt not."

Mary laid a hand on Jesse's arm and whispered, " He hath inherited your father's dislike of any music and singing that is not religious. But in a moment or two he will be making his evening round of the place——"

He felt her close in that small conspiracy as he had not felt her even when he had rested his head on her breast at their last meeting. Tenderness flowed in him for her, and gratitude because now, at last, they could be simply and easily together, without the feeling of constraint he had felt in her even when she had walked a little way along the road with him that last time and he had been aware of her friendship at last.

Now he could ask her, when they were alone, " Tell me—did you marry John because you fell in love with him? "

229

She bent her head low over the music she was sorting through.

" No."

" Might I ask why, then? "

" Because he was your brother."

The wound in him could not have been deeper if she had said a bitter thing.

He said at last, painfully, " It seems a strange thing to marry a man's brother when you could have had the man himself."

She told him, as painfully, " Pride is a strange thing, Jesse."

She straightened herself and moved over to the spinet, seated herself, then smiled at him, as it seemed to him a little piteously. He came over and stood behind her whilst the thin sweet notes ran out under her fingers, and in a moment her voice, a little tremulously at first, then steadying itself as the song filled her spirit, was lifted on the dusk of the room.

> ' There is a Lady sweet and kind,
>   Was never face so pleased my mind ;
>   I did but see her passing by,
>   And yet I love her till I die.'

Jesse moved away from her and went over and stood by the window, looking out at the trees darkening against the sky's pale amber. The stillness was full of the evening scent of flowers and a sense of the earth breathing out the warmth poured day-long into it. O sweet and gentle countryside hiding such pain ! The music ran like a golden stream over his soul, cool and limpid and beautiful, then Mary's voice rode upon the stream—

> ' Her gesture, motion, and her smiles,
>   Her wit, her voice my heart beguiles,
>   Beguiles my heart, I know not why,
>   And yet I love her till I die.'

He looked back at Mary, but her face wore the rapt look of one moving in an immaterial world. Was it her intention to express for him through this old and lovely song everything for which he had no words but had known ever since that summer day when she had stood beside him in the smithy, caught by a shaft of sunlight piercing a cobwebby window and alive with dancing dust?

> ' Cupid is wingèd and doth range
>   Her country so my love doth change ;
>   But change she earth, or change she sky,
>   Yet will I love her till I die.'

The vehemence of passion in that last line sent a shiver down his spine, like the youthful thought of men marching with pikes in spring sunlight. The last notes escaped under her fingers and then she turned and smiled at him.

"Thank you," he said, "I shall remember it always. When I am out alone in the curagh it will run through my head and you will come close. The other song was all Jessica. This one will bring you."

She smiled, but her eyes were soft. She forced herself to say, lightly, "'Tis pretty, but I think the poet only loved his dream. Had he known the lady better it might have been a different story!"

Jesse smiled then. "The point is he was not permitted to know her better, and so he knew he would love her till he died, whatever else changed. Just *because* he did but see her passing by. . . ."

She rose and began putting the sheets of music together. Jesse, watching her, said, abruptly, "Tell me one thing more, Mary—whose idea was it to call the children Jesse and Jessica?"

"John's."

"John's? But why? I don't understand. . . . How could he wish his children named after the black sheep of the family? And our parents—what had they to say to it?"

"They were both dead before Jessica was born, but they wanted the boy called Jesse . . . to replace the Jesse Hallard who had gone from them. But 'twas John who first suggested it."

"So that there would be a Jesse Hallard to inherit Valley Farm one day?"

"That was your father's idea, but with John 'twas different." She straightened herself from bending over the music-stool and looked at him. "John has a great devotion to you—underneath—Jesse. He admires you."

"How can that be? He disapproves of everything I ever was and everything I am. I drank and poached and went with loose women, and now I am poor and unsuccessful and unprogressive and an outcast!"

She insisted, "All the same, you are all he would have liked to have been. He would have liked your looks, the charm you had for women, to have had your success with them. To have had your temperament and gone drinking and poaching. He would have liked to have been popular with the poor as you were. To have had your courage and rebelliousness, and your indifference to all the things he values! His disapproval is nought but jealousy—as much now as when you were both lads."

"'Tis I who should be jealous, surely—since 'twas he who married you in the end, and me you sent empty away!" He smiled ruefully.

231

She turned away. "He knows very well 'twas you I loved, that only an echo and a shadow of you in him that drew me to him." She sighed. "Ah well, 'twill always be true that as we make our beds so we must lie in them!"

"And yours is a feather-bed, and mine a straw mattress, but mine the softer of the two at times, I doubt not. Poor Mary!"

"Oh, no, no, please!" Her eyes darkened with distress, and there was an agitated movement of her hands. "Not pity, I beg of you! I have more happiness than I have ever deserved. John loves me, and I have little Jesse and my darling little Jessica, and this new child coming to me. I permitted my wretched selfish pride to stand in the way of the happiness I could have had with you and drive you to Sally Lane and all that followed—I deserve nothing. . . ."

"If 'tis to be reckoned like that, then you gave me Ireland and Ria and my children. He hesitated a moment, then said, "Has John told you yet what happened to our sister Jessica?"

She shook her head, and he told her, briefly. She was silent for a minute, then she said, "She had great courage. She was not afraid to go out boldly after her happiness. Was she"—her eyes filled with tears suddenly, "was he handsome—her gipsy?"

"Very." He took her hands. "Thank you for being on Jessica's side," he said, simply.

Then they moved apart and she fetched a silver candelabra—a wedding present, she said—and they kindled the candles, and their light fell upon the bowl of roses on the table, and sent long shadows over the heavy old beams and the blue-washed walls and filled the room with a soft radiance.

"'Tis time the children were abed," she said and laughed, a little unsteadily, still shaken from their talk. "We usually shut them up at the same time as the fowls, but 'tis hard to get them in these long light evenings. They are probably in the orchard in the long grass——"

"I'll go and find them," Jesse said, and was moving to the door when John came in. He was pale and had a tense look.

He spoke rapidly. "Mary, I want you to go to your room and stay there and take Annie and the children with you. There is no need for alarm. 'Tis merely a matter of dispersing a rabble coming along the road with a good deal of noise. The squire's men are here, and there is Jesse." He looked at his brother. "We will go down to meet them," he said, and went over to the gun-rack.

"Certainly I will go, but not with a gun," Jesse said, firmly. "Those men out there are my friends."

"They are certainly not mine!" John snapped.

"They could be—if you'd let them."

" You are a fool, Jesse! You don't know these labourers as I do." He turned back to Mary, his gun under his arm. " There is no need for alarm," he repeated. " They will never reach the house."

She clung to him. " John—Jesse is right. These men could be our friends! Once again I beg you to grant their demand—'tis just and fair. . . ."

He put her aside, gently, and turned to address an elderly woman servant who had come in with an arm round the shoulders of each child and a scared look on her face.

" Annie, go with your mistress to her room and stay there till we return," he commanded.

" Yes, sir. Very good, sir. They won't burn the place down, will they, sir? "

The boy, his eyes sparkling with excitement, called out from under the wing of the protective arm, " Will they set fire to the ricks, Pappa? 'Twould be a great blaze! They say you could see Mr. Johnson's for miles around! "

" They will not come within a hundred yards of a rick! " John said, violently, but even as he spoke there was a thud of marching feet and a clatter of horses' hooves, and a confusion of shouts and cries, coming nearer, steadily. . . .

IV

By the time John and Jesse had reached the rick-yard gate the mob had already crowded into the narrow lane that led down to the farm from the post-road. It was a raggle-taggle army in ragged smocks and broken shoes, and armed with pitchforks, sticks, catapults, pruning-hooks. At the head of it rode a highwaymanlike figure wearing cloak and mask and riding a blood horse—the chestnut Jesse had seen on the ridge that morning—and by the straightness with which the rider sat the horse he recognised, instantly, the mysterious stranger with whom he had talked. Immediately behind the rider Jesse saw old Mortimer, Wainwright, and the man, ' Joe ', who had first spoken to him in *The Ship's Bell*.

Not merely every man who worked on Valley Farm's two hundred acres was there, but all the squire's labourers and tenants—in fact the entire peasant population of the valley. The lane was packed from gate to gate. They were like sheep penned for a shearing. Faces ceased to be individual and became part of a mass face.

The rider halted a yard or so from the rick-yard gate and the procession shuffled to a standstill behind him. They were a formidable company, with their set faces and grimly determined air. If they decided to swarm into the rick-yard, Jesse thought, John and the squire's two assistant game-keepers with guns were not likely to stop them ; it would be like shooting at a burst dam. . . .

"Speak civilly to them," he urged John as they advanced together, with the other two men one on either side.

At the gate John addressed the leader. "I have not the pleasure of knowing you, I fear, sir."

"My name's Swing," the rider answered him, curtly, "and I have come to demand justice for your labourers. You refused to see the last deputation. You are now given your last chance to pay the demanded rate for this parish. Failure to comply means the loss of your ricks."

There was a growl of endorsement from the crowd, and one man called out, derisively, "Make up your mind, Farmer Hallard, we can't wait here all night !" and there was some laughter.

John said, "I see no reason to discuss my business with a stranger, Captain Swing, and the men are already acquainted of my terms."

Wainwright stepped forward then.

"We are giving you a last chance to be reasonable, Mr. Hallard. Valley Farm has the finest ricks in the parish and 'twould be a pity to see 'em burn."

"I have agreed to the Arundel rate," John stated, "and I am not to be intimidated into paying a penny more !"

"Could you raise your own family on two-and-threepence a day, Mr. Hallard, or even two-and-six, come to that ?"

John said, coldly, "I am not prepared to debate the matter. You have my decision and you can take it or leave it. As to you, sir," he turned to Swing, "may I point out that you are trespassing on my land ? "

"May I in turn point out to you, sir," Swing retorted, "that you are trespassing against human decency in your refusal to pay a living wage to your workmen ? "

He wheeled his horse round and addressed the men. "When a man renounces reason, my friends, 'tis useless to argue with him. We have been called criminals because we have smashed machines that put men out of employment, and because we have razed to the ground the barns and hayricks of farmers who spend in their pride what you, the common people, gain for them by your toil. Is it *your* wives who wear fine gowns and drink tea out of china cups ? Once a year at the harvest-home you are treated like men ; the rest of the year you are merely the oxen that tread out the corn. . . ."

John stood listening to these impassioned utterances with a scornful smile, muttering to Jesse, "What kind of a charlatan and play-actor is this, pray? He hath the windy wordiness of the Mad Priest of Kent!"

But Jesse was troubled; these men were ripe for violence. Captain Swing's oratory might be a poor imitation of John Ball, so much wind in John's opinion, but it was a wind that could fan the smouldering fire of hate and anger into a leaping flame that would very easily reach to the ricks. It was quite clear that this Captain Swing, whoever he might be, was inciting the men to defy the four guns at the gate and pour into the rick-yard. That he was sincere in his bitter denunciation of injustice he did not doubt, but he was, nevertheless, inciting the men to their own ultimate self-destruction.

"'Tis not too late to agree to meet a deputation now," Jesse urged. "What's threepence a day more or less?"

"'Tis the principle involved," John insisted, stubbornly.

"Farmer Hallard of Valley Farm must learn a lesson," Captain Swing concluded. "He has to learn that the employer is not always right, and that money and position are not always the last word in a dispute. He has to learn that the poor also have their rights, and when they are not freely granted them know how to seize them!"

There was another deep growl of assent, and Captain Swing reined his horse in to the side of the lane and the crowd began to move forward. Instantly John and the two assistant keepers brought their guns up to their shoulders.

"Anyone attempting to pass this gate will be shot!" John called out.

"We can do a bit o' shootin' oursen!" someone shouted, and immediately some shots were fired into the air.

As the crowd came on John and the other two men backed towards the ricks.

"By Christ, this is daylight murder!" Jesse cried, and mounted the gate.

"Men," he cried, "this won't get you what you're after. 'Twill get you nothing but jail and transportation and, if there's any shooting, the gallows!"

Someone shouted, "What's it to do with you, stranger?"

"Aye," said Wainwright from the front of the crowd, "what right have you to meddle in our affairs?"

It came to Jesse then, in a flash, that the only way he could get a hearing was to reveal himself to them—and he had to get a hearing, not merely because of the bitter, tragic futility of these men committing themselves to acts of violence as a means to their end, but because he was Jesse Hallard and could not stand by and see the Hallard ricks, the finest in the parish, burn. There was that old innate loyalty that had made it impossible to poach on Valley Farm land. . . .

And in that moment of revelation in which he knew that he must speak to these men as Jesse Hallard, he saw his ancient enemy, Tom Surridge, at the back of the crowd. For a moment he hesitated, as a man might hesitate on the edge of a wide crevasse before deciding to risk the jump, and in that brief interval was aware of the rising impatience of the mob and the need for immediate action.

" Come on, lads, let's do what's to be done," a man near the front urged those around him.

" Aye, 'tis deeds, not words, that's wanted ! " another affirmed, and again the crowd began to surge forward, whilst those by the rick stood tense, guns to shoulders.

" Stop ! " Jesse shouted. " I'll tell you what 'tis to do with me—I am no stranger ! Many of you here have known me since boyhood—you, Wainwright, you, Mortimer—I am Jesse Hallard ! And I tell you you can't destroy yourselves in this way, and you can't destory the farm that gives you a living ! 'Tis still possible to reason with my brother, I tell you, but not by menaces ! "

The crowd stood still again, and for a few moments there was silence, then old Mortimer edged his way to the front, went up to Jesse, looked closely at him.

" 'Tis you right enough, lad," he said, wonderingly, and turned to the crowd. " 'Tis Jesse Hallard sure enough, lads," he told them.

Above the murmur of the crowd Jesse raised his voice again.

" Let a delegation representing you all come forward. We will get round the table together, your delegates, my brother and I—we will talk the matter out. Let the rest of you bide here peacefully, but only those who work for Valley Farm—let the rest be gone and not trespassing on my brother's land."

He appealed to Captain Swing. " Bid those who have no business here follow you, sir. I promise you the men shall get what they want without bloodshed or burning."

" May I point out that you are not your brother's keeper, and that therefore it doth not rest with you ? Your brother hath already twice refused to listen to reason."

Again that growling murmur of assent rose on the still twilight.

" My brother resists argument backed by force and threats, like all Hallards. This time 'twill be different. Call your men off, Captain Swing, and we will to business ! "

Swing turned his horse and rode back down the lane and a number of the men fell out and followed him. When the gate on to the road had banged on the last of them Jesse opened the rick-yard gate, and Wainwright, old Mortimer, and ' Joe ' passed in. John came forward to meet his brother, and to Jesse's astonishment he held out his hand. " Thank you, Jesse," he said, simply. He turned to the squire's men. " I'll not need you tonight, after all."

236

" Will you have sufficient guard for the ricks without us, sir? " one asked, wonderingly.

" My brother has ensured that the ricks will not need guarding," John said, and addressed the three delegates. " Go on ahead to the house and await me there. I will join you in a few minutes. I want a word with my brother in private."

Two of them went on, but old Mortimer stopped to speak to Jesse. " 'Twas good work ye did, lad, good luck to ye—but don't linger here —Tom Surridge was here this evening, keeping an eye on the squire's men who were supportin' us, and he'll lose no time in informing the police you're back. He's likely riding back with 'em now ! Ye gave 'em the slip once, lad, 'twould be a pity if they caught up with ye now, after all these years ! "

He pressed Jesse's hand and went on.

John said, " Old Mortimer has said what I was going to say. You must get away at once, Jesse." He looked intently at his brother and said earnesly, " I wish I had one tenth part of your courage, Jesse ! "

" There was no courage in it, John. I have seen enough of the misery caused by what they were proposing to do, and I know it leads to no good, and I couldn't see it happen to them, or to Valley Farm. I knew the only way to prevent them destroying both themselves and the farm was to speak out."

" That you should care what happened to them I can understand —you were always on the side of the poor. But why should you care what happens to Valley Farm? "

" I don't know, Johnny—something to do with being a Hallard, perhaps—in spite of everything ! You'll give them what they're asking, Johnny? "

" Yes. You've made it possible. I refused to be bullied or scared into doing it. When you haven't courage or personality or much else your pride is very precious—it's about all you have ! "

He smiled, wanly, and in that moment he was the thin, pale, book-ridden boy again, passionately envious of his dashing elder brother's popularity ; the unhappy youth who also wanted to be liked and loved and happy.

" But you must go, Jesse," he added, urgently, and began hurrying him to the house. " You must get away to Plymouth and pick up the steamer there. It will take you the better part of two days to walk it, but the ship doesn't leave Oldport till the day after tomorrow, you said. The ports are sure to be watched, as 'twas thought you got away in a ship last time, but you will take some old clothes of mine and change into them before you reach Plymouth and then walk boldly down to the quays. You can get your beard trimmed and make yourself presentable, and when you get back your wife will fall in love with you afresh—you'll be ' Handsome Jess Hallard ' again ! "

It was the first time Jesse had ever heard his brother make a joke. When he was flushed and excited as now he was quite good-looking, he thought ; he ceased to be cold and remote but became alight and alive. For the first time in his life he felt drawn to him.

When they reached the house Jesse remained in the kitchen and talked with the men, whilst John ran up the stairs to fetch clothes and to bring Mary to put some food together.

" To think we talked with ye in the inn and never knowed ye ! " old Mortimer said, and volunteered the news Jesse was longing to hear : " Jack got back from Australia, thanks be to God. Worked his passage back, the lad did, in a grain-ship. He's working in a mill now, and has a wife and two childer."

Whilst they were talking Mary came breathlessly into the kitchen, followed by John.

" There's no time to lose," she cried. " Surridge is riding along the post-road now with three other men——"

She bustled from kitchen to pantry and back again, wrapping food and stuffing it into the bundles of clothes, whilst John tried to persuade his brother to accept some money, which Jesse refused, insisting that he had all he needed.

" Hurry, lad, hurry," old Mortimer urged, repeatedly. Between them they almost pushed Jesse out of the house.

At the door of the back kitchen John said quickly, " Cut along the old tree across the pond and make for Plymouth through the King's Mead and over the hills. Keep off the post-roads. When Surridge and the constable get here we shall swear that you were never here— that you disappeared in the crowd that followed Captain Swing." He gripped Jesse's hand. " It's goodbye now, Jesse, but if things go badly with you in Ireland don't hesitate to write for the passage money to ship your family here till better times. If there should be another famine, for example——"

Mary laid her hands on Jesse's shoulders and her eyes were full of tears. " We can never thank you enough for saving the farm, Jesse, and taking such a risk in doing it. God bless you always ! "

Jesse looked from one to the other of them and had no words.

He said, with difficulty, because of a tightness in his throat, " Bless you both. Kiss little Jessica for me, and tell your parents how much I'd like to have seen them, Mary—give them my love——"

" Hurry, hurry," old Mortimer beseeched behind them. " They're comin' down the lane now—can't you hear the horses' hooves? "

The sound came to them quite distinctly as he spoke, and then there was the crash of the rick-yard gate.

Jesse bolted from the door and down to the pond and scrambled across the fallen tree-trunk. He took the leap and landed into the little copse in which Jessica had confessed to the hawthorn tree, just as Surridge and a constable marched up to the door of the back kitchen. . . .

V

JESSE pelted across country like a hare in the warm summer dusk. He had no time for thinking. The immediate necessity was to get away, to beat Surridge a second time, and this time for good. By the time a starry darkness had closed in he was under the hills and, he estimated, a good eight miles from the farm. Then he slowed down, and with the night-wrapped English countryside all round him again he was taken back to his poaching days, instinctively listening to every movement and seeking to identify it. The air was full of a scent of meadow-sweet and hay, and occasionally, as he skirted a hedge, of the warm smell of cattle. He thought with satisfaction of Surridge, whom he had so often fooled in the old days, hunting him now a second time but having lost scent.

He sat down in a dry ditch under a meadow hedge and ate some of the food Mary had hurriedly thrust into his bundle. When he had eaten he lay down on his bed of dry leaves and bracken, drew the coat from the bundle over him and fell asleep almost immediately.

He wakened in the dawn with the birds and walked some way before stopping to break his fast. He wanted to cover as much country as possible before the arrival of workers in the fields would force him out into the lanes. He was determined to take John's advice and keep off the post-roads and also to avoid passing through villages. He had no doubt that every mail-coach that went out of Oldport would carry the news to the police in each town and village it passed through that the ' wanted ' Jesse Hallard had turned up again in this part of the country.

When the sun was up, turning all the cornfields, with their standing sheaves, to a warm gold, the scene seemed to him so steeped in peace that it was difficult to imagine the unrest everywhere, and that at sun-down ' Captain Swing ' rode those quiet lanes with a hungry ragged horde at his horse's heels. He was struck for the first time by the gentleness of the English scene, the gentle undulations of the corn and meadow-land, the gentle swell of the hills, in such striking contrast to the wild bare hills and stony wastes to which he had grown accustomed. It was smug-looking country, he found himself thinking ; it so obviously belonged to landed gentry, with its stately parks and its carefully fenced game preserves. And he longed for the sight of floods of grey water heaving against brown rocks covered with golden seaweed, and teeming grey rains beating down upon grey stone, and cloud reflected in brackish bog pools, and the blessed smell of a turf fire. Now everything in him strained to be home again, heart and blood and mind and ' home ' was a wave-washed rock with gulls screaming over, a white-washed cabin with an earth floor and hens at the door. And the warmth of Ria's breast, and her wild dark hair streaming over him in the night, and his children swarming about him with their wild grace. All that was wild and free was home. Here he was nothing but a hunted hare with a pack at his heels.

Towards mid-day he came to a stretch of unenclosed common land where the gorse blazed in the sunshine and heather made long purple patches like shadows. He was looking about for the best place in which to settle and enjoy more of the home-made bread and cheese Mary had put together for him, when his attention was attracted by a thin blue spiral of smoke a little distance off, behind a clump of furze. His heart leapt with the thought of a gipsy encampment and he moved quickly over in that direction.

He came to a hollow, full of bracken, at the bottom of which was the fire, and beside it a tramp whom a moment later he recognised as the one he had seen in *The Ship's Bell*. He grinned up at Jesse.

" Lift the latch and walk in, brother," he commanded.

Jesse descended the slope of the hollow and sat down away from the fire.

" 'Tis hardly a day for a fire, brother," he suggested.

" A poor man must do his cooking, brother. I have potatoes in the ashes here, and you're welcome to one when they're ready."

" Are you Romany? " Jesse asked.

" No such good fortune, brother, though I have lived with them from time to time along the road. Are you going far, brother? "

" I want to get to Plymouth by tomorrow to join a ship."

" Then 'tis fortune has thrown us together, for I am going that road myself, though not to join a ship—I had my fill of ships in my youth.

Jesse said quickly, " I am taking short cuts across country—I'd not be a good road-companion, for I have an aversion to roads."

But the tramp was not to be shaken off.

" I am as willing as any man to go over a hill rather than round it," he assured Jesse, and reached forward and raked two potatoes out of the ashes with a piece of stick.

" Help yourself, brother," he invited.

Jesse in turn offered some of his bread and cheese and a Valley Farm apple. For a few minutes they were busy eating, then Jesse

240

said, " Did you ever happen to know a girl in Oldport called Lucy Williams? She used to go every night to *The Ship's Bell*. I knew her years ago and wondered what had happened to her. She had a heart as big as the world."

" Aye, I knew her. Welsh she was, and pretty as a picture and a sweet disposition—not like some of her kind. Not like that Jezebel Sally Lane. There was a whore for you! Not a good honest whore like Lucy Williams, but the kind that sneaks out of your bed to get into another's and then lies herself black in the face about it!" He spat.

" She came to a bad end, by all accounts," Jesse ventured.

" Aye, she did that, and the feller got clean away, and good luck to him. 'Twould be a pity if any man should swing for the likes of her!"

" They seemed to think in the tavern that the one they wanted on account of her death was innocent."

" Innocent men don't run away, brother."

" Perhaps he had no intent to kill her."

" Wenches like Sally Lane don't get killed by accident. They go about for years inviting men to murder 'em and one day it happens."

Jesse was silent a moment or two, then said, " What happened to Lucy Williams—d'you happen to know?"

" 'Twas said she married the bo'sun of a clipper-ship and sailed away with him on the next voyage to Baltimore. Another story hath it that she stowed away in his cabin and he didn't discover her till the ship had sailed, and then the captain had to marry them at sea for the look of the thing. Or maybe they wanted it that way. One thing is certain—she went off with him and never came back."

Jesse's eyes shone. " I hope 'tis true she married him, at sea or ashore." he cried. " She deserved happiness, if ever a woman did!"

" Aye, she was a good wench," the other returned, laconically, and pulled out a flask from some inner recess of his rags and held it out to Jesse. " Drink to her happiness, brother. 'Tis good smuggled French brandy."

Jesse took the flask from him and took a gulp and was reminded of Sunday afternoons at the Lanes'.

The tramp, when the flask was handed back to him, drank deeply from it. " There'll be more from the same source when we reach Plymouth," he said, and offered Jesse the flask again.

When they left the hollow the turf and heather underfoot seemed more resilient than before, and there was no exhaustion in the afternoon heat.

They walked for the most part in silence, skirting cornfields where the harvest was being gathered in, cutting across the stubble where the sheaves had already been carted home, resting sometimes in the shade of trees, when the tramp would take another draught of brandy, and Jesse would look about for a spring or stream.

Towards the end of the afternoon they came to a small market town, and the tramp suggested that they should find a tavern.

"I have no money to spend in such places, brother," Jesse told him.

"Then you are in luck, brother, for you have fallen in with one who has."

"I have had drink enough from you," Jesse insisted.

They argued for some yards, and at the point where a road ran down into the town and a path sloped away over fields, parted company, the tramp going on into the town, and Jesse, much relieved at the separation, cutting eagerly across the fields. He passed a number of labourers going home at the end of their day's work, but he attracted no attention, a shabby tramp of a man with a bundle under his arm, a poor man walking the roads.

He went on until the dusk became too deep for him to distinguish path from ditch, and then making out a cartshed, with a loft over, in an adjoining field headed for it. 'Twould be better than sleeping in a ditch or under a haystack, he thought, for the dews were heavy in the mornings now.

He climbed the ladder to the loft and found plenty of hay. He shook down a bale and made himself comfortable with his bundle under his head and his boots off to ease his feet, and was soon asleep. Sometime tomorrow he should reach Plymouth. It was a satisfying thought to sleep on.

2

He wakened with a start and an impression that a thunderstorm was crashing about him. He lay, confusedly listening, and then realised that the loft had been invaded, and that the thunderstorm was the invader blundering about in the darkness.

By the tremendous smell of spirits which filled the close atmosphere Jesse knew that the tramp had found him again.

"Hi, brother," he called to him, "it seems you found a good tavern!"

There was a thump as the tramp finally came to rest in the hay beside him.

"The place was full of Jezebels," he said, thickly, "but no Jezebel is going to betray Peter Vinney a second time! Once is enough, brother, once is enough! Have a drink, brother!"

In the darkness Jesse felt the movement of the flask being waved vaguely in his supposed direction.

"I've had enough, brother," Jesse told him. "Keep it for the road tomorrow." Peter Vinney, his mind echoed, Peter Vinney. Where had he heard that name before?

"No man has ever had enough, brother, except of women. A man can have one too many women. One day he goes out to meet her, and he finds her with someone else and accusing him of being the father of her child and commanding him to marry her. How would you like that, brother?"

Jesse's heart was beginning to beat very fast. The thick drunken voice raving into the night was splintering darkness and letting in light.

He said, deliberately, "I should feel like murdering her, brother."

"Murdering her, did you say? By God you're right, brother! 'Twas that handsome young farmer fellow, the one they were speaking of in the inn—the one that had all the women. I come back from sea and she tells me it's all finished between him and her since Christmas, and then the very night she is to be meeting me I see them meet and go down to the rocks together. But I was too smart for her, I tell you—I hid in the shadows and heard every word that passed between them. He wanted no more of her, and that made her mad."

There was a pause whilst the flask was conveyed once more to the speaker's mouth. Jesse felt as though his heart would burst the bounds of his body. It seemed strange to him that the other man did not hear its loud hammering. He said into the darkness, cautiously, "What happened then?"

"He went off in a temper and left her. She was going to jump up and go after him after he'd flung her down——"

Jesse's heart seemed then to leap almost out of his body.

"Then it couldn't have been him that killed her——"

"How do I know?" He was on the defensive, instantly, whining, "She was found dead, wasn't she, and he was the last person seen with her, and sneaking back ways out of the town, and he ran away, didn't he, like a guilty man?"

Jesse said, soothingly, "True enough, brother. Innocent men don't run away."

There was a sly chuckle in the darkness. "That's where you're wrong, brother, for that one did—that handsome one. He didn't see her start to get up after he'd walked off in his fury, and he didn't see me come out of my dark corner. And no more did she, the Jezebel! I was on her before she knew what had happened, and when I'd thrown her down she didn't try to get up again. It was the end of her."

There was a pause, and then a combination of hiccups and maudlin weeping.

"Women like her drive a man to crime, brother, and even now there's no peace from her. She keeps drawing me back to Oldport. Down to the rocks where it all happened. I tramp the roads to try and keep away, but in the end I always take the road back. If I go to sea I always come back to Oldport harbour if the ship berths a hundred miles away. That's what 'tis to be haunted, brother."

" 'Tis bad luck on the other one to be carrying on his conscience the burden of a crime he never committed," Jesse said.

"Am I to go and confess to him and put the rope round my own neck? You must be drunk, brother! Besides, he disappeared—years ago—afraid to come back—afraid to—come back . . ."

The voice died away into the darkness and the flask fell from his hand with a clatter to the floor-boards of the loft. There was the soft drip-drip of the liquid flowing away through the hay and dripping down through the cracks into the waggons in the shed below, and a powerful smell of spirit on the air.

Jesse did not lie down again. He sat leaning against the wall of the loft, and up and down in his brain like a carillon of bells went the thought, ' I did not kill Sally Lane! I am not guilty! I am innocent! I am a free man. At last! At last! '

With the first grey light he pulled on his boots, gathered up his bundle, and crept out of the loft, down the ladder and into the still sleeping fields. It would be some time yet till sunrise, but his whole being was a blaze of dawn; the black night of the soul was ended; whatever happened now he was free.

VI

When Jesse came off the steamer in Cork harbour he was wearing the rough ragged homespun in which he had set out from Rull. The sight of himself in the mirror in the barber's shop in Plymouth, when he was having his hair and beard trimmed to a neatness to match the clothes John had given him, had startled him. It was not that he could not feel that the clothes belonged to him, but that he did not belong to them. They were worn and shabby, but they remained nevertheless the clothes of an English yeoman farmer, and had he put on a priest's cassock he could not have felt more of a masquerader in them. They would have been the world's wonder had he worn them back to Rull, and every man, woman and child would have come fingering the machine-made cloth in awe and reverence and envy, but he had for too long identified himself with the poor and disinherited to wish to be different from them in any particular, or to be reminded that he sprang from a different stock. He gave the clothes to one of the crew and walked off the ship as he had walked on to it.

There was a fine mist-like rain drifting on the mild air as he stepped ashore, and an old apple-woman in a black shawl and a red petticoat observed to him that it was ' a fine soft day ' ; he laughed with pleasure because of the Irish intonation and the Irish weather, and bought some of her bruised green apples for the children, then strode along the quayside with his blood singing. Wind and rain in Ireland were better than sunshine and clear skies anywhere else in the world.

It was a fair-day and the wide main street was full of frightened lowing cattle and frantically crying sheep and squealing pigs. There was ordure everywhere, spattering pavement and road alike and splashing the shop-fronts, and urchins laughing delightedly as the cattle mounted each other, their blood defying even the terrors of the market-place, and men standing about in apparent aimlessness in small groups, or leaning against limestone walls with vacant expressions. Nobody minded the fine small rain. Well, and why would they be minding it? In Ireland, Jesse reflected, picking his way through the mud and mess, there were only two kinds of days : there were ' fine ' days, whether grey or sunny, and ' fine soft ' days when it rained. At first it had startled him to be greeted on a grey lowering day with the observation that it was a fine day, but why not? You took what God sent and were thankful.

A farmer driving a high-wheeled gig gave him a lift along the road, and he came to Kinsale by noon. The rain had ceased and the sun came out, palely, and the little town seemed to stand with its feet in blue water at every corner. There were the spars of ships and a kind of indolent busyness along the quays.

There was, Jesse knew, no chance of reaching Burra that day, though he plunged on briskly through a landscape that grew wilder with every mile. He walked until the stars were out, and then leaned upon the half-door of a white-washed cabin, gave the occupants within God's blessing, and asked if they would shelter him for the night—though he knew he had no need to ask.

There were a number of people gathered round the turf-fire talking animatedly in Irish. Only an old man who seemed more like an old gnarled tree than a human being had any English, and he had been in America as a boy. Jesse had by then a little Irish, and between them there was speech enough. They looked at him with eyes black as mountains after sundown ; there was melancholy in their faces broke

245

by a wild laughter, like sunlight breaking through clouds. There was hunger in their faces, and a faith in something beyond this life. The young women eyed him furtively and whispered together like children, with little bursts of laughter, and their black hair fell about their shoulders straight as rain, and, as when he had first come to the country, Jesse was filled with wonder at the strange natural beauty of these people.

They gave him poteen with hot water, and a shallow bowl of thin broth and potatoes. They sat staring into the fire and occasionally rearranging the sods of turf, and a young man told a story and they all laughed, and the old man asked Jesse questions, as to where he had come from and where he was going, and had he a wife, and what did they think of Dan O'Connell in England. Presently the company broke up, fading away by ones and twos into the smokiness and shadowiness beyond the range of the fire, and the old woman came to life and raked the fire down for the night, then she and the old man gave him God's blessing and retired into the inner room. Jesse made himself comfortable on the earth floor beside the fire, his boots under his head for a pillow. He thought of Ria, and was impatient for sleep to close in on him, bridging the night with the day that was to bring him to her.

2

He reached Burra in the late afternoon of the next day, and had the good fortune to find Angus Byrne on the pier.

"Glory be to God!" Angus cried, "if it isn't himself back again before we've hardly had time to miss him!"

"I couldn't get back quickly enough," Jesse told him, "and if you're not returning to Rull immediately I shall swim out!"

"Man dear, hold on to yourself a wee while, and don't be spoilin' the beautiful patches on your clothes! The fastest curagh from here to there is leavin' for Rull this very minute," and, laughing, Angus leapt down into his boat tied up to the side.

Jesse followed him, and asked, as they pulled out of the harbour, "Has anything happened since I left?"

"Ach, no, unless 'tis news that Weaver Reilly's overdue sow has farrowed at last, and his reverence has the hay-fever two months after the hay is taken in, and your brother-in-law gave an Orangeman a black eye in Faherty's bar the other day for sayin' ye couldn't throw a stick over a poorhouse wall without hittin' one of Dan O'Connell's bastards. . . . Which reminds me that your own family are all well, praise be to God."

Jesse's eyes twinkled. "Are you suggesting my family are all bastards, Angus?"

"Ah, divil a thing of the kind did I mean, at all! Aren't you the bold one to be after twistin' the raisonable meanin' out of the poor innocent words!"

Jesse felt a great upsurge of affection for the young man. There was something of Clancy in him, he thought, he had the same brilliantly-blue eyes, bluer than the sea on a summer's day, the same careless gaiety and good humour. Mother of God, 'twas good to be back amongst such people!

When they reached the island he helped Angus pull the curagh up over the beach, and was immediately surrounded by his children, who seemed to spring to life from nowhere and everywhere, and came leaping and bounding excitedly about him. Patrick was for rushing away to the house to tell their mother that their father was returned, but Jesse restrained him.

"All of you wait here," he commanded, distributing the apples he had bought in Cork, "I will go on up alone and surprise her."

He found her sitting outside the cabin, her hands in her lap, look-in at the sea with a far-away expression, and the sadness in her face smote him. Ah, beautiful she was with her high cheek-bones, and the thick braids of her black hair, and the proud lift to her head. . . .

When she saw him hurrying to her between the boulders she sat staring for a moment, unable to believe, then jumped to her feet with a little cry and ran into his arms.

After the first blinding moment of clinging hands and lips was over he could hardly wait to tell her, "'Tis most wonderful news I bring you, my darling. If I had not gone to England when I did I should never have found out that 'twas not I who was responsible for Sally's death! Think of it! To have such a burden lifted from my conscience at last! Wasn't it right for me to go, now?"

She looked at him with love and joy. Ah, the dear, the blessed creature, living all those years with such a black weight on his innocent heart!

She smiled at him with tears in her eyes. "There was the hand of God in it, sure enough!" she said, and they went into the house together with their arms about each other as on their wedding night.

He knew that night for the first time what he had had that deep need to know, 'the rest that peace begets', the peace that holds on waking; because for the first time he knew the wholeness of personal integration.

Waking in the half-light before the dawn he saw Ria's sleeping face beside him. Privation had tightened the skin across the bones, and anxiety drawn lines across the forehead; but her hair was black as a raven's wing, and her mouth had the sweetness of a girl's. He was filled with a profound tenderness, and drew her to him and slept again.

London, Sept. 1941—*Feb.* 1942.